CW01506859

Radio
Silence

Radio Silence

Silence

CHARLIE CHEUK

First published in Great Britain in 2020

Text copyright © Charlie Cheuk 2020
Cover Image by Charlie Cheuk
The moral rights of the author have been asserted.

All rights reserved.
No part of this publication may be reproduced, stored, or transmitted in
any form by any means, electronic, mechanical, photocopying or
otherwise, without prior written permission of the publisher.

This book is typeset 11pt Bembo

To my family and my friends
who've remained by me ever since,
and to all the lives that I've touched –
I'll take parts of you wherever I go.

To live without hope
is to cease to live.

- Fyodor Dostoevsky

prologue.

"It's going to work," he insisted, hand drawing the curtains back and eyes fixed on his car.

Darkness had fallen like rain upon his side of the world and he couldn't imagine any other way to spend it. He could, actually, because he didn't want to be on the phone.

He heard an impatient sigh from the other end which infuriated him.

"What if it doesn't?"

His eyes narrowed. "When did you become such a pessimist?"

A pause. "We'll see."

A distant car alarm. His mind dragged away from the sleep he'd clung onto. He hung up, allowing the curtains to drift back over his window, and listened to the wailing sound, like a cry. Minutes passed before the sound was silenced and it left his thoughts to himself. He returned his attention to the outside world, his hair the colour of sand when the tide came in, his expressionless gaze a peaceful blue that captivated anyone against their will. He thought about what he was

1

going to do that day, planning and executing his plan efficiently.

"It's that time again, isn't it?" he said softly to nobody in particular.

Taking his phone out, he sent four separate text messages and as he clicked send, the voices became quieter, finally satisfied. He sprawled himself on his bed and stared up at the ceiling, his forearm draped over his forehead, letting the cogs in his brain whir gently in his ear.

Outside, the city of Runswick lay quiet in the morning as the fog settled comfortably onto the grass, forming beads of dew that decked the grass with shining pearls.

Detached houses sat with the people inside at the outer suburbs, where the rich lived, lining the streets like soldiers: uniform and purposeful.

Nobody was out at this time, not even the people who posted letters or junk mail. It was six o'clock and the town hoped for the peace they finally deserved after a week of working.

Wherever you went in Runswick was the smell of bakery – what the place was known for, and the smell of superstition that lingered in some homes.

Also known for its single infamous double homicide. Twenty-seven years ago, a couple had been dragged out of their homes at the dead of night and axed to death in the woodlands far away and the perpetrator had never been charged, the trace so faint it evaporated with the air. But there was bound to be a trace out there, people just didn't look. Or they didn't want to.

Never in his life had his mind shut up, it was constantly chattering like knives and he secretly didn't mind it. Nobody knew how cunning he was, not even himself. Constantly, he had to keep tight reins on his mind, or it would snap, just like last time.

His phone received a message.

Smiling, he put down his phone beside his head and continued gazing up at the ceiling searching for a flaw. Today would be the day. The day where the people he had manipulated would fall and he would finally rise again and be something he'd only hoped for in himself. Just like their parents had been. It was only a matter of time.

PART I

one.

In a house tucked away in the quiet part of the suburbs, Robyn Wolff was up in her bedroom, a cold blue hue bathing the room and softening her features. She lay awake in her bed gazing up at the ceiling where a gentle crack had formed in the very corner, a frail line of a spider's web had strung itself to the two walls forming a triangle. It drifted along to a non-existent breeze and she turned away absently and focused on her phone on her bedside table. The clock beside it read 6:01.

Seven hours since he last called. She wondered where he called from. But one thing was certain – she thought about him a lot and it made the insides of her stomach feel unpleasant.

Robyn sat up, eyes trained on the desk that was on the opposite side of the room. Desk full of revision guides, completed homework, and exam papers she didn't exactly remember doing. Robyn did well in school. Joining clubs was a hobby of hers not only for her CV, but for her own enrichment, and if that wasn't enough, she always volunteered at the weekends at the library. Sometimes. She was what others aspired to be like. Book smart.

Robyn got out of bed and crossed over to her mirror, eyes mirroring sleep. Hazel like her dads. Instead of looking warm and kind like her his, hers constantly had stormy clouds glazed over her irises, coming with a matching scowl. Like her mother's. It was so dark she could hardly see her pupils.

She picked up her faded grey hoodie that lay strewn over her chair and changed, a determined expression on her face. It was well worn by now after a year and she liked that.

A text pinged up on her phone screen and her heart vaulted, though it was only small, she didn't need those emotions. She grabbed her phone and stared at the notification. Heart tumbling, it was a reply from yesterday's conversation with Eliza. She felt bad for not replying but today she was going to go study at the museum library just in the centre of town and maybe buy some weed off her dealer – if she felt like it. She pocketed wads of cash just in case. That was how she kept on top of the game: weed.

Robyn strode out the room right after checking the cash stayed squeezed between two books on her shelf and headed to the bathroom. As she got herself ready, she couldn't help but wonder if Will thought of her every morning as she did. Probably not. Meeting online was the last thing she'd expect, really.

She scowled in the mirror and once again realised how unfriendly she looked. Her eyebrows arched way too high and her eyes were often cold. She always wore her shoulder-length hair down because she felt she'd go bald if she kept tugging it into a ponytail. Bald was not a nice look for her. But recently she'd bought a new hair tie, the ones which were overrated.

She took the scrunchie from the sink and tied it high, to match her eyebrows.

"Meh," she said and pulled it out and felt the velvet material between her fingers, like an endless sea of blue. Blue didn't suit her. Green or red did more.

"What's so great about them?" she had asked, standing in front of the rack full of hair ties.

Eliza had told her it made you look cute, but she was sceptical. But after a few more minutes of being coaxed into getting one, she had impulsively bought the blue one and tried not looking back, regret piling up in her chest. She wasn't easily pushed into doing things that others wanted.

Robyn exhaled and retied her hair this time at a medium height and it looked okay. She looked in the mirror gazing into her own eyes wondering. Sometimes she'd look in the mirror and not know who was looking back. A stranger even to herself.

Deciding it satisfactory, she walked downstairs making sure not to wake her dad whose bedroom door was closed. But her dad was downstairs boiling the kettle and he turned, dressed in his navy-blue dressing gown, bleary expression in his eyes.

"Hi."

Robyn smiled and greeted him, asking why he'd kept his bedroom door shut.

"Need to air the room and didn't want to cause a draught," he answered.

She nodded and opened the fridge, eyes sweeping over its contents. Tons of butter for some reason, lots of meat which kind of grossed her out, and lots of juice and onions.

"Do we have milk?" Robyn turned to her dad who stood nonchalantly beside the kettle avoiding her gaze.

"I think we're out then."

"I thought you were going to find a job?" she pointed accusingly.

Her question remained unanswered for a few moments. For the last couple of weeks, they'd become tight on cash because her dad lost his job at the local accountancy which had pretty good pay. But then some other things happened

9

and before they knew it – no money. Robyn had come home and regretted buying so many books that day when her dad had told her. To add to that mixture, her mother had left them two years ago and recently they'd found out she was engaged to someone else who looked almost identical to her dad. Robyn had tried tracking the guy down and stumbled upon his Facebook which was scandalous.

"I have applied to other things in Runswick and further, but they haven't got back to me."

Her dad stiffened and then relaxed again, the click of the kettle signifying it had finished boiling.

"I'll get a job—"

"This is my problem. It shouldn't be yours too."

Robyn had suggested this every time the money problem came up, but he'd always refused. This time he sounded less certain and more considering.

"I live here too. It won't be hard for me to get a job… my CV and references are great because teachers love me. I mean, who wouldn't—"

He laughed bitterly. "I failed your mother, I can't fail at being your dad too. I should be the one providing. You just started sixth form. You don't need to concern yourself with this."

She scoffed and rolled her eyes. "First of all, you didn't fail her, she failed us. She left. And so what if I'm in sixth form? I have nothing to do at the weekends apart from volunteering. I'll do it."

Her dad was contemplating this. The fridge started making a noise because she'd left it open for more than a minute, so she shut it. Her dad busied himself with the sink.

"You can sit down, you know."

Robyn sat down warily, looking down at her thumbs and then back up to the clock. It was still 6am. Time was always so slow which bothered her. Slow things usually did.

"Why are you up so early?" she asked.

"I was actually going down to the supermarket to get some groceries. Also return something because I found the cheaper version online, but I don't want it to look weird when I return it."

She shrugged. "Just tell them that your friend you were buying it for died."

Her dad twitched backwards. She counted six blinks of alarm

"What?" she protested. "Not only is that a legitimate reason, but they'll also offer up their condolences too."

"What if I jinx it and my friend actually does die?"

He cocked an eyebrow.

"Jinxes aren't real. And you have no friends apart from me."

She looked up and studied his face. Worried. So worried. "I was heading out anyway to study at the library. I'll get them."

"You made a list yesterday, let me get it."

Her dad jogged out of the room and up the stairs.

She really wanted to help pay the bills in this house, she hated seeing her dad struggle. Robyn sighed and checked her phone and saw a new notification that hadn't made a noise for some reason.

It was from Will. Her heart instantly picked up the pace, stumbling over itself.

There's a party at a friend's house and I was wondering if it would be your scene?

And an address attached in another separate text underneath including the postcode. She liked people who included every bit of detail. She clicked the address and led her phone to Maps. Robyn was grinning but her smile instantly waned. It was five miles away. That meant he lived closer than anticipated, she thought he'd live somewhere vague. It wasn't too far. She could take the train that would be one mile from the location and would take a good twenty minutes until she reached the location itself.

Frowning she texted back an 'Okay'.

Robyn wasn't stupid, she'd face timed him and met him in public places. However, she'd always forgotten to ask where he lived. Will read the text and reacted with a thumbs up.

Robyn's dad jogged back in, a crumpled piece of yellow note paper in his hand.

"It's still really dark outside so wait until eight," he said, leaving the list beside her.

She glanced outside and noticed how dark it had become since September, daylight hours still fading fast every day. He left the room swiftly, slippers scuffing the floorboards, the tip of his dark hair almost touching the door frame. Some people hated their height, but there was her dad who loved it. His six-foot-six stature was intimidating but his face told the opposite story; people often turned to look.

She surveyed the brightly lit kitchen contemplatively. All usual kitchen appliances, nicely tiled and colour themed. Green and grey were her dad's favourite colours. Her mother always went along with what dad thought. Kind of like a parrot. Then there was the sink and the floor – spotless. And the cupboards that concealed plates and glass cups stood still. Of course, it stood still they weren't alive.

Robyn had two hours to kill and she didn't know what was better than finishing incomplete tasks. She had a checklist on her phone that reminded her to water her plants, feed the goldfish and all that. But first, she had to eat, or she'd faint. It always happened now because of her iron deficiency and not bothering to actually take the medication every day. The pills weren't even hers, they were stolen. And neither was she diagnosed. Her dad didn't need to know.

Robyn got up and opened the cupboard that was built beside the fridge. Her eyes searched downwards until they settled on a box of cereal half eaten and rich in iron. Perhaps all that would substitute three weeks of not taking her medication. She made a grab for the cereal box but as she did so, a sticky yellow note slipped out from the top cupboard onto the floor. Robyn made a slight shriek thinking it was a rat but quickly recovered and bent down, still holding the box of cereal. Her own note paper she used at home.

Whatever you do, don't go out today.

Confused, Robyn turned the note over and breathed a sigh of relief when she realised there was nothing else at the back. She began studying the handwriting, frowning to herself. It looked familiar – almost like her own but she wouldn't write a note to herself. Definitely not her dad, he would've confronted her by now. Robyn headed over to where they kept the bowls and cutlery and took what she needed and sat at the small wooden rectangular table, joined by two chairs. While she ate, she studied the penmanship on the note. Evenly spaced, pointed handwriting and written in pencil.

Robyn finished her breakfast doing without milk and got up to look at the time. 6:23. Was that it? She took a swift look outside through the blinds. It was lighter, the sky still dark blue but a lighter, more welcoming shade but the grass looked like dark blades of gleaming knives. She shivered, feeling the coldness of the window and let the blinds swing back to their original position. A quiet laugh echoed through the halls.

"Dad, are you watching without me?"

A slightly sheepish muffled voice came. "No."

Robyn smiled and pocketed the note. She'd go to the library later and figure it out. She headed to the living room, shuffling her feet and standing by the door. Her dad sat on

13

the sofa with a leftover pizza from last night and a coffee she presumed which he sipped happily.

"I'm going out tonight," Robyn said quickly, the words tumbling out like a basket of spiders.

Her dad's smile glazed over, and he turned his head robotically to face her.

"If that's okay with you," she added hastily.

"It's a Saturday. We usually throw slippers at each other and you laugh at my good jokes," he said slightly stricken.

Crap, she'd completely forgotten. How could she forget something like that? It was tradition, something that always happened like clockwork.

"I'm sorry, I promise. I can be back in time – by nine," Robyn assured.

"All right," he mumbled and turned his attention back to the TV. "I just… this is what happened to your mother and I don't want to lose you too."

"You won't. This is a one off, when do I ever go to parties?" she tried her best to sound convincing.

He considered it. "Okay."

Robyn waited for him to say something else, but he didn't. "I'll go," she said torn between feeling awkward and annoyed. But she didn't feel guilty. She never did.

"Take the keys."

And so she did.

Robyn shut the door quietly, making sure not to wake her dad who was half-asleep on the living room sofa. She'd dressed herself in a trench coat that stopped short at her knees, striped top, blue jeans and black Converse, and armed herself with her laptop and charger.

She studied her dainty, empty neighbourhood noticing how bipolar the weather was. Now the sky was a brilliant blue and cumulus clouds sailed by calmly like a child's bedroom wallpaper. Robyn drew in a lungful of air that dragged itself harshly through her airways and lungs. Just an hour ago she'd checked the weather and it would become cloudy by three and rain would fall by evening. She steadied herself against the doorway as her vision partially blackened and when it had gone, she pocketed her phone, ignoring a crumpling sound and walked to the bus stop just down the road. The streets weren't as empty as she had hoped, an elderly couple hobbling by and two people on skateboards. They zoomed past, the guy glancing back twice at Robyn, Robyn paying him with just a small flicker of her eye. He wore a white collared shirt underneath a baggy green sweater with fitting grey jeans. She wondered why he didn't wear a coat.

She tallied up the coins in her hand one more time before flagging down an exhausted bus which sagged over its tyres and smelled strongly of combustion. The driver took her money, thanking her. Robyn stepped on and gazed at all the different people on the bus. There were commuters and they looked exhausted. Or bored with their lives.

She took a seat nearer the back and checked her phone once again. No messages from Will, or anyone. Somehow her heart sank, and she gazed out the window all throughout her journey, tight lipped and unsmiling.

two.

Leo Luong watched as a girl strode past, a bag slung low over her shoulders and holding a laptop case. She had glared at him – well maybe not glared but had stared back with hard eyes. Leo was mildly intrigued. The girl looked around his age give or take, and she looked somewhat familiar, perhaps someone from school.

"Are you checking her out?"

His friend Priya raised an eyebrow and grinned slyly, skating alongside him.

He raised an eyebrow back. "She's not my type."

They skated by, narrowly swerving past the lamp post he had kissed his ex against. He cringed and stopped as a sharp pain had formed in his side.

"I gotta stop."

Priya laughed and they moved off from the centre of the road and sat. She sat on her skateboard and took the hair tie from her wrist to tie her long black hair up.

Collapsing against a brick wall, Leo took his phone out instinctively and checked his phone.

There's a party tonight at a friends. Do you want to come with?

A party? The thing was, having no real friends at school meant the last time Leo ever attended a gathering was when he was twelve and that was only because everyone in the class was invited. And even if he was invited, he declined because parties weren't his scene. His only actual friend was Priya which was honestly quite sad. She on the other hand had so many other friends and it was puzzling as to why she only hung out with him. But with Will it was different. If that meant seeing him again after weeks, then he would do it for him. There was an address below that directed him straight to google maps. Surprisingly not far away from where he lived, just several miles. He texted back with a faint grin on his face.

Earlier that day, his mouth had run away with him and he'd told his parents that he was gay, and it did not go well. First was the denial from his dad and his mother had to pour her coffee over his dad and second when his dad realised that everything added up. Why he 'dressed that way' and why he 'talked that way', all fuelled by stereotypes. His mother was more accepting than his dad though. Leo remembered the harsh words he'd beat into him and how his mother had coaxed him to stop. They'd let Leo leave, making sure he wasn't going to meet his early morning lover or something. Leo almost pissed himself laughing when he exited, arm around his skateboard protectively.

Leo looked up from his phone and marvelled at his surroundings. The sky was painted a perfect azure blue by some artist no longer alive, light brushes of golden beams that stretched like scars across the sky. He'd been out for ages now, since then the sky had grown lighter and birds had woken up. A text message appeared on his screen and his heart tripped over itself. It was just his dad.

Where are you??

The text radiated anger, he could feel it. Two question marks. Demanding. For this one time he wasn't going to reply.

"I want your opinion on something," Priya said suddenly and scooted over to where he sat. Taking out her phone, she showed him two screenshots of a cat, both different in colour: one black and one grey.

He shot her an inquiring frown. "They're both adorable."

She sighed. "Which one?"

"Both." He shrugged.

She rolled her eyes, smiling widely. "You're no help."

"Why don't you ask one of your friends then?" he grumbled and switched off his phone.

"They'll laugh at me."

"I'm laughing at you."

"Not right now you're not."

"In my head."

"Well, you don't count."

"Thanks."

"No problem."

"Are you getting a cat?" he asked.

"No," she said with hostility. "You know I love dogs more."

"Then why are you asking me which cat is cuter? All cats are cute."

"It's my friend's. You know, Rose? I was just clarifying something for her."

"Oh."

Upon seeing his face, her smile softened. "But you're my favourite friend."

18

"I am?" he said nervously.

She nodded her head and her curls shook with her. "You're my platonic soulmate. Honestly, Leonard, we've been friends since we were thirteen you should know by now."

He reddened and gave a nod, not trusting himself to speak without crying. "Don't ever use that name," he reminded.

"Only for you," she snickered and stood, pocketing her phone in the back pocket of her green jeans. "I gotta go."

"That's fine," he replied and stood with her.

"I'll see you on Monday."
She gave him a two fingered salute.

"Yeah," he nodded and watched her skate off back in the direction of her house.

After a minute of staring at a nearby tree in melancholy, he propped his skateboard horizontally like a compass pointing north and skated off in the opposite direction. He knew where he was headed to; there was a large plain of field that seemed to stretch like endless currents of green sea. It was where cows were kept but that didn't bother Leo because the more the merrier.

Passing his ex's house was part of his daily journey and slowly throughout that year, he'd grown accustomed to the fact he wasn't coming back, and he should cut ties completely. Those endless nights he wept without sleep, tears flowing like a leak in the ceiling, asking himself why. Why did bad things happen to good people? He never got a reply from the universe. However, something good had grown out of his breakup – Will. Not only just Will but his taste of music and clothing had changed, probably for the better. He regarded him as a rebound and girls in school talked about it in hushed voices. They'd asked before, but he let them think what they wanted to.

Leo rounded a corner and slowed to a halt. He'd stopped wearing his helmet after his breakup because, to put it quite plainly: he didn't care if he had an accident. Priya said she'd care but he questioned it.

Standing in a dazed trance, Leo rocked slightly as a light gust of wind zipped itself past, picking up wisps of wavy hair. He needed a haircut. His feet sank slightly into the wet mud, he stood facing the fence that opened up to the garden of green where he usually went. He'd never introduced this place to anyone. It would tarnish the quiet and peace it gave to him. He watched as the sprinkles of dandelions danced sweetly to-and-fro across the field almost like they were at a school dance. Leo really wanted to draw that. Too bad he couldn't draw.

Sighing, he slumped himself against the fence, drawing his feet out the mud and sitting on a relatively dry patch of grass, gazing into a small puddle. Staring into his own reflection he realised that his hair was dishevelled and greasy and someone had drawn dark lines under his dark eyes. Sometimes he wished he were a different person with a different life that was easy, everything handed to him and he wouldn't need to overthink every little thing. Maybe if he had the power to teleport or read minds, he'd be happy.

"I knew I'd find you here."

A sneer from behind him which startled Leo and made him swivel round, almost dislocating his neck in the process.

"Jesus," Leo muttered before heaving himself up and backing away from the fence, feet sinking in the puddle of his reflection.

His dad stood there beside the gate on the other side, in his safe space, with a slightly amused expression on his face. Suddenly he felt very vulnerable and he hated that feeling to the core.

He surveyed the field in mock interest and turned back to Leo with a deepened sneer.

"Are you allowed to be here?"

Leo didn't reply, instead thoughts about bolting came to his mind but quickly fleeted away when his dad's expression changed.

He sighed in frustration pinching the bridge of his nose. There was a moment's pause and when he looked back up, he looked almost emotional. Leo didn't back down nor did he feel bad.

"You don't need to hide."

"I'm not hiding," he snapped. "I'm in plain sight," Leo said, his grip tightening around his skateboard.

"You're our only child and I've realised…" he pinched the bridge of his nose harder and visibly grimaced. "that it's okay to be different. Just know that it's something that can change, you know… sexuality. A phase really."

He adjusted his demeanour and smiled distastefully.

"Okay," he said calmly, struggling to not feel the need to yell or stumble over his words. "Looks like you being straight is a phase too."

His dad realised his mistake but didn't bother replying, like he didn't hear him in the first place.

"The thing is – it's okay. Your mother is here for you."

"And what about you?" he said coolly.

His dad didn't say anything but continued to stare at him, a slight hint of a frown emerged, eyes shifting to the place behind Leo's shoulder. He didn't turn around in case it was another trap so he could try and kill him.

"You're not welcome here."

Leo turned his head and the fire inside was put out like a lid closing on a candle and he broke into a relieved smile.

The man who owned the empty field was stood before him, a bucket he gripped in his left hand that tilted his whole body slightly like scales. Both of his dark eyes were different shades to each other, his greying afro hid beneath a woollen hat and he was much taller than Leo, and Leo was tall. The clothes he wore were clean in a way that would be suitable for a farm but too fraying for perhaps a supermarket trip without attracting attention. Leo really wanted waffles in that moment.

Carter wasn't looking at Leo but his dad, eyes relaxed but hard.

"Who's this?" his dad asked but nobody replied so he walked out and closed the gate behind him. His safe place was finally safe. Carter dropped the bucket down slowly, his eyes fixed onto Leo's dad.

"I've heard about you." Came his short reply.

It was true, Leo had been caught lounging in his field behind a barn one day, but Carter had brushed it off and instead they became friends. They discussed the weather and the individual animals that sometimes flitted by and occasionally shared beer. He questioned if that were legal, but it wasn't like he'd get drunk there beside some sheep. They'd judge him too hard.

Leo's dad looked to Leo and back at Carter. Leo barely registered what was happening, it was so fast until a fist made close contact to Carter's face before it was strained backwards, and his dad was sprawled on the floor. Leo's jaw dropped in awe and he felt incredibly embarrassed for himself and his dad. Carter however dismissed it with a wave of his gloved hands, straightening up from his bent knees and picking back up his bucket.

"I'm going to press charges," his dad groused, wincing as he slowly sat up, squinting angrily up at Carter. He had a hand clamped around a bruised jaw.

"You hit me first," he countered.

Leo's dad swore under his breath and said something racist. That was the tipping point, the frustration and anger pooling onto the floor.

"Fuck you."

"Leo, let it go," Carter said.

"I'm gonna go, I won't be back for a bit," Leo declared loudly and off he went, pointing his skateboard away from the field like a surfer before trundling off, barely being able to stop himself from screeching.

The innocent blue of the sky from morning slowly faded to a lazy blue as it allowed the sun to sail slowly across the sky at noon. Leo sat in the crime thrillers section of the library and gazed completely lost at the shelves of books. He'd been sat there for almost an hour and he was starving as he didn't have lunch and it was almost one. There came a sigh from the bookshelf behind him which he ignored but light footsteps began and stopped directly to his right which Leo again chose to ignore. They'd probably go away.

"Are you following me?"

He raised his eyes from the most exciting title of a book and met the eyes of the girl he'd seen earlier - the bus stop girl.

"Oh," was all he said.

She stood her ground and encouraged him to speak with her eyes.

"No, I happen to live by here. I love the museum library, it's like my home. Home is where the heart is. And my heart is here. Right now..." he trailed off and frowned to himself. "physically and metaphorically."

The girl didn't say anything but sat opposite him and glanced at the book beside him.

"I've read that. The ending isn't very good," she sniffed disdainfully.

"Oh," he said again which pretty much put the end to his misery of anticipating the ending, feeling slightly disappointed. Instead, he took out his phone and saw a notification from his reminders to take his meds which he chose to ignore because he wasn't home. The girl was silent for a while before she spoke.

"Don't you go to Riverton Grammar?"

He looked up and narrowed his eyes. "Why? Are you in the year below?"

That was a stupid question, every year was the year below to him.

"Year twelve."

"Yeah, figured. You look dead."

"Sorry?"

"Year twelve does that to people."

"You don't think I look alive?"

"Uh, yeah. As I said, year twelve does that to you. Makes you exhausted."

Silence again. They looked anywhere but at each other although sometimes their lines of sight would cross, and they'd stare. The girl was slightly weird.

"I don't wanna be rude, but I might just get some lunch from the café," he said.

"I'll come!"

She stood up eagerly before he was even up. He stared bewildered but shrugged.

Leo realised he had no money with him, so the girl chose to pay for him and herself which he thought was quite nice.

24

They chose a quiet two-seater in the corner that peered out to a park full of people walking.

The café itself was spacious and modern, yet the place itself was older than they imagined – it was a room that led directly to the exhibition of dinosaur bones and other interesting artefacts which interested children an unhealthy amount. It had an echo to it and the chatter that rose was recited back.

The girl propped down the tray that held her coffee and wrap and Leo's burger and lemonade.

"Not the healthiest option," she pointed out.

Leo thought that was an unnecessary comment, so he ignored and took his seat, checking the time. Just gone half one.

"I'm Robyn by the way," she said whilst ripping open sugar in paper and letting it flow down into her coffee. It made a satisfying noise. Robyn stirred and took a sip. It was blistering hot and she almost dropped the cup, collected herself to save the embarrassment, and directed her attention to him.

He stared, his phone uselessly in his hand. "Did you know that you're really strange?" he said.

"I did not."

"Well, now you know."

"I feel enlightened."

"You should."

She swallowed and put down her coffee. Her hazel eyes retreated into the depths of her mind and she thought about what she was going to say next.

"I just felt bored and I realised that I once talked to your friend. He was with a blond guy? I've forgotten what he looks like. You were there when we talked so I thought it would be... okay."

It was Leo's turn to splutter on his lemonade and it wasn't nice. It fizzed his brain and made him sneeze. She muttered a bless you before he replied, dabbing at his face.

"Oh yeah, I remember you. You just look different without uniform."

She waited for him to continue and when he didn't, she asked, "Did something happen?"

"The blond guy. James. We broke up," he croaked.

Her eyebrows went up a fraction and it didn't escape his notice.

"If you're gonna say something rude you can take your food and shove it up—"

"No, I wasn't. That's stupid."

Leo could feel her eyes on him as he unwrapped his burger reading the paper wrapping: *I am made of 100% recycled paper.* He laughed to himself before stuffing his face. Wow he was starving, each bite made him feel even hungrier.

You're going to get heart disease when you're older.

He composed himself. "Yeah, James and I broke up. It was a mutual thing, really. Didn't really communicate properly, you see. Don't do that," he babbled on covering his mouth as he chewed as quick as he could.

A small smile appeared on Robyn's face. "Okay."

"The thing is, I thought James was my soulmate. Literally. I loved him, he loved me, and life got in the way. I hate this world, don't you?"

"Uh, yes, sometimes yes. Most of the time I kind of just… don't care." Came Robyn's reply before taking a cautious sip of her coffee afraid she'd burn off half her tongue again. She thought it suitable to drink and took a larger sip. Wincing, she put her coffee down and shrugged. "Too hot still."

"You're so weird."

26

"I heard," she replied. "I've never dated anyone in my life, and I don't know how it works."

Leo agreed. "Two people have to be so lucky to like each other back, against all the odds."

"I don't think much about romance."

"Oh? I wish I were like you then."

"Caring more about school? It's exhausting, really."

"Why are you here then? School work? How's year twelve? Trust me it only gets harder."

A faint blush spread slowly throughout her face and deepened when Leo smirked. She glanced to her left and right comically, searching for anyone who could possibly overhear. There were many people there as it was lunch time and it was a Saturday. Families, mostly.

She leaned in. "Volunteering. But my dealer is supposed to show up. Maybe seven minutes ago but she's always late," she stated and returned to her seat and the red across her cheeks disappeared.

Leo's eyes widened and his jaw unhinged. "*You*? Not ecstasy, right? That stuff is probably—"

"It doesn't matter, just never do weed yourself."

He didn't stop staring. "That's so bad, you need to stop," he commanded, voice in astonishment.

"Don't tell me what to do, I'm in control of my life," she snapped and unwrapped her wrap, taking a small bite.

"Sorry, I just feel invested in you now you confessed your undying love for me."

The scorn fell from her face and the grin returned. "I never said that I loved you, you're just skater guy."

"No, I'm library guy," he scoffed, falling back in his seat and crossing his arms huffing.

"Skater guy," she insisted.

"It was nice meeting you."

"Likewise."

"How do you know James anyway?"

"I don't, I knew the other guy with him," she replied.

Leo drooped visibly and Robyn offered a sympathetic smile tilting her head to one side.

"You'll find someone else, someone who'll stay."

Leo instantly brightened, grinned, and took more bites out of his burger, satisfied.

three.

Elena Morais watched with a mild fascination the blood swirl and mingle with the water, so different against the porcelain of the sink. It circled once before sneaking down the drain and she shut the tap, sealing her eyes shut and wiping her nose of blood. She heard the microwave downstairs ping five times and the door popping open. Her dad was still home. A shaky sigh slipped out of her and she met her own guarded eyes in the mirror. Her phone received a text and she stole a glance at it. She groaned irritably.

She stood by a lamppost, hoping to catch the attention of her friends who would soon arrive and relieve her boredom that Saturday had to offer. The sunlight filtered its way through the tree above her and casted flickering sunlight across her face – a devil and angel simultaneously. Her dark hair was almost black but not quite, though she'd dyed it red several times. Her eyes were a mahogany brown and they looked at everyone with meekness.

As always, the blue sky above her showed her the endless opportunities she had in life and the roads around her were busy with life. She was dressed in a beige sweater, black jeans, and an olive- green coat, her trainers scuff-free. It was forecasted to rain and she only hoped she'd be home by the time it did.

Elena smiled to herself as a figure appeared from a corner, turning and on seeing Elena, broke into a light jog. He approached and she enveloped him in a hug.

"I haven't seen you for twenty-four hours," she exclaimed, a wide smile that stretched itself across her face.

"Too long for you?" he said.

Elena didn't notice the snarl in his voice or how pathetic he thought she was. They embraced again.

Elena's boyfriend Mark Doyle stood much taller than Elena herself, brown curly hair and calming green eyes flecked with brown.

"Guess what?" said Elena.

"What?"

"You have to guess!"

"I'm not good at guessing."

"You're no fun."

He grunted.

"It's almost Christmas!"

"It's November."

"And it's almost your birthday!"

"I'm aware."

"How's life been then?" she asked as they pulled away from each other.

Mark considered that for a second. "I just finished my English lit. essay which I spent almost twenty-four hours on, it's so time consuming," he responded, not burying the dislike in his voice. He turned sharply at an angle and lit up a cigarette, unsuccessful on the first two attempts. She would've asked back how he was by now or even offered him a joint if she were him. When it became clear he was going to do neither, she painted a fake smile to her face and told her how she was anyway.

Momentarily, Elena and Marks' other friends joined them, and they made their way together as two groups towards the park: Elena with her friends and Mark with his. They knew they had a problem, but Elena tried hard to cling onto their relationship. She thought back to Will. They'd met at a bar open at day several months ago and they'd both got along well, exchanging numbers, and talking over text. She'd actually gotten a text off him earlier that day saying there was a party that wasn't too far away, and she should go. At first, she'd said yes but now she was thinking about it, she wouldn't know anyone there but him which made her vaguely uneasy. That meant nobody could help her if she got into trouble. As a matter of fact, she couldn't even remember what Will looked like anymore.

"So, Elena, guess who's legal today?" her friend Vienna piped, doing a little dance. Her blonde hair danced along with her and she stood several inches taller than Elena like most did.

"You," she retorted, trying to give a convincing grin.

"Yes, isn't it great? We'll buy you drinks tonight. It'll be fun. I don't really know how the whole procedure works but I'll show them my birth certificate or something."

Elena laughed until she felt like crying and the thought of the party she'd go to slipped into her head.

"Actually... I'm out tonight. I've got something to do," she started.

Vienna's eyes widened fractionally. "Okay. What are you going to do?"

Elena thought about telling the truth, but it would be better lying. Besides, she was good at lying it was almost second nature now.

"It's my dad's birthday and we have to go outta town," she settled on eventually.

Vienna's eyes narrowed into slits. "Your dad's birthday was last month."

Shit. Had she already used that excuse? A breeze swept past them and she shivered.

"That was the pre-party, it's the real thing this time," Elena responded quickly.

Vienna stared at her for a few seconds and nodded understanding. "I get you. Wow, you're busy," she said.

They picked up the pace as the wind continued blowing stronger.

They made their way behind a shed located in the middle of the park. Mark took swift glances in all direction and flicked open the rusty lock which resonated against the damp wood and slinked behind the door. Their crowd of people all wore calm and indifferent faces and didn't even shiver, while Elena shook violently against the thin fabric of her coat.

"What are we doing?" Elena asked suddenly aware that the situation was strange. She couldn't help the squeak in her voice. "I thought we were here to find your little secret stash of—"

Mark emerged with a grin of victory on his face, a gun held discreetly under his jacket. Elena's eyes widened in dread.

Mark turned to Elena and winked. "Don't look at me like that. I'm not going to hurt anyone here."

"Anyone here?" she repeated shrilly.

"Yeah. I thought you were in on this?" Mark's voice became dangerously accusing.

Elena held her arms up hopelessly. "I didn't read the group chat, okay? I thought... I dunno..." she trailed off awkwardly.

"When did you become so boring?"

Her friends around smirked and she felt it a slap in the face. She didn't know what to do next. She wanted to say something back but the look on his face stopped her. Mark shrugged and fiddled with the safety. It was small but had a deadly looking stare and the barrel looked up at Elena like a dead animal.

"Shoot some pigeons, test it out," he said casually.

Gulping, she shook her head, taking a slow step back. "That's weird, I'm not killing anything," she said firmly.

Vienna rolled her eyes. "Relax, this isn't illegal. Mark's parents own this shed, so legally everything in there is also his."

"Is that the truth or what Mark made up?"

Mark turned on Elena slowly, eyes like a storm brewing in the depths of the Atlantic Ocean, harsh green waves and black clouds. He didn't say anything, but his smile rotted and his face uninviting. Elena shrunk back.

"Who votes that Elena should leave?" he said, voice emotionless.

Her mouth fell open in horror and she struggled to keep the hurt off her face. Vienna raised a hand, eyes trained on Elena and so did more than half of their group. Outvoted. A wave of nausea overcame her, and she took another step back in betrayal.

Mark was like this often, but she always brushed it off. They had been dating for years so things like this wouldn't be surprising.

"Mark," Elena began desperately grasping at straws. "Are you struggling with homework stress? I know exams are coming up…" the last of her words died on her tongue when Mark gave her the look. The look which asked are-you-dense-or-crazy?.

"Have fun at that party of yours," he sneered.

Her eyes dropped to his hand which held her phone threatening to fall by the top corner.

"How did you—"

"Things like that don't go unnoticed. Not when you're my girlfriend," he growled tossing her phone back to her. It spun across the air like a manic helicopter and she only just caught it in time before it fell in a puddle. She stared back at him defeated and they left, leaving her standing there.

Elena didn't let herself cry on the tram as she stood with a hand wrapped around a pole and eyes downcast. The vehicle swayed back and forth with intensity and purpose as it moved its way and the people inside through the city. Elena moved with it and she felt her brain rattle in her head and a headache crept along. Glancing down at her nails she noted that she needed to repaint her nails and looked down to her shoes which had clumps of mud attached to them.

The train stopped and a man hobbled off, so she took his seat, collapsing against it and stabbing herself in the elbow in the process. Elena was so used to these situations in which Mark turned her own friends against her. Did he even love her in the first place? She certainly still loved him; it was maybe just school stress. Elena cringed to herself when she relived the memory of her own friends voting her out of their group because she didn't want to involve herself.

Sometimes she would think back to the nights when they were years younger. She'd wait for Mark's mother to come home while his stepdad was miles away at work, but she'd never show. They'd always sat in the front garden, on their little rise of ground overlooking the houses below that huddled together like overcrowded teeth. Mark would always tell Elena to go home but she wouldn't budge. And his mother would never return until she needed something from Mark.

Elena averted her gaze from her shoes to the window opposite her, watching the midday sky exhaust itself and the blue mixed with the inevitable grey clouds. It was definitely going to rain now.

Rows of houses ran together like a blur of grey and red watercolour and soon vanished altogether revealing the countryside; a wide strip of green that seemed to run forever like time.

She thought about her dad at home who she left to hang out with Mark, and she regretted that so much it hurt. Her phone startled her; her ringtone were drums that banged absurdly. It earnt a few looks from other passengers.

"Emma?" she said into her phone's microphone.

"Hi, Elena."

"What's up?"

"Want to hang?"

"Uh," she peered at the time. "Not right now, I gotta get home. I'm on the tram."

"That's okay. Maybe tomorrow? We should work on the computing project, it's due next Wednesday."

"Oh, I forgot. Yeah, tomorrow then. At yours?"

"Sure. Four o'clock?"

"Okay."

"Bring food!"

"I will."

Time marched by in the next hour on the tram as Elena stared blankly at the different people getting on and off like a hamster on a wheel but she felt like she was the one running frantically on it and the people watched. Thoughts passed like day and night in her mind as it strayed further away from the events of today which she welcomed as change.

She cursed the geography of Runswick as she took a step off the tram onto the platform, slightly dazed from her headache and the constant rattling of the tram had done to her in the past hour. Making her way to the vending machine that stood like a sympathetic butler waiting after her journey, she took out some loose change. Selecting an inconveniently expensive bar of chocolate, slotted the right amount of coins in and she stabbed at the metal numbers. Elena watched the coil of metal slowly rotate and the bar dropped with a low thump and she reached down to take it. She was meant to have lunch with Mark and her friends afterwards, but it never got to that point despite her hoping. You should never count on people. Passengers around her walked by in their separate paths inside their little heads. She took a bite of her chocolate and felt a little better.

It had been twenty minutes and Elena walked with a slow pace not bothering to check before crossing roads. She lived on a very busy A road which wasn't wise. She came to a small junction leading off to another road

"Elena." Came a slow and deliberate voice behind.

Elena whirled around and instinctively flinched as the person ran wildly towards her, hands wrapping around her throat in an attempt to block her airways. She gasped and she kicked desperately at her attacker's legs and she felt her soul temporarily leave her body as she looked up to their face. She saw an attractive face of a male before he covered his face again hastily with his hood and she struggled as he pushed her to the floor, knocking the air out of her lungs. Then they were gone, and Elena lay there taking controlled breaths and clutching her neck in pain. A few moments passed, the bruising showing around her throat and her headache had worsened thanks to being slammed onto the floor. Sluggishly she raised herself to sit and she checked her surroundings before attempting to stand. First, she got to her knees and finding a street sign beside her, she hauled her lopsided body up. No cars had been nearby. How convenient. She cursed in the two languages she knew as her eyes swept by the bar of chocolate that lay discarded and half eaten on the grass. Elena breezed by avoiding the accusing glare that it seemed to throw at her. Just a few more minutes and she'd be in the safe vicinity of her safe neighbourhood. Well, what she thought was safe.

There were black and dark purple smudges that framed her right eye and Elena couldn't remember how that had been inflicted because she didn't remember pain on anywhere but her throat. She swallowed and it hurt. She experimented with her voice and it hurt. Standing there in her bathroom half-dressed made her realise how sickly she looked; her arms were stalks and her hair which she thought was nice didn't shine anymore, not even in the sunlight. Maybe it was a change in conditioner? The television was still on downstairs and she'd heard it when she crept back home and before she left to meet Mark. Her dad would be sat in his armchair watching the headlines with wide eyes and thinking tortured thoughts. She felt bad of course she did but she didn't know what to do or help in any way so instead she kept out of his way hoping he would appreciate the peace that came with it. However, she didn't know it did him more harm than good.

Elena re-dressed taking her time and tried smiling to herself in the mirror. It looked more like a grimace and so she took a makeup brush by her sink and dusted lightly around her eyes to cover up the bruise. She began missing her chocolate even more. A muffle of a crowd cheering presumably from the TV made its way to her ears and she thought about checking up on her dad. He'd appreciate it wouldn't he? The pain around her neck had not subsided and Elena thought back to the attacker's face. Her thoughts trailed off into an unsure whisper. What made him leave? He had fled the scene as quick as he had come and not even spoken a word to her. He had known her name but that was it. The TV was loud and disrupted her train of thought as a virtual crowd cheered again.

Elena took the stairs to the living room slow and deliberately, not announcing her presence just yet. Her house was a semi-detached and she'd like to think hers was the more maintained one out of the two as the outsides wasn't intertwined with vein-like vines that seemed to strangle and choke the windows on the first floor. She shuddered and reached the ground floor. Taking a look around she noticed how sad the oil paintings were that hung within the same proximity of each other across the white paint of the walls. The carpet was worn and a faded maroon colour that seeped into every corner of the floor like furry blood in a way. Up at the ceiling she noticed the ceiling's paint was cracking like someone had used a knife to slice a line across and the paint had erupted around. She was going to take a detour to the kitchen and get his lunch that he'd left in the oven. The kitchen wasn't much fancier, the colour scheme didn't seem to match the rest of the house or itself, but it was tidier than the rest. Lasagne sat forlornly gazing through the oven door like a mourner out a window. She grinned and took it out; it was still warm but most of the heat had left since and she took a fork from the cupboards. Stomach growling lowly, she made her way to the living room. Elena pushed open the living room door open slowly and peeked inside, expecting to see her dad imprinted in his armchair with a Sprite can squeezed between his pudgy fingers. Everything seemed fine one minute, but she noticed the needle on the floor and her dad wasn't sat upright, he was slumped over the sofa and he looked almost blue. Elena took each step with caution in case his dad woke and scared him, but he was unmoving, and his eyes gazed towards the heavens blankly.

She clamped a mouth over her mouth, dropping the lasagne and fork down with a crash. The colours around her seemed to have sharpened and her feet started to feel unsteady, bile rising in her throat. But she had to check. Reaching a hand over, she gently nudged her dad.

No response.

She turned to his neck. It was cold. So cold.

Cold sweat sprung on her skin like weeds and she felt her heart start to run. She bolted out the room and stumbled blindly out into the open air, trying to calm her breathing by listening to the cars on the road. Elena fought the tears, but she started mumbling to herself hysterically, walking in circles, debating whether to call someone. There was always her mum. But she didn't care.

"Elena."

Elena turned and her heart stopped.

"What are you doing here?" she said turning to face him fully.

She was seconds away from having a full-blown meltdown.

Mark stood just inside her driveway and he had his arms folded like he owned the place, barring her only way out.

"He attacked you."

Tears welled in Elena's eyes and she scowled, not knowing why she was crying. "Why do you seem to just show up everywhere?" Her voice cracked and her heart shook. "I don't wanna see you. And I certainly don't want you fighting my fights."

"I wasn't fighting your fights."

"Look, my dad is dead, I don't know why you're here and I didn't walk out here so you could annoy and insult me—"

"No, you look—"

"Shut up. Please, just shut the hell up," she screamed exasperated.

Mark's face suddenly softened, and he reverted to calmness, dropping his arms.

Elena sighed too and she felt the ice inside her begin to melt away. Before she knew it, she was sobbing into Mark's shoulder while he held her tightly, both unable to let go.

four.

Business was always slow and quiet on Saturdays. Especially at this time of day.

Roman Sheridan counted the last of the pickled jars and heaved a sigh, fetching a cloth to wipe one of the lids. His best friend Cahil sat at the till watching the outside through the glass. It was smashed at a corner and they'd tried patching it up as best as they could after Roman dumped his bike carelessly against it, but it caved in further.

"Can you come and help me?"

Roman stopped trying to reach the top shelf after a cramp had formed in his foot.

Cahil stood blinking awkwardly. He was taller than Roman by an inch or so and carefully took the tray down. None of the other employees were here. It was their shift and theirs alone.

"Short white boy," Cahil grinned.

Roman rolled his eyes and took the tray from him and resumed wiping the lids with a cloth with grim determination. Cahil watched but got bored and looked at the shelves of pickles and other unidentifiable slime in their jars.

The shop was small and only sold non-perishables and both worked trying to pay off the money they'd lived off from their parents. It was a boring job and they profited nothing but at least they got to talk.

"So," Roman said quietly, looking up from the tray.

Cahil raised an eyebrow warily. "Yeah?" he said.

"Can you drive me there? I would ask my parents, but I haven't been home for really long," he said.

Cahil made a thinking face and fiddled with the string on his hoodie. "You should go home. Or tell them at least," he muttered.

"No thanks."

Cahil shrugged helplessly. "Fine."

"Fine you'll drive me?" Roman asked hopefully.

He grunted.

Roman grinned.

"But we have another hour and a half of our shift."

"We'll close it early, who cares what Bartholomew says?"

Cahil scowled but grudgingly agreed. Roman stood to bump him lightly on the shoulder and headed over to the cashier desk.

He'd been friends with Cahil since he moved to Netherwood. Sure, he had other friends, but he was his closest despite being a bit of an air head. He was a good kid with good intentions and you barely found anyone like that around anymore.

Roman sat at the desk, inspecting the gum on display. Nobody even shopped at this hour. They never really shopped at the place anyway. He stared into the dusty dimness of the ceilings. He noticed the roof was leaking, writing a mental note in his head he'll never read. Cahil came over, dusting his hands and edging nervously away from the spilt jar of pickles by the window they dropped earlier.

"Wanna leave?" he said with a tired smile. Roman smiled.

"Is it down this road?"

"No, I just said it was the one that specifically says Carston Ridge. That says Third Wood Drive."

"All right but aren't all roads linked together like the motorway – oh wait, is it this one?"

"Goddammit, Cahil. Can you read?"

Roman in the passenger seat slumped downwards and seethed with annoyance as Cahil gulped and continued driving on, waiting for a Carston Ridge to show up. They were driving to a friend of a friend's house and they were stuck on the same main road stopping at every junction because he was so thick. The car they were confined inside was an old red sedan and drove with a similar speed to the elderly crossing a road. Roman took a glance at their rear-view mirror and a couple of cars were queuing up behind them impatiently, matching their snail-like speed. He caught the eye of an angry driver and she sounded her horn sharply. That scared Cahil and he blinked.

"Can we drive any quicker?" Roman asked. "Look behind us."

"I'm going just over twenty."

"You see that sign over there? It says thirty."

"Do you think they'll hate us?" Cahil asks sounding mildly worried.

Roman groaned. "Why don't you ask the nice lady behind?"

"She's not nice," he said glumly.

"Suppose not."

"I think this is it."

This time they braked slightly and made a slow turn into Carston Ridge. He felt the passive aggressive sound of acceleration pass them.

The neighbourhood around them looked tastefully tidy and wealthy, all houses detached and separate from each other's noise. Trees lined the pavement all cut in the same fashion and cars parked in driveways that gleamed in what was left of the sunlight that day.

"They're loaded. Do you think they'd let me borrow their car?" Cahil muttered slowing the car down even more and searched his right side for the number twenty-seven.

"I don't think he'd even let us in yet, it's only four."

"Then what are we doing here? Hey, help me look for twenty-seven. Oh, wait this is the even numbered side. It's on your side."

Roman rolled his eyes in irritation and turned just to see them passing twenty-seven. "Stop," he commanded holding up his hand.

Cahil braked harshly and they jerked forwards, seatbelts cutting into their necks. They turned to look at twenty-seven in synchronisation. It wasn't much different from the rest, but this house was much more decorated. Fairy lights were adorned thoughtfully on the hedges and a table was already half set up in the massive driveway. Drinks table, he assumed. Will's friend was fancy.

"I wanna make sure I don't show up at a random person's house. You have to be prepared sometimes," Roman replied answering Cahil's question from a few moments ago.

He nodded dumbly. "Are you okay for a lift afterwards?"

Roman hadn't thought about that. "No, you're gonna have to drive me."

Cahil deflated.

"Roman, nice of you to drop by."

Roman closed his front door with a click and turned slowly to face his dad who was stood by the landline phone, a flyer in his hand. The look on his face was unmatched.

They stood in silence for a moment, one glaring and the other just staring blankly.

"None of your excuses?"

"Not this time, I'm going out tonight."

He made his way to the stairs, but his dad stepped in front, his eyes darkening.

"Do you mind?" Roman snapped.

"Not at all. Your mother and I were worried," his voice swerved meticulously away from breaking.

"It's literally the same time I get home from school."

"You've been gone for twenty-four hours. Have you even showered?" His dad wrinkled his nose.

"I'm not careless like my sister was, chill," Roman treaded lightly on his words and met his dad's gaze evenly.

He didn't say anything so Roman dodged by him and carried on, not looking back.

Clouds shrouded the blue sky and the daylight had dimmed slightly, soaking the buildings of Runswick in a grey filter, escaping into each room.

Roman sighed and collapsed on his bed and shook off his dark green jacket, flinging it carelessly to the wall. Feeble anger boiled in him, but he managed to contain it as long as nothing else was added to the mixture. His parents were always so worried about him despite him being seventeen and smart enough, so he'd have no trouble kicking ass. But then he always forgot about his sister. How she had died. Roman shook his head angrily and sat up over the edge of his bed. Sometimes he did miss her.

Sofia was two years younger than him, making her fifteen if she was still alive today and their relationship had been complicated. He regarded her as stupid and she regarded him as stupid. Simple. He caught his own eye in the mirror by his desk and it was like staring at a male version of his sister, chestnut brown hair and dim green eyes. But where his eyes were green, hers were a light brown. They both also had strange smiles which looked more like a smirk and their friends had always commented on that. Roman never smiled, he just socialised with different people and made friends, then lost them because he always yelled at them for being too stupid or too clever. It was quite hypocritical, but he didn't really care most of the time.

Roman rubbed his eyes and admired his room. Three years ago, they'd moved out of a small town called Dawson City in the north-west of chilly Canada because they needed a new start from Sofia. Typical, really. He had only been fourteen so he had just gone along with it and so they'd moved to Runswick in the north-west of England. Sometimes he'd miss his small town which hardly even populated two thousand people which was saying a lot about the size. The school he now went to itself already had half the amount of that population. Crazy world. Roman had had a few good friends and the rest were what he considered as acquaintances; they were there for the sole purpose for him to lean on if he fell and vice-versa. Kind of sad. It was easy adjusting for someone like him. Roman continued being civil to his parents, students in his class, his teachers, his new friends. And not long later he'd become one of the well-known people in his grade which suited him just fine. He had the automatic pass to know everyone, be invited to parties and become mutual friends with all that were like him. Roman wasn't sure if he liked it but he definitely never turned down an offer to a house party.

He had recently changed the style of his room and ripped down all his posters from three years back with all the singers he used to like. The colour scheme also changed from shades of green and blue to mocha, greys, and blacks. His parents let him do whatever he pleased in case he snapped just like Sofia did.

Roman stood on the back of his shoe in turn to take them off and he heaved himself over to his wardrobe at the very corner. Now, what would someone wear for a party? A hoodie? Just a jacket? Birthday suit? He grinned laughing at himself and took out a faded red hoodie and ripped black jeans. That'd do.

He headed over to the bed and laid them down for later.

Taking one last fleeting glance over his room, he turned and was startled as his door opened right in front of his face, his mother stepping in with his backpack he'd forgotten to pick up when he entered the house.

"Roman," she breathed relieved and dropped the bag, enveloping him in a tight hug.

"Did you guys thing I'd left the country or—"

"You're so stupid. Here's your bag you left by the door, don't leave it again or I'll think you want it thrown in the trash."

She let go of him.

"Uh, yes. Yes, mom, I know," he replied, taking his bag and placing it under his bed.

"Did you see the removal van outside?"

"New neighbours?" Roman mused and stumbled over to his window and peered out. Indeed, there was a removal van just opposite his house and he saw an elderly couple stood watching the people move about their furniture.

47

Roman sagged. "I thought it would be someone my age," he sulked.

"Immature and making their parents worried all the time?" his mother wondered.

"What? No. They're old. Why do old people constantly move onto our street? Aren't old people supposed to prefer quiet places? There's a main road just outside, don't you think they'll fall over one day and be ran over—"

"I heard you and your dad. You're going out just after disappearing for a whole day? Do you think that's wise?"

"I'm not doing drugs, okay? I promise, I'm not that type of person. This is Will's friends party and he's in Law Society like me. He's basically a saint."

His mother regarded him with a withering stare. "Does that automatically make his friends the same?"

"I hope so? I could go on about him being great. He's rich, funny, he has quite a nice face too to some extent."

"You like him?" his mother asked raising a laughing eyebrow.

Roman scoffed. "As if, mom. We don't talk at all, but he invited basically everyone he knows."

He hoped this was enough to convince her. It's not like he lied in any part of that though because it had all been true, he just didn't make it sound very convincing.

His mother sighed, averting her gaze to her clasped hands. She looked up and met his gaze. "Fine. Just stay outta trouble."

Roman suppressed the need to laugh. He nodded and smiled instead. "I'll try my best."

"That's all I ask," she smiled and patted him on the shoulder.

Rain began to dribble from the sky at 8pm just before the party started and the sun had long gone and taken the rest of the day off for the moon to take over and shine. It wasn't doing a great job because it shone behind thick rain clouds which obscured any light coming through.

Roman closed the blinds to his bedroom window, watching thin lines of dark blue race downwards. Cahil would be there in a few minutes, he was always on time.

Roman's mother came into the room without him noticing and he shrieked when he turned back from the window.

She giggled. "Have you charged your phone?"

"Don't worry about me. I've done this many times," Roman responded, walking by his mom and stuffing Lotus Biscuits inside his backpack. When he noticed a silence that had settled in the room, he turned, and his mom had eyebrows in her hair.

"The food might be really bad," he said dumbly and continued packing mints into a pocket in his jeans.

"When I was your age, if the party food wasn't good, we'd get a Domino's."

Something soft was thrown on the floor by him and he looked to see a small wad of cash containing a few notes.

"That's all I'm leaving you with, don't give it to anyone unless they're dying."

And she was gone.

A car horn echoed through his street that shook him. His phone chimed and it was Cahil.

Roman got into the passenger seat and clipped his seatbelt in just before they took a sharp turn of a corner. He didn't even indicate.

"You took long. I bet you were too busy in your bedroom," said Cahil, two hands on the steering wheel and tapping a thumb against it rhythmically.

"I was actually," he said. "Tidying is good for the soul. Marie Kondo says so."

"You watch that?" He raised an eyebrow at the windscreen.

"Of course," he said dryly.

Minutes fell by as the rain lashed against the windscreen and the wipers swept the water off in merciless manner. They drove in complete silence. He didn't like silence.

"Can we turn the radio on or something?"

"Sure."

Classical music filled the car and Roman groaned rubbing his face in irritation. He did that a lot.

"What's wrong with classical? It's good for the soul," Cahil explained.

"It's perfect, don't sweat it," Roman grunted.

"When does the party start?"

"It started at eight."

"It'll be really late when you get there."

"What can I say, I'm fashionably late."

Roman sighed and shifted his gaze to the view out his own window. The world was dark around them and consumed their entire being, it seemed that the only light that emanated was the lights alongside them on the highway. A constant rush of wind that ran against the vehicle was present and the roads were tarmacked well because Roman didn't feel the need to apologise to the tyres. He leaned his head against the window and closed his eyes for a few moments, letting the warm glow of orange wash over his face as they hurtled a little over seventy along the motorway.

Cahil decelerated and they stopped outside number twenty-seven Carston Ridge. Roman barely noticed until he was nudged.

Loud music from inside pulsed its way outside and there were a few people already drunk near the drinks table they saw earlier. The lights strewn over the hedges seemed to be flares of welcome and they glowed with a warm intensity. They hadn't found it difficult to find a parking area because everyone had come on foot as they lived nearby.

Roman turned to Cahil with hesitation. "Hey, how about you come join me," he offered. "If you're not doing anything tonight. I'd like a friend."

Cahil remained still and staring ahead blankly, running his thumb over the symbol on his car keys. He finally nodded curtly. "Thanks, Roman. You're the coolest Yank I know."

"Uh, I'm Canadian—"

Cahil had already shut the car door behind and was waiting for him to get out so he could lock the doors. Roman stumbled out, clutching his backpack by a strap and he felt his mind tip over from being in that shaky car for almost an hour. Together they made their way to the front door.

"Is Will here? Do you know?"

"I dunno. I'm gonna go to the kitchen."

"No, wait. Can we take a picture at the front so I can print it out?"

Cahil was already taking out his phone. Roman felt bad so he complied, and they quickly took a picture. They checked the photo and Roman grinned. Cahil's hair was dark and it joined the blackness of the night as one.

"Nice," Roman said.

"Do you mind if I go pee? I had a Pepsi before I left, and you know me—"

"Yeah okay, good for you," Roman cut him off, not wanting to hear what came next.

Cahil smiled gratefully and jogged inside, consumed by the music. Roman wondered if the neighbours here cared. Surely, they would.

He took his phone out and glanced at the time. 7:54pm. Usually Roman wouldn't have noticed if anyone was staring at him but he saw in the corner of his eye a girl his age that stood by the car that was parked in front of them. He turned and met the girl's gaze. She was smirking for some reason and Roman frowned lightly.

The girl kept her distance and continued her unnerving stare, her face partially darkened as the small glow from the streetlight stopped halfway across her face.

"Hi," she said, raising a nonchalant eyebrow. "Who might you be?"

"I might be Roman," Roman responded confidently.

The girl laughed and she stopped sounding so tense and made her way to stand in front of Roman. She was tall, around the same height as him.

"Roman's such a funny name, don't you think?"

"I was named after the city I was conceived in."

"You're obviously not from around here." She started sounding gruff again. "Mind if I ask where?"

"Not at all. Canada."

"Wow."

"Yeah," he shifted uncomfortably. "I'll go now."

She nodded and she made her way inside, glancing behind her once to look at Roman. Some of the drunk people at the driveway were staring but they quickly went back to screaming along to a song from inside. *Payphone* by *Maroon 5*. Roman didn't let himself be shaken by her because he wouldn't leave without knowing what she wanted.

five.

He watched as she set the drinks on the table in the garden, working efficiently and lining them up rim to rim.

She stopped and looked up to him with an amused expression on her face. He gave her the thumbs up and she scowled, trailing back indoors and reappearing by his side in seconds.

"Do you know when he gets here?" he asked, tearing his eyes away from the night sky.

The clouds had blocked out the stars and the only thing that emitted light were the streetlights.

"In the next few minutes," she replied and leaned a head on his shoulder making them both stumble slightly backwards. She giggled but his face remained cold as he turned to her. Immediately, her laughter ceased, and she stared back at him.

He didn't like what she pulled on him, those little jerks of affection but he made no attempt to tell her it was stupid. But inside his mind, he smiled because soon she would be dead, and it wouldn't matter to him anymore. Out of the picture just like that. So he decided to play along just for tonight and tonight only.

"You're looking pretty today."

"Oh," she said. She didn't smile but he knew she was good at keeping it in. At lying.

"Who do you like more? Me or him?"

"You," she replied with confidence.

"But I know you also love him very much."

"There's enough room in my heart for two."

He didn't say anything but continued to gaze at her with a look of interest crossing his face.

"And you like me back."

He chuckled softly before leaning in and kissing her softly and slowly. They hung there together for a while because he pulled away. She searched his eyes for his love for her and didn't find it. Or it was never there.

"When the party's over, we'll pick this up," he assured her. A lie.

"We have ten minutes," she grumbled, hands twisting to his chest.

"Which isn't long. Remember what you're supposed to do," he said firmly.

"Scare her," she replied bitterly.

"I'll be giving you this." He gave her something small and heavy which made her eyes widen in awe. "I'll have a matching."

She blushed.

A car decelerating and parking outside.

"Can we—"

"He's here. Get going. Now."

She adjusted her clothes and took one last look at him. He didn't look back and continued to gaze out the window calmly.

"You never liked me, did you?" she said with dismay.

"Good luck and goodbye."   The sound of a car approaching made her shrink into the shadows and she closed the door and left to the cold world of outside

six.

Robyn checked her phone once more to make sure the address was right. It was correct and she raised her hazel eyes to the house she stood in front of, a hand stuffed in her trench coat pocket.

The train ride there was a blur and she didn't remember if she'd spoken to anybody on the way.

The house was enormous and when it was enormous it meant that it must've been three acres, the driveway was as big as her back garden. The rock music from indoors was audible from the outside and she wondered if the neighbours minded. Although, it was sophisticatedly decorated with LED lights that pierced the thick darkness around. People her age were constantly arriving, and they were in groups with friends. Immediately regretting her decision, she decided to step inside the driveway to make her seem less out of place. Everyone was dressed in clothes that showed a lot of skin even though it was early November. Crazy. She hadn't bothered to change. She didn't even remember what she did that day. A large table was sat in the driveway to the side serving all kinds of drinks that were no doubt spiked. Robyn edged away from it, keeping her distance from all the people who were drunk already. It was only 8pm.

She stepped inside the house and she felt the music flow through every vein in her body, reawakening the angry and dormant migraine that she had a few hours ago. However, the house was beautiful, marble floor and the hallway itself was a few metres tall, stretching into a dome. She wouldn't have known if she hadn't stepped inside. Large portraits hung on each side of the house and the room led to a few others: the kitchen, living room and bathroom. Suddenly she remembered Will and she took a deep breath and all she smelt was the strong stink of alcohol. She didn't like it.

"Forget it," she muttered venomously, turning back and instantly walked into a solid wall. Though it wasn't a wall, it was a person, and that person was Leo. Her heart skipped an uncomfortable beat and rubbed her nose as tears stung in her eyes from the impact. Blinking them away, her eyes met his who looked at her in equal surprise.

"Are you following me or something?" she snapped irritably.

"No, I was invited," Leo said defensively, raising his voice above the sheer volume of the music. "Short notice but my parents were too busy arguing so I snuck out."

"Oh. Small world."

His dark eyes began scanning the many people dancing to bad music and his gaze came back to Robyn. "I hate parties."

"Me too," Robyn agreed.

He laughed for no reason. He was dressed in what she'd seen him in earlier that day. "How'd you get here?" he asked.

"Train. Not worth it," she gestured to the air around and rolled her eyes. "What about you?"

"The tram fares are way cheaper and they're good for the environment. Did you know they run on electric and—"

56

"I know that," she scowled.

"We'll get the tram together if you want?"

"Perhaps."

Another song came on and it blasted even louder than the previous. A really bad one. They were all bad.

"Do you wanna leave?" Leo asked turning curtly to Robyn. Before he had even said the word leave, Robyn nodded frantically. Leo smiled sympathetically and they made their way to the front door again. But a girl barred the way, eyes hooded and she switched her eyes lazily between the two like she was playing slow badminton.

"Where are you two going?" she questioned, running a casual hand through her blonde hair.

"Leaving. Is there a problem?" Robyn replied as politely as she could.

She shook her head mockingly. "No, you can't just *leave*. You were invited, weren't you? Nobody will step foot out of this house until it ends."

A tall girl strode past and she didn't even look her way.

"What about her?" Leo quizzed, patience slipping away.

"I trust her. I don't trust you two."

"We don't even know you," Robyn stated flatly.

"Yeah, I reckon if you really got to know us, you'd love us. We're hysterical."

The girl had nothing to say to that and stayed silent for the longest, most awkward moment. Robyn and Leo stood waiting in anticipation.

"You're with Will, aren't you? He'll be disappointed." And she slipped into the living room where the main entertainment was. The moment she disappeared from sight, they both swivelled around to look at each other in unison.

"You're with Will? Atwick-Pierce?" Leo asked.

"You are too?" Robyn replied frowning, betrayal showing on her face, so she disguised it.

"We're actually dating too. Sort of. It's complicated," Leo mumbled.

"Oh."

"He probably invited a helluva lot of people then, huh."

"Yeah."

Leo sighed and slumped into a sitting position in the corner inside the house. Robyn was going to do the same, hesitating for a second before sitting opposite him, one knee up and one leg outstretched. They remained silent for a few seconds, letting the loud music echo through their bodies and overcome them, becoming part of the party. Leo began watching the door, watching more people enter than leave.

"How do you know Will?" Robyn questioned.

"From the internet," he responded in resignation, not bothering to hide his shame.

Robyn raised her eyebrows. "Me too. This is crazy. And he asked you today? To come to this party. Because it was his friend's?" Robyn tried to stay calm.

"Yeah, let me show you his texts."

Leo took his phone out and a few moments later, he showed the screen to Robyn who drank every word in, wishing his heartfelt messages had been to her. Too full of meaning to be to a friend. Her eyes narrowed as she looked to Leo.

"Is Will your rebound or something?"

Leo looked attacked but made a halfway nod and laugh. She showed Leo her texts too. They gazed at each other wordlessly and both exhaled.

"How did she know we were with Will?" Leo wondered.

"I don't know – some list or something, with faces. Maybe we can find it and see who else Will invited. Maybe his whole year."

"Robyn, that doesn't exist—"

But Robyn had already stood shakily and was halfway across the hall. Leo wheezed and followed suit. They reached the living room and mutually concluded that it wouldn't be in there.

"I feel so dizzy, I stood up wrong," Robyn muttered leaning against the wall and closing her eyes.

"Is it the music? Is it that bad?" Leo had a grin on his face and Robyn could hear it through her closed eyelids.

"Health reasons."

"Sucks." Leo stood patiently and spotted a stairway that harboured nobody.

"Hey, let's have an adventure upstairs."

After a second, Robyn looked to where Leo was pointing, and a grin tugged at her mouth.

Once successfully at the landing they were in awe at the length of the corridor and the decorations. The carpet seemed expensive, a deep blue with golden spirals that curled the whole length of the floor, doors every few metres and chandeliers hung stylishly, clear diamonds that sparkled with gusto. At the ends of each side was a window that was tall as room itself and the smell was slightly more relieving. The music was also quieter, and they didn't need to shout anymore. It was also slightly colder.

"Do you think Will's house is like this too?" Leo mumbled.

"I don't know. Okay, choose a room."

He went to the first door on the left and examined the intricate carvings of the door.

"We'll just go left to right," he said, and Robyn agreed. Before opening the door, Leo giggled nervously like a crazed fan. "I feel like a detective."

Robyn rolled her eyes and prodded him to open it. He inched it open and peeked in. When nothing seemed to pose a threat, they entered and closed the door behind to make it look normal on the outside. It was the bathroom, the floor a sepia marble, matching the glossy bathtub and sink, grey and blue mosaic tiles a few centimetres thick that laced itself halfway up around the room.

"If I had a bathroom like this, I'd pee every day," Leo said in amazement.

"Do you not pee every day?"

"Fine, I'd take a dump every day."

Robyn wrinkled her nose in disgust, but she agreed. It *was* beautiful.

"It won't be in here."

"Look at the toilet paper holder. It looks like it's made of gold."

"I could do with that. Sell it online for good money."

"I'll bid it off you."

"Good luck with that."

They left the room laughing and discussing the amount they'd bid it off for and left it the way it was. Robyn entered first and it was a bedroom. Massive again, a double bed, big decorative window and well carpeted. Although, there was no wardrobe or beside table.

"What do his parents do?"

"I bet they're both lawyers," Robyn said in envy.

"I think they're strippers."

She shrieked, laughing.

There was a door at the very end which was probably the ensuite.

"Is there anything behind that door, you think?" Robyn pointed a finger to it.

Leo frowned, silent for a moment. "Robyn. I think we should leave," his voice had turned hard and it came as a low whisper. "Listen. I think there's someone showering."

They listened, straining their ears and they could make out the sound of running water and music, though they weren't sure if it was coming from the door or downstairs.

"Oh. Okay. Should we take their mints too? There's a basket of wrapped mints over there."

Leo considered it for a bit and eventually shook his head. Then his eyes landed on something on the floor and he gasped. "Look."

Robyn looked to where Leo pointed, and froze. A gun with a silencer and it lay beside the bed like an ornament.

"What should we do?" Leo whispered.

"Leave?" she suggested.

Leo nodded. They slipped out through the door.

"I'm still pissed at Will," she muttered.

"Don't sweat it, he probably invited all his friends."

"Yeah," she said sulkily. She glanced at Leo and realised she'd never properly looked at him before.

His hair, his hair was black and freakishly glossy, his eyes also reminded her of whisky when it came into light. She shook the thoughts out of her head as they opened the door of the third. It was empty. Just like the others. Completely empty. Not even carpeted – it was dull grey and there was a single window and naked bulb that hung looking lonely.

"I have a good feeling about this," Robyn said, cautiously closing the door behind them, not taking her eyes off the room.

"I have a *bad* feeling, this is where we die," Leo said, but he didn't move. He waited for her reply.

Robyn inspected the room, hands on hips, a frown settled on her face.

"Yeah, this is so weird," she muttered.

"Maybe they're refurbishing?" Leo suggested attempting to reassure himself.

61

"Probably not," Robyn replied and made her way to the only window, Leo eventually following reluctantly.

"I smell dust, this room isn't used a lot – I'm such a detective."

"Congrats, you can smell."

"It takes a lot to smell."

"I'm sure."

"I wish there were another two people to help us look, that way there are people on the lookout," Leo said as he approached Robyn. Robyn peered down at the people in the back garden, all drinking and chatting away like it was the best day of their lives.

She sighed bitterly, hands on the windowsill to steady herself. "I can't see Will."

"I thought you didn't care?"

Robyn turned and she seemed to be in her own little world, a sad smile appearing on her face. "Of course. I don't."

The two of them gazed outside in silence and wondered. They always seemed to be in silence, but it wasn't uncomfortable. Robyn went from each face down below to the next searching for Will, but none matched. Leo pulled her out of her own mind.

"What does Robyn mean?"

"Huh?" Robyn blinked. She wasn't even expecting that, it kind of threw her. "I'm assuming it means the freedom of a robin," she replied, and her smile morphed into a grin. "What does Leo mean?"

"Lion, probably."

"Oh, because you're so scary?"

He laughed and after a few moments it withered to a silence.

"Robyn with an I or Y?"

"A Y. It's German."

"Nice."

"Let's get out. It's horrible in here," Robyn said finally.

Leo agreed and they left silently.

The next four doors were just other bedrooms and a nursery. Nothing that was worthy of notice.

"We found nothing. I told you," Leo sighed and fell to the floor. Robyn joined him.

"What a waste of walking."

"Walking is never a waste if it was fun."

"You found that fun?"

"Well, it wasn't boring."

She laughed.

"That girl was so weird though. Do you know her?"

"No, of course not."

"Why did we listen to her?" Leo frowned to himself. "I hate not questioning things."

"She was scary tall," reminded Robyn.

"I'm taller," he insisted. "I find it hard to believe they only have two floors. If they don't have another maybe there's a basement."

Robyn made a thinking noise. "Let's go ask."

Robyn and Leo came to a stop several metres from a couple who looked sober – a guy who stared at his shoes glumly and a girl that was glaring into the crowd. She assumed they were a couple and her assumptions and intuition were most of the time correct.

"Do you want to ask?" Robyn nudged Leo who recoiled violently.

"No, they're strangers, that's weird," he hissed and pushed Robyn forward. The couple didn't even notice, they continued whatever they were doing so Robyn started waving at them.

"Hi."

The girl turned from the crowd and stared at both of them with a laser blue stare. If looks could kill they'd be on their way to purgatory already. If that existed.

"Hi," she said back slightly questioning.

"Do you know the guy who lives here?" she asked, twiddling her thumbs. Robyn also smiled maniacally. The guy stared at her with fear.

"Lorcan. Why?"

"We, uh…" Robyn looked to the sky. "Do they have a basement, perhaps?"

The couple turned to look at each other, wondering whether Leo and Robyn were crazy.

"They do but it's only for authorised personnel," the guy spoke up for the first time. He was Australian.

"Yeah, you can't just simply waltz down there, you'll need access to a code," the girl said nodding along with him.

"Are we talking about this house or something else?" Leo finally said.

The couple stopped and stood.

"We know the code. But you have to give us something in return."

Robyn hated that people still said that. "Uh, I don't think so. Do you know what's down there?" Robyn said.

"No, we never go down there. I mean, Christian here has but he doesn't remember it."

Christian nodded solemnly. "I was drunk."

"We kinda wanna go down there. Explore, you know. Stretch our legs," Leo said.

"Okay," the girl said.

"You don't remember anything at all?" Leo pressed.

A gasp. "Oh my God, you're Robyn," the girl said quickly, her face merging into surprise.

Robyn blinked and jerked backwards like she'd been shot.

"River? Holy crap."

"How do you know Lorcan?"

"You know each other?" Leo asked.

All three nodded.

"Old family friends."

"Until her mother left them."

"So now it's just her dad."

"Loner forever."

"Shut up."

"Listen, we'll give you access if you give us some of your good stuff," River said rubbing her fingertips together.

"I don't have weed on me at the moment," Robyn lied. The only time anyone ever needed her was drugs.

"Sorry, then we can't help you."

River took Christian's hand and led him out the door. The girl who had stopped Leo and Robyn nowhere in sight.

"Do you still want to leave?"

Leo thought a bit. "Can we get some drinks?" he asked awkwardly.

Robyn blinked, somewhat astonished. She'd blinked in surprised so much that night she thought her eyes were permanently going to fuse together.

"A drink?" she echoed.

"Yeah, nothing too strong."

Robyn shook her head. "You're going to lay unconscious and drown in your own vomit," she said.

Leo shrugged hopelessly. "So?"

"For one, that's fatal—"

"It doesn't matter," he muttered and took out his phone. "Please can we get some drinks. I'm bored."

"Is my holy presence not enough?"

"I wouldn't go as far as to say it's holy…"

She looked annoyed. "I would."

"Can you give me some of the good stuff?"

"No," she firmly. "Do you even have money on you?"

"I'll pay you tomorrow," he said.

"Tomorrow's a Sunday."

"I know."

"Sorry, I can't. My clients are usually people I don't know, and I know you."

"So that makes it right?" He raised an eyebrow.

She sighed and splayed her palms upwards. "My hands are tied."

"Well let me untie them."

"Funny," she said sarcastically.

She didn't know what caused his mood to shift so much. Maybe it was Will. Or being out of options and hitting a wall.

"Sorry. I can't."

He avoided her gaze, eyes fuming as he drummed him fingers on the floor.

"Leo, let's go home—"

He met her gaze with no problem and her heart did a strange dance move, like a lurch but more graceful.

"When did you start talking to Will?" he asked. His eyes were so dark, and they stared back at Robyn with an unwavering stare. She'd never felt so intimidated in her life.

"I don't know. I don't remember. It was around end of August. Why is this relevant—?"

"I started talking to him in March."

Robyn waited.

"Do you know what that means? It means he probably grew tired of talking to me and went to you instead. After the breakup with James in February I hit up Will and we were so good together."

"I didn't ruin this intentionally, Leo. That's not fair on me. For all we know I meant little to him and you meant the world. He never expressed anything more than friendship," Robyn said hoping it would stop Leo from crying.

He seemed like he had gone through too much and stood up. "Then why isn't he here?" he said, all emotion emptied from his voice.

"He might be stuck in traffic?" Robyn suggested, standing too.

"It's eight."

"So? Roadworks."

"Can we go check?"

"Of course."

They made their way in silence, Leo at the front by several steps and Robyn behind keeping a distance and making sure he wouldn't blow up again. His anger was like no other – quiet and passive aggressive, not loud and tearful like others. But it made her think twice about where she went wrong, and Robyn never let herself feel that way.

The music got louder and swallowed them up like a monster as they entered. There were more people now and a few people had already flooded out from the living room. An awful lot of litter too. Leo tensed and stared at someone from the crowd. Robyn craned her neck to see who it was but none of their faces were familiar to her. When she turned back to Leo, he was gone. She felt a panic settle inside her like darkness, and it spread through her blood like a disease.

seven.

Leo slipped away from Robyn, anger simmering inside him and it increased exponentially when the dancing bodies beside him pushed intrudingly into him.

He wanted to scream.

The one time he loved someone, and they'd loved him back, he realised he also liked someone else. Maybe not love but nonetheless it made him feel insignificant. It was somewhat irrational, but he couldn't help it.

Leo made his way to who he thought was Will, he saw him drinking out of a red plastic cup like he'd done it a million times and was chatting to someone with red hair. Flaming red hair. Leo stopped where he had thought he'd seen him, trying his best to stand still despite everyone rocking the building and singing along. No blond stood in the vicinity and no red head either. He cursed and made his way to the drinks table, hesitating and rethinking his life choices as he neared red cups identically placed in rows and columns. His hand stopped near the furthest cup away because it was less likely to be
spiked. He made a grab for the one he had his eye out for. He'd never had anything stronger than beer. Before his brain

could object to his impulsive decision, he tipped his head back and downed which caused him to splutter as some crept down his chin. The alcohol burned slightly in his throat and it even had a warm feeling which replaced the anger from before. It muted his mind. However, it wasn't enough to suppress his thoughts of Will, so he downed half of what remained which wasn't a lot. He realised it had already been drank from and blanched. Then just as quickly as he'd drank it, those thoughts faded and he felt the need to laugh and cry at the same time, it was a strange sensation. Leo stumbled out of the room, shoving people out of the way this time and found himself in the kitchen.

The kitchen window was smashed, and it was chilly, but Leo felt fuelled, so he sauntered over to an island in the middle which held boxes of pizzas. There were lots of people in the kitchen and everyone seemed to know each other, everyone was practically vibrating with energy. It was less packed though which meant Leo wasn't breathing in human skin anymore. It wasn't as half as comfortable as being stuffed in a coffin though.

He picked a plain margherita and began stuffing his face, not realising how hungry he was, and he took another before others did. He seated himself of a stool which faced another window this time intact with glass. It overlooked the front garden and driveway and he could see there were still people pouring into the house. He wondered how it was possible to invite so many people. He guessed the house contained a few hundred people and he was sure he didn't even know that many people in his lifetime, never mind at this moment in time.

Sighing, he dusted flour off his fingertips and eyed the remaining slices of pizza that were left untouched. The cheese looked so amazing. So he took two more slices and chewed happily, savouring every bit. A chuckle came from behind him which he didn't think much about, but another reflection joined him as Leo stared out the window. A lean figure stood beside him and he was smiling. Leo

turned and instantly felt like he needed to stuff the pizza back into that cardboard box because he was embarrassing himself.

A guy around his age stood with wavy blond hair and deep-set blue eyes that shone in the chandelier's light. But his heart sank when he realised it wasn't Will, not even close. He made his disappointment clear on his face.

"Hey," he grinned ignoring the look on his face. "Are you gonna share that pizza with the rest of us?"

Leo frowned and stopped chewing. He felt his sense of authority heighten like never before and he liked it.

"You wanna share my germs or something?"

"Maybe I do."

He raised an eyebrow. "I had a cold last week."

"Are you sure it wasn't the coronavirus?"

"That's not funny," Leo grunted and was going to turn back.

"I was trying to flirt with you, idiot. Or are you too drunk? Would that be considered as taking advantage of someone?" He pretended to think, blue eyes glittering and tapping his chin.

"Not if they're both drunk." Came Leo's reply.

The guy cocked his head to a side, gazing at Leo like he was a mystery to be solved. Leo stared back levelly.

"You want a drink?"

"Only if it tastes nice."

He took three drinks from a nearby table and gave them to Leo who grabbed them one by one and downed them, ignoring his bladder pressing him to go and piss. It always told him to. He went through them like tissues leaving one partially empty and eventually he finished off with some more pizza.

"You're taking advantage of me," Leo stated coolly. A bit of cheese got stuck on his face.

"I like you."

"I like me too."

The guy shook his head, eyes laughing, and he finished Leo's drink for him.

Leo glowered. "I was gonna drink that." Leo finished his pizza. "I wanna go home."

He chortled. "Poor you."

"I wanna go and talk to James. Or Will."

"You're looking right at him."

"No, my James and Will. You're the knock-off version," Leo snapped.

"Excuse you."

"You have nice hair though. I'll give you that."

"I *am* James."

"James Bond?" Leo echoed.

James laughed but he stilled, like a heartbeat finally stopping. Leo watched him. The gentle slope of his nose and his strong set jawline – features he suddenly recalled from his memory.

"Leo," James breathed eyes wide and guilt stricken.

"What?" Leo mumbled blearily and he took everything not to throw up. He'd eaten his pizzas too fast and he had bladder paining amounts of alcohol. He needed to pee now. Badly.

"I– Leo, it's me. James Munday."

"Funny name," he said, and he bolted, rushing through the crowds like a crazed fan, ignoring James' cries to stop. He remembered the bathroom upstairs he'd visited with Robyn and made his way up the stairs. Robyn. Where was she? Probably screwing Will somewhere and he dusted her out of his mind like dust. Shutting the door behind him and locking what seemed to be the lock he threw up in the bathtub because it was big enough. After a few moments he sighed and went to wash his face then wash his hands and peed. Instantly, he felt better but another bout of nausea overcame him, and he vomited again this time in the sink. There was a knock on the door, it was urgent, and every knock jerked harshly in Leo's mind. It twisted and wriggled into his brain and he grit his teeth.

"Go away, James," he yelled.

"It's not James. It's me. Open the door, please."

"Who's me?"

"Robyn!"

Leo sagged and turned the shower head on, washing away the vomit. He shuddered.

Another knock came and it was louder and longer, penetrating his mind like nails. Being sensitive to sound wasn't what he bargained for.

"Okay, I'm coming, I'm coming, Jesus." He snapped the lock open and Robyn stumbled in, toppling over Leo and they slammed onto the floor together. His head hit the floor with a smash and his vision distorted, imaged pulled sideways and a high-pitched ringing sang in his ears like a cardiac monitor of a deceased heartbeat. Robyn was somewhere screaming obscenities and he saw her figure looming over him like in those movies. Was he in a movie? Then suddenly, he took hold of his vision and it stopped pulling at the edges, becoming clear again and he yawned, ears popping. Robyn was practically on top of him, but she didn't seem to notice. Leo mumbled something about being alive and Robyn shook him by his shirt collar.

"Hey, don't you dare rip my shirt."

"Leo, don't die," Robyn cried still shaking him like she was trying to find a phone in a blanket – the phone being his consciousness.

"Uh, yeah, please let go," he said.

She shrieked and let him fall, hitting his head against the bathtub which in a way hurt less. He sat delicately and felt his head expecting blood when he withdrew his hand but there wasn't anything there. Thank whatever God was out there.

"Follow my finger, can you see it?" Robyn held her index upright and moved it just in front of Leo. His eyes unfocused again and he slumped backwards, this time Robyn tugged on his collar, so he jolted to a stop.

She sighed in relief. "I'm sorry, Leo. I saw you run up the stairs and you looked green and red at the same time—"

"That's racist," he murmured and sat again his eyes open but not seeing. He dragged his eyes to hers and blinked. Recognition clicked and he cringed. "Did I have a seizure?" he asked.

"Pretty damn close," Robyn said breathlessly.

"There goes my dignity."

Robyn continued to look at him, worry etched on her face. She was pretty in a way but obviously not his type, he went for heartbreakers. His eyes shifted to the door behind her and it was closed.

"Okay." Leo stood stiffly and his vision felt all right. Good enough for him and he turned to walk by her, but she stopped him.

"Where are you going? Don't stand up, stupid." Robyn led him to sit at the edge of the bathtub and she sat beside him, an awkward arm slinked around his shoulders. She rubbed absently and bit her lower lip in thought. They sat in their usual silence.

"I have to go," she said.

73

The words came slow to Leo, but he turned, eyes calm.

"Because you feel guilty?"

"What? No. Because I promised my dad I'd be home by nine."

He turned away. "I only have one back you can stab," he said. Leo didn't know what he was saying anymore, and the words flooded out, losing control of the gates. "I was talking to James. My ex."

He could sense Robyn tense, but he carried on.

"I didn't recognise him. You know because I was drunk. And at school I always avoid looking at him. He looked different. Good different." He turned to look at her for the first time and she'd dropped her gaze to his feet, chewing lightly on her lip. Leo waited for a reply, a snarky comment but none came.

She sighed. "I'm going home, Leo."

"I wanna go to the moon. You know, I look out there sometimes and wonder where that flag is. I never find it. Because the moon landing was probably fake."

"How could they have faked it?"

"I dunno, some sorcery shit."

"I've never heard you swear before."

"I'm pretty sure I have."

"You're not the type."

"You dunno me at all."

They descended in a tense silence, listening to the uneven sounds of dripping from the shower nozzle and feeling the soft vibrations of music from beneath their feet.

Robyn shifted slightly and out of the corner of Leo's eyes he could see her take a yellow slip of paper out from her pocket and she quickly returned it, looking to the window. He chose to ignore that and turned to the door as a knock sounded.

"Leo. Are you in there? It's James."

The door handle shook as the person behind the door attempted to open the door.

"It's locked," Leo called.

Robyn glanced at the door and looked to Leo with an expression he'd never seen before.

"I'll leave and you can stay with James," she said gently.

Leo didn't blink. He stood slowly and went to the door, opening it with just a turn.

"Oh. It wasn't locked," he said.

James stood there a panicked expression on his face and he looked at Robyn.

Leo rolled his eyes. "Get over yourself, I barely even know her."

Hurt flickered behind Robyn's eyes and James stepped back when Leo stormed past. He continued past the living room full of noise, numbness spreading through his entire being. When he reached the driveway, he was stopped by the same girl.

"Are you following me?" Leo snarled.

"What did I tell you?" she said, her voice slow and scornful.

Leo had had enough. "You think you can keep me here against my will? Fuck you," he spat, and the girl pushed him harshly back in the bounds of the house.

"I'm doing this for your safety," she whispered, and he could've sworn there were tears in her eyes.

"Is everything okay, Leo?"

Leo spun around and glared. James dragged Leo in the safe zone of the house away from the girl who stood perfectly still. He would've burned with embarrassment if he weren't still drunk, but he couldn't care less.

"Who was that?"

"Such a creep," Robyn muttered, and Leo turned hazily in surprise. Both James and Robyn dragged Leo back indoors and they sat him on the stairs that nobody seemed to be going up on. They fidgeted without talking to each other for minutes and gazed at the crowd who were getting drunker by the minute. Leo could feel the vibrancy growing like a shadow from it and it reached out to him with a beckoning hand and touched him.

"I might get another drink." He stood purposefully and ignored his friend's looks of disapproval. "Anyone wanna join?"

"Let's take a back exit, she'll never know," Robyn suggested.

"I changed my mind. I might stay."

"Fine."

Leo scoffed. "I thought you wanted to go home?"

"I texted my dad, said I had to study for a test."

"You can't outrun your problems, Robyn."

Robyn glared and stood too but stayed silent. Leo rolled his eyes and walked but Robyn grabbed him by his hand.

"Let's find Will," she said firmly.

"Who's Will?" James said but Robyn ignored him.

"Don't you want to meet the person you talked to for so long? Confront him? He's not even here and we've been here half an hour. Don't you?"

Something clicked inside Leo's mind.

Yes, he did want to know what he was thinking. To know once and for all if he liked him in that way. Robyn felt him hesitate.

"If you don't want to do the confronting, I will."

Leo tried a grin and they walked to the back door, tips of their fingers still touching.

They reached the door that led to the garden and they exited, dodging past the intoxicated people stood breathing in what was left of the dry air. It would rain soon. Nobody stopped them this time and they got to the bottom of the garden. It was big and the trees stood tall outside like a side dish to it, fairy lights tangled within the fir branches that staggered to the roof of the house. Less people hung out in the garden than in the kitchen, so they didn't have to speak too quietly.

"Text Will," Robyn commanded, and Leo took his phone out.

Seconds passed.

"I've sent a message. Hopefully he'll respond because he was last seen seven minutes ago," Leo said, and Robyn nodded in response.

They waited in silence, staring at Leo's screen hoping for it to say 'Online'.

"You know the word obese. It just looks obese don't you think? All the letters are curved."

Robyn struggled to hide her laughter. "Being curved doesn't make you obese."

"I know. But think about it."

The two laughed but Leo's turned hostile. "He hasn't even bothered texting either one of us. Had me fooled."

Robyn tilted her head and her face shaped into something close to sympathy. "Me and you both." Robyn's smile reduced and she looked to the sky.

The sky seemed to be clouded with thick grey cotton balls that drifted alongside the wind, guiding them elsewhere, away from this place. A starless and empty night which made him uneasy even though there was a party raging inside.

"So, James. You have a thing for blonds?" Robyn teased.

"No, I have a thing for backstabbers." Leo trained his eyes on Robyn and she sighed.

"Are you still drunk? How much did you have?"

"Enough to wanna throw it back up again," he answered hotly.

"When we get back to Riverton, I'll get you some coffee on the way. Then you can tell me about James, it'll help with the anger."

This was Robyn edging near to comforting someone.

Leo grumbled. "You have to be home by nine though. It's—" Leo checked the screen. "You're not gonna make it."

"I told you, I'm staying," Robyn said gruffly. She fiddled with her hooped earring. "My dad is the only person I have that's close so lying wasn't easy."

Leo waited for her to say more. "What about your mother? Siblings?"

"My mother left two years ago. It's just us."

"Typical," Leo said.

Robyn nodded and averted her gaze to her shoes. They were covered in dirt.

He sighed and surveyed the garden, mind wandering as his eyes landed on everyone, thinking up what their life could be like. His eyes landed on James who was manoeuvring himself through the crowd towards them, a drink in hand. Robyn spotted him too and her eyes narrowed as he stumbled in front of them.

"James," she said uncertainly.

"Some guy, some blond, he wants to see you guys. Says he wants to talk to the two who were with me. I'm assuming it's you guys because you're the only people I've talked to – unless I'm even drunker than I thought—"

Leo immediately thought of Will and his eyes widened. "Did he say where?"

"At the driveway there's a Mercedes. Really shiny."

Leo and Robyn emerged from the front door and stopped as they fixed their gazes onto the girl who'd previously stopped them. She stopped texting and looked at them, then resumed. Leo could taste the freedom and desperately wanted to get away from the party clamour. Robyn led the way and barged past her, Leo faltered but Robyn widened her eyes angrily and they got halfway down the driveway before realising there was a black Mercedes idling with headlights puncturing the darkness. They doubled back and peered into the driver's seat and frowned.

"He left his keys in," Robyn whispered, pointing a slow finger to the ignition.

Leo sighed frustrated and that was all he remembered because afterwards there was a blinding pain to the head which made his body stiffen, stars dancing mockingly in front of his eyes. And then another hit, and he collapsed and then blank.

eight.

Elena arrived at the party glamorously late and already half drunk in the back seat of a cab. She paid the driver who looked at her with slight fear on his face. He probably thought she'd puke any minute. She was dressed in a cropped purple cardigan and a black denim skirt and black boots. It made her feel powerful. Especially being taller. Good feeling.

"Aren't you cold?" the taxi driver asked her contemptuously.

"Thanks, dad," she said before slamming the door and staggering to the driveway, gripping her phone in a hand.

She could feel the alcohol lingering in the air, and she stepped inside, wiping a stray tear that slipped out of reach from her eyes. The music seemed to press against her skin like water, forcing into her ears until they became deafening. She would probably step out of the clatter and her ears would still leak with noise. Her heels went from concrete to carpet and she headed to the drinks table in the kitchen. She parted the crowd easily because she was thin and slipped by anyone's notice. Not for long, she'd soon become the life of the party and everybody would know her name, that was her goal.

The house wasn't even a house, it was a mansion – big windows that would've let the sunlight gloriously shine in if it were day and when empty and night, the house would hold its breath and lie in wait for the unwelcome. She could only imagine.

The thought of Mark slipped silently into her head and she scowled as she thought of earlier events. How did he know? Her passcode was the date and year she realised she no longer loved Mark. 151219. She scoffed as she realised the sentiment behind that. Grabbing the nearest drink, she drank like she had been starved of water for days and instantly she felt a bubble of warmth and an emotional boost.

Elena made her way to the centre of the room fuelled by music and screaming people enjoying their nights like they didn't care about anything else. She bet half of them snuck out and lied to their parents, that's what Elena would've done if she had any parents left to lie to. She thought about her mum who lived in some unknown place and she scoffed.

"Hi! Hello," she called out to everyone.

A few people turned to stare at her blankly, but they returned to screaming along to the lyrics of some overrated love song.

Stand on the table.

She didn't know why she did the things she did, but she clambered onto the drinks table, knocking cups full of liquor over and seeping onto the floor. To her brain, four feet in the air was dizzying and she swayed. Then she screamed at the top of her lungs and lunged backwards and came crashing through glass of a window. The wind was knocked out of her and she flipped impossibly quickly down the length of the garden and a bout of confusion came over her as she came to a halt on her face. Glass was sprinkled like dust over her clothes and she grumbled, picking them off like drawing straws. Standing awkwardly, she looked around her and people crowded her snapping pictures discreetly on their phones. Good, recognition. Even if it wasn't the good kind.

Someone tall pushed through the crowd and stopped, facing Elena eyes ablaze and mouth set in a hard, straight line.

"What is wrong with you?"

The person's face blurred as she was hauled over someone's shoulder and they made their way back indoors, past the smashed window and up the stairs.

Elena groaned as her head made contact with floor and she could smell cheap perfume that suffocated the air like viscous liquid. A punch was inflicted on her jaw and she gasped, turning away and heaving herself up on an elbow. Or she tried. Another punch and she choked up a sob.

"I knew you were lying. You use that excuse every time."

A soft click came from behind her as she lay on the floor facing a double bed. The room she was in was a bedroom well decorated with matching carpet and bed covers. There was another door too in the corner that she felt was probably a bathroom. A single open window and outside was fresh air. Elena whirled herself around and her eyes widened in alarm.

She stood one hand on her hip and a gun levelled at her in her left, finger on the trigger. Was it loaded?

Elena turned back to stare at Vienna. "Uh, what are you doing?"

"Shut up and sit."

Elena did what she was told and scrambled onto her knees, arms gripping the fabric of her skirt, fear biting at her edges. She felt almost sober now. "I came here to have a good time, Vienna," she muttered desperately.

Vienna scoffed. "Why is it always about you?" she snapped allowing the anger to creep into her voice which stung Elena to the very core.

"That's not true," she said in a quiet voice. "Where did you get that?"

"Mark," she replied coldly. "Thanks to him, I can finally kill you."

"Oh, joy." A tactic formed in Elena's mind and her confidence sparked. "If you're gonna kill me, please don't do it. So you kill me. What then? Will you be satisfied?" Elena said, eyes on Vienna.

She didn't say anything, but her gun didn't hesitate. It still pointed to her accusingly, the barrel like a black cave.

"I can handle it. It's what I've wanted for a long time. Because of you, Mark doesn't even talk to me."

Elena thought she was one of those people who waffled before they were going to kill their victim. She knew how those ended. But she let her continue.

"You guys have been going out since you were *eleven.* Isn't that such a long time for someone like you. And Mark? Are you not bored of each other? I know that Mark's bored of you. Definitely showed today."

"I didn't know you liked Mark," Elena said uncertainly, and she waited until Vienna took her eyes off her before she continued poking around under the bed with her hand. She came across a cold long pole and gently took hold of it by its end.

"You don't notice things, do you? You never have. But Mark and I spoke today. After you left."

Elena stopped as her gun dipped downwards so if she shot, she'd shoot at the space in front of her knees. She could afford that. "He came to me today at my house."

Vienna's face contorted in anguish. "You're lying. Not that I care. You'll be out of the picture soon." Vienna relevelled her gun and her finger began squeezing the trigger.

83

"Someone will hear," Elena said, doing her best to inject laughter in her voice.

"Over the music? I have a suppressor," Vienna snarled and tapped the silencer twice with a manicured nail. That was new, she didn't have those earlier.

In that moment, Elena realised how fucked she was. She realised her dad was dead, her mother had started a new family in Wales, Mark was gone, the Vienna she knew was gone, and she was soon going to lose herself. It was a nice place to die, she supposed. If she died on the bed it would be less painful maybe.

Then there was a voice. A voice outside their door. No, two. Vienna's gaze hardened as she stared at Elena. The voices became louder and her eyes widened. Saw her take an angry glance at the window. "You've gone and ruined it," she hissed and then the trigger went off.

There was a cry and Elena realised it was from herself. She expected to feel like blinding pain in her racing across her body or death sooner or later, but she felt nothing.

Realising she had squeezed her eyes shut, she took a peek and saw Vienna slumped against the door, eyes widened in mild shock. Elena clamped a hand over her mouth and resisted the urge to scream. Even sat down, she felt the room spin and a feeling of detachment caved in her. The shot had been so loud, it was as if the silencer hadn't worked.

She'd shot herself in the head and blood painted the door behind her like spilled alcohol, the gun loosened in her hand. The voices were now outside the door. Before Elena realised what she was doing, she had dragged Vienna's body face-down inside the ensuite and fastened the lock. There was blood spatter on the door, and she hoped whoever was outside walked by, but she heard the door open and there wasn't a close noise. Breathing hard, her eyes darted around the room as voices started. Her eyes landed on the shower head. It was a bathroom. Wallpaper a cream colour, a shower block, a toilet at the far end and the floor was marble. Maybe if she pretended she was showering, they would avoid coming in. After all, they probably didn't live here.

A laugh echoed – it was female. Elena hurried over to the shower and turned it on. It drowned out their voices and Elena shuddered, taking another look she couldn't control to Vienna. The sides of her head wept with blood and where she'd dragged her was a trail of it. Why had she shot herself? Wasn't that a little dramatic? There was no need. Her thoughts muddled into each other like paint and formed a brown monster of a thought. The gun was still on the floor outside and they'd see it. Perhaps there was blood on the carpet too in view. She had to do something about Vienna's body and a startling image of her burying her crept up from behind her.

"This is crazy," she whispered.

"No shit."

Elena yelped and spun. She hadn't noticed a guy stood behind the wall beside the toilet she was too busy panicking.

"Mark?" she cried in shock.

He frowned and looked around him. "What?"

"Y-you're not Mark," Elena sighed and slipped downwards against the door and burst into tears.

The guy's frown deepened. "Don't cry."

Elena sniffed and looked up to glare at him. "What were you doing in here?" Voice wobbling like a car with a missing wheel.

"I was emptying my bladder and I heard voices. And someone is now dead," he said pointing to Vienna.

She was bleeding profusely from her head and on the other side was the exit wound, she didn't know which one was which. Blood stained the floor like tears and swirled in red patterns. Elena felt like hurling.

"I saw a bathroom downstairs, why didn't you use that one?" she asked suspiciously.

"The queue was long, and I saw my friend come up here. Said there was a bathroom in here. This, though. What a plot twist."

"I didn't kill her," she said defensively.

He nodded. "I wasn't gonna say it was you."

"I wouldn't do such a thing," she grumbled.

"Stop looking scared, you'll sort this out."

Elena visibly relaxed and gave him a grateful smile which he didn't return.

"Good. Now I'm gonna leave and forget this ever happened." He shrugged on his backpack which rustled loudly, and Elena shushed him.

"You can't leave, you're in this with me."

"I didn't witness her death though, did I?"

"What should I do?" Elena gestured hopelessly to Vienna.

He stared at Vienna and grimaced. "Tell someone downstairs, they'll call the cops."

"Where are you from?"

"Not here," he replied vaguely.

Elena rolled her eyes. "Are you American? Canadian? I can't tell."

"Doesn't matter. Now go downstairs and tell someone—" he cut himself off and searched the floor. "Where's the gun? Was it a gun? I heard something loud as fuck."

Elena felt her face crumple. "It's still outside," she whispered. "And there are people in the room. I dunno why they're there, but they're there."

He sagged. "I need to find Cahil. He'll know what to do. What am I kidding?" he was muttering to himself now and he stood, hands on his hips looking from the ceiling to the floor, anywhere but the body. Suddenly he got on his knees and took hold of Vienna's arm and pressed a thumb against her wrist. He was trying to find a pulse on a dead girl. Elena waited patiently for him to announce she was still alive, hoping against all odds. His thumb paused on different areas and he frowned. "How do I find the pulse? People just find them but it's difficult—" he trailed off and pressed his thumb to his own wrist and waited. "—I can't even find my own."

Elena got to her feet and found Vienna's vein immediately. She was still warm, of course she still was, it had only been a matter of minutes. There was no pulse though and with the caution of a quiet animal hunting, she turned Vienna's body face up. She stooped to the floor and watched to see if she breathed. She gathered up all the hope she'd felt and threw it out the window.

His eyes widened. "I spoke to that girl."

Elena frowned. Silence stifled the atmosphere.

"Can I look at the gunshot wounds?"

"What can you do now she's dead?" Elena mumbled flatly.

He ignored the comment and looked to both sides of her head, moving her hair out the way.

"Oh, this is good. Entry on the r—"

"I don't care. She was my friend and now she's dead." Elena sat back and let the tears bite at the corners of her eyes.

"What were you hoping for?" he laughed.

"This is crazy," she repeated.

He nodded and their eyes met for the briefest second and something stirred in Elena's mind.

"You know what else is crazy? I thought you were someone I knew," she said.

He raised his eyebrows surprised, not looking away. "That's because you're drunk."

Elena nodded, breaking eye contact awkwardly. "Who are you then?"

"Roman. What did you say your name was?" Roman asked cocking his head to the right.

"Oh, I didn't. It's Elena. Spelled E-L-E—"

"I know how to spell it. E-L-E-A-N-O-R."

"No. E-L-E-N-A."

"What's the difference?" Then he stopped and looked down to Vienna. "You gotta do something about your friend here."

"Vienna," she muttered darkly.

"Yeah. I think we bury it."

"What? No! We tell someone—"

There was a muffled shut of a door and silence. Elena went to shut off the shower as she felt wary of the water wasted but then thought to the owners of the house and how they'd have no trouble covering the bill.

"I was joking. But why is she dead?"

"Mark," she sighed, "I think she killed herself over Mark. But I wouldn't know."

"But what actually happened?"

Elena judged Roman for a few moments and Roman stared back evenly, waiting for something to happen.

"I've been with Mark a long time and she was jealous. Then someone was outside the door and she shot herself." Elena finally spoke.

Roman considered this. "Should we check if she has anything on her? A phone? A note? Did you ask where she got the gun from?"

"Mark again. His parents own a shed in the middle of a park for some reason and it's loaded with ammunition and firearms and stuff," she trailed off. "I could raid it if I wanted to."

"Not today. Come on, go and leave her here. We'll lock the door. Funny, actually, because I remembered locking the door, but you still managed to come in."

Elena took one last glance at Vienna's lifeless form and how her eyes gazed towards the ceiling like glass.

That's what death did. Took your soul but kept the body in the same snapshot forever.

She'd lost two people in one night.

"My dad died today too," she said and stood.

Roman stopped and his expression formed disbelief. "You think this is connected?"

"I didn't say that," she frowned, "but he did heroine or something."

"Oh," he said eyes wide and unblinking. He soon recovered and checked the time on his phone. It was an old model and the screen was smashed – glass shattered like the patterns of a cobweb.

"Let's just leave," she said.

"I came here with Cahil. I need to find him."

"Cahil?"

"My friend."

"Where's the name from?"

"I dunno. He's Turkish though."

"I need to find Will," she said.

Roman looked at her with a shock he tried to mask. "I know a Will," he said slowly.

"Okay," she said shrugging and she put a hand on the handle and unlocked the door.

"Will Atwick?"

"Atwick-*Pierce*, yeah," she replied and turned her head. "You do too?"

"Where do you live?" he asked suspiciously.

"Strontham. A few miles from here. I got two cabs it was that far."

"I live on the other side of the city. You heard of Netherwood?"

"Yeah."

"There's a school there too."

"Sagittarius?" she breathed hopefully.

"Uh, no. I'm a February. Sorry to disappoint."

"I have a boyfriend," Elena snapped angrily. She didn't know why she felt angry or why she felt defensive. And she didn't know why she felt the alcohol return, hungry to control her mind again, confidence brimming.

Roman didn't either and he raised an eyebrow. "Good on you."

"You piss me off."

Roman's eyes shifted and became cold but didn't say anything worth of mention. He sighed, annoyed, and surveyed the bathroom for a few moments and picked his next words carefully. "Why don't you stay here, and I'll get help? Somebody who isn't drunk down there. Then we tell them what happened. Have my number."

"With a dead body?" she hissed shrilly.

"Fine, wait in the bedroom."

"What if someone—"

"Look," Roman said holding her gaze impatiently, "All you have to do is keep your phone in sight so if I do call, you answer. Straight away. Then once everything is wrapped up, we walk off into the sunset and enjoy the rest of our lives and we never see each other again." He broke into a grin, but his eyes remained a cold green glimmer.

"It's night outside," she pointed out, feeling slightly disappointed.

Roman scowled. "Figure of speech, Elena," he said.

They traded numbers and she couldn't keep the blush off her face. She didn't think he'd notice, and he probably didn't because he left, giving her a quick thumbs up and no complimentary remark.

Elena took a deep breath and searched Vienna's pockets in an attempt to find anything. But how was that going to help? If she found a note, great. If she found a phone, she could call her parents. No, she had a passcode. However, she came up empty handed apart from the penny in her coat pocket. She inspected the coin. Small. Copper. A batch from the seventies. Cute, it was basically vintage, so she pocketed it and continued searching. She felt something lukewarm and groaned as she withdrew her hand and it was Vienna's blood coated thickly on her fingers. Elena retched and threw up in the toilet, feeling suddenly hungry. Of course, she hadn't even finished her bar of chocolate and her bruises patched on her neck spoke out.

Getting up unsteadily, she staggered to the sink and washed her hands thoroughly. Elena groaned and slumped against the toilet, tears welling as she stared at Vienna's lifeless form.

nine.

Checking left and right, Roman nudged his way out of that cursed bedroom. He didn't know why he did that, he wasn't a spy. He'd seen the blood spatter against the door and had ran past it. Now with sweaty hands trailing down the bannister and descending the stairs.

Heart making painful knocks on his chest, he reached the ground floor and realised how many people there were. He'd only come here because there was free food and he could pretend to be anyone here with Cahil because he wasn't judgemental. But now he was dragged into some incident because of a girl he didn't know and Cahil had gone somewhere without him knowing.

Anybody would do so he made his way to a girl with blue hair and a pierced lip that stood casually against the door frame of the living room. She was smoking. Her disapproving dark gaze drifted and settled on Roman and for a moment it looked as if she was going to say something before she coughed violently and stubbed out her cigarette on her shoe with contempt.

"Can I help you?" she asked, shifting her weight. Her eyes were so dark it was difficult to see where the pupil and iris started, and it reminded him of Elena. Drunk and afraid up there.

Roman hesitated, "I don't know how to tell you this."

The girl stared back expectantly, features screwing into annoyance when he struggled to find the right words. "Is this a prank?"

"Someone's dead. Shot."

The girl's dark eyes widened like plates and she barked a loud laugh and it scared the shit out of Roman.

"I don't know whether you're lying or not," she said.

"It's upstairs. Do you know who lives here? Are they here?"

"Yeah. I'm Lorcan's sister. He's out and I don't live here but I'll call him."

He waited for her to get out a phone to call Lorcan, but she made no attempt to do so and began lighting another cigarette.

Roman glared. "What if I were asthmatic?"

"But you're not."

"I could be. I could be coughing my lungs up right now."

"Breath taking."

He glared.

"You don't need to care about others if you're this rich," she muttered and inhaled into the smoke.

"Are you gonna call him?" Roman snapped.

Her lip curled cruelly. "Listen, I'm not here to play random games—" she stopped, and her eyes narrowed. "How old are you?"

"Eighteen," he blurted quickly. "I'm not playing games, I—"

"Roman!"

Roman turned and his anger began to boil. Elena was rushing down the stairs and she emitted fear, especially clear on her face.

"What the fuck are you doing here, get back up there and keep watch," he cried furiously.

Elena stood on the very last step of the stairs with her eyes widened like a scared animal. She hesitated and looked to the blue haired girl with dread.

"You were gone a long time so—"

"Is—" he checked the time, "—seven minutes long for you?"

Elena shook her head for the sake of shaking her head. Then turned to the girl. "Great, you have someone. Can you come upstairs for a minute?"

The girl's eyebrows raised for a fraction and to Roman's amazement he followed in Elena's wake without another word. Was he that unconvincing? It didn't matter, he dampened the flames of annoyance in his chest and went after them. Elena paused outside the bedroom and adjusted her skirt, looking back to Roman and the blue haired girl.

"I can't keep referring you to blue haired girl in my head, what's your name?" Roman asked.

"Millie," she grunted.

Roman almost cried. What a name for a girl like her.

"Right. Millie. Don't be afraid of what you're gonna see. It's, uh… see for yourself." Elena held the door open and Millie approached it with a hint of caution and a guarded expression in her eyes. She stopped short by the door frame.

"There's a gun."

They peered and the gun sat there on the side like a bomb.

"You think I was lying?" Roman said.

Millie rolled her eyes and frowned. "Holy crap," she breathed as she edged her way past the blood that spattered the door.

Soon she disappeared and Elena and Roman stood together in a painful silence. Elena cleared her throat. Roman noticed that Elena was picking at her nails and she kept her gaze to the floor.

"Stop looking at me," she complained.

"I'm not *looking*, I'm *judging*."

"This isn't funny."

"I'm funny."

Elena finally looked up and couldn't keep the disgust out of her tone. "You're really mean," she said.

He shrugged. "I'm aware."

"Fuck off."

"You first."

"I told you first."

"Ladies first."

Millie stepped into view with a sardonic expression in her eyes. "There's blood. But no body."

Roman felt his stomach drop and turned reproachfully to Elena who looked at him with an equal amount of shock that mirrored his.

Millie's lip twisted in animosity similar to a villain. "Whose blood is that?"

"Elena," Roman said with a harsh quiet to his voice. "What did you do with the body?"

"I literally left her for a few seconds! Millie, I think you're lying."

She pushed past Millie who had a scornful smile on her face.

"You can go," Roman suggested coolly.

95

"Yeah," she sneered and left leaving a whiff of cigarette in the air.

Roman ran through the room and stopped when he almost walked right into Elena.

"Watch it," she snapped.

Vienna's body was nowhere in sight. Roman checked the bathtub but it lay empty and puddled with water. There were also no drag marks in the blood, it lay pooled by their feet like venom they avoided.

He rounded on Elena, a furious look on his face and he struggled not to hit something. He really wanted to though.

"Did you bury it?"

"Vienna isn't an it. She's a she. And no!"

Roman turned away, the anger simmering inside him like broth that desperately needed a lid taken off it. He counted from ten to nought slowly, eyes clenched and he spun round with a tight-lipped smile. Elena shrunk gawkily back and didn't notice when her expensive black heeled boots sunk in a dark puddle of blood, neither did he bother telling her. Let her have it.

"This is so messed up," he said gravely.

"Be positive, please," Elena pleaded.

"This is so fucking messed up," he cried through a cheerful grin, throwing his arms up for good measure as Elena winced.

"What do we do?" she asked hopelessly, crossing her arms and taking her foot gingerly out of blood.

"I'm leaving you here. I'm done. I don't wanna be caught up in this because hell," he gestured to where the body should have been hysterically, "someone winds up dead and disappears off the face of the earth."

"Roman, listen to me. You're in this now and you can't get out of this, don't be such a Mark." Something strange flashed in Elena's eyes that Roman had never seen before and he felt the impulse to back away. They stared at each other in silence.

"I'm sorry. Mark mustn't be a great guy," he said quietly.

"No. He isn't."

He frowned. "Then why are you with him?"

She met his frown with a frown of her own. "Because I love him."

Simple as that. Love. It made you do crazy things sometimes.

"You don't."

"Excuse me?"

"You don't love him."

"You have no say in who I love."

"No, but I have a say in if I think he loves you."

"You have never met him."

"I don't have to have met him to know he's stupid."

"Stay out of my life."

Elena pushed past Roman, a shoulder colliding his elbow. He narrowed his eyes.

"You contradict yourself a lot."

Elena stopped by the bedroom door.

"Do you want my help or not?" he said.

Elena glared as she turned suddenly looking as if she was so done with everything. "Yes."

"What do you think we should do?" he asked, attempting to keep the peace.

She grumbled. "Find Cahil."

"Do you know Cahil?"

"No, but you do. Call Cahil."

Roman watched as Elena picked the gun and examined the barrel with unnerving closeness to it. He thought she would shoot herself or maybe him, but she dropped her hand down to her side and gave him a short smile.

"Call Cahil," she repeated brightly.

"Okay."

He took his phone out and gave Cahil a call, praying he'd pick up. It rang four times, and he answered.

"Cahil," Roman started but the line cut. He pulled a face. "Weird. No service. Do you have service?"

Elena reached into the pocket of her skirt and checked her bars and nodded.

"Three bars. I'll call him."

A ring whistled through the air and made them both jump.

Roman answered hastily. "Cahil. Hi. You're on speaker."

The sound on the other line was muted but Roman could hear the sound of loud music which matched what was going on beneath their feet.

"Roman. What's up?

"Where are you?"

"I'm having the time of my life."

Roman's eyes rolled, eyeing Elena. "Can you come upstairs for a second. We just need your help."

There was a sharp intake of breath. "You need my help? Great. I'm out. Where are you, upstairs? The bathroom?"

"No, we're in a room. It's a bedroom."

"We?" he echoed, and glee launched into his voice. "You got yourself a girl already?"

Roman's anger scrunched itself into a loud ball. "No, gross. Get up here." He ended the call gruffly and stuffed his phone in his hoodie.

"You seemed pretty intent on saying I wasn't with you," Elena remarked.

"Well, you're not, are you?" Roman said.

"Hell no," she murmured through clenched teeth. "If I'm being frank—"

"Why would you wanna be Frank?"

"Stop trying to be funny," Elena warned.

"I'm not trying, I just am a naturally funny person," Roman countered but his gaze landed on the gun still in Elena's hand and he kept his mouth shut.

The door opened, smacking Elena in the arm.

"Roman! His friend! What's happening?" Cahil waltzed in like he lived there and walked past Elena who was rubbing her arm with a scowl implanted on her face.

"I'm not his friend," Elena mumbled.

They formed a little triangle in the middle of the room.

"All right. So, what are you doing here? It certainly is cosy." He eyed the bed enviously and looked between Roman and Elena. "What are you doing here?" he repeated.

"See for yourself," Roman said.

Cahil gasped and staggered a few steps back, standing on Roman's foot who kicked him off angrily.

"Is that…?"

Elena and Roman nodded in synch and Cahil turned back to stare at the blood pooled in places. He turned to them with a strange expression.

"How did this happen?"

Roman turned disdainfully to Elena who slumped.

"She committed suicide," she replied wanly.

"Suicide?" he echoed, eyes widening.

"And fuck up over here left it and now it's gone."

Elena glared at Roman.

Roman sagged and walked out the room, thoughts in shambles. He'd tried piecing the little bits of information into one little chunk, but it dispersed again, out of reach. He groaned and collapsed on the bed. And then a message.

Can we meet just outside? Also, bring your friend Elena, I want to meet her.

He texted back.

Sure. Driveway?
See you then.

Roman crept up to the partially closed door to the ensuite and heard them both conversing in hushed voices.

"Elena. Will wants us," he said.

Elena turned so Roman could only see one of her eyes through the gap in the door.

"I've called the police and I'll talk to someone downstairs," Cahil said.

"Cahil. You're the best."

"I know. And you owe me," he said.

Elena bounded out the room and stood beside Roman. He gave one last parting gaze to the blood.

His stomach made a twisted noise, but he ignored his hunger and made his way down the stairs and to the door with Elena in tow. The party was wild, and it reached out to Roman like a dying person grasping for the last shreds of life. FOMO.

"Where did she go? Someone must've moved her," Elena whispered fearfully.

Roman rolled his eyes boredom settling in. He'd gone in circles with this. "I wonder whose fault that is?" he said as he opened the front door to let himself out first.

Elena didn't notice and instead her glower never left Roman. "Did Will say why he wants to talk to both of us? I can't believe he knows someone like you. You're an ass."

"And you're a fuck up," he shot back, pushing past some drunks in the driveway who tried to kiss him.

It was too dark, and it was too cold, and he didn't like it. A cold that rattled the breath of Roman and left him breathing cold liquid. Elena shivered violently as they made their way to the end of the driveway.

"What did you expect wearing nothing?" he said, reading her mind.

"Don't body shame," she snapped.

"I'm not," he snarled.

She held a hand up to silence him as she reached to rub her temple. "Should I have taken the gun?"

"No," he said frowning.

"Good. That would look weird wouldn't it? And the fingerprints. *Fingerprint*s. They have my fingerprints," she breathed and shook again. He didn't feel bad for her.

"Then we'll stay to tell them the story," he said calmly.

"You don't get it," she muttered finally.

"What's there not to get? Trust me, it'll be fine."

"I'm so dumb."

"It's okay. We're all varying degrees of dumb. Sometimes some are dumber than others."

"Let's go," she muttered, and they walked past Cahil's car and to a black car parked with headlights on.

"Will," Roman said.

Will sat in the driver's, an elbow resting on the window and a hand holding his head, window down. Will's expressionless gaze rested on Roman and then to Elena.

"Hey. Get in the car, it's two degrees out there. I got food."

"Great. I'm starving."

Will unlocked the car doors to the back and they ducked their heads and sat, leaving the middle seat empty. He handed them a portion of chips and ketchup to share. Elena cried and ate and Roman tucked in, thoughts of sharing and disgust deserting him. Will laughed. His green chequered shirt looked almost grey in the light.

"Your friend's house is massive," Roman stated.

"That's because they're wealthy."

"I wish I was rich," Elena mumbled.

"I thought someone like you was," Roman laughed, and Elena glared then turned away from Roman to Will.

"My dad's dead."

"I'm sorry to hear that," Will said.

"There's also a dead body on the loose."

Will stared. "Sorry?"

"Yeah. Someone died in that house," she mumbled though a mouthful of chips.

"Have you told someone?"

"Yeah. The police are probably on their way right now."

"Is that so?" Will said grinning.

They didn't know why he was smiling.

Elena's chewing slowed.

"We've finished. Should we stay here so the police can question us?" Roman asked, dusting salt of his fingertips but the grease trapped most of it.

"I don't think that's necessary."

"Roman. You're blurry."

Roman frowned through his own fuzz just as Elena spoke, his vision distorting.

"What do you mean?" His voice sounded like someone else's.

"You have a big face," Elena laughed.

Roman laughed back and they both threw their heads back and laughed while Will sat at the front with a wicked grin that filled his entire face.

PART II

ten.

Robyn felt her shoulders shake and her arms were about to be wriggled from their sockets. Who was doing that? It wasn't time to wake up yet. Perhaps she'd got it wrong, it was a Monday. Wasn't it Sunday? It was. The shaking didn't stop so her eyes snapped open angrily and her anger melted away and it was replaced with nervousness.

"Oh, thank God. I've tried the others, but they're still knocked out."

Robyn sat up and the girl who woke her sat back. She had deep brown hair, with medium skin, pretty brown eyes and a fearful look on her face.

"Huh?" she muttered disoriented. The back of her head hurt an awful lot. Bruised. She reached a hand and felt and withdrew. Dried blood. Robyn shrieked.

"We're in a van," she said gesturing to their surroundings. Robyn peered into the darkness and saw two guys slumped on the floor beside them. Leo was one of them. The place was empty apart from the four of them. A single filament gripped a handlebar in the corner and cast shadows over the place. Huh.

"Who are you?" she said, the fog still persistent in her mind.

"I'm Elena. Look, it's important you don't black out again. That was probably an hour ago. It's hard to tell."

Robyn couldn't work it out but there was a strange smell in the air. "You talk an awful lot, don't you?" Robyn mumbled and sat with her back against the vehicle, pain racing through her head. The wall against her back hummed with exertion and something clicked in her mind, taking one step out the cobwebs. "We're on the motorway."

Elena nodded. "Yes. We are. What's your name?"

Robyn regarded her suspiciously. Had she been at the party too? She was definitely dressed like it.

"Robyn," she replied holding back, a shake in her voice.

Elena smiled and gave Robyn's arm a little pat which Robyn mistook for attack, so she stood, knocking Elena back, her head smashing to the opposite wall. The vehicle was big enough to fit anybody below two metres. It didn't reassure her.

"I'm not attacking you, Jesus," Elena seethed with pain her face scrunched up in agony.

"I don't know you. I don't even know why we're here. My head hurts like hell," she said hysterically. She was never hysterical, so she calmed herself. Thought of clouds. Clouds were good.

"Believe me when I say I have no idea why we're here either."

"Do you even know how we got here?"

Elena thought for a moment, shadows danced across her face as she thought. It took an awfully long time.

"I was in someone's car and then—" Her eyes widened when the memories came. "I was drugged. Will drugged my chips."

Robyn's eyes narrowed and heart ready to fall. "Will?"

"Yeah," Elena nodded. "A friend. He invited me. And Roman over there. Oh my God, the dead body."

"Dead body?" Robyn repeated raising an eyebrow, but Elena wasn't listening, she was hyperventilating.

"He wants to kill us."

"Kill us?"

"Oh no, oh no," Elena whimpered to herself.

"Elena. Elena's a pretty name. How do you spell it? Anyway. Elena. Calm down. No need to worry like that, we're all in this together—"

Elena took a sharp intake in breath and shook violently, tears welling in her eyes.

"Hey," Robyn snapped her fingers in front of her face. "You've got to breathe. Let it go. Like Elsa in Frozen."

"I'm sorry," she managed to mumble before curling in the foetal position and sobbing. It wasn't awkward any longer because she didn't think Elena even realised she was there anymore.

"Elena," she cried, tapping her.

"Yeah?"

"Please, calm down. Listen. We'll be okay. All of us. I'm sure we're just in a massive limousine or something. Or maybe the house has a disco, how fun would that be?" Robyn said. She knew this was all a lie. They were in deep shit.

"My brain feels like it's just downed ten shots." Elena sat upright. Her hair was a mess, but she visibly tried relaxing herself.

"Thanks, Robyn," she gave a wan smile.

"Yeah," Robyn regarded her with wary eyes. "What time is it?"

"My phone is gone."

Robyn cursed. She should've worn her wristwatch today but of course she didn't. She knew she should've stayed at home. Her dad.

Tears came to her eyes, but they were gone in an instant. They would get out of this place. Will couldn't be that terrifying.

"Well. I guess we just wait. We'll probably be dead by the end of today," Robyn exclaimed cheerfully.

Elena made a pained expression like she desperately wanted that to be untrue and Robyn sat back down, flipping her trench coat like a halo around her. She felt for the hooped earrings her dad had given her three years ago. Still intact. Good.

"So. How old are you? Where are you from? You're really pretty by the way."

"Why do you wanna know?" she asked.

"We have nothing else to do," Robyn replied.

"Okay," she laughed weakly. "I'm seventeen and I'm from Brazil. I lived there until I was five and moved to Strontham. You know Strontham? Yeah, thought so. I didn't realise I'd end up in this situation." She motioned to the air. "I wanted to be all right and happy and do well in life. Now we're probably gonna be tortured for some information none of us know about and killed and they'll dismember our—"

"Hey, hey, hey. Not that talk, I don't need to hear that right now."

"Sorry," Elena apologised. "What about you?"

Robyn was careful about the information she chose to disclose. "I'm seventeen too. I turned seventeen two months ago. I live near you. Sort of."

"And you're white?"

"Uh, yeah. My family are all German."

"That's cool. Can you speak it? What's your last name?" Elena seemed almost excited.

"Not really, no. They never really had the chance to teach me. It's Wolff with double F," she said. A thought popped into her mind and she fiddled around her pocket and was relieved to feel the cigarettes still there. But lighter was gone. Her keys were also still in her jean pockets. "My lighter," she sighed in dismay.

"Maybe it got sick of being an arsonist, so it took a day off for a walk?"

Robyn couldn't help laughing. "Will probably took it so I couldn't do anything with it," she murmured darkly.

They listened to the silence that hugged them and the sound of tyres on the outside.

"Nice roads. No potholes," Elena grinned.

"That's because it's the motorway."

"Still. Nice roads."

"You said you tried to wake the others? Leo, and who was the other one?"

"Roman. He doesn't like me much," she replied sadly.

"Why?"

"We just don't get along. And I hate when I don't get along with others because I feel we're at war."

Robyn blinked and noticed a flicker in her vision. "Oh. Well. We can ask him because he's waking up."

Elena turned and stood, walking shakily to Roman. She shook him violently by the shoulders just like she'd done to Robyn. She grimaced as Roman choked and woke. They gathered around him as he came to his senses.

"Elena?" he said, green eyes unfocused in their sockets.

"Yeah, it's me."

"I feel hungry and I wanna hurl," he complained bitterly before throwing up to his side.

Robyn wrinkled her nose and Elena groaned. Robyn realised the stench in the air was vomit.

"Roman, we don't know long we'll be in here, you didn't need to do that," she muttered annoyed.

"Don't talk so loudly, please."

"Nobody can hear you."

"Weird. I hear myself just fine." His gaze switched to Robyn. "Who are you?"

"I'm Robyn," she began before being cut off by another retch and he vomited.

"Sorry," he mumbled and gave Robyn a confident smile. Robyn returned it awkwardly. "You're Robyn. Cool. Do I know you?"

"No. But we're stuck in here, so we need to find a way out."

Roman visibly paled. "Oh hell," he turned to Elena, "he gave us those fries and—"

"They were probably drugged," Elena finished nodding grimly. She turned to Robyn. "Were you struck on the head? I saw you touch your head before."

"I probably was. Me and Leo were getting out the house and that's all I remember."

"Hmm," Roman said.

"Hmm what?" Elena said.

"It's my thinking noise. Shut up."

"Well think faster."

"I think faster than you."

"Think. Faster."

"Shut. Up."

Elena seemed to inch forward and readied herself to yell at him, but she decided against it and shrunk back beside Robyn. Roman's eye fell on Leo's unconscious form.

"Who's he?"

"Leo. He was with me."

"Are you the same age as us?"

"I'm seventeen."

"Me too."

"Let's get outta here, I don't like this."

Roman got up unsteadily to his feet, a hand supporting his weight against the side of the vehicle.

"How? I don't think we've braked for ages."

"How long have you been awake?" asked Roman.

"Ages," Elena said glumly.

"But we were drugged at the same time," Roman said, a hint of suspicious creeping into his voice.

"Yes. And you took all the chips meaning you took most of the dosage."

Robyn's gaze darted from both and she could see the untold anger between them. She didn't want to be caught in that crossfire.

"Does anyone know the time?" Roman asked before reaching into his pocket. His face twisted in frustration. "Did he take our phones?"

"Took mine," Elena said.

"Maybe I can kick down the doors?"

"You?" she scoffed and Roman tried stamping the angry expression out of his face.

"Yes, me."

"Go on."

"I shall."

Roman walked to the doors of the van and studied its size. He rapped his knuckles against it, emitting a thin metallic sound.

"Are you testing it?" came Elena's voice, a hiss.

Roman didn't answer but took a few steps back and hurtled his shoulder into the door. It echoed in surprise but didn't move. Roman gritted his teeth, walked backwards half the room and rammed his shoulder in again. The whole vehicle seemed to shake. He made a groaning noise before collapsing backwards into Robyn who steadied him to his feet again.

"You guys can try it."

Elena shouldered past him and took a running kick to the door. The metal seemed to vibrate, and its atoms collided heavily into each other but nothing. She walked to the opposite end of the van and ran, the look of concentration evident on her face. This time she used her shoulder. The doors protested but stood its ground. Robyn felt the hope between her fingers slip.

"Let's try it altogether," Elena suggested breathlessly.

"What if we do open it and we're out on open road where cars are going seventy. We'd die," Robyn said, arms folded.

"I'd rather break my neck than die because of him." He pointed to the front of the vehicle who she assumed was at Will.

"Robyn. Try it," Elena mumbled, breathing heavily. Robyn did the same as the others, only winning a groan from the doors. Her shoulder hurt.

"Does anyone have anything that can do harm?"

Roman shrugged off his bag and rifled through it. He came up with cookies and cash and he cringed. Something told her that meant they would never need to access that money because they weren't ever going to get out.

"If nobody's hungry I'll be having these."

When nobody said anything, he shook out a packet and opened it and ate.

"Mmm," he moaned, and Elena groaned in disgust.

"Do you mind?"

"Not at all," he mumbled, taking another bite.

"Can we try Leo?" Robyn said, ignoring Roman.

Elena held a hand out to signal a go ahead and Robyn knelt beside Leo. He looked peaceful despite sustaining a blow to the head. He almost looked as if he was smiling. She gripped his shoulders and shook him lightly, afraid of breaking his body.

"Leo," she said loudly.

All eyes were on her now and she shook him harder. "Hi. Leo?" she said. His head shook with his shoulders, but he didn't wake. She shook again and this time, his brow twitched but he made no attempt to awaken. "Leo—"

"Let me try. Leo." Elena was beside Robyn and slapped him across the face. His whiskey brown eyes widened in shock and he gasped.

eleven.

Leo felt the dull throbbing ache at the back of his head. It wasn't as bad as he thought it would be after realising he'd been hit. By instinct he reached his hand to where it hurt, and his heart accelerated when clotted blood smudged his fingers. He remembered the sensation; it rattled his brain in his mind and the pain tore down his spine. It was awful.

Leo blinked in the dim light and saw three faces peer down at him, guarded. He saw Robyn among them and felt relief.

"Hi. Is this a party game?" he asked nervously.

There was a rumbling noise from beneath him and he knew they were on the road. Maybe not a party game.

"Afraid not," Roman replied.

Leo's gut twisted and he turned to his side and threw up.

"Was he drugged?"

"No. Must be the alcohol," Robyn replied. "That's Elena and Roman. We're all stuck in here."

Leo grunted what sounded like an acknowledgement.

"Leo, can you try the door?" Roman asked.

He turned to the wall on the far end and could just make out the shape of two doors firmly held in place.

"You want me to run into it? With a head like mine?" Leo asked outraged.

"All right. Fine. We die in here," Roman said and sat back down, munching.

They all retreated hopelessly and sat apart from each other, in their own little heads. There was something beside Roman.

"Don't litter," Leo said, pointing to it.

Roman frowned and picked up a yellow note. Squinting, he slowly got up and made his way to the light and was silent.

"*He is after you*," he read numbly.

"That's cheery stuff," Elena said.

"Yeah, we're gonna die," Roman mumbled, scrunching the note up and throwing it to a far corner beside the vomit.

"Was that just there?" Robyn asked.

"Beside me, yeah."

"If anyone else is going to throw up, do it in that corner. We don't want more places to avoid," Robyn said.

"Are we all stuck in here?" Leo wondered.

"What does it look like, big guy?"

"Are we special?"

"No? I'm normal!"

"Why us?"

"We have nothing in common."

"I suppose not."

Leo sighed and searched for his phone. It wasn't there and his heart made a plummet. "What does Will want?" he grumbled.

"Well, we all know Will. That's one thing in common," suggested Roman.

"How do you all know him?" Elena asked.

"The internet," Robyn and Leo both responded.

Elena didn't hide the scepticism off her face.

"He goes to my school and we join the same club," Roman replied. "I thought he was normal, you know. Especially since he never loses a debate. Normal as in not psychopathic. Not like someone who locks four people in a car and drives them somewhere."

"I met him at a bar," Elena said at last. "It was one of those family ones at noon."

He suddenly really wanted steak and he hated steak. "I'm starving," Leo mumbled. He stood unsteadily, shadows appearing before his sight and walked to the doors.

"Have some of these."

"It's okay."

He knocked his knuckle against the doors. He rammed his shoulder in it and the door gave way with a mechanical lurch and Leo tumbled out, a look of surprise on his face. And landing right in the arms of—

"Will?" Came Roman's voice, like the rain before the storm.

Leo disentangled himself from Will who stood with a hand on the door, a perfect calm. They hadn't realised the vehicle had stopped.

"It stinks," he said. His peaceful blue eyes wandered from person to person, a neutral face. Nobody dared say a word and he felt the others stiffen. He himself felt a tremor coming to his knees.

They were parked at a gas station and in the distance, Leo could see fast food restaurants and book shops. They were at a service station. Which meant they could get help. But the sky was different. It had stopped raining hours ago and the moon was stitched high in the sky. There were only a few stars to guide their way.

"We're out of petrol and food. Use the toilets, we'll get food and be out."

"You're gonna drug us again," Roman said.

Will turned to him. "Don't be so childish. Nobody likes children."

Roman glared.

"Where are we driving to?" Elena interjected fearfully.

Will's expression didn't change. "To the Safe House," he replied. "And don't even think of trying to run, we have eyes everywhere."

The others stepped out with Will bringing up the rear, Leo trailed behind Robyn who gave him a frantic smile which he returned with a tremble. The ground would've been a welcoming sensation to his feet if it wasn't for present circumstances. Leo wobbled slightly and noticed the floor was damp with rain. The light from the station lit up the floor with a tinted blue that shone quietly. They walked through the cars parked and Leo kept his eyes straight ahead. Only several cars remained parked. Not unusual.

Reaching the entrance, Will made his way to the front and issued instructions. "You're going to the bathrooms. I don't want any more vomit in my car." He shot a pure look of venom at Leo.

Leo paled.

"And you're to come straight back here. Remember, I have eyes everywhere so it's going to take more than running at one hundred and twenty miles per hour to outrun us." He grinned. "Off you go."

Bile rose to his throat like water up a straw and Leo ran inside past the shops and the troubled glances, to the bathroom, not waiting for anyone else. He entered the brightly lit men's and found a cubicle and threw up in it. A sigh of relief overcame him as he flushed and slumped to the

119

floor. It was filthy but Leo didn't have a care in the world. They were all trapped there with no means of a way out. Perhaps forever by the looks of it. Tears came to his eyes when he realised he may never see home again and his future was uncertain. He sniffed hastily as the door swung open from outside. He didn't know whether the other cubicles were empty. Footsteps made their way to the sinks and a rush of water briefly blocked out his thoughts.

He didn't want to unlock the door until the person was gone so he decided to pee. Might as well. Then a thought came at an alarming speed, punching him right in the brain.

He peeked from beneath the gap in door and saw the back of a guy whose head was covered by a thick woollen hat.

"Excuse me?" Leo called out quietly.

The man didn't turn or acknowledge him. He didn't think he'd even hear him.

"Hello," Leo said, louder this time over the rushing water.

The man turned. He wasn't a man. It was someone his age and he was wearing the wickedest of grins, eyes glinting.

Leo shrunk back suddenly going red. He stood waiting for him to say something, tap running. It bothered him that he didn't turn off the tap.

"Do you know the time?" The question came out of Leo before he even thought. "It's just that I've lost my watch."

The guy dug his phone out and Leo eyed it longingly like an animal watching its prey. He was up and a punch was flung against the hinge of his jaw. Leo thought wow.

He recoiled with anger. Anger but not surprise. Fingers dugs into his eyes and then an elbow slammed into his face which the guy answered with a grunt but did not fall. He quickly recovered and punched Leo right in the jaw, rattling his teeth, causing him to cry a cry that sounded like a sob. He fell, pain jostling and clouding his mind.

He turned back to the sink and the squeak of a tap and the water stopped. With a relaxed turn he dried his hands with a paper towel and left the room, stepping dismissively over Leo's outstretched body.

Standing, Leo winced as his muscles cramped and he fell like a brick against the wall of a nearby cubicle. It seemed to shake but recovered. "Sorry," he whispered. He didn't know how long he had waited there staring after the guy he encountered. His jaw ached like hell and resisted the urge to curl up and cry. Something tapped at the corner of Leo's mind, nagging him to consider this through. He stood straight and washed his hands by the sink, staring dazedly in the mirror. No mark yet. The water ran like time and he watched it swirl in the basin and realised how terrifyingly thrilling the whole situation was. Not thrilling. Surreal. A face he recognised but didn't at the same time, he couldn't match the guy's face to anyone he knew. He just didn't know yet.

After Leo met the others, they'd made their way back to the van in silence with food. He tried looking for a license plate and found one hung over the end and noted it in his head, pausing after the others. Will had laughed at him and told him they'd switched plates every hour and there it was, the last ray of hope snatched away from him. Elena had told him to remember the first half and she'd remember the second. The license plates belonged to somebody and it could give an indication of any stolen vehicles and their whereabouts.

The doors whirred shut and they felt the vehicle unbalance to the right. Will had got on and they knew he was driving. Backing out, they drove back onto the motorway along with other cars, picking up speed.

Leo sighed. He still didn't know the time.

The four of them huddled by the light, examining the yellow note that Roman had found earlier. Extremely crumpled.

Leo felt sleepy and he yawned.

"It's exactly the same as mine." Robyn held a second note beside the one that Roman held. So they were. Both yellow and in the same pencilled handwriting.

"And you found yours when?"

"This morning. It was in my leaky cupboard."

"*He is after you*," Elena read and made a face. "Yeah, thanks. We know." She sat with her face in her knees.

"It might be Will. You know, with the reverse psychology and all that shit. *Don't go out today*. It makes you wanna go out," Roman explained.

Robyn judged him with derision. "I was going to the library. I didn't think I'd end up dying."

"The library? Why not study at your own house?"

"It's quieter."

Roman's eyes narrowed quizzically. "It really isn't—"

"It doesn't matter. They're in the same writing, that's gotta be something," Leo said before voices raised.

Robyn turned to Leo who stared blindly at his fingers. "Finally got the alcohol out of your system?"

He gave a bitter smile. Now was his chance to tell them. "Yeah. I also got punched by someone."

The three blinked wildly.

"By who? Just then?" Roman said in surprise.

"How should I know? I kinda attacked him first though," Leo mumbled.

"In the toilets?"

"You hit someone?" Elena gasped with amazement.

"I was going for his phone. Maybe I could have called the police, I dunno." He fell back against the wall and hit his head which hurt like hell.

"It was smart," Elena said dropping her gaze to the floor then back up to meet Leo's gaze. She smiled wanly and Leo returned it.

"Are we going to eat that?" Robyn pointed to the floor opposite them.

Paper bags containing fast food. It was almost comical how they sat miles away from it, afraid of eating it and falling unconscious again.

"How could he have drugged it? I was the first one out of the toilet and I watched him take his order. I was with him the whole time and didn't see him do anything," Elena said.

"Let's vote on it," Leo proposed. "Hand up if we eat it." He raised his own hand and his stomach grumbled in approval.

Elena raised her hand and after a moment of hesitation, Robyn too raised her hand, but it stayed half up like she didn't want everyone to know she was eager.

Roman shot a glower at the food. "I've eaten twice in the past few hours. They're drugged, I'm telling you. Or the drinks are."

But Elena had already reached the bags of food and was handing them out. She reached a hand in and unwrapped a burger, taking a grateful bite.

"It's nice of him, really. To give us food. And clean up the vomit."

Robyn laughed for the first time in that van. "I am so hungry."

"I still have cookies in my bag— holy shit, where's my bag?" Roman looked around him and stood, anger in his eyes.

Elena snickered. "Poor cookies."

Roman's eyes flashed with annoyance and he sat back down.

"If you're not gonna eat yours, we'll happily eat it."

"Fine. Knock yourselves out," Roman said through gritted teeth, crossed his arms and turned away from them.

Elena smiled brightly, "We will." And took Roman's.

"I mean that in the literal sense."

Leo sniffed at the bag of fries with a guarded expression and couldn't smell anything unusual. In his bag was also a burger just like the others. There was even two sachets of ketchup and he felt a strange jolt of warmth which he knew was ridiculous. Will had locked them in a van and drove them away. They didn't even know where this Safe House was or what he even intended to do to them.

Harm.

The chips tasted warm and salty and he closed his eyes and savoured them. This could potentially be their last meals.

"So. Let's all get to know one another. We might die in each other's arms," Elena said.

Robyn grunted and Roman rolled his eyes. "You think this is funny?" he mumbled and lay down on the cold floor.

"Shall we put you in the recovery position?"

Roman faked a laugh directed to Leo and turned away from them.

"Leo?" Elena looked expectantly at Leo.

Robyn had her gaze trained on him and nibbled on a fry.

"What do you wanna know?" he asked weakly.

"The basics," Elena replied.

He hated these things because he'd either tell them something that they'd be bored by or overshare.

"I'm seventeen," he began slowly. This pained him.

"We gathered. Year thirteen?"

"Yeah. I'm half Vietnamese." He knew they didn't care.

"Wow. I didn't know that," Elena said.

"Yeah, it's because I look more like my dad," he mumbled. "And I wanna go home. Even though I hate my parents and I have no siblings and friends." He sighed heavily.

"I don't have siblings either," Robyn said.

"It's okay, I have no siblings either. It's just me now," Elena said.

"What about your parents?" Leo asked.

"My mum left years ago. My dad is dead. He died today actually."

They descended into a terrible silence and Leo felt Elena squirm underneath their gazes. It was enough to stir Roman. He turned and sat and listened.

"I have no siblings too," he said, and a look crossed him. A look of something in his mind clicking.

"So we're all only children? That may be a link."

"Maybe. Maybe Will wants siblings?" Elena grinned.

"Perhaps he wants to exterminate all only children?" Leo suggested.

"Why us?" Roman pondered.

"What about schools?" Leo suggested.

"Grammar," they replied in unison.

Roman's eyes flickered to Elena with a note of disbelief, but nobody noticed. Only Leo.

"Okay. Carry on Leo, you're interesting," Elena prodded Leo's arm. He reddened. "Seriously?"

"We'll ask questions then," Elena answered.

"When was your first kiss?" Roman's voice came from the corner. He sat with a hand propping his chin up and a look of curiosity and interest.

Leo reddened even more.

"Seriously?" he said deflated. Roman didn't say anything but continued staring.

"It was with James. It was on a street. We were listening to something on our earphones and he just…" he trailed off and his face flushed with heat. Remembering something like that was horrible now he had nothing to do with him. It was more than sadness. It was a loss.

"Wow. Earphones. They're vintage, now aren't they?" Roman chuckled. "How come I feel like you and James aren't together anymore?"

"Because you're right. He left. And I found Will."

"Woah Will is gay?" he said, surprised.

"I don't know anymore."

"What's your star sign?" Elena chimed in.

Leo's lip curled and he found himself smiling again, taking a quick sip of his Pepsi. "I'm a Taurus."

"I'm a Leo. How ironic."

"Leo, remember the book you were reading in the library?"

"Uh, yeah. The Art of Revenge, was it?"

"Yeah. I feel like we're in that situation right now."

Elena and Roman looked to Robyn, waiting for her to elaborate.

"In the prologue, there's a person stuck in the back of a car and then they die there. Starvation?" She turned to Leo who confirmed it.

"That's cheerful," Roman muttered and soon silence wrapped itself around them. It was suffocating. Daunting. They listened to the whir of tyres beneath them and the sound of them cutting through the air and covering far distances.

"Let's tell jokes," said Elena and inched closer. "What's big and small simultaneously?"

"The world?" Leo suggested.

Elena shook her head. "Any other guesses?"

"Life," said Robyn.

"Don't care," said Roman.

She laughed. "A brain."

They stared. She laughed again, this time nervously.

"Big brain, but small in size…" she trailed off.

"We get the joke, I just thought it was stupid," Roman said coldly.

Elena's smile wobbled. "Tough crowd." Elena fidgeted some more and stood like an injured soldier.

"I'm gonna talk to Will." She made her way to the front of the vehicle and hammered on the wall. It emitted a hollow noise. "Will. We know you're there. Let us out or we'll call the police."

There was barked laughter on the other side and Leo was surprised he would reply.

"The police?" he repeated scornfully, muffled by the screen.

"Elena. Stop," Leo hissed. He knew this wouldn't end well but Elena stubbornly stayed.

"I have a phone on me you didn't take," she lied. "Listen to me Will. You pull up at the next junction and you let us out," Elena continued. "You hear?"

To Leo's amazement, a small compartment door just big enough to fit a human, slid open and there was Will. With something long and black and metal pointed to Elena's temple. She faltered but remained stood, eyes shining with cold.

"You're not going to leave," he said. His gun was still and mirrored Elena's determination. There was a quiet which was deafening, and everyone felt it. It chilled Leo and his blood froze along with it.

"No," came Elena's reply.

A jerk of a gun, the close of the compartment, the fall of a member. Elena screamed and clutched the top part of her right arm in agony. The others rushed forward and held her to the floor where she writhed in pain. Her cropped jumper around the wound was no longer a sunny lilac but a deep crimson that drowned the colours and gave silent warnings. The three exchanged looks of concern.

"It hurts," Elena cried, and Leo hugged her, careful of the red. The smell of gunpowder was strong in the air.

"Stop moving, we need to stop the bleeding," he whispered.

But it was like she never heard and carried on sobbing and thrashing and trying to take people's eyes out. Robyn backed away and looked to Roman who looked to Leo who shrugged helplessly. Roman looked down at her gravely and pinned her wounded arm down which earnt him a scream higher in pitch.

"Is it even possible to stop the bleeding of a gunshot wound? Is the bullet made of lead?"

"Maybe it exited," Leo said.

Robyn looked around in the dim glow of the light for a bullet.

"It was at close range. I don't know if it's stayed in or not."

"Elena. Calm down," Roman yelled and started unbuttoning the buttons on her cropped sweater.

"Woah, what are you doing?" Leo said.

Roman threw a gritted glare to him and shrugged the jumper off her. Thank God she was wearing another top underneath. He examined the bullet wound which dripped mercilessly with blood. To everyone's relief it had only grazed her shoulder. Around the wound was the shape of the barrel of the gun which Leo thought maybe was the result of a bullet being fired directly on the skin. Elena suddenly stopped thrashing and went limp.

Robyn shrieked. "Is she okay?"

"We need to stop the bleeding. It's gonna be harder now she's not awake."

"What are you doing to do?" Leo asked, shuddering as he glanced again at the blood.

"At school we did something like this. Tie something really tight around it." He looked at Robyn and Leo. "Any spare pieces of clothing?"

"I have a sock," Leo offered.

"Just tie her jumper."

And he did so with the skill of someone who went by the book. Minutes later, he tied the knot of the sweater harshly and Elena jerked awake.

She looked down at her arm and paled. "I was shot."

"Wonderful, your eye receptors are working," Roman said and withdrew his hands.

She stood which surprised everyone. They stood too.

"Thanks, Roman." She tried a wry smile and Roman nodded to the floor and muttered something like don't mention it.

"Does it hurt?" Leo asked.

Elena shrugged. "Hurts like hell. But I've had cramps worse than this."

"What?" Robyn shrieked.

"We can't find the bullet. We think it's still in your arm. Maybe lodged in bone," Leo added.

"I'll live." She cradled her arm awkwardly and sat so everyone else did so robotically.

"Do you guys think we'll ever get out?" Leo said in a small voice.

"Of course we will," Elena said hotly.

"I hope so," Roman nodded.

Robyn sighed.

"We will," Elena insisted feverishly.

"I don't know but wherever this Safe House is. We need to get out."

"We might as well have a snooze," Elena mumbled.

Everyone's startled gaze settled on her and she didn't even realise.

"Maybe," Robyn said. She set down her burger and slumped against the wall, eyes closed.

Roman's eyes widened in alarm and he went over to shake Leo who felt nothing at that moment. He noticed the blood smudged on his fingertips.

"Bro, you've gotta stay awake. I told you guys not to eat that."

"But Elena saw—"

"Screw what Elena saw."

Leo frowned through the fuzziness of everything.

Roman sighed. "I can't be the only one awake. Come on, fight it. Fight the drugs," he protested, giving him another shake.

"It's really hard."

"Yes, I know, I went through it too. My fries were fucking laced with something hardcore. It's hard but you have to fight it. You can. You barely touched your burger."

"Why does my mouth taste bitter?" Leo murmured and then started laughing hysterically.

Roman punched him across his bruised jaw and he gasped, a hand to it.

"Sorry. I'm trying to keep you awake." He took an anxious glance at the others.

"Yeah. I feel no different," Leo said. He was swimming against the strong currents, and it kept dredging him under, not allowing him to take a breath.

"Leo?"

Leo felt it at last and he took one look at Roman whose eyes were anything but smug and let the waves take him over, dipping into unconsciousness.

twelve.

Elena woke to the sound of a short burst of clanging metal.

It was Roman stood by the van door.

She sat and her arm buzzed with numbing pain which made her cry out like a cat and noticed her bare arms that stuck out like sticks. Her sweater was wound around her arm and it was just tight enough to stop the bleeding. She poked at her arm and clenched her teeth through the spike in pain.

Roman turned and his agitated face remained agitated.

"Great. You're awake. We've stopped driving."

"For how long?" she said blearily.

"Half an hour."

"Half an hour?" She echoed, dazed. "How did you know?"

"I counted the seconds and converted them into minutes."

"Wow," she said.

"Now get up. Help me bust down this door. It can't stay closed forever."

"Who did this?" she gestured faintly to her arm.

He seemed to take a moment. "Do you not remember?"

"Nope," she mumbled.

"Well. I did tell you the food was poisoned. I'm surprised it hasn't killed you."

"My mouth tastes bitter too."

"I remember the feeling."

Elena lifted herself gingerly off the ground and staggered to Roman who went back to kicking. Each kick was like a kick to her arm and it was continuous and on the brink of unbearable.

"I tied it," he said gruffly.

Elena blinked and everything she thought of him changed.

"Oh," was all she could say.

"You were bleeding out, I had to," he said, like he wasn't proud of what he did.

Her heart fell. "What do you want me to do?" she asked feebly.

He turned to look at her arm and back to her face. "Kick."

She nodded and they kicked the door for a few minutes, each taking a running to it. Leo and Robyn remained slumped unconscious and didn't stir.

"Maybe we should try prising the door open with our fingers?" Elena suggested, slightly panting.

"Just kick," Roman snapped savagely.

She kept her mouth shut and she leaned against the wall, watching him in futility. He was sweating, she could tell. Each kick came slower than the last until he stood with his hands on his knees gathering in long intakes of air.

Elena sauntered over to the door and scrabbled her fingers into the small crack and pulled. She didn't expect it to do anything but one time she was in a van similar with her dad and it had opened just like that.

Roman watched in dismay as they opened and revealed a dark bricked wall. They were in a garage.

"Your ego must've expanded."

"It did."

Roman walked out, wriggling his fingers awkwardly.

She noticed he did that when he was wrong and that wasn't often. Elena felt triumph stir in her and a crazed smile lit her face for a brief second before Roman walked back to her.

"The door is locked."

Happiness never lasted long enough for her.

"Let's find a key or something then."

He nodded sulkily and helped Elena out the van.

"So the van's doors swing both ways."

"Seems so," Elena said.

It was a small garage, but it had the height to fit the van. Metal racks stood forlornly against the wall, peppered with rust and strewn with cobwebs. The floor was a grey stone that probably gleamed years ago and in places there were deep holes. Bullets, maybe. A single dusty clock hung on the wall and read eighteen minutes to three, but Elena didn't know how reliable that was. It could have slowed down or had been switched forward because of the seasons. Two bikes lay at the end, fallen and sad and the garage door that led someplace else was securely locked. No obvious key in sight at first glance.

"It smells like damp," Roman complained and kicked at the wall. Something from the other side of the room fell against one of the racks with a clang. Elena turned and blinked. An axe.

"Let's hack down the door," she said and manoeuvred the axe out from behind the rack, careful not to clash both objects. It was heavy and wooden and cold in her hands and she felt a grin form on her face. Roman wiped it off for her.

"Let me do it."

"Uh, no. I can do it myself."

"You can't even hold it properly."

Elena adjusted the axe, so it was balanced in both hands. "Happy?" she said raising an eyebrow.

He kept his arm folded and a glare sketched on his face.

Elena walked to the door. It was a navy blue which was a contrast to the greying of the rest of the garage with a single window centred squarely nearer the top. Elena could see through despite being the shortest out of the four.

"We don't need a key. We just need to smash the window," she said and swung. A crunch to the small window of the door and the glass fell to the other side. She didn't think it would be that easy.

"You're gonna wake up the entire neighbourhood."

"Maybe that's a good thing?"

"Your stupidity is limitless."

"It adds to my characters, doesn't it?"

Elena could part the curtains to one side. Her jaw fell. They were in a house. Not nearly as big as the house party but it still had the most majestic air. The room was a big kitchen and it was dressed in the shades of green. Even the cupboards were a shade of beige that matched. Elena thought back to her own kitchen and heaved a sigh and shivered.

"I don't think we can get through there."

Elena withdrew her hand from the curtain and glowered. "That's because you're fat."

"The pane of glass is still jagged. See? You could fall against it and impale yourself," Roman stated.

Elena let another slow groan slip out of her. "Then we'll cut down the door."

"Go on then."

Elena aimed and made a dent in the door.

"Let's find a key."

"I'm not that short," she huffed.

"I never said that."

"I can tell by the way you're looking at me. You're judging my height. Well I'm sure the taller you are, the more expensive your coffin will be. And the more your parents will have to weep with their hands clasped before clicking add to cart on their overpriced wooden box for their only little boy."

Roman didn't say a word and callously grabbed the axe off Elena who allowed herself another smug smile. He trudged over to the door and let the axe fall against it, propped upright.

"Prices don't vary by height, by the way," Roman mumbled softly and turned away from her, looking at the shelves.

Elena raised an eyebrow detecting a change in his voice. She decided not to push it.

Half an hour passed between the two. Elena sat over the edge of the van, chin in hand and Roman kept peering through to the other side. They also figured it was too small for any of them to fit through, even Elena. Realising it would be better a group decision they waited for the others to wake. Not one word was spoken between them in that time. Elena felt calmer than before and she accepted that she was in the situation she was in. Maybe they were held for ransom and their parents needed to offer Will money and they'd be free. She scoffed quietly. No. They'd probably die.

The van toppled to the right and Elena turned. Leo sat beside her and grinned, eyes flocked with sleep.

"Hi," he said.

"Hey. How are you?"

"Bad. It was the kinda sleep that knocks you out. But you wake up and you're still tired," he replied. "How's your arm? Are you cold?"

Elena pulled at the purple fabric appraisingly. "It'll be fine. Maybe lead poisoning or something," she muttered. "Roman and I found an axe. We're in a garage."

"Yeah, I heard you talking ages ago, but I think I passed out again," he said shrugging.

"Oh. Well we found a way out, but we need a key. We broke the glass, but nobody can fit through."

"Let's get hunting." He stood and wobbled but walked over to where Roman was practising swinging an axe.

"Woah," he said, barely dodging a swing that whistled past his eye.

Roman stumbled backwards in alarm. "Sorry, Leo."

"It's fine."

"No, it's not. I could've killed you."

"You didn't."

"Close."

"Why are you doing that?"

"I'm bringing it with me, and I can swing it at Will's head," Roman replied joyously.

Leo nodded.

"Is Robyn awake?"

"Not yet," Leo replied and diverted his gaze to the broken glass on the floor that shone like dirty crystals in the dim light. He only realised that the van headlights were shining and the only source of light. "Should we mess with his car?" Leo said.

Elena frowned and held her injured arm and Roman blinked.

"Mess with the mechanics?"

"Yeah, so he can't drive it."

"Hadn't thought about that. I suppose we could," Roman muttered.

Leo stared through the broken window and it gaped ominously like an open black mouth.

"Let's do it. Do something with the gears or something?" Elena waved her arms around and stood from the van. "Who knows anything about cars?"

"Not me," Leo and Roman replied.

Elena sagged but snatched the axe. She walked to the blue door and lifted the axe high in the air and it almost unbalanced as she and swung to make contact with the door handle. The handle fell with an awkward clunk. A hole was left where it used to stand, and Elena stooped to look through. It was too small to fit anything more than a few fingers.

"Elena. Please tell me you can get us to the other side," Leo said quietly.

"Trying," she grumbled and twisted her arm even more to an impossible angle.

"What the hell are you tryna do?" Roman cried shoving Elena out the way. Her hand jarred and bent and she yelped.

"You broke my good arm," she howled hysterically on the verge of tears, her fingers wrapped protectively around the hand which was once stuck in a door.

"I didn't," Roman snapped.

"What's going on?"

All turned and Robyn stood by the van. Her hair was a mess, but her eyes shone twice as bright.

"I have the key. I found it. Let's see if it fits."

She made her way with ease through the waiting gazes and reattached the handle to the door. Then producing a key, she gently slotted it into the keyhole and turned.

Nothing.

Nothing happened and the anticipation dissipated into the stale air of the garage like smoke.

"That was not what we were hoping for," Leo pointed.

The handle then fell once again in defeat.

Robyn cautiously traced the edges of the jagged glass with a finger.

"What are you doing?" Roman asked.

"I'm going to climb through this window. It shouldn't cut through my coat." She turned and shot them all a grin. "This was my grandad's coat in the war, and it left him alive."

"But it's just fabric," Roman countered.

"Your grandad?" Elena echoed.

"Yep."

"What about your jeans?" Leo asked.

"Will be fine," Robyn muttered. She judged the window carefully and looked to the room.

"Would someone be a dear and give me that and turn it over?"

Elena answered and tipped a small bin of its contents. Dust, dust and more dust She flipped it, so the base was now on top and Robyn stood on it. And she scrambled her way through. It was a struggle but already half her body fit through.

"Can someone push me through?"

The three left on the other side glanced at each other in terror.

"Elena. You do it," Roman hissed.

She looked aghast. "I don't wanna cut her by accident," she exclaimed.

"Just push my feet."

Elena heaved at Robyn's feet and it pushed her to the other side, curtains snapping shut. Robyn cursed but moments later there was a click and she stood by the door with a triumphant smile.

"Why didn't I think of that?" Elena demanded angrily as she gripped the axe, she'd so desperately wanted to break the door with.

"Hmm," Robyn said, brushing off the looks of amazement. "Elena, let me see your hand."

She walked numbly to Robyn and she inspected her hand.

"It's fine," she announced with a quiet smile.

"Are you sure? I—"

"Can we get out of here?" Robyn asked, addressing everyone, pocketing the key.

All four exited the gloomy room grateful for the change in scenery. Instead of smelling cooking and sun it smelt of cold and unfinished business.

thirteen.

"So. We're in a house," Roman said slowly.

Elena grumbled still holding the axe in both hands. He would have thought she looked like one of those badass movie characters if she wasn't so mortifyingly annoying. "No shit."

Roman ignored her and made his way to the kitchen sink, where the window was above. The blinds were drawn, so he parted them to look outside. He squinted but all he could make out were the dark still shapes of shrubbery that looked ominously like they could move any second.

"Woah," exclaimed Elena to his right. She marched up to him and presented a milk carton right in his face. Roman fought to urge to punch her backwards.

"Best before *27 July '93.* This milk is literally green."

He raised a curious eyebrow and opened the lid to sniff the unrecognisable liquid. Bad idea. The pungent smell filled his lungs in a way that made him turn away and stop himself from vomiting.

"I've got a plan." Came Leo's voice.

Roman turned and the others stood glumly in a circle staring at the same spot on the tiled floor.

"Okay?" he said.

"We're gonna split up and look around—"

"Isn't the most logical thing to do is just run to a door and leave?" Roman interrupted. "Break this window or something? Elena's axe can be put to good use."

"Yeah, you can do that, but we need to find Will first," Elena replied glaring.

"Find Will?" he repeated. "He's a psychopath."

Roman stalked off through the kitchen but Robyn swooped in to bar his way.

"What are you doing?" he snapped.

"What does it look like? We need to stop and think what to do next," Robyn answered.

"Leave?" Roman suggested and dodged past Robyn and made his way down a weakly lit hallway. The floor was wooden beneath his feet and creaked happily alongside him like a dog.

"Roman. Stop."

"You see that door there?" Roman pointed to the door several metres in front of him, simultaneously walking. "I'm walking out of it in a few seconds."

"It's probably locked."

He reached it and pulled the handle and was shocked by how cold it was. It didn't open.

"See," Robyn said behind him.

He turned and pushed past her and walked back down the hall. "Why are there no other doors?"

The hallway was long, and it only led from the kitchen to the door. It made Roman feel small and that didn't usually happen. He took a glance at the wallpaper which was vertically striped green and white and faded at the edges. No doors. He stopped and turned. Robyn almost walked straight into him.

"Robyn, get out your key," he commanded.

"I doubt it would work."

Roman shot her a look and she complied. They walked back to the door and Leo and Elena had joined. Robyn bit her lip and turned the key, a click resonated through the wood. She turned the handle and it opened to a large living room. There was a single grey sofa that faced a coffee table and a plasma television stood with the remote on top. A rug over the wooden floor, a cabinet at the other end that held priceless antiques and a black grand piano in the very corner. It was still open, the keys dulled with dust and manuscript pages on the stand. But the greatest find was a door that led to another room and another door that seemed to lead somewhere else. The room seemed to breathe quietly and watch the four intently. It was disconcerting.

"How old is that TV?" Elena had gone right up to the television and was inspecting its width. Roman asked himself the same and the question lingered in the air.

"Maybe from the nineties?" Leo said.

Elena turned her attention to the couch and her eyes widened comically. "Look at the sofa. Is that blood?"

There was a deep coloured stain across the seat of the sofa it almost seemed black.

"I dunno," Roman said uncomfortably. If it was, whoever had bled there must've died there.

"Right. My plan," Leo said uncertainly. "So, let's split into twos and find what's beyond those doors," he said.

Elena eyed him warily and folded her arms self-consciously. "Can I go with you, Robyn?" she mumbled.

Robyn looked to Roman and Leo but they both had their gazes turned to the floor. "Sure," she shrugged. "Why not?" She smiled and that made Elena smile. Almost too happy.

"Right, Roman. We're going through that door. The basement." Leo pointed gleefully to the door nearest.

Roman tensed. "How do you know that's the base—oh. There are windows on either side."

They both shuffled over and peered through like they were checking if something was dead. It was so dark it seemed like there was nothing below them.

"I think this leads to a bunch of stairs," Elena's voice wandered over.

"Does anyone know the time?" Robyn asked.

"No, then I'd be outta here, wouldn't I?"

Robyn scowled and ushered Elena and herself through the door. Elena still held a tight grip on the axe and Roman almost laughed. There was a clamour of footsteps up stairs and then silence.

Leo felt the uneasiness in Roman as his eyes darted nervously from the basement door to the door Robyn and Elena had just gone through.

"I'll go first," Leo said and opened the door.

He stopped and stared into the thick smog of darkness and it seemed to mix and boil threatening to spill up towards them. Then cool light expelled the darkness and Leo blinked. Roman had found a switch and gave him an easy grin. The light switch was old and one of the ones you flicked up and down. His school still had them. Beneath them they saw an empty room with dozens of boxes stacked to one side bathed in light. Roman could feel a colder temperature swim against his skin.

"Let's go look at the boxes," Leo whispered. He didn't know why he was whispering it wasn't like there was anybody there to overhear them.

"I don't know," Roman whispered back. "I hate basements," he said with a tinge of shame.

"Okay. How about you stay by the light up here and I'll go search in the boxes? Maybe there's something in them connecting this house to the owner."

Roman mentally thanked him for not judging his irrational fear and sat, watching him slowly descend. He caught a glimpse of something dark by the stairs and froze. "Is that a rat?"

Leo followed his finger and studied at a distance what it was. "Uh, no. It's a shoe."

Roman felt relief and almost cried. "I wonder who actually lives here."

"Probably not Will. I don't think it's very him." Leo reached the bottom of the stairs and onto the cold grey stone floor. He took a moment the gather himself.

"Really? How come?"

"If he owned a house, it wouldn't be this. I've known him a couple months."

"Were you guys actually official?"

Leo began easing the highest box of the pile down to the floor. "Yeah, now he just wants to kill us," he said.

"I thought he was a cool person. I know him personally from school."

Leo began peeling of the brown tape that clamped the box shut. It made an unsatisfying peeling noise. It didn't even peel satisfyingly either. A spark of paper tainted the air and he wanted to sneeze. "Oh, yeah you said. Are you guys close?"

"Never spoken. Perhaps once."

"Maybe you knew him well enough to know why he's doing all this."

Roman laughed and leaned forward, elbows on his knees. "If I knew then we wouldn't still be here."

Leo nodded quickly and sighed. "Hey, take a look at this."

"Can you hold it up in the air?" Roman asked, fear running back into his system.

Most of the time he always contemplated why he feared certain things. Rational and irrational. He wanted to understand himself better so nobody could fool him. Fear of basements.

It was seven years ago when he was ten and in his old home in Canada. They had a cat. He felt bad for forgetting its name, but it was something along the lines of Stones. Oh, Pebbles. His younger self was searching for him in the kitchen because it had been a while since anyone in their household had seen him. And him being the oldest, had to search high and low for the small greying cat. Roman didn't mind basements back then, so gripped the handle and trudged down the stairs calling his cat's name. Cats don't reply back, not like dogs, so he reached the ground and looked. Looked everywhere. Close to giving up but he didn't want to, despite the hunger in his stomach that left him feeling sick. What made him vomit eventually was the cat. Against the radiator, its head stuck in the grills and eyes wide open. He never saw cats or basements the same again.

Leo began pulling a long strip of tape from the box and it didn't stop until it lay like a snake around him. Even from metres away, Roman could see it had the word 'Police' repetitively worded along the whole thing.

"Okay," Roman said slowly. "Maybe whoever lives here is a cop?"

"I found photos too. In frames. Can you come down and look it's not too bad down here. Just cold."

Roman took a hesitant glance at the light switch and trekked downwards, biting his lip. He sat by Leo who brought framed photos out from the box and laid them around them.

Taking one he stared into the face of two people. A woman in her late twenties in a white t-shirt who seemed pregnant, short brown hair that just brushed past her ears and smiled serenely at the camera, blue eyes shining. Then a man by her side with a grey t-shirt and fringed ginger-brown hair sat equally as happy but his brown eyes didn't shine. The backdrop was a plain blue, so it must've been an organised photo shot at a place professional. But something struck him as odd.

"Do you know them?" Leo asked.

Roman shook his head. "No. I've never seen them before."

"Look at the back of the frame. It says January 1992."

That was it. The photograph was washed with a strange filter that distorted the colours into a different shade than they must've been in real life.

"It feels creepy looking at this stuff," he commented.

"They look around twenty something. These people now must be…" he trailed off as he did mental maths.

"Around fifty," said Roman.

Leo glared.

"Is there anything else?" Roman asked, eager to look away and placing the photograph back in the box.

"There are more of these photos. Look. They have a child in this one. Maybe they're a couple. Or maybe they're all siblings."

"Ew," Roman muttered as Leo handed him another frame.

It was true. In that photo, the two weren't smiling at the camera but at a baby perched in both their laps. The baby was looking at the camera though and its blue eyes were rolled big and wide. It seemed that they were a couple because siblings would not look at a child like that. Like they were the luckiest people in the world. He couldn't tell its gender, but its clothes were blue. People were traditional back then, so it was most likely a boy.

Roman turned the frame over.

March 1993.

"There's more," Leo warned.

Roman was handed a photo album, heavy and faded in his hands and he flicked to the page before the photos began. To the very front.

Clyde J

March 1992–1997

Your the most beautiful baby in the world xx

"They spelt 'you're' wrong," Leo grumbled.

"Shitty," agreed Roman. He turned to page one and was overwhelmed with photos tucked into pouches of a baby just born and still covered in blood. The same woman from the photos was in a hospital gown and held the baby in her arms and then another with all three in the picture. How people loved babies was beyond Roman. A date was pencilled at the top corner.

7th March 1992.

That must've been Clyde's birthday then. Roman did some quick maths and it meant that Clyde if he were still alive today would be twenty-eight. Roman kept turning the page, watching Clyde grow bigger and by early July 1993 he was sitting up. But after that, the pouches remained empty. He double checked.

"It stops here. At the front it said 1992 to 1997. There's nothing after that."

Leo eased the book from Roman, swore he saw him shake, and saw for himself. "Maybe they didn't get him vaccinated so he died. Measles was a big thing back then," Leo suggested.

"You mean smallpox?"

"That was eradicated in the late seventies."

"Maybe," Roman mumbled. "Funny to call someone Clyde."

Leo laughed but his face dropped. "You think we could find Clyde's room in here?"

"We could."

"Unfinished photo album—"

A scream paraded the air and panic exploded in the both who rushed up the basement stairs and arriving back in the living room but there wasn't anybody there. Roman was secretly glad to be out of that cold basement.

"They might still be upstairs," Leo said. "Do you think that was Elena or Robyn?"

Roman didn't reply and tugged Leo along with him. They raced to the door and didn't stop to admire the mahogany of the staircase and the carpet that draped over it. Both reached the landing and peered panicking into each room in turn. Leo found Elena and Robyn in a bedroom.

"Is everything okay?" Leo asked urgently. Robyn was stood by the mirror with her back turned to it and Elena sat on the brown covered bed with a vacant expression on her face. Robyn looked surprised to see them there. For a minute they both looked very out of it.

"Yeah?" Elena said with a small frown.

"We heard someone scream," Roman said looking between the two who looked at them oddly.

"I didn't hear anything. Did you, Elena?"

"No. But we discovered none of the windows open because they're locked and double glazed."

Leo looked to Roman desperately.

"We heard someone scream. It came from upstairs. Here," Roman pressed.

"We're telling you, we didn't," Robyn maintained.

Roman stared at her for a moment and saw something strange flicker behind Robyn's eyes. His eyebrows creased together. "Are you sure?" he questioned.

"Yes, you're scaring us. It isn't funny especially now—"

"I shit you not, we heard a scream from upstairs," Roman reiterated slowly. "Are you absolutely sure?" Roman was now scared himself. Scared shitless.

"Yes," Elena said and stood, arms folded. She seemed to shiver without her sweater.

"Leo. We both heard it."

"I guess we heard wrong. What did you guys find?"

Roman stared at Leo in disbelief.

"Windows are locked and there's just garden out there, but we saw a door earlier," Robyn replied. "And another key." Robyn held a silver key that was the same silver as the one she'd found earlier.

"Where was it?"

"On top of that wardrobe. Dusty as hell."

Roman gave a side glance to Leo hoping to catch his eye but he didn't see. Or didn't want to.

"Great."

"The outside leads to a garden and then a wall," Elena mumbled.

"Well that's just as well. Wherever this Safe House is, it's probably up in Scotland for all we know," Leo mumbled.

That thought hadn't occurred to Roman until then. If the time in the garage was right, then they'd been away for hours. And in that time, they could have travelled anywhere. Even overseas. That scared Roman more than he could admit. He caught sight of himself in the full-length mirror Robyn was stood by and looked at his dishevelled appearance. Drugged Roman wasn't a nice look.

"Wow, I'm really feeling myself tonight," he said admiringly, hands in his pocket and feeling the mints.

"What?" Robyn said.

"What?" Roman said.

She shook her head.

"I look high." He bent closer to his reflection and saw his pupils were so dilated even in the bright light of the bedroom. He turned and grabbed Robyn's face to peer into her eyes.

She shook him off angrily. "What are you doing?" she snapped.

"The drug Will gave us. We've all fallen unconscious because of what we ate. Look at our pupils."

Leo glanced into Elena's eyes and they both confirmed.

"I hate mirrors," Robyn muttered.

"Why?" Leo said.

"I scare myself," replied Robyn shrugging.

"That's because you're looking at the wrong angle." He smiled and she gave a funny grin.

"Can we leave? This bedroom is creepy," Elena muttered.

The bedroom was average and in colours of neutral tones. Nothing out of place. Maybe it was the fact that only two out of four people heard the scream in a completely silent house.

"Have you checked the drawers?" Roman asked.

151

"Yeah. We think this is a girl's bedroom, there's clothes and stuff," Robyn said. "Did you find anything in the basement?"

"Some photos. There was a photo album of a child, but it stops after they turn one," Roman responded half-heartedly.

"And we found police tape," Leo added as an afterthought. "We would've looked for more because there were a few more boxes but we heard a scream." He gestured to the air.

"We'll go back some time. Right now, I think the best option is to find more keys. We have two already."

"And for some reason it was placed in a specific place," Leo said.

Robyn raised an eyebrow.

"Think about it. You found the key in the garage which opened the door in the hallway. That is not a coincidence," Leo said.

"Yeah, where did you find that key?" Roman asked.

Robyn seemed to take a tentative moment to answer. "It was actually near the wheel of the van. It was taped there," she responded.

"Let's go find some more keys then," Elena said.

Robyn nodded and headed out the room, Elena in tow, dragging the axe along the floor like a child with a toy.

"We're going to check the bathroom; you can check outside. The door unlocks. Or continue with the basement, we need this whole house searched," Robyn said.

Roman noticed that Elena was always under the command of Robyn. That girl was hopelessly lost.

Both left and silence rained down on them.

"Do you think they're lying?" Leo mumbled in a low voice only audible to himself and Roman.

"Without a doubt."

fourteen.

Robyn blinked and Elena was kicking the door open. How quick time had gone. Robyn turned to smile at Elena reassuringly as they entered the bathroom. Elena carried her axe in her left and it scraped along the floor, carving the floor in its wake.

"It's definitely colder in here," Elena said shuddering in only a black top.

"Isn't it." Robyn welcomed the cold when they walked into the bathroom, it was suffocating in the garage.

A pearly white bathtub, a matching sink and a window that gazed glassily out to the gardens. Robyn watched the stars blink their tired eyes at the world below them as the world turned on. With or without them.

She knocked against the window and sighed as she realised it was double glazed. Absolutely nothing in the house could cause these windows to break. Earlier they'd tried throwing the lamp through the glass, but it didn't even dent. It had been an old filament lamp with a shade. Perhaps a heavier piece of furniture would suffice.

"Don't you think the others acted really weird before?" Robyn said.

Elena looked up from surveying the tiled walls and gave her a look. "A bit, yeah. Maybe when we tried smashing glass it sounded like a scream," she mumbled quietly and resumed, crouching to the floor and touching the mat. "It's so dry it could break if I bent it."

Robyn watched her as she looked under the mat and shrieked. Dead moths, dust smudged around them like soil.

"How long do you think they've been there?" she asked, recovering, and replacing the mat.

"Yeah everything in this house is really outdated," Robyn said. Come to think of it, the fact that everything seemed decades old nudged something in Robyn's mind which she found familiar. But when she asked herself what it was, her brain didn't answer.

"And my arm aches." She gave a sharp laugh which impaled itself through Robyn.

"I was held at gun point by one of my best friends who is now dead and then I was shot by a guy I thought who was good. And attacked," she smiled to herself weakly. "And my dad died today."

"I'm sorry," Robyn said unsure. She wasn't sure of anything now that they could only see a few centimetres into their future. Kind of like a car's headlights in fog.

"People surprise you, don't they?"

"They sure do," Robyn replied, thinking back to her mother.

"And then I get into a fight with my boyfriend. It's like life hates me. Maybe God had this planned out all this time," Elena added giving a hopeless thump to the wall. Something above crumbled.

"Predestination?" Robyn said amused.

"My mum was religious, and it made me low-key religious too," she said. "Then she left."

"If it helps, my mother left too."

Elena laughed bitterly. "I don't know what to do."

"Well tell me what your dad was like. Or your best friend who tried to shoot you. Or your ex. And whoever attacked you. Wow, this list is exhaustive."

"My dad? Was the best. He took care of me. I guess. I looked after him too because he had diabetes and most of the time, he's sat watching TV," Elena said.

Robyn nodded, encouraging her.

She coughed awkwardly. "But then I got back home, and he was dead. Gone out cold. I rushed outside, and Mark was stood there. We called the ambulance after that. I told him I was coming here. Well, not here. The party."

"Did he offer to drive you?"

"We fought so I took two cabs."

"We were going to leave when this person stopped us from leaving. Twice."

"Oh," Elena said.

"Oh, indeed. She was tall and intimidating. And I'm never intimidated by anyone."

"Sounds a lot like Vienna," she said sadly. "She dragged me into a bedroom and shot herself afterwards. It's a shame because I would've loved to wear her top," Elena added that as an addition.

Robyn frowned to herself. "A dead person's top?"

"I'm not creepy. It's just it was red and lacy, and it would—"

"Red? Lace? The person who Leo and I were stopped by was wearing that."

"Was she blonde?"

"Yes."

155

"Grey eyes."

"Probably."

"Talks like a girl?"

"She is a girl," Robyn said raising an eyebrow.

"But she's like a proper girl. Traditionally."

"Her voice was really high."

"I think Vienna tried to stop you from leaving," Elena said finally.

Robyn frowned sceptically. Elena's friend had stopped them from leaving. And if she hadn't, they would probably be home now sleeping through into Sunday dawn.

"Do you think Vienna knows Will?" Robyn whispered afraid suddenly of the tiled walls. They caged them in.

"Maybe they were working together. But I don't get how. Vienna was a normal person. She's definitely not a psychopath."

"Yeah, well people surprise you."

They fell silent and Robyn began to wonder whether they would ever get out. Or who else could potentially be involved in everything. She wondered if they were ever going to make it to the next sunrise.

"What about your ex?" Robyn said quietly.

"We dated for a long time. Several years. He was my rock. But lately I've started to realise he doesn't really like me."

"Why's that?"

"I don't know. His stepdad and his mum own this shed. It's full of guns. And…" Elena wavered, and her eyes darted to her arm, "and I think what Will shot me with was Mark's gun." She said it so softly Robyn had to catch the words before they escaped into the cold air of the bathroom.

"How could you tell?"

Elena frowned. "They're both the same."

"All guns look the same."

"No, they don't."

"They do—"

"Were you held at gunpoint?" she snapped.

Robyn sealed her words. She began to feel sorry for Elena. Despite her fights with people she was willing to start and the stupid need to do everything herself even if it was lousy. Her life really sucked and maybe that was what made Elena do what she did.

Elena grumbled to herself, glancing at her arm.

"If it gets worse, you tell us," Robyn said kindly.

Elena looked to her and watched her for a few moments. Robyn got the impression Elena was deciding something and she stared back her smile frozen into place.

"Yeah," she said at last. "Can I have a hug?"

Robyn blinked. "Now?"

"Yeah."

Elena stood and Robyn embraced her, hand rubbing her good arm in a brusque fashion in an attempt to make her feel warmer. Elena smelt like baking and the scent of washed clothing. It made Robyn think of home and her dad and her face crumpled. She recovered when they moved apart.

"Do you think I'm annoying?" she asked suddenly.

Robyn frowned. "No. I think you're cool and determined."

"No, I'm not," she said.

"Yes, you are."

She made a thinking noise. "Maybe the cool part."

Robyn grinned.

"And the determined bit too."

Robyn's grin wandered off behind her face. "Have you checked the drawers?" Robyn pointed to the cupboard under the sink.

Elena stooped and peered into them. She shook her head, disappointed. "Absolutely nothing. Just furniture and no trace of a human ever living." She stopped short. "Apart from the big stain on the sofa and the clothes."

"Let's go to the next room."

The cold that lingered between her clothes and her skin had long outstayed its welcome.

"It's locked," Elena pulled the handle and pushed but it only rattled stubbornly. She gave it a kick. Robyn noticed she really enjoyed kicking open doors.

"Let's try the second key, I doubt it'd open this door especially considering our luck—"
It clicked open and it creaked threateningly on its hinges. Elena heeled the door open and Robyn flicked the switch on, and light jabbed painfully into their eyes. They couldn't believe it. The room was small but several columns of black screened televisions like the one downstairs on top of one another sat in their sight. And in the middle was an old computer and the monitor.

"Holy crap," Robyn said.

"Surveillance?"

"Maybe."

They walked in cautiously, with Elena watching by the door. Robyn pushed the button at the bottom of the screen of the thick screened computer. She grinned as it glowed white and then green, the screen lighting up blue. It was still a version from long ago. 1992.

"You got it working," Elena said in disbelief.

Robyn's face fell as a username and password was required. As expected.

"Come look, this is old. The electricity in this place works." She couldn't hide the excitement in her voice. If she had her phone, she'd send a picture to her friend Eliza. She missed home. "Let's go see other rooms and tell the others."

"Oh, the others," her face dropped noticeably.

"What's wrong?"

"For a minute I forgot Roman existed." She smiled sadly. "Just... don't provoke him."

"It's hard when he disagrees with everything I do."

They'd checked the rest of the floor but came down empty handed as they came back to the ground floor. The door they'd not entered previously was slightly ajar. Elena used to her foot to nudge it open and Leo and Roman stood hands in pockets in the open space, backs facing them. It was freezing but on the bright side, there was a pool. They were in a garden which was big and bordered around it was a high brick wall that seemed oddly out of place and colour. Apart from the small pool and deckchairs that looked dusty and bleached by the sun, it was empty.

"Hey," Robyn said.

Roman turned instinctively, stepping back and Leo jerked.

fifteen.

They cleared the stairs and Leo turned back to stare at the ceiling where the others would be above.

"What are you doing?" Roman questioned already at the door.

"I'm just weirded out," Leo replied, and he turned to where Roman stood, a hand on the handle.

"Me too," Roman said.

"I wonder what's behind that door."

"Maybe it's a ballroom. Who even knows anymore, these people are rich."

"Open it."

Roman tugged and beyond the door was the outside world. Cold breeze oozed into them and it cooled the sweat that lingered on Leo. It wasn't just the outside world, there was a dark pool that lay still, throwing the wave's reflection on the wall behind them. The light came from the bottom of the pool and a few white deckchairs were placed around. The entire place was surrounded by a brick wall tall enough to block out anything but the sky.

"There's a pool," Leo exclaimed.

"Why don't we try and climb over the wall?" Leo suggested.

Roman grinned and followed him. He then backed away suddenly and ran back flinging his arms to the wall as he vaulted. He didn't get anywhere near.

"Let's try getting a deck chair, here. Help me."

Leo dragged the nearest chair to him and up against the bricks. They clambered on, both had to make a small jump to cling to the very edge. Leo felt the hard brick against his sweaty palms but managed a leg over and then the other. Roman was a few seconds later but they admired their surroundings. Like a picture book laid open, hills and greenery lay beyond them rolling like the sea.

"We need to tell the others," Roman said but then frowned looking at his hand. He held a silver key and he thumbed it carefully.

"Where did you get that?" Leo asked, suspicion flaring.

"It was digging into my knee just as I got up."

They got down and dusted their hands. Leo had a small cut on his hand from scrabbling, but he hardly felt it. Excitement buzzed in his mind from the new find and he turned back to look at the wall. It held them in, but they'd found a weak spot.

"Hey," said a voice behind them.

Leo's heart toppled and both turned. Robyn and Elena stood like silhouettes against the yellow light. Robyn's expression was questioning, and Elena stood small with a half-smile.

"Sorry," Leo said, avoiding Robyn's eyes. She frowned but didn't think much of it.

"Find anything?" Elena gestured to the space.

"A pool. And a key," Roman held up a silver key that flashed in the moonlight.

"It was on the wall over there. I think Will's putting them in places on purpose."

"Maybe he wants us to let us out after all?" Elena said.

"Leave that to us, we've found a way out," Roman said, and he grinned proudly. He pointed to the wall and beyond. "We saw to the other side and there are fields. That's our way out."

Elena sighed in relief, dropping the axe and Robyn's face brightened evidently.

"Come look," Leo said, and they went over to where the wall was. They took turns in standing on the chair and peering over the wall. Leo clung to the wall and smiled to himself. Around them at a slight elevation were empty fields of dark green patches and it beckoned them silently. All they had to do was climb over.

"You think we're still in England?" Elena whispered.

"It looks pretty English to me," Leo said.

"We found a surveillance room. We think," Robyn said.

Leo turned. "But I haven't even seen any cameras anywhere."

"I know. Which is why it's weird, it may not be CCTV. The computer still works though."

"Roman. I think I should look after the keys, you're being irresponsible," Elena scolded from below. Roman was sat on the wall tossing the key up like it was a coin and whooping. He snatched the key before Elena could take it from him.

"Relax, it's not like I'm gonna drop it," he laughed.

But Elena didn't laugh and suddenly pushed Leo and Robyn off the deckchair so she could climb to Roman. Leo toppled and fell with a thud on the stone floor, Robyn along with him. The pain in his head knocked like dice in his skull and for a minute he thought he saw stars in his eyelids.

"Give me the key, I don't trust you," Elena snapped.

They were fighting over the key and to Leo's dismay, Roman seemed to move further to the edge of the wall. Half his body fell, and he swore, completely forgetting about the key. Elena took hold of it and was going to pocket it but Roman kicked her hand and the key went veering off. It slipped noiselessly into the dark stomach of the pool and there was a struggled silence when the water gurgled.

Elena gave a scream of torment and walked to the edge of the pool, Robyn following behind. Leo stood and helped Roman back upright. He seemed almost green in the face.

"We can't—"

"Come on, let's get that key," Leo butted in and dragged Roman down with him back to the ground.

They went over to join the others and squinted into the dark pool. The watery depths weren't clear enough to see to where the key was or the bottom. It wasn't even close. Inside was a mix of twigs, shrubbery and another type of dark liquid which swam gloomily alongside. Oil. Or maybe blood.

"We don't need the key anymore if we're gonna leave over the fence," Leo said to Elena who stood with a crumpled expression scribbled on her face.

Elena said nothing and stole a glance at Roman and Leo knew what would come next. The tipping point.

"This is your fault," Roman snapped.

She blinked. "You kicked it out of my hand," she cried back.

"You know," Roman laughed bitterly, "you dragged me deep into this mess. I think you're to blame for why I'm here. Maybe all of us."

Leo fell silent and all thoughts to stop them fighting deserted his mind. Robyn's eyes were trapped wide open and she looked from Elena to Roman in panic.

"You've been rude to me ever since the beginning—"

"I thought you were all right but then you went and left the body and then it disappeared. It *disappeared*. It didn't walk off, Elena. Somebody took it and they wouldn't have if you didn't leave. You hear?"

"You're yelling, why wouldn't I hear?"

"I told you to stay with the body."

"I didn't like being left with her. She stared at me," Elena said squirming.

"Then look away," Roman hissed.

"What body?" Robyn said. But nobody replied. It was like there was nobody else around but Elena and Roman and they continued tossing abuse at one another, almost painful to watch. Leo felt Roman was screaming at him from where he was stood.

"You're dead to me," Roman snarled and his tone was so quiet and foreboding.

Elena didn't say a word, but she blinked from underneath her messy brown hair. Leo noticed there was a red residue on one of the tips and he knew it was her own blood.

"Have you quite finished? Both of you?" Robyn said.

"Not quite," Roman said grimly.

"No, you're both done," said Leo firmly. He turned away from the three and looked to the mansion that towered above them. The windows and doors were railed with balconies with vines spiralling themselves along the surface. A dark shape loomed in one which he was just able to make out before it was swept out of view. "There's someone up there," Leo said, aiming a finger like a gun to the window where he'd seen the movement.

Heads snapped to look up guardingly.

"Are you sure?" Robyn asked.

"Yeah. They looked at us and then left," Leo said. "Can we stop fighting about the key? And just go?"

"We can't," Roman mumbled coldly.

"Why not?" Robyn said frowning.

Roman looked to the three of them even Elena who avoided his eyes. "Come look."

Again, they strode over to the wall and Roman stood, Leo with him raising an eyebrow. Roman pointed directly below them and Leo's heart gave a horrible lurch. He hadn't even looked downwards.

"Can we see?" Robyn asked patiently from behind them. Leo stared for a while longer and gripped the wall beneath his fingertips tighter, steadying himself against the non-existent wind he felt was going to blow him over the top.

"We're on the edge of a mountain and if we drop, we die.

sixteen.

Elena's face became buzzing with horror and she stepped to an empty space on the deckchair to see for herself. Indeed, they were on a cliffside that was only centimetres from the very edge but without looking down, the hills seemed to be almost level with where they were standing only slightly lower. After the cliff dipped, it plummeted several hundred feet like a canyon before sloping upwards to meet with the fields. Like someone had dug a trench around the perimeter.

Ideas whizzed like bees in her mind as she stepped away and down to the ground. Robyn took her place and came down with a blank face.

"So there's no way out," she said.

"I think we should scale the wall then get to the roof."

"Can't. The roof is too tall."

"We're in the middle of nowhere," Leo heaved.

Robyn looked over her shoulder, a deep frown upon her face. Then as if the expression were literal, her face lit up.

"I think I know what's going on here." Her voice sounded on the verge of hysteria. The others waited glumly and when nobody spoke, Leo nudged her. "Oh, right." She blinked like she was disoriented. "I don't know if I have this right."

"What?" Roman prompted.

"The outdated furniture, the landscape of this place, the emptiness."

"What about it?"

"Didn't you guys say you found a photo album?"

"Yeah," Leo said.

Robyn blinked again and turned to look at the sky, thoughts racing. Elena turned to look up too and she thought about how the sky closely resembled the darkness of the pool.

"I read about this," she muttered and then she looked back to the rest of the group. "You heard of the murder twenty-seven years ago? A couple axed to death?"

The three exchanged blank looks and shook their heads. Elena felt she always had to do that in her life. Living in Runswick all her life and never once had she stumbled upon that.

"I read about it this once."

Elena raised an eyebrow and Robyn grinned embarrassedly.

"Can you tell us the whole story?" Elena asked.

"Okay. So there were four people all in their late twenties. Two of them were just friends but the other two were a couple and they had a child. Clyde—"

Roman and Leo eyed each other warily. "The kid was Clyde J. We saw his photo album."

"Yeah. Clyde Jackson. They didn't put his name in the media, but it got out anyway. So the four friends were at a party and then as the night progressed, they got drunk like teenagers and found themselves in the woods. And the couple, Mabel and Keith were murdered. With an axe. The other two got away and I googled. They're still alive. Some thought that because the couple were Jewish, it was a hate crime."

"Was it?"

"No, it was random."

Elena remembered the axe she carried, and she thought about the ghost of blood that could have stained it. "I don't see the link."

"This house," Robyn gestured to the house that loomed. "Is Mabel and Keith's house. That's why it's left like this. From the nineties."

Elena took a step back from the house and her shoulder made contact with the wall. She had never felt more trapped. Leo and Roman exchanged troubled looks.

"Mabel and Keith's parents struggled to sell their house after their death, so it's remained like this," Robyn continued. "I don't know if Clyde is still alive, but the perpetrator or perpetrators were never charged.

"And this is linked because we're in their house. The four of us. Kidnapped and brought here. If you ask me, we're going to end up in a similar fate."

"By the same people, you think?" Leo asked.

"But Will is only the same age as us. He wasn't alive in the nineties," Roman said.

Robyn shrugged in response.

Suddenly, Elena felt the anger and fear whirl inside her, and she strode past them back to the door and inside, picking up the axe as she went. Shouts of protest came from behind, but she brushed them aside. She needed to get out and she knew how.

All her life she felt confined only to feel certain things. They'd taught her not to be so sensitive, to be able to take jokes even though they left you feeling like shit. And she'd listened. She backed down out of things beyond her and she let her best friend and her ex speak for her. They weren't very good speakers. This was something she'd do by herself, without the help of others. A journey alone.

Back into the living room, she unplugged the TV cable and held the TV in her arms in an embrace, the axe wedged awkwardly between. Her wounded arm gave an ungrateful throb of pain. The TV was heavy as she heaved herself up the stairs and into the bedroom Robyn and her had been in before. The TV was dusty as hell too. Carefully she tapped the glass at the window and lifted the TV over her head. She balanced it there for a couple of moments, muscles humming with pain. Then she remembered she had an axe which was easier to hold. Sounds of quick footsteps echoed up to where she was, and Elena quickly kicked the door shut with her heel. With strength, Elena smashed the window with her axe and with renewed determination, she began hacking away at the window. Hearing the sprinkle of glass as it sprinkled to the pavement below, she grinned. The door handle turned, and a figure stood.

"Not now," she barked through clenched teeth.

"Elena."

"Can't you see—"

A hand was on her shoulder and she shuddered as the hand was cold and seemed to sear through her bare skin. She wouldn't be surprised if it left an imprint.

It was Mark.

The Mark she was so in love with and seeing him there awoke her dormant feelings for him. Elena faltered and she blinked the surprise from her head. "Good God. What are you doing here?"

"I followed you," he responded calmly.

Elena's instincts heightened in alarm. If he'd followed them, then he'd been here with them for hours.

169

"You followed me?" she croaked.

"The car and your three best friends," Mark said with the same casual tone, but something showed Elena the hostility behind his words.

"My three best friends?" Elena repeated incredulously.

"Yes, Elena. You don't need to repeat every phrase I say. It'll get quite boring," Mark snapped.

She frowned, trying to ignore that comment. "Why did you follow us? Did you know we were in trouble?"

"No."

"How did you get in?" Elena questioned.

"Front door."

Freedom was at the tip of her tongue as she took hold of the denim fabric of Mark's jacket. "Let's get out of this together," she implored. "My friends and I aren't here because we want to be. We were kidnapped." She shook him to make sure he was still there with her.

"Why should I help you? All of you?" he said.

"Just show us where the door is. Not them, just me." Some part of her felt bad but after what they'd all done. But they were a team and one fall meant the rest would fall so they were just as bad as each other.

"I thought we agreed on a break?"

"You can just help me. Think of it as even. After all the times I stayed with you," she pleaded. It was manipulative, but it had to be in these times. "Please. You can do whatever you want with the others but I wanna go home. My dad—"

"Is dead," he finished coldly.

Elena nodded frantically, clinging onto the subject. "There are doors everywhere that we can't access, and I need you to tell me where the front door is." Elena held Mark's gaze for what felt like minutes, but it was really seconds. She noticed the green in them gleamed in the light, but his face remained as blank as ever.

"No," Mark retorted finally.

Elena shook her head in frustration.

"She's gone mad."

Roman.

The three blocked off Mark's exit and they looked from him to Elena.

Leo gasped. "He's the guy who attacked me," Leo said hand over his mouth, wide eyes imprisoned open.

"Who are you?" Robyn spoke, her voice guarded.

"What is this, a little sleepover?" Mark's eyes glittered strangely. "Did you save snacks?"

"Elena actually has a boyfriend?" Roman stared, hand on his head. "I thought she was lying. So, you're Mark."

"Why did you attack me?" Leo said.

"You attacked me first," Mark said dismissively.

Leo's eyes narrowed. "You've been following us this whole time. Why?"

"It doesn't matter," Roman hissed. "Can you get us out? You got in."

"I would but—" Mark shoved a sheet of paper into Elena's hand roughly.

"What's this?" Elena said sharply, dropping it immediately like it was a bomb.

Mark picked it back up and handed it back to her. "I'm going to leave now," Mark said.

The four ignored and surrounded Elena reading off the same sheet of paper. It read like a contract and looked like one too. But there was one key aspect that stood out as most important.

Your personalities all align together well and you're here to solve something, something that hasn't been solved in years, and if you managed this far, you're doing something right.

But there are rules. And there's only one – don't try any shortcuts. That's breaking things, cheating.
Any rules broken will result in the extermination of a party member.

In my world, the currency is in secrets. A secret given is a secret traded. To get by, secrets will have to be exchanged. Secrets bigger than others will equate to a larger sum.

–WILL

Elena looked up shakily to the window she had so desperately broken, dropping the paper to the floor. She shouldn't have.

"We're gonna die because you broke that stupid window," Roman said bitterly. "And the fucking glass in the garage."

"How did Mark find this?" Robyn asked raising an eyebrow.

The slam and click of a lock startled the four. Mark was gone and their door was locked.

Panic rose in Elena's throat and she ran urgently to the door and tried turning the knob. "Psychotic son of a bitch," she cried and crossed back to the window, looking down at the pavement below.

"He didn't help us because their stupid breakup."

"Stop yelling. We'll go through the window," Elena said. "He's gonna kill all of us. Not just two of us like before."

He didn't flinch, his face was dark with anger. A wave of rage possessed Roman and he came at Elena, a fist striking her in the head, pain resonating through her bones. He was held back by Leo and Robyn, both had arms around one of his arms. Roman shook them off violently.

"I hope he kills you first," Roman said, quiet and monotone.

Elena swallowed the little burn in her throat hard. It felt like barbed wire was being pulled slowly up her throat. She didn't want to show any weaknesses. And the headache Roman had resurrected.

"I hope he does too," Elena said trying to sound indifferent and brushing off the comment he'd upturned so angrily into her face. She looked to the window and soon enough she was on the window ledge. On the outside. The cold night air was refreshing to her now because her face felt red and her brain throbbed. She clung to the ledge precariously and tried her best to empty her mind. The attack earlier on her way home and all of this.

"You sure about this?" Leo asked peering out concerned.

"I'm gonna find that exit myself and I'll tell you all," Elena said. She was lying. She was going to find that exit by cheating and she wouldn't tell any of them. Fuck all of them. The pavement seemed closer now that she was outside and took a breath and launched right onto the lawn. The grass was incredibly overgrown but not in some places. Weird. Her knees bent and she crouched, palms on the ground. The grass was cold and wet. She looked back to the window for a last time. They were all looking at her but not sadly. Almost in relief. Maybe. She was bad at reading people. Roman wasn't there. If she stayed with them, she'd be dead and if she cheated and left, she may still have a chance of survival. And fuck, she'd left her axe. She took off out of view and rounded a corner and couldn't believe it. The wall ended and a picket fence stopped her only way out. She was at the entrance. She walked backwards and then ran, breeze threading its way through her hair.

Nothing mattered anymore. Not them, not Will, not Mark. Not even her dad. She needed to get out. And she was over the fence, barely a scratch on her or her clothes. Her arm felt okay too. Around her was the driveway. It was massive. And nothing lay ahead of her but greenery. A car was parked just out of view, but she could see the headlights on.

"Hello? Help!" she screamed waving her arms. She began running towards it and realised who was in it and started sprinting in the opposite direction, dread jumping about in her. The car began to move, and it sped towards her as she made her way down the hill. And then she was on the floor, lying on her back, body splayed in confusion. The engine cut off sharply and there were gentle footsteps that inched towards her. Someone peered down at her. Even in the dark she could see the green glint of Mark's eyes.

"Mark," she mumbled, her hand twitching.

Mark's foot crunched onto her hand, stopping the twitching which made her pierce the air with a shriek. "Give me your finger," he said impatiently.

Elena began sobbing half in relief and half in fear. "You're marrying me?"

"Give me the fucking finger you use for your phone," he snapped.

Elena didn't stop sobbing to herself in dismay. "Why do you need my finger? You know my passcode, right? I haven't got my phone on me."

The pain in her chest cramped like a shrimp and she struggled to breathe. It did not help her headache. Her hand was crushed yet again, the pain sprinting through her arm and her heart kicked and thrashed like a baby. "It's my thumb, it's my thumb on my right!" she said quickly.

Mark knelt beside her and cradled her crumpled hand almost in a gentle manner. She watched his slow and deliberate actions with suspense, her sobs subsiding. He titled his head, so their faces were in line with each other and smiled gently. "Maybe in another world we'd be together forever," he said softly.

"I'd love to be in that other world right now," she said eagerly.

Their eyes met and she clung there for seconds. Mark was the first to look away, something in his hand from his denim jacket.

"Me too," he said.

Elena screamed when the silver of the blade made contact with her thumb and she didn't stop screaming when it cut straight through the bone to the other side. But she did when her vision darkened like the end of a winter's day.

seventeen.

And then a scream. A long agonising scream that shook the air.

Roman didn't even have to think about whose it was. Leo and Robyn ran to the window and leaned out, both careful to avoid the shards of glass that stuck out like teeth. Roman stood still, his left clutching his right hand.

All his life he'd had issues with his emotions, especially the stronger ones like anger. It wasn't a secret. He'd usually resort to violence and he knew that he got it from his dad. While his dad had gone to a shrink to talk about his feelings, Roman had bottled it up. It was a small ass bottle because he always felt like exploding every time Elena spoke. Even if they'd sat in silence, he would still find something to be annoyed about with her. Ever since they'd met. Spoiled girl. With a sad life. Pity points earned.

"I can't see her," Robyn said.

Leo turned desperately to Roman who stood nonchalantly. "Why did you punch her? You don't go punching people. I get that you're angry but this—" he pointed with his thumb to the window, "is what we want to avoid. Conflict."

176

Roman shrugged like it didn't bother him but deep down it did. It scared him to his bone what he did. "Oops."

That angered Leo and Roman could tell it took him everything not to yell at him. His skin usually a pasty cream colour was red. He couldn't blame him.

"I heard a car peel out," Robyn said.

"A car?" Roman raised an eyebrow.

"Mark?" Leo suggested.

Mark. The guy who he found extremely peculiar.

"The door is locked," Roman said hopelessly. "She threw the key in the pool."

"We have to find Elena," Leo responded. "I don't like that Mark guy anyway. He attacked me."

"And he also followed us here," Robyn reminded darkly.

Roman stumbled to the window and poked his head out. The cold air provided a temporary relief to the heat in his head, cooling his angry thoughts. He watched the dark sky, cloudless and empty and the wall. And somewhere, Elena was out there. In pain. Eventually, he realised how unfair he'd been to her. She couldn't help it, but neither could he. It made Roman's face turn sour but on the other hand...

"Let's follow her," said Leo.

Roman and Robyn glanced at each other.

"What if she's dead?" Robyn said.

"We can find a way out and then find her."

"We'll go to the garden. We haven't searched it properly. And the basement," Robyn said.

Leo turned to Robyn. She looked back at him anxiously.

"But she needs our help. The door's locked."

Something was slipped beneath the door and all turned.

"Another set of instructions?" Robyn said, walking over and picking it up. "We know you're there Will."

No reply.

They huddled together and read.

Secrets aren't meant to be kept.
Money is meant to be spent.
When was the last time you slept?

-WILL

Robyn bit her lower lip, Leo blinked and Roman narrowed his eyes.

"I think we do a trade," Robyn said.

Roman rapped his knuckles loudly against the door. "Poetic much."

"So, what? We say a secret out loud and we get out?"

"Perhaps."

"Well, we gotta try."

A heartbeat of silence.

"This is a little unnecessary if you ask me," Robyn said. "Let's sit."

They crouched far from the window and looked solemnly down at the sheet of paper lying in the middle. Will would be listening outside; he was sure of it. If he wasn't, it certainly felt like he was.

"I'll go first. To get it over and done with," Leo said.

"What? You're really following through with all this?" Roman asked.

"Yes," he said.

"Okay. Fine."

He scuffled. "Does it have to be a big secret?"

"If it's big for you."

"Right." He frowned at a speck on the floor. "I attempted."

They blinked and a second went by.

"Attempted what?"

"What does it sound like?" Robyn said apathetically. She turned to Leo and nodded to him. "Why?"

"That's two secrets," he complained.

Robyn nodded sympathetically. Roman as quick witted as he was, finally understood and didn't say a word.

"Okay," Roman said. "I guess it's my turn."

"I guess so," Robyn said looking away from both.

Roman gathered up his thoughts and began wording his sentences. He really didn't have many secrets, and if he did, they weren't worth mentioning.

He made a face. "I don't know."

"Use your brain."

"Don't have one."

Robyn rolled her eyes.

"You think Will is actually just gonna let us out after we tell our secrets?" he said and all signs of anger rushing to his face. "With no strings attached?"

"I don't like strings," muttered Leo.

"It's our only option."

Roman sighed. "Fine. I've never had a crush on anyone."

"Okay," said Leo.

"No, seriously. I've never had a crush on anyone in my life. No girls, no guys. Nobody."

"Maybe you're asexual."

"Like, plants? Bacteria?" He raised an eyebrow.

"You've never slept with anyone?"

"Jesus, no."

"Right," Robyn said awkwardly.

Roman stifled a groan. Robyn shuffled around and decided to move from her crouch, so she was sat cross legged.

"My mother left us two years ago," she began, voice calm but Roman could detect a pinch of sadness. "She left us for

179

this guy who looks exactly like my dad. And since then, it's just been us. We're not exactly financially stable either—" Robyn stopped and took a deep breath. "So I drug deal."

Roman's mouth snapped open, but Leo didn't look surprised.

"I thought you just did them?" Leo said.

"Nope, I help distribute drugs. I'm a felon. I use the money to buy my own," she said and sagged. "But I could've helped with the bills." "Wow, you're a druggie," Roman said in awe. He thought Robyn was smart and not the type to do drugs. But they all surprise you sometimes.

Robyn's eyes jerked into slits. "Don't ever tell my dad as long as I'm alive. That would break him."

Something heavy scraped and a lock clicked. Robyn was the first to jump up obviously uncomfortable with sharing details. The door opened with ease and she ran out, looking left and right for Will.

"That was quick, you wouldn't even think there was anybody there," Robyn said.

"Look at the sky. It's the only good thing," Leo pointed to the sky above.

"I guess so."

"I could write a poem about this."

"It wouldn't be very good."

They were sat on the wall, cautiously looking down the mountain with the cold between them. Elena was the only thing missing. Robyn scowled. Roman noticed she did that a lot.

"I need to pee," grumbled Leo.

"Gross."

"It's been hours."

"Someone needs to get that key at the bottom of the pool."

Leo eyed her carefully and looked to Roman when she turned away.

"Make Elena," Roman muttered.

"She's not here because you attacked her," Robyn snapped.

"I didn't *attack* her, I just *punched* her."

"That's the same thing."

"Roman, stop. We need to search the garden, we didn't do it properly last time you were too busy arguing," Leo said looking accusingly at Roman.

He rolled his eyes stubbornly but knew they had a point. Roman's eyes swept fleetingly over the garden and something drew his attention. A patch of grass around the tiled floor previously wild and tall was gone. Like a shave. "Did someone put something there?"

Robyn switched her attention to where he was looking at as Roman leaped down to the floor, wobbling alarmingly as his ankle fractured and gasping in pain.

"Did I just break my—?" he cried, sitting and twisting his injured foot experimentally and flinching. A jolt of pain in his ankle shocked him and shocked him even more when tears sprung to his eyes.

"That's not funny, don't make a joke like that," Leo said from above.

"I'll go check whatever's there," Robyn announced, letting herself carefully onto the ground beside Roman. Roman looked desperately at her knelt beside him. "Next time, don't be an ass."

Roman glared through a layer of tears. Robyn walked off frivolously.

Leo groaned and dropped to the floor. "Have you ever broken a bone before?" he asked.

"Well, one time I punched Cahil really hard in the shoulder and I dislocated it for him," he responded, a wobble in his voice.

Boy, he missed Cahil and that stupid pickle store. Leo looked to Robyn without turning his head and they traded a silent look that Roman barely registered. Robyn used her index and rotated it around her ear with a grin.

Leo chuckled. "Try walking," he commanded with firm persistence.

"Are you tryna break my foot even more?" Roman snapped.

"Stand up."

He stood himself and offered him a hand. Roman took it after a moment's pause and with surprising strength, he was off the ground without shifting a muscle. He put a light pressure on his foot and then harder until his whole weight was concentrated on his right. It didn't hurt too bad, so he took small steps like a baby. Roman laughed breathlessly in relief.

"I've had one before and it was because I did the same thing as you," Leo pointed with a bored voice and let go of his hand, making a beeline to Robyn. Roman didn't want to be left behind so he walked over with excruciating slowness in case it broke any further.

When he got there, Robyn and Leo were knelt and looking at something pale in the mud. He was right, a whole patch of grass was missing and what was left was damp soil. His eye focused on the object and the blood in his face drained to his feet. It was a human finger. Two in fact. The second and third, composed like it was reaching for something. They poked out like a sapling growing. Roman thought to Elena and a startling panic wriggled in him.

"It can't be Elena."

"What do we do?" Leo said.

Both their faces were slack with alarm.

"We dig it up, that's what," Roman replied like it was the simplest solution, giving the fingers a watchful prod. Cold as ice like his own. They were too pale to be Elena's, but he didn't know how drastically the skin changed colour after death or how long it took.

"Using what? We're not using our hands," Leo queried.

Roman pointed to Robyn who had both keys. "Keys."

Robyn and Leo set out with grim determination digging at the ground with the two keys. Roman sat by nursing his injured ankle, occasionally grabbing the key from one of them and digging himself. He thought they looked like a bunch of grave robbers and that was exactly that.

Fifteen minutes later, they'd dug around the body and all that was needed to be done was uncover the layer of soil on the top. Robyn looked as if she'd pass out, Leo sat back and looked nervously between Robyn and Roman, Roman was ready to leave.

"It can't be Elena," Robyn repeated, flicking gently at her key encrusted with clots of soil.

"How did he bury them without us realising?" Leo murmured.

"We were locked in that room, he could've done anything," Roman told him.

They sat in a tense silence, each one waiting for someone else to respond. The sky was still bristling with stars and the more you looked, the more you'd see. Leo was right. He could write a poem about this. A souvenir from his past to his future.

"Let's just do it," Leo said brusquely. Leo didn't wait for them to respond; he used his hand despite what he said earlier to scrabble and dig at the remaining mud etched onto the skin of the body. Part of the forehead was uncovered, then the nose and the startling open eyes that were throttled with debris. Leo froze, fingers hovering over the face. That was all that needed to be seen to make the body identifiable.

"No," he whispered hoarsely.

eighteen.

"I'm telling you my daughter would never run off like this. Not without a text or call."

"Sir, sometimes teenagers do this kinda thing. Run off." The detective used a finger to nudge her glasses back up her nose. She gave Matthew a short smile. "We'll keep an eye out for her."

Robyn's dad scowled. It was a family trait. "You're not going to file a missing person's report? A search party? You're just going to *keep an eye out*?" he seethed, a fingernail against the palm of his hand in irritation. It was close to digging in and drawing blood.

The detective's partner who was male turned from looking at the kitchenware and gave her a look. His ginger hair caught the light and became a fuzzy outline.

"As we said." The detective spun round rigidly to face him again, a tight-lipped smile hung on her lips, "to make a report, you'd need to wait twenty-four—"

"I know. But this is out of character for her. Her phone seems to be off and her last tracked location was Carston Ridge in West Grange."

185

"You keep track of her phone?" The detective's eyebrows raised marginally.

"I want to know that she's safe, I'm not restricting her," he told her.

She nodded contemplatively and then turned to her partner. "Wasn't an emergency call placed there?"

The man shrugged but nodded. Matthew's hope flared.

"It was a hoax," she quickly said, a hand in front of her, the splinter of hope gone.

"Can't you consider this as a circumstance where you'd send out someone immediately? She might be at risk."

"We're assessing the risk, sir," she replied, a hint of steel in her voice.

"Not quick enough," he grumbled.

The detectives pretended not to hear.

The atmosphere in Matthew's kitchen was quiet and cold. The light that hung in the centre of the room did hardly anything to expel the gloom at the edges of the room. Matthew clung onto the table behind him, fingernails burrowing in. He'd called the police right after eleven, two hours after the time Robyn was supposed to call. She'd said she was staying over at a friend's, but he knew she was lying so he waited until ten. Then eleven. Two plain clothed detectives had arrived fifteen minutes later. One female who was tall and the male who was short. Their car wasn't even a squad car, just a plain Ford. Matthew did his best to be assertive and he couldn't help feeling proud despite the circumstances. He was never assertive.

"We should be going now," she said, letting her hand holding the notebook drop to her side and glancing quickly to her partner. The man turned away again from inspecting the kitchenware to Matthew. Matthew subtly rolled his eyes.

They walked together through the hallway and he opened the door for them. They stood on the door mat, the fake smile still on their faces. It soured into sympathetic ones.

"Keep calling her. I promise we'll be in touch."

He grunted in reply, looking to the floor in worry. She tilted her head to one side so her long cornrows spilt over her shoulder like a black river. The man looked at his watch impatiently.

"You'll see Robyn again," she said.

"Yeah," he said dryly. His eyes shifted to the man. "You're not much of a talker, are you?"

He surprised him with a long reply. "No, I'm exhausted, and we want to go home. We were both off duty and going for a drink until we got called down here. And honestly, we hope you find her. Thank you for your time. We'll get someone to see Carston Ridge."

"Can't you go now?"

"Not our jurisdiction."

"Then can you ask someone who has jurisdiction?"

"Crack of dawn," he confirmed firmly.

But he knew the crack of dawn in the winter wasn't until commuting hours and by then it would be too late.

Matthew watched them drive off down the road and away. Taking out his phone, he gazed at his phone screen. A picture of himself and Robyn together on their birthdays. Their birthdays were days apart, so they celebrated it in the days between. It was Robyn's fifteenth and she grinned at the camera, hand clutching a knife that was halfway through slicing a cake. He had an arm around her and gazed fondly at the cake he'd made himself.

Giving himself a faint smile and then pressing Robyn's contact and the call button, he put his phone shakily to his ear and waited. Half a minute later, he placed his phone down on the shoe rack dismally, watching the amber of the streetlights through the blur of glass and began softly weeping.

nineteen.

Alivia took one last measured sip of her black coffee and set it down on the table. It was cold. She hated cold coffee. Her husband entered to room, face folded in worry.

"What did they say?" she questioned, wrapping her navy cardigan closer around herself protectively.

In the living room light the glow illuminated his face in a way that emphasised the lines like a palm on his face. The clock beside him read just past midnight. Jason gripped his phone in his hand and crossed over to her, avoiding her eyes.

"They said two other kids Leo's age in Runswick have disappeared too. They might be linked."

Alivia's gentle eyebrows knitted together in alarm. "Did they have something to do with his disappearance?"

"They think they've all disappeared *together.*"

Alivia slumped against the wall with a defeated expression on her face, close to hysterical tears. "But Leo…" she started.

"Has no friends," he finished with grimness.

Alivia removed her ring from her fourth finger and held it out to Jason. The diamond glittered in a quiet manner, just like how their marriage had dimmed in their years. She'd been twisting it round and round her finger all night like she was trying to twist off her anxiety.

"I will never forgive you if he doesn't come back," she said, voice tinged with anger.

He didn't fight back this time and took her ring, slipping it in his pocket with a soft sigh. She swept past and outside to the porch, seating herself on the cold stone. Twiddling her thumb anxiously, she dialled Leo's number again, but it went straight to voice mail. She grabbed at her wispy brown hair and tugged the hair tie out and let it cover her shoulders from the cold.

"Come back inside, you'll freeze out there."

"Not now," she said caustically. She traced the outline of her phone and her frown melted into a nostalgic expression.

A scuffle of footsteps and soon Jason was knelt beside her, taking darting glances between her and the place he sat nervously. "I know this is my fault," he began regretfully, "that our son is not home. But you'll freeze out here. Have another coffee."

"My last coffee was cold."

"Didn't you use the kettle?"

"Yes, but it went cold."

Jason looked away thoughtfully and seemed to weigh up his options. Not like he had any.

"We were arguing when he left. I heard him shut the door," she said with conviction, obviously slamming intrusively into his thoughts. He stared shamefully at a blade of grass.

"Do you remember what we were arguing about?"

"Alivia—"

"Pegs, Jason. The pegs on the bathroom door. You never remember any argument we have because we have so many." She sighed exasperated and tilted her head softly to the

190

heavens like she was searching for an answer. But there was none to see.

"What are you trying to say?" he said after a moment's reflection.

"We can't go on like this. After we find Leo – if we find him, I am leaving with him," she responded. She expected him to flip out in a rage like he did with Leo, but he continued staring at air. "Whether you like it or not," she added.

For the first time since, Jason looked to her. Brown to blue.

"What about me?"

Alivia let out an shocked laugh. "What about you? I'm going to find *him*. And I'm going to bring him home."

twenty.

Quinn heard the unmistakable sound of his wife's voice echo down the hallway and knock in his ears. She was on the phone with someone and she struggled to remain calm. He shuffled his weight onto his other foot as the other began aching from leaning towards the crack of the door for too long.

A vague thank you was muttered, and Jenny held open the door. Quinn just about dodged the swing that came centimetres from his face.

"I was on the phone with Cahil, Roman's friend. Said he was last seen at that party he was at. Also that Will wanted to see him and another girl accompanied him." She groaned softly to herself and covered a hand on her face, attempting to dispel the tiredness out like cobwebs. "They could be anywhere by now."

Quinn found it difficult to over worry about his son's whereabouts and it became increasing so as that was what his new normal had become. Slinking out to parties or to God knows where and not coming home until the next day. It was frustrating as a father. He just about developed all the wrinkles on his forehead in the past year alone and he was only forty-five.

"Why is this time more different than last time? He probably went off with that girl," he offered.

Jenny's green eyes flashed.

"Did you miss the fact I told you that some other kids have disappeared too? They're all from Runswick," she said almost agitated.

Quinn splayed his hands in front of him, attempting to calm her. "Okay, all right." He lowered them. "But the police told us they can't report him missing because it has not been twenty-four hours and neither is he in danger." His face softened when he saw the look on her face. "Hey, hey. He's okay. The other kids they mentioned are probably unrelated to this. I'm telling you: our son is safe."

Jenny let him peck her lightly on the lips but stayed stiff and staring forward glassily. "I don't know. I just feel something really bad has happened," she muttered.

"Your gut is barely ever right. Not just yours, it's everybody's. It's just human anxiety," he explained with false cheerfulness. In his own gut he knew that Jenny was always right with her gut instincts and his smile fell away.

"Yeah."

"Come sit." He took her lightly by the shoulders and steered her to the kitchen table where they sat beside each other.

She didn't say anything when he told her about his day in so much unnecessary detail it was almost pornographic, and she still didn't say anything when he microwaved a glass of milk for her.

"It will soothe your mind, I promise. In twenty-four hours' time, he'll come waltzing in like he thinks we're not expecting him." He mimed running his hand along an

193

imaginary line like he was revealing the plot of a story. "I'll talk some sense into that boy, so we never have to worry ever again," he promised.

"You promise?" she mumbled, meeting his eyes. Her eyes shined with intensity that almost fazed him, but he wouldn't let that deter him.

"Promise," he nodded solemnly, placing a reassuring hand over hers.

All Jenny did was offer the flicker of a smile.

twenty-one.

They all backed away considerably and a collective intake of breath was heard.

Lying in the soil there was the same Vienna who'd confronted Leo and Robyn and the same Vienna who Elena had gone on about who was shot. She really had shot herself. Her body didn't look like it was decomposing but the obvious signs of injury was the two bullet wounds in the sides of her head that gaped like eyes.

Robyn shuddered.

"I've never seen a dead body before," Leo said in a hushed voice, breaking the trance Robyn was in.

Roman's eyes stayed widened. "What is she *doing* here?"

Robyn remembered her talking to Leo and herself at the party. How she knew Will and now she ended up there. Dead. "Everything is linked," Robyn realised.

Roman blanched. "When Elena left the bathroom, it must've been Will who took it."

Robyn and Leo both looked at each other in confusion.

"We were upstairs, and I told Elena to stay with the body, but she left afterwards. Must've been Will."

195

"Did you call her *it*?" Leo said a note of disbelief but not anger.

"Well she isn't alive anymore, is she?" Roman countered.

"Would you call her an it if she were someone you loved?" he hissed, still not angry, but close to it.

He muttered an apology.

"What do we do?" Robyn wondered aloud.

"Maybe if we kiss her, she'll come back to life?" Roman suggested.

Robyn's head just about snapped off when she turned.

"What?" Roman protested. "Technically if you kiss a corpse it isn't cheating because they're no longer a person."

Leo pulled a hopeless face and Robyn looked back to Vienna grimly. A haunted expression crossed her face.

"There's something sticking out." She swept the leftover soil from her and it revealed her hands crossed over her chest with a crumpled note. "It's really wet," she muttered prising it out of her fingers warily and smoothing it out. It didn't even crinkle, it had soaked in the moisture from the soil.

"What does it say?" Leo demanded, shuffling over to peer over Robyn's shoulder as she read. She could smell him, the smell of sandalwood and the fizz of oranges. Weird combination but she didn't mind it. Roman picked the keys up and pocketed both.

"*One down, three to go. Consider this a warning,*" Robyn read in a dull voice. She looked up and her face was a whole mass of conflicting emotions. "I don't get it."

"Give me that," Roman snapped, slipping the sheet out of her hand. He read and then he scanned the garden angrily.

"Do you think he's referring to Elena?" Leo said.

"No, she's not dead," Roman said. But there was something intangible buried in his voice.

"I need to pee," Leo repeated.

"Your timing is incredibly off."

"Excuse you, my timing is excellent."

"I don't get it," Robyn repeated. She had a habit of repeating her own words now. Her voice dialled down a notch and her eyes skimmed the surroundings anxiously. "I think there's two people in on this."

Roman pulled a disgusted face. "Will has no friends."

"Think about it. We were in that room for just minutes and then Elena screamed. Then Vienna with the note. How can someone dig a one metre deep grave in that time?" she hissed indicating at the corpse. "Unless Elena leaving was planned."

"Mark," Leo said, eyes lighting up strangely.

Robyn watched him steal a glance at Roman. "You don't attack a stranger in the public bathroom."

Robyn considered that.

"What do we do with her then?" Leo said.

"I—" Roman started but his words were savagely cut short when three gunshots rang out in quick succession.

Bullets flecked the area around them, and they quickly dived for cover. Robyn shrieked realising there *was* no cover. Her eyes darted around the garden crazily and saw a figure on the wall silhouetted like a cardboard cut-out against the blue and they held a firearm. Maybe a rifle. Something clicked in Robyn's mind as the bullets zipped past her.

"Get back in the house!" she screamed fervently at the other two who had thrown themselves beside Vienna, arms shielding their faces. It was a futile attempt to save oneself. Roman stood first and scrambled into the safe zone of the house with a noticeable limp. Leo struggled up, eyes straining to see the attacker and Robyn silently slipped her hand in his, tugging him along like they were escaping a war zone. They were.

The door unlocked and they turned to run through the house. Somehow in the space of time they were gone, all lights had turned off, their filaments rosy with the last of the dying heat. Robyn thundered up the stairs, the noise hushed by the carpet and Leo at her heels. His hands were clammy and thin between hers and she kept losing her grip. They entered the bathroom she was in earlier and locked the door shut with an old-fashioned silver lock. It didn't fit into place, so Robyn kicked it hard.

The place was also in darkness, with just the light of the moonlight cleansing their souls. It was colder than she remembered, and she thought back to Elena who was out there somewhere. Dead or alive.

Robyn stood taking in lungful of air and came to the realisation Roman wasn't there with them. Leo was bent down and retrieved something yellow from underneath the sink and had frozen into porcelain.

"Another note," his voice quavered, and he held the note out after finishing reading to Robyn who inhaled sharply. Their hearts thrashed in their chests in symphony while Robyn read, the world silent and breathing over their shoulders.

"*If you go, you won't ever come back*," she said in a leaden voice. She took an impatient breath. "Why does Will keep leaving us these notes?"

"I honestly hope Roman is all right wherever he is," Leo said staring out the bathroom window to the skies.

Robyn affirmed.

"I agree with you, by the way," Leo announced, breathing coming out shaking. "I think there's two people in on this."

And then he fell to his knees and toppled, hand cupping his shoulder with a frown where his usual expression would be. She felt the worlds shrink and she scrambled in front of him, a hand on his knee. Then the dizziness hit, and she remembered she hadn't eaten since they were in the van. Eliza had told her it was cool she was iron deficient because it meant it kept her alert of her body's needs. However, she knew it was just another thing that made her more fucked.

He took a breath with the tears scalding his liquor brown eyes and the grip on his shoulder tightening.

"Let me see," she said softly.

His grip relaxed and in his shoulder was wedged a bullet wound that looked just as angry as Elena's had. Crimson red that tainted the green fabric of his sweater and made her breath catch. She checked for an exit and entry and both were there.

"I've never dealt with bullet wounds before. It's Roman who somehow has the experience," she said apologetically.

Leo laughed brightly as if he weren't injured at all and then held out black blocks of glass that Robyn could see her reflection in. Their phones. Her mouth fell open and she quickly singled out her own, feeling the cold glass wordlessly. It turned on and the time read **02:23**. No service. Words had never disappointed her more than those.

She snapped her attention back to Leo who was looking at the ceiling blankly. "How did you get these?"

It seemed an age before he spoke.

"I saw them beside the body," he grinned. "Any service?"

"No," she mumbled and pointed to his shoulder. "We have to do something about that."

"Like?"

Robyn couldn't clean the wound or stop the bleeding with his sweater on. Or his shirt. She didn't even have the cleaning equipment. She snuck a glance at the toilet paper that hung by the toilet and didn't know whether that paper was sterile. But she had to do something.

"Leo. You've got to strip."

199

twenty-two.

Even before the words came out her mouth she cringed, and Leo could tell she regretted even thinking them. He blinked and then grinned. "No need to blush," he said.

"Are you going to do it?" she snapped. She didn't mean to snap but Leo continued smirking at her. Then the grimace returned.

"Can you help? I can barely move my left arm without crying."

Robyn bobbed her head slightly dazed and began shrugging his pine green sweater over his head, careful not to catch on his shoulder. It was like peeling away another layer off him to reveal another equally as complex characteristic. His white shirt was even worse than the green because the red popped out like it wanted to be noticed.

"Yikes," she mumbled and paused at the top button of his shirt.

Leo was looking away from her and avoiding looking at the red. Instead, he stared at him own hand covered in his own blood dumbfounded. He also felt the dire urge to pee. "Is it bad?" he croaked.

Robyn shrugged and with a readying breath, she began unbuttoning. Only halfway so Leo wouldn't freeze and enough to deal with the wound. A compromise. There was a bullet sized hole through the fabric and Robyn struggled to stop looking, he could tell because she kept trembling. He felt detached from reality with the spiking pain in his shoulder and it definitely outweighed being attacked in the toilets and being hit on the head. Shot. With an actual gun.

In his life he'd endured varying degrees of physical pain. Six and he'd fallen off his bike and the children laughed at him. They wouldn't have laughed if he was their friend. Ten and fell one storey which wasn't too bad considering he fell into a pool. Thirteen and was driving in his dad's car, crashing it into a wall. His forehead bled for days. But none quite matched the severity of this, and Leo couldn't help smiling.

"What's funny?" she grunted.

"I think I've gone hysterical."

"The fact that you're older than me is hysterical," she muttered onto the second to last button.

"This is what Elena felt."

Leo looked back and their eyes met for a slow second. Something woke in his mind, but he stayed put and waited for Robyn to do something. She stared back with her coffee stained eyes then she dropped them back to his shoulder. He frowned. Robyn tugged the collar of his shirt down until it reached below the bleeding and she stopped taking a breath, eyes squeezed shut.

"What?" he said amused. "Blood scares you?"

"It's not that," she said with her eyes clammed shut. "It's…"

"It's normal. Especially because it stapled a hole through me. I could be a souvenir keyring."

She finally opened her eyes and smiled reassuringly for a moment. "We stop the bleeding first and then we clean it, okay?"

"Has anyone tried the taps?"

Robyn leaped at the chance to look away and Leo watched as she twisted the faucet. It gurgled and spat out pressure violently, but no water escaped. She looked down at him apologetically. "How about the pool?" she suggested.

Leo thought back to the murky depths of the decade's old chlorine waters and pulled a face. The dark liquid that floated like a shroud also made him shudder.

Something from the outside clicked, paper was slid beneath the door, and slow footsteps receded. Both traded alarmed stares. Leo sat up properly and stood, drawing a deep breath. Robyn tried the door and shook with anger. Then Leo watched her for the next minute as she assaulted the door with her foot and screamed herself hoarse. She staggered to the bathtub and perched herself on the side, tired of her own breathing. Leo sat with her. Only exhausted breathing was exchanged between them. Leo's eyes were getting tired like a contact lens was stuck at the back of his eye. Every time he blinked, there seemed to be something lodged there. He stuck a finger in. There was something in his eyes. His contact lenses. He wasn't meant to wear them for more than a few hours, and his dad had told him he'd go blind if he did. Scepticism had been the next thing. But right then, he took them out. Just in case. It wasn't too much of a difference, he just couldn't see closer objects. He'd take that any day instead of short-sightedness. Sometimes when he felt that tired, he'd yawn, and it'd go away. But it wasn't just tiredness. It was the trauma that was carved into his mind and even if he closed his eyes, it would be in his mind's eye staring back. His old life wasn't even that bad compared to now. At least then he had a strained sort of peace and he wasn't constantly at the controls of death whenever he turned.

Once the silence had become so deep, Leo felt a black hole settle in his chest and in some way, it drove his mind away from his shoulder. He wondered what Priya was doing now.

"Weird how doors can lock from the outside."

"Yeah," Leo said. "Should we look at what he wrote?"

"You can."

Leo inched forward and snapped the piece of paper from the floor.

When a door closes, another one opens.
An eye for an eye,
an arm for an arm,
but this time – Robyn's.

-WILL

"What's that supposed to mean?" Leo gave the paper to Robyn who worked it out immediately.

"He wants me to shoot my arm."

"You what?" he spluttered. "You're not doing that."

"Oh, I know I'm not."

"Then what?"

Robyn sat back on the bathtub and Leo pulled the toilet seat down to sit. They gazed at the same tile on the floor.

"It's been twenty seven years since," Robyn said. Leo waited for her to say more. "I remember reading about this crime and thinking how dreadful it would've been. For their family, especially their son who would grow up orphaned.

"Having no family is the deepest of pains and it scars you. People talk about family every day and everywhere. In schools, they'll bring your parents in to talk. At Christmas, they'll expect family over. And Clyde doesn't have any of that." She took a solitary sniff, eyes fixed and shining on the sink opposite. "Nobody to hug him. Nobody to watch him grow as a person." Robyn turned to Leo and her eyes burnt intensely into his. "Nobody to love him."

Leo chewed slowly on her words and they digested with uneasiness. He wasn't used to Robyn showing so much emotion and frankly it scared him because she was the reluctant leader of this group. The only one who he thought truly knew what she was doing. Decided, firm, unemotional.

"Not necessarily," he whispered.

"What?"

"Not necessarily." He paused and thought about the best possible way to phrase his next words so they avoided reminding Robyn of her mother.

"He would have had friends. Maybe even a partner. You don't need parental love. Sometimes where there should be love, there isn't."

"I know, it's just sad how both his parents are dead. And we don't even know where he is."

"Or Elena and Roman."

She nodded and turned away.

"I thought you were a robot."

She looked at him. "Sorry?"

"I've never seen you look sad."

She laughed. "Every time I do it's just me malfunctioning." She smiled. "Let's fix you."

Leo didn't realise he was shivering, the cold spread like butter over his bare skin. With them both locked in the bathroom, there was only one possible exit and that was through the window. But he was injured and falling several feet wouldn't help. And that would also be considered cheating.

"What are you gonna do?" Leo questioned.

"I'm going to do what Roman did and tie something on it. The pressure should stop it from bleeding," she replied, reverting to her old self.

"I mean about the arm thingy."

"Oh."

"I was thinking."

"I think I break my arm."

"You're not doing that."

Robyn sighed. "Let's fix you first."

"Maybe not?" Leo muttered squeakily but Robyn already had his jumper halfway around his shoulder. He turned away once again and swallowed the forming lump in his throat when she tied a harsh knot. Sometimes he wondered if she hated him.

"Sorry," she mumbled.

"Fine," was all he could say before his breathing came out as severed sobs.

He sensed Robyn recoil and stare at him with horror.

The tears bubbled angrily down his face and he struggled to keep them at bay, wiping at them. Angry for not keeping it together. For some time now the increasing realisation they may never go back home was edging closer and closer in his mind and it finally fell face first into his fears. "Do you think we're gonna die here?" His voice came out chipped and higher than usual and Robyn slowly put a hand on his in the attempt to comfort him. Instead, it made him bawl his eyes out even harder. It usually did when people offered him sympathy. Maybe it was because he felt he didn't deserve it.

She shuffled around on the floor awkwardly and gave his hand several pats, her face half cautious and half worried. "It's becoming increasingly likely," she responded truthfully.

Leo nodded and suppressed his tears with his wrist digging in to stop them from exiting. He thought about himself looking down at them from the corner of the ceiling, a disdainful expression written on his face. The pain subsided and his sobs lapsed into sniffs. Robyn looked almost too relieved, but she quickly buried it under.

"Better?" she whispered.

Leo shrugged and gave her a half smile that didn't quite reach his eyes. He stood and went to the mirror. His eyes. Such a strange brown with soft flecks of black and an endless entrance to a dark tunnel. Red rimmed like a hoop around a ball. "My nose looks big."

"It looks fine."

"Don't lie."

"I think it's gorgeous."

"No, but look," he insisted, tilting his head to a different angle.

Robyn laughed. "So what?"

Yeah. So what? Leo never thought about that. This time he grinned a genuine smile. He buttoned up his shirt and stifled another shudder as he looked down on his blood streaked hand, now drying and browning. It scared him how there was so much blood in a human being. So full of life. The fact that the human body relied so heavily on it. It scared him so much.

"We're going to get this window open."

Leo tore his eyes away from his hands. Robyn stood with a hand on the latch and the other held out ready to take his hand. He walked over to join her and gazed down into the shrubbery below at a dizzying height. The rose bushes so wild and tangled like a dark mass of tentacles uprooted in a shipwreck. Robyn risked a glance at him and gave him a wounded smile.

"How do we open it?" he asked dumbly.

Robyn's eyes scanned the room and settled on the toilet paper holder. It was metal and long and sturdy. She took it, flinging the toilet paper to the floor and used all her power to haul it at the window. A clanging smash and better yet, she'd nudged the handle upwards, so it opened. Leo flinched.

"Did you and James do anything that calmed you down?"

"What makes you assume I was never calm?" shot Leo raising an eyebrow.

"Most people with depression have anxiety."

"Well, that's a generalisation," he muttered.

"Leo. This is life or death. We have to cheat and save ourselves."

"If we cheat, would any of the others die?"

She frowned. "I'd hope not."

He shook his head. "There has to be another way."

Robyn paused. "Are you afraid of heights?"

Leo had never been afraid of heights. He wasn't afraid of falling. He'd fallen so many times in his life he'd always pick himself back up and pretend it was nothing. Like it didn't hurt or break anything in him. But this. This *was* life or death. And he didn't like not feeling in control.

"Yes," he lied hoping she'd say something that didn't address the truth and make him cry again.

"I'll be here," she said softly. Tears sprung.

"What if I break a bone? If I break something important—?"

"Calm down," she instructed soothingly.

Leo looked back from the rose bush and to the sky. Then back down. He couldn't stop looking. "Well, when I had panic attacks we'd sit in James' car and talk," he spoke.

Robyn waited.

"He has a car. It's his parent's but they don't use it." Leo wondered if Robyn even cared. "And when I felt panic come along which was always when I talked to my dad, I'd call him, and he'd always answer. Then he'd drive over in this beat up Corsa." His voice broke and he smiled. "We literally live a few minutes away but car's quicker. And we'd sit at the front and talk. Like some therapy session." He grinned through the blur at Robyn who smiled back.

"What would he tell you?" she asked.

"That I've been in this situation before and I got through it. That it won't be any different this time. And… he said he believed in me," he finished and gulped.

He decided to slip his hand into hers.

"This time isn't any different. You're in a situation that you need to overcome. And you may not have James, but you have me. Robyn Wolff." She grinned to herself like she made the speech of her life.

"Two animals in your name with such a contrast?"

Robyn looked complacent. She looked below to the rose bush once again which spared Leo the embarrassment of seeing him blushing.

"Must we?" he said doubtfully.

Robyn gripped his hand tightly in a bone-crushing way. "Will's blocked off all our exits. Let's break the rules." Her smile shone eerily in the moonlight, her face almost tinted silver and her eyes flickered with elation.

For once, Leo swatted away the doubt, hoping for hope. The window swung sideways, and they stood on the ledge, it was tall enough even for Leo.

"I believe in you," she whispered so close to his ear he might as well have had her voice in his earphones. It tickled and felt like a quiet breeze in winter. And together they plummeted.

twenty-three.

She'd just had a dream. It was very brief and not very interesting but nevertheless: a dream. That was what she thought anyway. Elena woke and the dream still lingered in her mind like old perfume. Couldn't place a finger on what the scent was but it left her thinking. The first feeling that Elena felt was the sensation of her whole body swaying. And then the strange feeling in her thumb like an itch that was right under the skin. Eventually, the swaying stopped, and she thudded to the ground and she didn't bother getting up. It was too comfortable.

The room rocked and Elena felt herself jerk awake. Her thoughts slowly sifted through and she blinked away the darkness. She was at the very edge of a cliff of somewhere. Perhaps. But then she looked to the other side and realised it was where the four of them had looked over the wall from. She was back in the vicinity of the house. Then a pinging pain in both her hand and her scalp that made her want to keel over and cry.

Something behind her shuffled, like something making contact against dirt. It was rhythmic and Elena appreciated it so much she was almost lulled back to sleep. A grunt and the sound became clear – shovel and soil.

Elena turned wildly and the house came into view. It took another beat to see Mark. He didn't seem to realise she was awake as he dug a grave, showering soil over his shoulder with a mechanical jerk.

"Mark," she squeaked, standing and feeling the black flood into her vision. It leaked away slowly, and she blinked.

He stopped shovelling and stared hard at her. There was a menacing silence where not even nature made a noise.

"You're digging a grave," she stated.

"Not hard. You're not exactly tall, it didn't take long."

Elena didn't know whether he was joking or not and an itch of panic crossed her skin. "You cut off my thumb."

He nodded and held her phone in one hand.

Elena's heart stumbled. "Why did you need it?" she said.

Mark didn't answer, just stared. It was getting to the point of an awkward silence.

"Reasons."

"Why are you here?" Elena quizzed and it almost came out like a whine. She hated how pathetic she sounded but it didn't matter in that time. Mark did the unspeakable and held his arm in the air, swung, and her phone catapulted into the far distance, falling to the depths below. She didn't even hear it land. If it did, it would echo across the valleys like a cry. A roar was wrenched from her.

"How dense are you?" he snapped, shaking Elena by the shoulders. His eyes were frantic and calm at the same time. He was a walking contradiction. Her fingers dug into this arm in defence and she could see in her peripheral vision her thumb missing. A violent red that did not needed to be seen and she fought the urge to vomit.

"I'm sorry?" Elena demanded.

"I have to do this, and you won't understand but I have to." His voice scratched painfully in his throat and for a second, she thought he was going to cry.

"Why did you dig me a grave?" she whispered.

"Reasons."

Elena blinked. "And they are?"

"Vienna didn't kill herself," he spoke, and his voice crumbled like dry soil.

"But I saw," she said slowly. She saw with her own eyes Vienna shoot herself.

"No, did you know which side she was shot at?" he spat angrily, and Elena's fear bled through her face for all to see.

Entry and exit? She half remembered Roman telling her this, but she couldn't recall exactly what he'd said. No, because she cut Roman off when he was trying to tell her.

"Entry right, exit left."

"She's left-handed… so why was the entry in her right?" Elena wondered.

Mark just about exploded like the stars did. But he was no pretty star. He was a black hole that could trap and suffocate everything in existence. "There was a window, in that room," he said steadily.

"Wait, you were there? Have you got something to do with why I'm here?" A pang of guilt when she remembered the others. "And my friends?"

"Everything I did was for my parents. They are the ones that carried this legacy," he mumbled more to himself than to anyone. Just like Vienna, his gun remained levelled to her head.

"Do you happen to know Will?" she stammered.

Mark turned his attention back to her, green eyes sharp like hollies. "That's my brother."

"You don't have a brother," Elena argued. Mark had never been like this. Speaking like he'd lost something.

"My brother is Will," he maintained coolly.

Elena pushed Mark away and he fell backwards into the shallow grave. His gun spun back even further, closer to the house.

"I have to do this, and you won't understand but I have to," Elena retorted, and her eyes shed tears that she didn't realise were there. Taking the shovel in her left, she began shovelling dirt over his body. The grave was deep enough, maybe just under two metres. Mark writhed in the dirt that covered his chest and began clawing his way out. Elena was too slow especially with only one hand and Mark was out and had both hands on her shoulders. She hissed in pain and dropped her only means of a weapon.

"Don't use my words against me," he snapped.

"I'll use them all I want," she cried and yelped when her foot lost the ground and she realised they were hanging on the side of the cliff. She did not remember doing that.

"You're going to die," he said, voice devoid of heart.

"What's the legacy?" Elena shrieked trying to thrash around but he held too tightly.

"Robyn was right. She's always right. They never caught the people who did it because those people are my parents. They're smart people."

"Your biological dad or your step?"

"My step, of course. Their legacy was one of many. But they passed it to my brother and I."

"What about?" she hesitated.

He grinned evilly, the branches of barren trees casting claws across his face.

"You're here for a reason. All four of you. I'll explain it all later, but Will chose you. All of you."

"But why bring us here? To your victim's old house? It's a little creepy and unnecessary, don't you think?" she whittled on.

"Will wanted to add to the scenery. It's the only quiet place in Runswick. A place nobody can hear you scream."

"Cliché," she booed.

His eyes were wild and blazed like a thousand fires. It must've been her fuzzy brain, but she swore she found something familiar about them. She'd seen them in someone else.

"You finally figured it, haven't you?" he laughed sarcastically, and it dug painfully inside Elena like a splinter of glass. She didn't know how to admit it or even say it out loud. It would topple and crush her.

"I dare you to say it," he said.

But she didn't and looked away grimly to the mountains, dreading what was to come.

twenty-four.

It was hard running in the darkness. Even harder with an injured foot. He barely remembered any of the rooms, Roman thanked his lack of attention to detail. But he quickly remembered because the lights in the kitchen came on and stopped him from groping around in the fridge thinking it was a door.

Will stood at the doorway, a hand on the flick switch and an unreadable expression on his face and in that moment, Roman forgot everything and remembered he left the oven on.

"Shit," he cursed, letting go of the fridge.

Will revealed something from behind his back and in the gas lighting, the metal of a gun reflected light into his eyes. Will held it casually in his arms aiming between Roman's eyes.

"Do you have a permit for that?" Roman pointed.

"Do you know why you're here?" Will questioned inquiringly, taking a decided step towards him.

Thoughts flashed in Roman's mind and he tried not making it obvious his eyes were darting around the room for an exit. Hard when Will was right there and staring him in the face.

"Robyn thinks she does," he replied cautiously. That was obviously the right answer because Will nodded approvingly.

"And what's the reason?"

"A remake from twenty-seven years ago?" he said.

He took another step forward and Roman followed by taking a step back.

"I want you to know exactly what happened. Starting from your parents."

He didn't take another step further and Roman frowned. "What have my parents got to do with this?"

"Why don't you come sit down at the table?" He beckoned to the table in the middle surrounded by two wooden chairs.

"Yeah, no thanks—"

But Will was so quickly in front of him with the cold metal pressed against his head. Roman remained as calm and as cool as he could be, but he couldn't stop the fear from creeping out of his eyes.

"Sit, please," Will told him. They sat.

"I don't get it. I know you from school and you were the most normal person," Roman said eyes searching his face. In his clenched fist were two keys each with the sharper end protruding out. No match for the rifle in his hands but it was something. He wondered where Robyn and Leo were, he swore he remembered them following him.

Will scoffed. "You think everyone shows what they're really thinking?" Will looked at him with disbelief.

"Well, no."

"Your dad did a good job of covering it up then," he said.

"Covering up what?"

He snorted, fingers fiddling with the safety and flicking it back and forth. It pissed Roman off.

"His affair with my mother," he replied.

"My dad has never had an affair," Roman said slowly.

"How do you think Mark was born?"

"So you reeled him in too?"

"Who says he wasn't there in the beginning?"

He didn't disguise his baffled face. "Tell me the story then," Roman prompted, eyeing the gun and tightening his hold on the keys. Roman made a show of clenching both his fists so it didn't look like he had something in his right. The table was in the way, but he did it just in case.

He knew Will from law society and sometimes from across the classroom Roman would stare at him and ask himself why he was even there. He barely spoke unless he was encouraged to by the teacher. But when he did speak his thoughts, they were loud and violent and silenced the whole room into shock. They rarely spoke to each other themselves but sometimes Will would catch him looking and hold his gaze back.

Will had a yellow sheet of paper and pushed it across the table so it was facing him. Roman didn't take his eyes off him. He knew what he was capable of now they were here.

"What's this?" he grunted.

"Why don't you have a look?" he said.

He lowered his eyes until he saw the piece of paper. It was really yellowing. Starchy at the corners and the writing a faded grey. A family tree of three generations.

"Is this my family or yours?" he said.

"Read," he snapped, and his blue eyes turned to solid ice.

He read.

On the left at the very top were his grandparents. On his mom's side was Jean and Lane Kahn. His dad's side was Mandy and Broxton. Weird names. All four Canadian. It also included their date of births. He did not know his grandma had the same birthday as him. Then his parents Jenny and

Quinn and two connected lines downwards for both himself and his dead sister. He gritted his teeth and moved his eyes to the other side of the page. Impatiently scanning the words of four other grandparents, he froze when a link attached to his dad was attached to another woman.

Theresa Pierce.

And connected to her was a Peter Atwick. Roman's heart stopped when he read the names below.

Then it hit him.

The green eyes almost the exact shade as his.

His hair.

The voice.

The smile – more of a smirk though.

Mark and him were related.

All because his dad had a child with another woman.

He lifted his eyes from the page, mind reeling in confusion. "How come Mark's last name is Doyle?"

"Because that's his stepdad's last name. You can't really take the last name of someone your mother had an affair with," he replied dismissively.

He'd had enough and he stood. His dad had utterly betrayed him. Did his mom even know? Did Sofia? Did anyone apart from them? Was he going to die with this secret? Will looked callously back with a faint trace of a smirk, like he was proud of breaking the unbreakable. "When did my dad do this?" Roman asked. His voice had become low and his chest felt tight.

"Do the maths." Will grinned to himself like he was the one doing the figuring out.

"Never been too good."

He sighed disappointed. "They met in February 2002 and had Mark in November. You know, for such a smart guy with such a big gob like yours, you're really slow at figuring these things out." He smiled and opened fire, but Roman was already on it. He dodged and threw himself under the table and knocking his rifle out of his hands by dragging him under with him. Raising his right hand in the air, he struck Will on the neck. When he removed his hand, there was no dent. Will laughed piteously. His hand shot backwards to retrieve his gun but Roman wouldn't let up and climbed on top of him and began throwing punches. Mark hit his good leg and Roman laughed but he hit the other and he cried out in pain. Will flipped him from under the table and lunged after him.

"You want to do this the hard way?" Will bent his elbow and brought it down on his ribs. Another hit and he felt something move. Pain ricocheted across his body and he struggled to get off, but he managed to. He stood and pressed a hand to his ribs, the keys in his other.

Will stood defiantly his face covered in shadows.

"You won't stop, will you?" Roman said trying hard not to sound out of breath. He knew he was going to die sooner or later but it couldn't be today. He had to make it through. But all of that left him when he threw himself at him, hands around his throat and smacking him against the fridge. He knew it then. Thoughts of his friends, his family, his sister. And then Robyn, Leo and Elena.

"Don't do this. We're family." His voice pushed its way through Will's strong fingers, and he could feel his lungs long for the oxygen they needed. The dizziness came next and he thought his head would explode.

"You're no family of mine."

twenty-five.

Robyn shrieked when she saw her hand. Bruised and a few rose thorns sticking out like spikes. The coat had shielded most of the fall and she'd covered her arm over her face.

Leo grimaced and helped pull them out, the cold night air swirling around them. Darkness from the window above observed them, disappointed they no longer held them hostage.

"You okay?" Leo said raising a concerned eyebrow.

Robyn nodded and convinced him with a strained smile.

The night seemed much clearer out there and Robyn hadn't felt that freedom for so long. Somehow, they felt one step closer to the outside world. To getting home.

"Okay, so we've just gotta find the others. Then what?" Leo asked.

She lifted her shoulders powerlessly. She felt just as unsure as he did. "We just run," she told him.

They began walking along the fence waiting for the bricks to divert course and turn a corner. Until then, they listened to the silence around them – Leo with a defeated slump in his shoulders and pain in Robyn's hand. She had come so close to death: jumping out a window, being hit on the head, drugged. She didn't know if it would end, if all of this would end. The overwhelming regret of lying to her dad. It gnawed the edges of her and soon she'd be consumed by it. She missed Eliza – the only friend she really had. Her bright smile that shone in Robyn's darkness. She paused. She'd never replied to her message from earlier and it made her crumple that much more. Taking out her phone, she glanced at her signal bars, but they weren't there. How could a place have no service? What was the television doing in there?

"I'm hungry."

She hadn't realised with the adrenaline clouding her veins that she was too. And that meant she could faint. What did she have earlier that day? – another gap in her memory.

They stopped walking just before they rounded a corner. A white fence lined their exit and on one of the slabs of wood was a dim trail of blood.

"Elena was here," Robyn pointed and saw Leo pale. "Everything okay?"

Sometimes she never asked how people were. It made her feel a little bad, but then again, nobody really wanted to know why if you said no.

"Fine," he replied absently and inspected the fence and she watched him. His eyes flickered close to her but stopped at her arm. "Are you staring at me?" he said.

Robyn almost faltered and she made a show of looking down at her feet. "No," she lied.

He scoffed and he met her eyes. "Are you scared?"

"What kind of question is that?" she asked almost explosively.

He shrugged. "A question."

"Of course," she nodded to the sky and breathed in the blackness. "Of course I am."

They looked at each other and Leo's eyebrows creased like paper, eyes ignited strangely. "You know the yellow notes we've gotten?"

Robyn bobbed her head which signalled Leo to point to her coat pocket.

"Back at the party, I saw you in the corner of my eye."

Robyn didn't know where he was going with this, but she thrust a hand in her pocket, retrieving the note from the cupboard. Gently unfurling it like a butterfly, she lifted it to Leo who took it and inspected the writing. A pause.

"Do you recognise the writing?"

She wanted to say no but that would be lying. So she lied. "No."

She didn't know why she lied. But how would telling him it looked like her own make Leo think? It was definitely different to hers, but it wasn't dissimilar either. Maybe she was reading too much into it.

He inspected it further and traced the pencilled lines deep in thought.

"Do *you* recognise it?" she shot back.

"No, I don't think so."

"It's gotta be Will's."

"We've gotten a few. One in the van and another in the bathroom earlier. And the others that Will have signed – handwritten too."

"I know," she said slowly.

"I think they're Mark's."

"Mark?" she echoed dubiously.

Leo nodded and gave her the note back. She took it and shoved both hands in her pockets roughly.

"Who else could it be?" And began softly humming to himself, staring at the fence and tapping his foot against it rhythmically. It sounded like a song. After a few moments, he stopped abruptly and looked to Robyn studying her face for a reaction.

"Was that Beyoncé?"

"You got me."

She chuckled and he crossed his arms and started muttering to himself.

"Are you talking to yourself?"

"Leo and I have a lot in common."

Robyn held back a smile. "Such a weirdo."

He diverted his gaze back to the floor and she thought he did so shyly. "What are we waiting for?" he said.

"Death," she shrugged, and his face curdled into apprehension.

"I mean right now. We've not exactly got all the time in the world."

"I guess we could keep walking."

So they did, Robyn's hands in pockets and Leo arms folded against the cold. Felt their footsteps mark the time that passed and with every second was a new hopelessness that drove deeper.

"I feel like crying," Leo said as a new wave of emotion came over him.

Robyn stopped and he didn't notice until seconds later. They stood staring at each other. Again.

"Why?" she finally asked. She knew why. Everything. Nobody could blame him. But she wanted to hear what he said.

"Because I'd give anything to be back at home. My dad can yell at me all he wants, I can be at school sitting with Priya," he said, and his voice fractured. "I just want my life back."

"You'll get it back. Be strong," she reached out and gently knocked his elbow.

He tried smiling. "Why do we have to be strong all the time?"

"Sometimes you just need to be."

"What about those other times?"

Robyn blinked and gave him a look. "Then you're allowed to be vulnerable."

"Guess that's not an option right now," he mumbled.

"No. Not for any of us. Keep walking."

A cry ruptured the air nearby and both heads snapped in the direction. There in the tapered mountain side were two people veering dangerously close to the edge. Robyn realised Elena was the one further near the edge. Her heart picked up speed. They were maybe a hundred metres away and she could see a rectangular trench beside them. Maybe.

They began running, hearts clattering against ribs and the adrenaline at the tips of tongues. There was a small gate further down which Leo kicked open and Robyn followed in his wake. She hoped Mark wouldn't have heard and that it wouldn't be too late. The closer they got, the better Robyn could see there was something beside them – a shovel and something black. And then another figure in the distance, running towards them like two perpendicular lines just about to meet. They all stopped, switching gazes between each other in a kind of relief which came and went.

"You're both alive," Roman said like he hardly believed it.

"Where were you?" Leo asked.

Robyn noticed the slight swell under his eye, and he pulled at the fabric near his neck in discomfort. He himself looked disoriented.

"I just talked to Will."

"Listen, we don't have time. We need to get Elena and go," Robyn told him.

"Okay," he nodded grimly, and they hurried on ahead. They closed the distance quickly and by the time they'd snuck up behind, Elena had seen them, and her eyes slowly widened. Mark froze and turned, and he glared only at Roman who looked at him as if he could finally see him for the first time. What was different about Elena was the shock on her face and blood thick on her fingers. One push would do it all and that unnerved Robyn. Leo picked the gun up from beside the trench, checked the safety like he knew what he was doing and pressed it to Mark's temple. She could detect a flicker of a tremor, but he remained still and decided. A silence so terrible and sticky with expectation.

"Aren't you going to shoot?" Mark's eyes twitched like the tick of a clock and his mouth tugged into a sneer.

"Shut up," he muttered through clenched teeth. "Would you like me to?"

Mark blinked calmly. "You wouldn't."

Robyn's heart sank when Leo's face shadowed with reconsideration.

Elena's face crumpled in dismay. "Leo, please don't shoot."

Leo's eyes slipped from Mark to Elena.

"Don't kill him," she said.

His face became a conflict of emotions Robyn could barely count but what surprised her was he didn't step down.

"Please. I love him," she pleaded with her fingers digging into her arms.

Robyn risked a glance at Roman discreetly and expected him to say something, but his face mirrored hers: pure disbelief, but waiting. Kind of like watching a fight.

"Leo." Elena's voice was barely a whisper. More of a hoarse scratch in her throat. "Don't."

Leo took a small step back so the metal left Mark's head, a fearful look on his face. The gun looked heavy in his hand and it drooped in resignation. And then a powerful sound that collided against the world, rocking the valleys as they did so. Mark cried out and he curled downwards with a hand over his thigh, Elena choking back a scream. Dark blood laced like tributaries through his fingers and everyone could see it took everything he had not to collapse.

Robyn turned in awe to Leo, but he had his gun lowered to the floor, head turned back to the house. A lone figure by the open gate they'd ran through earlier. She couldn't see Will's face, but she knew it was him and he was running. Running towards them. Something told her that bullet wasn't meant for Mark, but for one of them.

Roman seemed to have regained his senses and was frantically pointing in another direction on the brink of hysteria. Stooped trees and an endless darkness that sat snuggly between. The woods.

So they ran, like never before. Elena bolting like a mouse, Leo just a step behind and armed with a small handgun, Robyn following a few steps behind, and Roman bringing up the rear. What a show they would seem to anyone watching.

PART III

twenty-six.

Seconds raced by and they ran with along with it. It was hard though because the trees gathered around closer and closer the further they went and soon they grew tired from having to dodge low branches.

Leo's skin tingled with perspiration despite not having an extra layer of clothing. He looked to Elena as they halfway walked halfway ran and she looked as if she were about to pass out. They had not had the chance to talk – none of them had, they were too busy running. He guessed it had probably been several minutes, if not shorter. And the only kind of reassurance he had was the gun still swinging in his hand.

Roman was the first to stop, bent and hands on knees in exhaustion. He threw a glance back the way they came and collapsed onto the floor with a grunt, a hanging branch snapping beneath him.

"What are you doing?" he asked him.

"Having a lie down." His voice came muffled.

"Fair enough."

Roman sat up with effort and pulled the leg of his jeans up to look at his ankle, turning to Leo. "Is it meant to hurt this much?"

"I didn't do any running with it so I wouldn't know," he replied. "It was a hairline fracture and if you can still run, yours must be too."

Roman nodded and muttered something inaudible. Robyn and Elena had stopped and were staring into the darkness.

"What happened to your foot?" Elena asked with surprise.

"Fell," he responded and smirked.

It was much noisier in the woods than what Leo would have imagined. Strange noises periodically from every angle and not to mention the sky was barely visible from where they were. Woods like a separate room and entity altogether from the rest of the world. He wondered whether Mark and Will would be able to find them in these conditions – if they died there, would the police be able to find them? The darkness around seemed alive and he knew if it was not for the other three, he would've gone insane with fear by himself.

"Everything hurts," Roman complained.

"Let's all sit," Elena said, voice starved of water.

It was a relief sitting. The hum of pain in his shoulder reduced when he lay it on the ground, and he watched the three of them grimace and sigh. He caught a glimpse of Elena's bloody hand and his face drained of colour. On her right hand where her thumb was meant to be was missing. Only four fingers remained and a stump.

"Elena, what happened out there?" said Leo having trouble containing the wobble in his voice.

Elena held her hand up flat like she was showing him a ring and gave him a brave grin. "He wanted it for my phone."

"He didn't think of just asking for the passcode?" Robyn mused.

"I probably wouldn't have given it to him." She frowned thoughtfully. "I still don't know why he needs my phone; he already knew my passcode."

Roman's attention switched to Leo and he pointed at his shoulder. "What happened to *you*?"

"I got shot," he replied with an almost grin.

"Elena and now you." He eyed the gun in Leo's hand. "Is there ammunition left in that?"

Leo fiddled with the gun for a few seconds and it was heavier than he anticipated. His fingers were still sweaty, and it was harder when he didn't know how to handle one. He pulled the frame back expecting it to be stiff, but it pulled back just fine and peered into the chamber. He was surprised to see two small bullets. Golden, small and harmless. But so deadly.

"I think I see them."

They passed the gun around and tried several ways of checking, and they all noted there were twin bullets.

Elena handed it back to Leo, her face slack. "He had a backup in case he missed."

"But he didn't need any, so it's okay," Leo tried.

Seconds trawled by and Roman looked blankly to the sky, sprawled on the floor and hands behind his head like he was on the beach. "Your boyfriend is my half-brother."

"*Ex*-boyfriend," Elena mumbled without missing a beat.

Leo and Robyn's eyes widened to double their size.

"Why didn't you let Leo kill him?" he asked still gazing upwards.

Elena laughed sadly. "Is it weird to say because I still love him?"

"Yeah, and really illogical," he said.

Leo was surprised a fit of rage hadn't overcome him and he remained remarkably nonchalant.

"What?" Robyn said.

"Will showed me a family tree. Our family tree," he said dully. "My dad had an affair with their mom and that's Mark for you."

"Sorry," muttered Elena.

Leo was surprised she wasn't screeching in pain, he knew he would be.

Robyn grinned, trying to be the hope in their darkness. "Leo managed to find our phones." She shot an apologetic look to Elena. "Not yours though."

"No way, where were they?" Roman said finally sitting up and holding his hand out greedily. Robyn gave him his, telling him Leo had found them beside the body and he checked his screen.

"It's the coldest my phone has ever been," he commented through a laugh. "Wow it's late guys, we should hit the hay." He looked up in time to see Elena's dismayed face being masked. "What's wrong?" he said.

The first time Leo had seen him say anything nice to her.

Elena made a face and Leo could see she was struggling not to cry.

"Thank God you guys are alive," she breathed and there was a feverish glow on her face.

Roman snorted gruffly. "He says you're welcome." But he gave her his first smile to her, and she returned it.

"Yeah, we're glad you're okay," Leo interjected and threw a nearby pinecone at Elena's foot. She giggled weakly.

"There's also something you should know," Robyn began.

Elena's face soured and resembled someone about to jump off a cliff.

"We found Vienna's body," she said.

She drooped and nodded in acknowledgement.

"That's where she went."

"So we've figured Mark and Will are in on this together."

"We should cover more distance between us and them. If we're lucky, Mark's too injured to walk without medical attention." Robyn stood with a renewed determination. The rest of them stood and all groaned in pain, especially Roman.

"What did he do to you?" Leo questioned.

"I probably have fractured ribs, lost a canine, fractured an ankle and he tried strangling me."

"Crap," Leo winced. And they started picking their way through the trees like they knew where they were going.

★

Half an hour later and Leo walked beside Elena and they discussed what their lives were like before. Roman and Robyn were just behind them and he could hear them talking about what type of trees they'd seen. Always fun to talk to Robyn.

"You know, if we ever get back home, my life will always be defined as a before and after."

"I get what you mean," Leo said softly.

"My life is a movie."

"It could be."

"You'll be one of the leads."

"I'd hope so since I lived through this."

They saw a dead squirrel and edged away from it.

"You still remember your half of the license plate?" Part of him didn't know why he even bothered. It was a similar thing to having a gun with no bullets in. Useless in their situation unless they found a way home.

Elena grinned and nodded, telling him the second half. Leo's laugh echoed through the woods and zipped back to them. He didn't even know why he laughed so he quickly told her the first half of it just like he was meant to. Like it meant anything in those woods.

"Where did you go after you jumped out the window?"

"I ran out to the front and Mark was in his car."

"Then you were on the edge?"

"No, we talked about shit."

"After?" he pressed.

"He used a knife to cut my thumb and I woke up with a grave next to me."

"What did he say?" Leo asked.

"He told me stuff," she muttered and recollected her thoughts. "A family legacy. Said he was doing this all for his family."

"Oh?"

"Yeah."

And that was that. Leo could feel she was holding something back but didn't want to pry in case she began crying. Sometimes he thought of her as a child; a certain amount of caution was needed around her. But then again, she'd been through a lot and he couldn't exactly blame her. Just her unfortunate circumstances.

"So, what were you like in school?" she asked with a brightly lit smile.

"I wasn't aware we were referring to everything in past tense."

"Sorry, Roman told be me being an optimist annoyed him." She shrugged.

"Well, some people are like that."

"I know," she mumbled. "Tell me."

"Tell you what?"

"What you were like before."

For the first time he realised he'd never talked to Elena by herself, he'd always been around the others. He didn't even know what she was like. The real her.

"You want me to start at the beginning? Like, when I was younger? Day I was born?"

"Sure, wherever you feel comfortable." She gave him a little pat on his arm. He glanced at her bare arms.

"Are you cold?" he raised an eyebrow.

"You get used to it," she replied vaguely. "You?"

"Freezing my ass off," he spluttered and laughed nervously. He clenched his eyes closed and after a moment's pause, he tripped over a root of a tree, arched out of the ground like it had grown uncontrollably and writhed for space. "So when I was in primary I was, like, the role model in school."

"Because you're half Asian?" she offered.

"Surprise," he said.

"Surprise," she said back.

"But I didn't feel like a role model. I was a roll, not a model. You should've seen how tubby I was back then," he laughed at the old memories that made his heart tighten.

The comment earnt a laugh from Elena. "When did you realise you were…?"

"I was what?" he frowned.

"Gay."

"Oh. I was thirteen and I watched Harry Potter for the first time—"

"And let me guess, you had a crush on Daniel Radcliffe?"

He could hear the tinge of a laugh. "And Tom Felton," he added.

They snickered amongst themselves.

"You guys okay?" Robyn called from behind.

They looked at each other and stifled their laughter. Elena was the first to sober up and she shot him another question.

235

"So you're gay, not bi?"

He felt the gun in his hand become heavier, like he could feel its real weight. He could even feel the bullet and the crunch the wet leaves made on the woodland ground.

"Yeah," he finally said, and he could've sworn something in the back of his mind reconsider. "Yeah."

"Okay."

"What are you like then?" he asked, keen to redirect the conversation back to more generic topics.

"You'll probably judge."

"Why would I?"

"I'm part of the well-liked."

"The pegs?" he teased but he looked at Elena in a new light.

"Don't call me that, I promise I'm not a bitch." Her smile dimmed, and she turned away from him and pretended to look for something in the distance.

"Sorry."

"It's fine," she brushed it off. "I'm basically the same as Roman. An ass. But I've changed, Leo. I don't want people like Mark and Vienna controlling me anymore and moulding me into their perfect posse," she said earnestly.

"That's good," he stated. "You know Robyn's a drug dealer?"

Doubt widened her eyes. "No fucking way."

"Hey, guys," Roman said.

They stopped and turned, expecting them to have found a new species of tree. They were on a slope and walked on a muddy pathway that was probably cleared several years ago, with thin trees that traced the edges. It was the most space they were going to get being temporarily out of the woods. Down below were fields. Roman indicated to something further in the distance and drew their attention to something big. It was a house, like a rock in the distance with a spot painted yellow. Someone was home.

"Is that a house?" Elena whispered.

"Already?" Leo said in a hushed voice.

"Yeah, look their lights are on," Robyn exclaimed in a whisper. They didn't know why they were whispering.

"Let's keep walking up and hope we get down there," Roman mumbled.

They began walking again, this time walking side by side. Elena, Leo, Roman and then Robyn. For the first time in a while, clarity hit clear and distinct, even the trees didn't seem as dark anymore and the sky was finally visible. A graveyard of stars plotted against the sky like a line graph. Leo checked the time.

"What's the time?" Roman asked, watching him.

"Three twenty-eight," he answered, and pocketed it in the back pocket of his jeans. It had been an hour since they were in the house. An hour that had slipped by his notice. An hour lost from his life.

"Do we really need that?" Robyn pointed and took the gun from him. She pulled back the top and moved her head about to look inside the chamber.

"Two bullets are quite valuable, don't you think?" Roman replied for him.

"I kinda like holding it too," Leo admitted sheepishly.

She raised a quizzical eyebrow but tossed it back to him over Roman. Leo continued staring at her even when she looked back forward.

"Did they try doing what we did? You know, the couple," Roman wondered.

"All I know is that they died in these woods."

The couple in the photograph came into view in the corner of his mind and he managed to push them back. He

237

remembered what Robyn had said about only two out of four making it out alive and if Robyn were right about the repeat, which she probably was, he wondered which two of them would die. Death grazed his mind and he coiled back, realising he didn't want to die. Not like this.

"How's everyone's injuries?" Leo asked in his normal volume.

Elena stood straighter and nodded, Roman shrugged and Robyn had no injuries to report. She was the lucky one out of the four.

It was almost four in the morning by the time they reached in level with the house. No longer in the woods or near any trees, Leo relaxed. The people who owned the house would help them. They couldn't just leave four kids stranded.

The house was a black slab of paper beside the sky and was perched on a cliffside. Their footsteps were muted against the wet soil and they passed the grassy area and onto plain mud. At first everything was fine as they carried on in silence but then they got nearer. A wave of nausea hit Leo and he stopped, rooted to the ground in shock.

"What's the matter?" Roman turned and frowned at him as did the others.

"That's the house."

Robyn's breath caught awkwardly, and she gawped before they retraced their steps, trainers slapping onto the grass and retreating up the mountain side.

Leo turned just in time to see two figures shifting below in the darkness out of view. "They're there," he hissed, and they all peered down into the darkness.

"He's gonna get what he deserves." Elena shouldered aggressively past Leo, grappling for his gun.

"Wait—" he cried.

Through the trees, the two people reappeared, and they stood with their backs facing them, Mark stooped over his leg. The golden of Will's hair was visible as the moonlight shone on it.

Elena ignored the whispered protests and she levelled the gun to the figures.

"Elena. Listen to me, don't shoot, they're not worth it now." Leo took hold of her good arm and shook, trying to shake some sense into her. But she proceeded to put her finger on the trigger, and she squeezed one eye shut so she looked downward on it, aim still true on Will. Or maybe Mark.

"Elena," Leo warned. "Stop."

"Shut up," she mumbled through gritted teeth.

Leo turned to the others for help. Robyn and Roman were watching the scene unfold, both faces reflecting Leo's. Doubt as much as fear.

"Let her," Roman said defeatedly.

"They're too far away," argued Leo.

"Eat shit," Elena said under her breath.

Leo's heart dropped as Elena squeezed the trigger, staggering backwards in surprise and a bullet zipped through the air towards them.

twenty-seven.

It missed.

Leaving a dent in the ground metres from both. They turned and yelled something inaudible to each other.

That's it, she'd just signed all their death warrants. She trembled in Leo's arms as she said over and over the same word like a mantra.

Sorry, I'm sorry, so sorry.

Robyn and Roman dragged them away from the edge and they took off running. Running until Elena's legs burned, until she kept stumbling, and she thought the heels of her shoes would snap right off.

The first time Roman pointed to the house and offered the only ray of hope left, Elena was stunned. Maybe they weren't going to die out in the open where animals and God knows what else out there with them would be bystanders of their deaths. And when Elena had finally convinced her mind they were going to be okay, they were hit with the realisation that they'd gone a whole circle about the house, displacing no distance whatsoever. She couldn't help but blame Robyn for that, for she was in charge of issuing instructions. It bothered her a little that it was her, like she knew more than them to be leading.

Now they were back to walking and dodging tree branches with low visibility. She'd given Leo's gun back too and they didn't utter a single word. Nobody wanted to use the torches on their phones in case their battery lives dwindled. Elena didn't even have her phone; it was down a cliff thanks to Mark. Another negative imprint he made on her life. She kicked herself for telling Leo not to shoot. But her gut told her Leo wouldn't have shot him anyway, she didn't think he'd hurt a soul. Every time they recovered, they'd cover more distance by running but it was hard with Roman stumbling and Robyn's unstable vision.

"I'm hungry," Elena whined. She didn't mean for it to come out as a whine.

"Really?" Roman said unimpressed.

"From all that running and sweating, I am too," Leo added, switching the gun from his right to his left hand.

"I've been hungry for so long," Robyn muttered and sighed in relief as she fell against a tree.

They halted and breathed in one of their many silences. Roman leaned against a tree of his own and hit his head back against it. Something flickered across his face and he reached into his back pocket for something. He withdrew with a small tube. Mints.

"I have mints."

Robyn perked up and walked over to him, as did Leo. Elena joined too hoping he wouldn't snap and laugh at her. He didn't and began peeling the paper, so the mints spilled out like diamonds over his open palm.

"Is your hand clean?" Leo wrinkled his nose.

"I think I dug up a dead body and opened a few rusty doors but apart from that they should be clean."

"Gross," Robyn mumbled.

Roman snickered and let them take two each. She popped both greedily into her mouth and felt her mind sharpen her senses. It was the kind of feeling that woke up her blood.

"Thanks," Robyn grunted and rest her head in the creak between Leo's good shoulder and head.

Roman grunted and ate three mints himself.

"So what's our plan?" Leo said. He seemed unaffected by what Robyn was doing.

"We keep walking and we might come across an A road and follow the directions back," Roman replied, popping another two mints in his mouth.

"Hey," Leo complained.

He complied and let the others take two each. The pack had twenty so only three mints remained. Elena chewed and eyed them but Roman stuffed them back in his pocket.

"Everyone has one more each, but we'll save them."

Elena looked to her arm where her purple sweater clung, parts of it mottled with a vivid red. It was drying and fading into a deep brown like the one staining the sofa. There was too much of it. At least she no longer wanted to gasp in pain whenever she moved her arm.

"God, I'm exhausted," groaned Robyn.

"We all are," Roman grumbled.

"Every time I turn my head my vision blackens."

"That's not good," Elena exclaimed.

"Were you hit that hard?" Leo sounded concerned.

Robyn made a strangled noise and inched away from him, so she stood unsteadily by herself, eyes unfocused on the floor.

"Come on, we gotta keep moving." Roman began trudging ahead, wading through the thick branches. Everyone followed suit.

Elena couldn't help being afraid of every sound that was made. The warped cries creatures made and sometimes the unsettling silences in between, like an erratic pulse. Occasionally, there'd be a skittering in the trees above and she was always the first one to hear them, shrieking in reply. Usually from birds and sometimes an animal they'd never seen before.

A bird made a hooting noise and they all paused.

"I've never heard an owl before."

"That was a pigeon."

Leo blinked and looked disappointed and they continued. Some of the branches that she avoided were as thick as her wrists and they were everywhere, and them, they were nowhere.

Four nineteen and a new sound had slipped its way into the strangeness of everything. Leo had been the first to hear it, so soft in the distance nobody but him thought twice about. But it got louder so they switched direction. The gushing sound of water leaving its source. A river.

Transcendental clear water that flowed freely and fought each other for room, jostling in the embankments, dodging chunks of stones and other objects that jutted darkly out the water. A new figure of guidance.

"Aren't I amazing?" Leo said.

"You really are," agreed Robyn.

"As the saying in Vietnam goes," began Leo. "One cannot give up on hope until hope has given up on them."

"Really?"

He faltered. "No. I made that up."

"It was pretty good."

"You think so?"

Elena racked her brain to her knowledge from the time she took geography. They were on a field trip and she'd overheard her teacher talking about the only river that darted across the length of Runswick and beyond. River Pel-something. Pelwyn- Pelwicks- Pelworth! River Pelworth. It had to be.

"Anyone know what the river's called?" Roman stood by it, hands on hips and an intense confusion written on his face.

That was her chance and she grabbed it by its hair and yanked it backwards.

"River Pelworth," she cried, a brightness burning in her eyes and trying to hide the excitement in her voice.

They turned and looked at her blankly. Then Roman seemed to think. "I think you're right. It's the only river that crosses Runswick and into Leykeshire, the neighbouring city." Roman seemed to smile through the bitterness his face always held.

She couldn't help grinning to herself and didn't bother burying it.

Leo frowned. "So we just follow it?"

"Until downstream."

"How long will that take?" Roman questioned, dread lingering on the edge of his words.

"Miles, but that won't be a problem because we'll pass civilisation," Robyn smiled to them all. "We're going to make it."

This time, Elena walked alongside Roman and they picked their way across fallen branches, Roman hobbling a little further behind. The trees became further apart so they had the space to breathe, but they weren't out of the woods just yet. Figuratively and literally. Robyn and Leo walked on ahead and laughed every so often. She enjoyed their laughter because it was the only normal thing left that she had.

244

"How's your arm?" Roman nodded to her and motioned for her to stop. "May I?"

"Sure," she winced, and she let him unwrap her sweater and he revealed her bullet wound. It looked even worse than before because it was on the way to recovery. At least it had stopped bleeding. "You think it's infected?" she asked weakly and looked away before she threw up.

"I dunno." He bandaged her arm up again but this time with the other side. "This okay?"

"Yeah," she responded and flung him a half smile. "But I'm freezing."

"You're not the only one."

Her smile stayed frozen on her face. It was silly because half of her wanted him to offer her his hoodie to wear but she knew it would be difficult to fit over the bulk of her sweater.

Like he read her mind, he scoffed and rolled his eyes. "You want my hoodie or something?"

"Jesus, no. You probably stink," she said pretending to be aghast.

"You're the one full of rubbish." He stopped walking and stood to face her. "Remember the first time we met?" His voice seemed urgent, but he was doing a shitty job at covering it up.

"Sure," she said finally. She didn't.

"Remember what you said?"

"Yeah," she nodded slowly. No, she didn't.

"You said 'Mark?', remember?"

Roman was smarter than he looked, he knew she didn't have a clue. Everything at the party before they were kidnapped was a little fuzzy. Something to do with the alcohol and her memory in general. But she remembered that part.

"I remember."

"I look like him, don't I?" He searched her face for an answer.

"I suppose you do."

He chewed on her words, waiting for something but he didn't find it.

"Catch up," Robyn called.

They started up again and Elena had her eyes to the floor, deep in her thoughts. Roman was too because he didn't say anything for the next ten minutes.

The river deviated and they snaked along with it as it widened, and the depth increased. It looked almost angry as it frothed. But it was an angry sort of hope and it was their only one. Until twenty minutes later at five o'clock, the river split into two like the forked tongue of a snake, forming a tributary.

"Shit, now what?" Roman said.

"We don't lose sight of both."

Elena didn't notice at first, but it became easier to walk. Her three-inch heels were making it difficult but the burn in her legs were weakening. They were heading downwards. And then someone popped the question.

"Does anyone need to pee?"

It was Leo. No doubt with all that alcohol you'd need to pee, and they hadn't been able to for ages.

"I do a little," Elena replied quietly.

"I'm fine," Roman said.

"I do too." Robyn.

"So, what, we pee in the river?" Roman gave an outraged bark of laughter. "Like cavemen?" His eyes darted from person to person and his smile fell. "You're serious."

After that, they continued on. The sky was a blue kind of black even though sunrise wouldn't be until seven at the

246

earliest. But dawn would be sooner. They weren't in the woods anymore; they'd passed that when they saw the river and around them were fields. Elena had only counted two aeroplanes that drew smoky lines slowly across and the last one she'd seen was an hour ago. So empty and alone out there in the wilderness.

"I'm sorry I said I wanted you to die."

Elena jumped about a foot in the air and yelped. He stared at her judgementally and laughed.

"I was thinking," she snapped. "But I guess it's fine."

"It's not, it was rude."

"Yeah."

"I thoroughly enjoy our time together."

"You do?"

"Yeah."

"All you did was insult me."

"I've never been a nice person and I tend to have a fixed idea of who people are in my head."

"Don't you think that's a little intolerant?"

"I do. And I'm sorry."

"Okay."

"I've never had a girlfriend before."

Elena did a double take. "That's a little random."

"I dunno, I thought we were opening up, so I thought I'd share something," he protested, and she saw a blush start to stir on his face. She'd never seen him blush.

"Wanna know why?" There was a laugh in his voice. "Because I've never liked anyone."

She really didn't know where he was going. "Where are you going?"

"Well, I'm going home hopefully."

"No, with this."

247

"There's something wrong with me," he responded. His face was resigned, and he avoided her eyes.

"No, there isn't."

"I think I'm gonna die alone."

"Nothing wrong with being alone."

"I'm kinda glad anyway. Nobody can cheat on me."

"I'm sorry about that," she attempted. "Do you think your mum knows? About the affair?"

"No, I don't think so."

"What even happened in there, tell me again," she said gently.

"Okay," he began and offered her a mint. She aimed him a look.

"Story time needs food," he insisted.

So she took one and the relief mint gave came back. Her last one.

"We were in the garden and we just found Vienna. There was a note alongside it, and it was just another one of those creepy ones.

"Suddenly, someone opened fire, Will on the garden wall, so we ran back inside but it was dark. No lights on for some reason. I ran blindly to the kitchen and I turned, and Leo and Robyn weren't there. Will was, though."

"And then?" She held her breath.

"He had the gun with him, told me to sit. He showed me a family tree of our families intertwining," he gulped. "My dad had an affair with their mom."

"Maybe it was all fake?"

"How? I look the spitting image of Mark – it all makes sense," he said dully.

"I'm sorry about that," she repeated.

"Then we were on the floor. I lost the two keys I attacked him with and then he tried strangling me." His voice suddenly sounded like he'd just been strangled and in need of water. "What bought me time was some emotional manipulation that I'm so good at." His smug self came back. "And maybe a kick in the balls."

Elena grinned. "Good on you."

"Right?"

"You've also gotta know Vienna didn't kill herself."

"Oh?"

"Will took a shot from the window."

"She's left-handed?"

"Yep."

"Oh."

"What's he like then?"

"Sorry?"

"Will."

His smile drained. "Honestly? I think he's a psychopath."

"What?" she said ludicrous and didn't look where she was going because her heel sunk slowly into thick mud. She groaned in disgust and heaved it out, brushing it against grass nearby to clean it off.

"Think about it. Unemotional, detached from society and crazy for bringing us out here to slaughter. Like we're a bunch of sheep."

"I guess it makes sense. But when I met him, he was—"

"Unpsychotic?" he raised an eyebrow.

"Th-that's not a word."

"Ha. Well it is now."

"Mark said it's some family legacy. To me, he seems less psychotic," she told him.

"Guess I've not got psycho in my blood."

"I mean, he did give me this." She gave him the thumbs up minus the actual thumb.

"I can't believe you lived through that. How's it not bleeding?"

"It had stopped when I woke… Roman, why are you suddenly being nice to me?"

Roman seemed to pause. Then freeze up. "Come on, I'm not evil."

"Where's the *anger*? I'm not used to this."

"You want me to be angry?"

"No."

"Okay then. I guess I realised I've been in the wrong the whole time."

"You always go round hitting people?"

"When I feel like it."

"You could be Mark."

He groaned. "Don't say that."

"But how would that work? Mark and Will aren't Canadian," she asked.

"Doesn't mean two people can't meet from two different countries and give birth to two fuck ups."

At first, she thought he was referring to her but realised he wasn't.

"Your parents are both Canadian?"

"Yeah. Last name is Sheridan."

"Sounds pretty normal to me," she mumbled. "So if Mark had a stepdad, his real dad must be—"

"My dad," he finished despairingly. "I did tell you that Mark didn't love you."

Elena scowled and tipped her head away from him. "Don't remind me."

"I'm just intuitive like that."

"Sometimes I ask myself where I'd be without you," she said sarcastically.

"Did you get a reply?" He waited for her reaction but all she did was roll her eyes with a chuckle.

"So how did you find your way out?"

"I just kicked down the kitchen window."

"In the state you were in?" Elena ruminated.

"Adrenaline was the only true friend of mine."

"I thought *I* was your only friend?"

They chortled.

"Holy shit, holy shit."

Roman and Elena caught up with Leo and Robyn who stood frozen to the ground and jaws unhinged. They'd come several yards from the end of the slope as it finally straightened to ground level. And the river still beside them ran stronger than anything.

"It's a farm," Robyn could hardly believe it.

"Are you sure that's not a shed?" Roman said unconvinced.

"It's a shed and you see those blobs? Animals!" Leo explained and smiled faintly.

She almost didn't see it because the trees and bushes were so wild to their sides. But just in the distance, the only part of the farm visible was half of a block. A shed. Something. "That was quicker than I thought."

Roman hesitated. "What if it's a trap?"

"Guys," Robyn took hold of Roman and Elena's forearm. "Were we anywhere near a river back at the house?"

"No?"

"Exactly. Come on, let's get walking," she said and dropped their arms, firing a grin at Elena which she couldn't bring herself to return.

She resumed walking beside Roman and behind the others. "If we ever get home, would you tell her?"

He was taken back. "Tell who what?"

251

"About the affair," she said treading around the words softly in case he exploded, but he hadn't done for so long.

He met her gaze with sadness. "Yeah," he responded firmly.

twenty-eight.

The question strayed so far from what they were discussing that it shocked him again when she asked. He didn't know when it would stop shocking him, but it wouldn't be today.

"If we get out of here first," he murmured.

"We will!" she asserted brightly. "Civilisation." She pointed to the farmhouse they were coming closer to. Either their saviour or their curse.

They became level with the ground and Roman thought he heard the sound of a distant siren.

"Civilisation," he confirmed to himself.

The farmhouse sat in the middle of the wet fields, silent and alone. Maybe it kept cows or pigs, but the smell of manure hit him – overwhelming and stark. A few cows were grazing by the edge of the field by a fence, separating them from another field. It reminded them that the real word still existed, and they were so close to it.

They stopped just a few yards from the shed and everyone seemed to be waiting for someone to do something.

So Roman said what anyone in their situation would say. "Shouldn't the cows be sleeping?"

Leo gave him a look and one of the cows looked up from its friend's butt and eyed him blankly.

"What?" Roman shrugged. "Cows need sleep too."

Elena giggled. "That one looks like a Bob."

Leo frowned. "No. Jeff."

"Only three cows and such a massive place. Waste of space if you ask me," Roman stated.

"I didn't ask you," Robyn scowled. "We keep walking until we find someone. A farmer or anyone," Robyn began striding away from them.

"My friend Carter is a farmer," Leo said and walked after Robyn.

"That's cool," Elena replied and did the same.

Roman turned to look at the cows one more time and all three were now looking at him, eyes following as he moved.

"Creepy cows," he shuddered.

Robyn stopped walking and seemed to sway a bit before straightening up again. She turned reluctantly to Roman and held her hand out.

"Can I have a mint?"

"Sure."

Only one more left for Leo. Some part of him didn't want to share but he knew that would be selfish. So he shared. "Leo, you want yours?"

"Later," he grunted and sat awkwardly on the grass. It was waterlogged with the rain, but he didn't seem to care.

"Why did we stop?" Elena asked.

"I felt dizzy," Robyn replied, chewing thoughtfully and looking into the distance. Probably the cows.

Roman was glad they stopped so he could check on his ankle. It looked okay. Okay for a fracture and he didn't know how much longer it would last like that before it broke for real. He missed the sound of the river running but after reaching flatland, they'd gone their separate ways.

"Maybe you have concussion?" Roman suggested.

Robyn's face paled and Leo made a face.

"Or brain damage," Elena added casually.

Robyn paled even further. "I do feel sick." Robyn inhaled sharply. "Look, it's a cycle path."

"Psychopath?"

"No, *cycle path*," Robyn pointed to where she was looking. Beyond the fence and past the neighbouring field was a line of tarmac just visible in their light. He could see the road sign for a cycling lane, he remembered after failing his theory test three times.

"Let's go," Elena exclaimed.

Roman stood hands on his hips with a withered expression on his face. Crossing the fence had been hard. Something dragged itself harshly across his ribs. It had to be broken ribs.

"This is it. Our way home," Robyn said straightening. Something in her voice reassured him to a point he felt he'd collapse against the fence in relief.

"Crap," said Leo halfway through the fence, his shoulder wedged sideways in the gap. "I told you I was tubby." He looked at Elena with a grin. Then Leo gasped and stumbled onto the ground, a leg stuck halfway through the fence. He loosened the sweater around his shoulder and grimaced. "It hurts," he said vacantly pointing to his shoulder.

They all crowded around him and Roman knelt level with his shoulder.

"I have to look."

"Do what you've gotta do," Leo said like he was out of breath. He handed the gun to Elena who placed it beside her warily.

Roman only knew the basics of gunshot wounds – stop the bleeding, clean the wound, and wrap something clean around it. He thought most people already knew that, but judging by the blank faces around him, he was the only one. So he untied the knotted sweater and receded when he saw. It was even worse than Elena's. Hers was a graze and it still had bled horribly. But Leo's was a full-on puncture right through bone and it had begun running with fresh blood.

"I'm gonna have to put pressure on it. It'll hurt," he warned.

"Sure," he said weakly and covered his eyes with the back of his hand.

Roman draped a clean patch of his sweater over the wound and readied himself. "I'm gonna use my knee if that's okay with you."

He groaned.

He took that as a yes, and he pressed his bent knee on his shoulder. Leo was good, he didn't make a sound, but he squeezed Robyn's hand tight. She looked on and flinched at every one of Leo's facial expressions.

Four minutes passed and Roman tied everything up. Leo had gone a considerable ash colour and he removed his hand from his eyes.

"What caused it to bleed again?"

"You fell on your shoulder." Elena nudged him gently and handed him back his gun.

"Maybe I do have concussion," Leo said.

"Let's keep walking." Robyn stood and offered Leo a hand which he took after dusting lumps of mud off his shirt.

The tarmac underneath his trainers was a welcomed sensation. Tarmac that belonged to the public and was trodden on by people, not tarmac of an old murder house. Roman wasn't the type to believe in haunted houses but if he ever went back to the house in daylight, it would just be the same. Other people's memories he was forced to live through. They passed the cycle lane road sign and Roman went to embrace it. All four did and he snapped a picture. Leo saved it as his lock screen and when they all raised an eyebrow he laughed nervously. Roman was notified his lives had filled up on his favourite game and as they walked, he was on his phone. Eighty-two percent was pretty high.

There was a slight breeze that tugged at their clothes and tussled their hair. Leo shivered and Elena sneezed.

"I'm gonna check my wound," Elena said and began untying. "Should I put a leaf on it or something? It's a little gross but it's stopped bleeding."

"Leaves aren't clean," Roman muttered, eyes still on the rows of colours on the screen. He found where the bonus was hidden and a loud applause from his phone filled the air.

"You should preserve your battery life," Elena said.

"I'm on eighty-two percent."

"I get anxiety when it goes below ninety."

Elena shrugged on her sweater and she hugged it to herself. "My calves hurt from these heels."

Roman finished the round he was on and pocketed his phone. "Snap the heels off."

"Hell no, do you know how shoes work?" she sighed impatiently and yanked one off and stretched her leg, then did the same with the other.

Roman decided to walk with Leo.

"How's the pain?"

He grunted in response.

"If it starts bleeding again tell us."

A nod.

"You're awfully quiet."

"Trying to conserve my energy," he muttered.

"Talking just exercises your voice box."

"My what?"

"Your larynx, dumbass."

A pause.

"Never heard of it? Maybe because you never use it."

"What are you on?"

"You don't know? Wow, I should talk to you more often. Expand your vocab."

"Sorry, I'm just thinking."

"Multitasking?"

"Something like that." He stopped. "Roman, I feel like you've done a character arc."

This time it was Roman's turn to be confused. "What?"

"I mean when I first met you, you were a little... above yourself."

"I was not," he protested pulling a face.

"I think Will punched you real good. Woke you up a bit."

"You're delusional."

"Aren't we all?"

"You're my homeboy, Leo."

"That's nice."

Elena stopped walking and gasped. She had her shoes back on. "There's a light on there."

A golden rectangle in the fields. A flicker of a shadow and they stood making a solid black shape in the light.

"Are we sure about this?" asked Leo.

"That's a farm. They'll have a working phone, maybe. And food. Or we can steal their car." Elena's eyes glinted with insanity. Sometimes he underestimated what Elena was capable of.

Robyn hesitated and eyed Leo's gun. Roman noticed.

"We gonna storm in like a SWAT team?"

Robyn laughed. "I was wondering if we go in armed or not."

"So we're storming?"

"I'm thinking." She chewed her lip shrewdly. At last she said, "Two people go. The other two keep watch outside."

"What are we, in school?"

"Got a better idea?" She crossed her arms defiantly.

"I was kinda hoping for SWAT team," he shrugged disappointedly.

"Who wants to volunteer?" Robyn swept a glance over everyone.

"I will," Elena said, squaring her shoulders.

"Okay. One more," Robyn said.

"There's no need. I'll go myself," Elena said automatically.

Robyn faltered. "We don't know who's in there, Elena."

"What, you think I don't know that?" she scoffed.

A shadow of anger skittered across Robyn's face, but she remained calm. Like she always did. "Then by all means, go."

All of a sudden Elena didn't look like she wanted to anymore. "I will," she said stiffly, and they drifted off the path, wading in mud once again. Elena hurried on ahead and when they reached the vicinity of the house she turned back to the rest of the group, hoping they'd reel her back in last minute.

"Who's the oldest here, just wondering," Leo said. He directed it at Elena and Roman as he knew Robyn was in the year below.

"I'm a February," Roman said. Nobody said anything so he grinned. "Cool."

"You'll just wrinkle first," Leo shrugged.

"I moisturise," Roman snapped.

"And I'm taller than you."

"Tree."

"Elena, are you absolutely sure?" Robyn turned to Elena.

Elena nodded confidently and observed the light on in the house. Roman could now see it was a kitchen, but the figure had gone.

"You guys wanna wait by that tree?" she asked.

The three moved off into the gloom of the tree and watched as Elena walked right up to the doorstep.

"Make sure they see the blood on your arm, so they know you're not a threat," Roman hissed.

"Are you dumb? It's all over her sweater."

"But also make sure you don't drip it everywhere. They might refuse to help because you ruined their carpet."

"Shut up!" Robyn whispered.

Elena ignored them and knocked and shot them a silent look of fear. A minute strip of light was flung onto the pathway Elena was stood on and it widened slowly after a pause until it swam warmly over her. Standing there in what Roman assumed were pyjamas was a guy with thick dark hair that covered his forehead and glasses. He was about his height and in his twenties and looked down at Elena's arm with shock. Then his eyes landed on her thumb and he paled. He looked ready to pass out.

"Hello," she said brightly, obscuring the fear in her voice.

"Hello," he said back uncertainly.

"Can... can I come in?" she asked.

"Why?" he said.

"... please?" she tried, maintaining the brightness.

"What happened to you?" He pointed a finger and his face squeezed into a wince.

"Can I borrow your phone?"

"There's no service in here."

"Do you have a truck? You got the keys?"

Roman watched desperately as Elena brushed past him and he protested. Eventually he shut the door and they were in semi-darkness again. A brief pause.

"That went well," Leo said.

"She's gonna die," Roman said.

"It's on her," Robyn grumbled and walked to the other side of the tree, out of view. Roman heard her sit. He walked to her and Leo followed behind. They all seated themselves and Roman felt the pain in his ankle jab him.

"Rob? Can I call you that? It's one less syllable." He flicked soil at her.

"Rob's a guy's name."

"So?"

"Do I look like a guy to you?"

"No, but it suits, don't you think?"

"Not really."

"You're acting really strangely," Leo stared at Roman. "Are you high?"

"She's the drug dealer, not me," he sniffed haughtily.

Robyn took out a pack of Marlboro he only just caught sight of and swung it absently into the darkness. It went surprisingly far for a swing that relaxed.

Roman's jaw fell. "You had that with you the whole time?"

"Yes, I won't need them now."

"What about when we get home?"

"I've decided to quit." She seemed to smile at her own words.

"That's littering," said Leo.

Robyn got up to search for it and came back, giving them to Leo to mind.

"You listened to me," Leo said and grinned.

"Good on you," Roman nodded.

A tense silence.

"What do you guys wanna do with your lives?" Roman said.

"Hopefully something meaningful," Leo replied.

"Like?" he probed.

He shrugged his shoulders high and grimaced. "I'm not smart, you know."

"You?" Robyn exclaimed sceptically.

"You're just downplaying yourself."

"You go to a grammar."

"I do but I really don't belong there," he said. "You should see my grades. I only just made it back into our sixth form, Robyn. Take one stumble back and I'd have failed."

"Wait, you guys go to the same school?"

"Yeah."

"Do any of you know Elena?"

"Nope."

Leo sighed heavily, because of his shoulder or the subject, Roman didn't know.

"I really wanna be a paralegal though," he said wistfully.

"Ambitious," Robyn told him with what looked like admiration in her eyes.

"Exactly, I'll never make it. Sure, I have opinions but I'm too awkward anyway. Instead of defending someone, they'll be the one defending me. I barely ever get angry."

Roman wished that were him.

"But considering law as a course makes you somewhat of a moral person," Robyn said.

"You want a mint?"

Leo glowered. Then nodded, holding his palm out. Roman pressed the last mint in his hand and he ate it.

"You want the wrapper?" he asked expectantly.

"No, my gift to you." He thumped his good shoulder.

"What about you guys?" he said. "What do you wanna do, I bet you're all really smart."

"I don't know what I wanna be," Roman said. "Something that gets me somewhere."

"Well what did you apply to for university?" Robyn asked.

"English."

They both looked surprised. He was surprised that they were.

"Well you can make your own newspaper," she suggested.

"Call it the Times New Roman."

Robyn grinned. "And you want to stay in the UK?" Robyn asked.

"Why did you move here?"

Roman shrugged. "My dad wanted us to move here. I don't mind it here. What about you?"

"What *about* me? Do I like the UK?"

"Jobs."

"Coroner," Robyn replied.

"Dead bodies?" Roman echoed.

"Why?" Leo said.

"You wanna deal with corpses?" Roman held onto his laughter. "I bet you had a hard-on when you saw Vienna." Roman collapsed in laughter, but Leo hushed him, darting a glance at the house. The kitchen light was now off. It worried them.

"What are they doing?" Leo whispered.

"I think it's time to go all SWAT," Roman said.

But a moment later Elena emerged hugging a giant plastic bag to herself. "Guys come on out."

Roman's heart lurched but Leo came into their view and waved awkwardly. Robyn and Roman did the same. The man stretched his mouth into a brief smile and Leo frowned.

"Are you all injured?" His smile stayed stretched a little too tight.

"Special effects. It's for the kids," Leo said and winked.

The man nodded but they knew he didn't believe them.

"You have to walk for another thirty minutes before you get to a service spot."

Roman tried seeing what was inside Elena's bag but he couldn't.

"Half an hour is nothing," Elena waved it away like it really was nothing.

"You want me to walk you guys up?"

"No, we'll be fine," she assured, and she turned to him and they seemed to silently communicate.

"And no, you can't have my keys," he groused and shoved a hand in his pyjama pocket, shutting the door.

Elena shrugged defensively and when she passed them all she grinned, and they followed. Roman nudged the handle of the bag out of the way and he peeked inside, and gasped.

"Did you walk into a store?"

"He offered."

"Oh, wow."

"You were really quick, what happened in there?"

"I told him our car broke down, so we stopped off here."

"He believed you?"

"Duh, I'm convincing. Anyway, I asked where we'd find service and if he had a truck. Also, we're in Ficklebury."

"Ficklebury," Robyn repeated, waiting for a clarification.

"Ficklebury. We're still in Runswick."

"Did he not have any medical equipment?" Roman asked.

"He already gave us all this food."

"But you already asked if he had a truck," Robyn countered.

"He told me he doesn't own a car, let alone a truck. He has to walk thirty minutes to get service down the road, wouldn't wanna be him."

"What would happen in emergencies? Jog a mile?"

"What's his name?"

"He wouldn't tell me."

"Did he say anything else?"

"Uh," She shifted sheepishly. "I asked what's been happening since we've been gone. You know, in the world. They found a new species of stingray."

"Life changing."

"Meh."

In the bag she held were a variety of foods. Fresh, canned and non-perishables. He even saw a raw broccoli still in plastic. That would last them a week.

"Anyone hungry?" she chirped.

"Do you happen to have aspirin in there?" said Robyn.

"Just foods, sorry, he said," Elena replied.

As they walked, they'd each chosen something from the bag and Robyn offered to carry the bag since she was the only one able to. Roman had picked a tub of cookie dough ice cream and he had never regretted his decision more. There was no spoon, so he'd had to use the fork from a meal deal they'd had to rip open. The road they walked changed and became unpaved and there were a lot of potholes. Roman had to keep his eyes down in case he trod in one. It was very scary.

"Ow," mumbled Leo. He stopped and pulled his shoe off, upturning it and shaking. A small stone fell to the floor.

"Guys, we should exchange numbers," Elena said halfway through a granola bar.

"Yeah, so when we get out of here, we're in contact," Leo agreed.

265

They exchanged numbers and Elena remembered her phone number, so they added hers too, Roman already had hers.

"I don't know what I'm gonna do when I get back home," she said sadly.

"What do you mean?"

"My dad's dead."

"Oh. Shit, yeah," Roman said.

"The police will do something," Leo reassured and snapped a bit of chocolate off for her which she took gratefully.

"What about your mother?" Robyn said finishing her dried cranberries.

"She lives in Conwy and we haven't talked for ever," she shrugged.

"Any nearby relatives?" Leo said.

"She's the closest. My grandparents live in Australia and Brazil and other places. My cousins live in Spain."

"I'm sorry," Leo muttered.

Elena nodded, deep in thought. "Come on, let's go home," she said.

twenty-nine.

Robyn's head hadn't stopped pulsing since they left that house, it was constant and relentless and stopped her from thinking clearly. There were random urges to vomit too but it had gotten better after she'd eaten. Or maybe she wanted to think that. Perhaps Roman was right with the concussion.

Roman saw her stumble and he raised an eyebrow. "Are you drunk?"

"No, why would you say that?" She caught up with the others. "My head just really hurts."

"Well, I could kick another body part for you? Make the pain in your head insignificant. Maybe hit your head, it might concuss you, but I think you already are."

"*You're* concussed," she muttered grumpily.

He laughed, throwing his head back.

"How long is thirty minutes?" Robyn said.

"Thirty minutes," Leo replied.

"We left at five thirty-one so... we should be there in five minutes," replied Elena. "Roman, did you eat the ice cream?"

"Yeah."

"I chose that especially for myself," she scowled.

"You didn't tell me."

"So does anyone have a plan?" Robyn said.

"For what?" Leo frowned.

"We reach service, great. Who do we call first, our parents or the police?

"Is it just me, or do their parents not know where they are?" Roman said. "Mine thinks I'm at Cahil's."

"Who's Cahil?" Leo asked.

"My friend."

"My dad's preoccupied," Elena shrugged her shoulders.

"I told my dad I was studying at a friend's." Robyn screwed up her face in thought.

"So? We tell them where we are and then we call the police so they can track our location and get us out," Leo said.

They reached a junction and a sign warning of cattle appeared, half of it covered in watered down mud from cars passing. It probably flooded a lot there.

She checked her phone and watched her phone screen. "Huh, still no service," she said. Then her phone carrier company appeared and one out of four bars of service. Relief flaring, she pressed the phone to her ear and waited for her dad to pick up while the others all celebrated. It rang out and immediately disconnected. Robyn frowned and checked her service bars again.

"Guys, the police aren't picking up," Roman said his phone and speaker. A disconnect sound. "I'm gonna call my mom."

"Absolutely nothing on my end. My texts don't receive either. Radio silence," Leo commented.

"Let's turn our phones on and off again," Elena suggested.

All did so but nothing changed.

"Let's walk further out and read the traffic information and directions as they come," Leo said and they walked, leaving the unpaved road behind them.

The road they walked on then was paved and smooth. It was called Sedley Road and Robyn put it in Maps. Her phone loaded slowly but eventually it did. She used her fingers to zoom in closer and checked for the nearest junction to the motorway. The quickest route to the motorway was about four miles if they kept walking which wasn't going to be a short amount of time. Six o'clock was dawning on them and Robyn realised again how long they'd been without proper sleep. Her head was still annoying her too.

"If we keep heading west, in four miles we'll get to houses and the motorway," said Robyn.

But it's as if they hadn't heard.

"Hello?"

Roman was facing her way and pointed to something down the road. She turned and her breath caught.

A vehicle. A black car with the headlights swamping the area in front and it was decelerating towards them. Without thinking, Robyn put a hand out and it approached, winding down the window on the driver's side. It was too dark to see through the windshield, so they gathered at the driver's window. Leo stumbled back like he'd been shocked, and Elena tensed. A gun flung straight to Robyn's head, but Leo pointed his own at them. Very slowly, Robyn pocketed her phone. Mounting terror pitched inside her and she struggled not to back away. The arm became a person and that person was Will. Beside him in the passenger seat was Mark and he was thumbing the barrel of his gun back. Both armed. But Mark was injured, and he maintained a calm kind of pain.

"How did you find us?" Elena thundered.

"Oh shit," Leo muttered and ran a hand through his hair desperately.

"What?" Roman frowned.

"They tracked our locations."

"Don't blame yourselves, we intended for that to happen."

"You put them there on purpose, so you'd find us?" Roman questioned and she watched as he began being consumed by his old rage. Then he started looking more scared than angry.

"Just like how we let you wander into those woods," Will finished coolly.

"So we didn't win?" Elena said dismayed.

"You can't win when you're only competing against yourselves," Mark snarled. Mark really was physically similar to Roman and she couldn't believe she didn't see it before. Even their voices were similar. She couldn't believe they were being followed the whole time either.

"What do you want? Really." Robyn had finally found her voice and she glared right into Will's eyes.

Will used his thumb to guide the hammer of his gun back.

"You shoot, I shoot," Leo warned, and his voice trembled.

"Answer my question," Robyn said slowly.

"Give me your phone."

She handed it to him and didn't make any sudden movements. It was becoming difficult to maintain eye contact, she really needed to blink. Her head protested.

"Get in the car."

She blinked. "Why?"

But before he could answer, if he was ever going to, Elena screamed like a banshee and dived headfirst through the open window. Mark cried out and Will had dropped his gun as she writhed on top of them. They wrestled in there for a few seconds and something sparked in Robyn's mind. She took the gun Will dropped by the floor and shot at his front tyre, jerking backwards. They made it look cool in the movies, but they forget the recoil still existed. Then the second one and the gun spat uselessly at the third. She tested it. Out of bullets. Her ears rang which didn't help her headache and the sharp smell of gunpowder overpowered her. She sank to the floor and blinked blearily. Someone hauled her up and they ran. She vaguely remembered dropping her gun and saw in her periphery Roman was with them. A white arm was dragging her. Leo. Where was Elena? She turned to her other side groggily and she was there, a purple and red arm hooked around hers. Her legs buckled but they didn't let her fall, they didn't let her go.

She collapsed and didn't get up. Something in her fingernails and she rubbed it experimentally between her thumb and index, eyes closed. Mud. Gross.

The ring in her ears was still there and she wondered when they'd leave. A voice in her head telling her to get up. She heaved herself up awkwardly on all fours, onto one knee, then onto her feet. Her vision swirled with black and three people came into view, backs facing her. They all stood between her and two other people. Will and Mark.

"Which one of you shot at us?"

Leo attempted to conceal his gun behind his back but Mark saw.

"I did," said Robyn. She didn't know why she admitted it, it was Elena. It was like she wasn't the one speaking anymore. Nothing made sense.

Leo turned back with shock printed on his face. Elena looked at her appalled.

"What? You can just take me instead. I'm way cooler," Roman said.

"It's not random, it has to be Robyn."

Mark's leg was positioned awkwardly as he pointed his gun to each person with a lingering pause. A warning not to overstep. Leo threw a punch which he seriously miscalculated and Mark knocked his gun against his shoulder. He screamed. Will stepped around the three and put two hands on Robyn's shoulders while she blinked sleepily.

"You're tall," she commented dreamily.

"And you're short."

She frowned. "Barely."

"You're coming with us."

"Okay."

In that moment it felt right. It was something she was supposed to do. She was in the backseat of a van before she knew it and the pain of a migraine blossomed in her brain like never before. And then something else, like something in her mind being intruded upon. A strange but familiar feeling.

An engine began purring and she felt her consciousness loosen its hold on her mind. She thought she shot the tyres? No, that was another car. At least her seat was heated, and it smelled nice. She wouldn't mind dying like this.

thirty.

"We should have tampered with their van when we had the chance." Leo watched, hand nursing his shoulder as they abandoned Will's black car and sped away in the van they were trapped in hours ago that was parked further down the road.

Roman's clenched fists trembled, and he turned away. Elena held onto her bag full of food with her left hand and wailed silently. All Leo could do was shake his head.

"We had her. We were going home," said Roman.

"I'm calling the police," Elena held her hand out at Roman who lent it to her numbly.

"He's rigged our phones. We can't call out to anyone." Leo's tone was flat and emotionless.

Elena shook her refusing to believe it.

Leo gripped the gun in his hand, and he could see the white of his knuckles. "I could have shot him."

"Mark had a weapon," Roman reminded gently.

"I didn't see an axe anywhere," Elena was pacing hysterically.

"We've gotta get help. Didn't she say four miles until we get to houses? We'll walk it." Roman nodded to himself.

"Yeah, we have food."

"No, four miles is a long time and my shoulder hurts," Leo said.

Roman walked over to him and untied his sweater and his face diminished. Leo didn't want to hurl so his eyes remained steadily staring at a rock nearby.

"Leo, I think you have an infection."

"Shit," he breathed.

"Don't look, I don't think that's a good idea."

"Well do you have any other good ideas?"

"Elena, do you happen to have water in there? Something clean?"

He watched her rifle through the plastic bag, and she grumbled angrily when she couldn't find anything. She dropped it to the ground and started throwing things out.

Roman became impatient. "Did you not see what he put in there?"

"No, I was too busy looking at his glass dog collection."

"Dogs are gross."

She gave an outraged gasp at his comment and took out bottled water and handed it to him.

"Anything like cloth?"

"I saw a paper bag with doughnuts in them."

"Give me that."

Leo moved his eyes and lingered at his shoulder. He cursed. Not only was his shoulder oozing with blood, it percolated with pus. A sound of the lid uncapping and he flinched. He met Roman's eyes and worry flashed across them. Roman held part of the paper bag in his hand and it was drenched in water.

"Hold still."

The pain was excruciating, and it took all of Leo to stop himself from screaming. He really did try but he ended up

274

crying obscenities at every touch. However, Roman did a good job of cleaning it and rebandaged methodically, his eyes never leaving the wound.

"You should join the army," he said.

Scoffing in response, he gave his arm a pat. "I know nothing about infections, but I know it's gonna get worse. So we gotta move."

They went on and Leo's steps were getting heavier with every step and his shoulder blazed with pain. They passed Will's Mercedes, the engine on and idling and Leo spotted something pale in the grass on the kerb and glanced at it before stopping. The yellow of the paper was a dead giveaway. "It's another note," he said and bent down to retrieve it.

"What does it say?" Elena looked over his shoulder.

"Where was it?"

"Right beside that tyre."

"Coffee, milk, bread, butter— this is a shopping list."

"Maybe they'll come back for it?"

"We're assuming these are Will's, right?"

"I'm guessing they're not. I think they're Mark's," Leo said.

"Oh?" Roman said.

"I've noticed the handwriting is different from Will's."

"I'll confirm that," Elena took it, almost snatched the note from Leo's hand and inspected it with a frown.

Seconds limped the way Roman did. Leo thought of his injured ankle and then to the shot Mark took to the leg. He almost laughed. He knew there'd been something strange about the two. Something intriguingly similar. Now he knew.

"This isn't Mark's. Not even close."

"You're sure?" asked Leo.

275

"His handwriting is almost illegible. I've seen it, it looks like they're stood in the wind," Elena nodded firmly. "That handwriting is way neater. A little too neat for anyone insane."

"Well there's nobody out of the two who are sane," Roman said.

Leo pondered and he was the left with the only person it could've possibly been. Dread shivered through his body and he almost swayed backwards.

"They're Robyn's."

"What?" Elena shrieked alarmingly.

"Maybe they're from a random passer-by?" suggested Roman. One look at his face Leo knew the possibility was dawning on him.

"But all those notes… they warned us, they were psychopathic," Elena said.

Something strange exploded behind Roman's eyes. "She found her first note in her cupboard, right?"

"I remember," Leo nodded.

"What did she say? There was another part of that sentence…" he trailed off in thought.

"She said she found it in the morning." Elena frowned and that triggered a memory and it loosened itself free from Leo's mind.

He gasped as he put it together. All of it. "In her leaky cupboard."

The two looked at him waiting for him to elaborate.

"The note she found was in pencil," he started.

"Does she still have it on her?" Roman shoved a hand in his pocket and his hand poked out from the other side.

"What does pencil do guys, you know this. Basic chemistry," he urged on the brink of crying. He didn't know why though.

"It writes?" Roman arched an eyebrow.

"If water touches ink, what does it do?"

"Messes up your work," Elena huffed.

"Exactly. A pencilled note in a cupboard with water makes sure it's still legible."

Roman unfolded his arms and his eyes expanded with shock.

"What, you think she wrote it for herself?" Elena said.

"I don't know why she'd write it for herself, but it makes sense."

"It doesn't," Elena mumbled.

"Let's not blow our brains out just yet, let's get outta here first." Roman waved a hand away at the conversation.

Leo really didn't know anymore, and he peered inside the front of the vehicle through the open window. They'd kept the car keys in, and blood bled through on the side of passenger seat where Mark had sat.

"We should search their car," Leo said.

"What, and drive it all the way back?" Roman's voice rose sharply. A suspenseful pause. "I'm so in."

"Should we see if there are any spare tyres?" Elena suggested.

"Why would anyone abandon a Mercedes?" Roman mused and he traced his finger over a small dent.

A black Mercedes purchased two years ago. Leo reached inside and tugged the keys out of the ignition and the engine automatically died. "What a waste of gas," he said.

They headed to the back of the vehicle and took two minutes figuring out how to open the trunk, but it did eventually. Leo expected to find another dead body stashed away in there, but it was remarkably clean. And no bodies. That, he was thankful for. Elena rooted around in there, lifting things and fiddling with bolts.

"So if we find a spare tyre, what then? Robyn put holes in two of them—"

"There's two!" Elena interrupted him and began heaving one out halfway before shrieking. "Spider," she pointed out awkwardly.

"Ew," Roman complained unimpressed. "Let me help."

Leo helped with the second one one-handed and they dumped them on the ground beside them, drawing in lungsful of air. They were heavy and lactic acid pumped itself around his arm.

"Anyone know how to change a tyre?" Leo asked through breaths.

"I've watched Mark do them."

"I don't think you should, your arm might collapse."

"Okay, Roman do it."

He receded. "I'm all right, I bent down just then, and my tooth started bleeding again."

"Huh, your weirdness is leaking to other parts of your body," Leo said.

"What happened to your tooth?" Elena asked.

Roman tipped his head back and showed her. It wasn't missing, half a chunk had been knocked off, but it was on the inside so when he smiled it looked perfectly fine. Roman even made a show of nudging it with his tongue. Elena stepped back, horrified and pretended to vomit.

"Your teeth are really straight," commented Leo.

"I had braces."

"Me too."

"Me three."

"Okay then, do any of you know how to fix a tyre? Leo?" She turned to him.

"Honestly, I wouldn't have asked if I knew," Leo said indifferently and pointed to his shoulder. He turned to Roman hesitantly and he rolled his eyes.

"Shall we get Elena's best friend?"

"My best friend is dead," she reminded dimly.

"I mean the guy you spoke to before."

"You said so yourself, he's half an hour away and Leo needs medical attention... all of us, I know how to do this," Elena implored tenaciously.

"Do it then. But if you must bleed out, make sure you've fixed all the tyres because at least we can get to a hospital."

"I need equipment, you think I can just switch them just like that?" she snapped. She went and rummaged around the trunk of the car again and then to the front. "Leo. Keys."

He unlocked the car and she leaned over the seats and checked compartments. Surprisingly, a toolbox.

"Okay. Let's go home." She rolled her sleeves up to her elbows and grimaced. "Does anyone here even know how to drive?"

"I do," Roman and Leo both said.

"I just passed," Leo said.

"I failed a few times, but I've had no alcohol out of the three of us, so I'll be driving."

"Great," grumbled Elena.

★

"Six thirty-five. Not bad." Leo pocketed his phone and grinned with joy as Elena returned the toolbox. He knelt by one of the new tyres and gave it a hard poke. "Hard as fuck. I think they're good," he said, barely concealing the thrill in his voice.

The sky was clear and cloudless, the bottoms had begun to tint purple and it was still blooming in its own time across the length of the sky, just like the pain in his shoulder. Stars gave out their light weakly, but they were still there, birds had already began singing animatedly and soon rush hour traffic would be upon them. Dawn. Beautiful, new and sweet.

They stood around the Mercedes with a new kind of hope. One that was promising unlike the others. Because that was their sure way home. They listened to the bird chatter and Leo huffed.

"Who are they trying to impress?"

"Other birds."

"They're a bit desperate."

"Leo, how's your shoulder?" asked Elena straightening up and wiping the sweat that lingered on her forehead. Her bloodied sweater clung to her loosely like it had suddenly enlarged a size. Stretching did that.

"Okay, but I feel really hot."

"That's because you are."

"No, like honestly I think I have a fever."

"Exercise does that to you."

"Right." Leo glanced at the note in his hand. A shopping list. Maybe Robyn's.

Elena followed his line of sight and sighed. "Are we really saying Robyn wrote all those notes?"

"No. Well, not no. But not yes."

"That makes no sense."

Roman walked over to them and held the note out against the sky like he wanted to check for outlines. After a strained silence, he made a thinking noise.

"Does this mean Robyn is working with them?"

"That makes no sense either."

"They did take her, and only her."

"No, this is stupid. I'm not believing this. Robyn isn't on their side. We're all in this together and she was just as confused and scared as all of us," Elena protested. "Why are you all quick to turn against her?"

That made Leo rethink everything. At the party when they both realised they knew Will, investigating in Lorcan's house and talking about their lives in general. No, that shopping list wouldn't be hers, it had to be someone else's. The note had been completely dry when he picked it up, so it could've been dropped any time between when it stopped raining and then. He had no way of knowing.

"I don't know, who else could this be?" Roman shook the note in his hand with frustration. "She was the only one uninjured out of all of us, I think that's conspicuous."

"Maybe Vienna?" Leo shrugged.

"Vienna's handwriting is joined and rounded," Elena shot.

"Have we considered maybe they changed their handwriting?" Leo said.

Roman made a sceptical thinking noise and Elena looked around for fucks to give.

"Maybe we should google this crime that happened twenty-seven years ago. If Robyn's right, then maybe we can predict what they do next," Roman proposed.

Leo took his phone out and was filled with dismay when a notification flashed on his screen. Twenty percent remaining. No, that would be fine. Just enough. He typed into Safari 'crimes in runswick' and hit search, praying it would let him. It did. The top result was the 1993 double homicide and he read the outlines aloud. "… Peters and Strangely both claim the Jacksons were driven away in a vehicle before returning an hour later. They briefly escaped into the woods and was pronounced dead at the scene. Lacerations to the head." Leo looked up and locked his phone. He checked the time and it was six forty. It had been just over half an hour since Robyn had gone.

"I don't get it. So Peters and Strangely both made it out alive and never saw the people who kidnapped them," Elena said.

"It said further up that the police drawings never identified anybody because no one came forward."

"Shit."

"Instead of puzzling over this, I think we should leave. Now," Roman nodded disgruntledly to the Mercedes.

"But what if they return? What if Robyn comes back?" Hope snuck into his voice without him knowing.

"Look what happened to the two. They died."

"So we're gonna let Robyn die?" Elena said indignantly. Then she wilted, tiredness pronounced on her face. "Two people I loved have died in the space of twenty-four hours. I don't want it to increase."

"You love Robyn?" Roman sounded startled.

"Well, we're all best friends."

"We are?"

"I thought so."

"That makes me feel nice inside," said Leo warmly.

"Okay, let's do a vote," Roman said. "All those in favour of driving to get help say aye." He raised his hand.

Elena's hand remained down, and she uttered nothing. Leo was torn. He'd half convinced himself the list wasn't written by Robyn, but his other half nagged at him because maybe it was. Perhaps Robyn wasn't who she seemed. She was the only one who conveniently knew about what happened twenty-seven years ago, she had been the one taking leadership the whole time, the one leading them. He didn't know what to listen to anymore.

"All those in favour say aye," Roman repeated, a hand still raised and looked at him zealously.

"What are we, voting?" Leo said confounded. But he found his own hand raising. In the pit of his stomach he knew he was doing the wrong thing. It was as worse as bitching about her behind her back. But he couldn't back down because Roman nodded resolutely.

Elena turned on him speechless. "Fine," she hissed. "You're both selfish."

Leo gasped like he'd been hit. "We're trying to save ourselves, Elena."

"Forget this whole vote thing, it's stupid. We're not politicians, we're kids. I veto the whole thing, you hear? We are staying until one hour is up. Robyn would do the same for any of us. If you disagree, you can leave but you're not taking the Mercedes." Anger stuck to the edge of her words, her voice was like thunder, with so much hostility and disaster waiting to happen. Leo couldn't help feeling intimidated. Also a bit light headed but that was probably due to his bullet wound. He turned to Roman for his reaction and his face was emotionless. Then he nodded dumbly for a few seconds. He looked like one of those figurines on the car dashboards where they wobble with impact.

"Okay. You're right."

"I am?" Elena raised a questioning eyebrow like she could barely believe what she heard.

"Yeah. We'll wait half an hour. But I'm serious, if nobody shows up, we are leaving."

"Okay," Elena agreed.

"Okay," Leo echoed. "Where do we go then? If nobody shows up."

"Hospital," Elena pointed to the injuries they all shared. Then her face crumpled. "Leo, your whole sweater is soaked."

He looked down and recoiled, retracting his shoulder as far as possible away from him. That was virtually impossible. The green of his sweater was like a raindrop in a sea of red. There wasn't a single green left in it, he might as well have dyed it. If it were possible, he felt even fainter and he was on the tarmac. They both hunkered down beside him.

"You're losing too much blood," said Elena and tried desperately looking through her plastic bag.

"Yeah," he said dazed. Looking at his arm made him even more faint. It was as if his vision was giving up on him.

"We're gonna have to tie something different around it. Even tighter than before," muttered Roman and shrugged off his hoodie. Underneath he was wearing a grey t-shirt that said, 'I'm Waiting for my Letter to Hogwarts' and an owl below.

Leo couldn't help grinning feebly. "God, you're such a nerd."

"I loved Harry Potter," he replied defensively.

"You look a bit like Harry Potter himself." Elena poked him in the rib.

"Ow," he snapped. He replaced his sweater with his and when he tied it, Leo threw up over his left. Luckily, they were both on his right.

"That's a nice red, Roman," he mumbled.

"Thanks."

"I'll wash it for you. Though there's no need, my blood is the same colour."

"Please wash it."

"Only if you don't steal my sweater."

"It's drenched in your blood."

284

"Trophy for my struggles."

He stood and Elena stood with him. Elena dragged Leo up and shoved him in the passenger seat, leaving the door wide open for ventilation.

"I call shotgun," Leo declared weakly. He'd always wanted to say that. Inside, it smelt like new car seats and lemons, and he spotted some mints in the compartment beside the handbrake. Sat down in such a comfortable place, Leo felt his control come back again. But only just. Elena checked the mileage left on it and nodded to herself.

"Half a tank, that's pretty good."

Roman scratched his neck uneasily from the outside. "I need to pee."

"You went a few hours ago," Leo objected.

"That's tough, because none of us need it." Elena crossed her arms.

"Can someone come with me? I don't like the idea of going alone," he said, uncomfortable. His eyes flickered from Leo to Elena. It took a moment for her to register and she grumbled.

"What are you scared of, the boogie man?" she scowled.

"It's dawn, Roman," Leo whined and threw his head back against the head rest. He was so tired.

"I know," he protested in defence. His voice lowered to a note above a whisper. "Did you guys see that sign back there?"

"What sign?"

"The cows."

"Yes," both replied, Elena annoyed and Leo groaning.

"I'm afraid of cows, okay? That's it. They're fucking scary, did you see them watch us earlier. Their eyes, their eyes!" Roman calmed himself down, eyes fluttering shut and stilling. "I don't eat beef because they're scary."

"It's okay, I'm scared of insects," said Leo.

Roman pulled a face. "Right? Why do they need six legs? We do fine with just two. You get me?"

Nobody said a word.

"I get me," he muttered quietly.

"I'll come with you just because you admitted you're not a rock." Elena heaved the plastic bag up and dumped it by Leo's feet and tugged at Roman's sleeve and did a little wave to Leo.

Roman gave him a salute. "Hold tight, okay?"

"Go empty your bladder." And kicked his legs up over. He'd sat in a car by himself many times but not one of those times topped the feeling of this. Pure freedom and adventure. Messing with some of the buttons, he tuned in to the local radio. Roman swayed to the song ineptly and closed his eyes.

Leo struggled not to cry watching him. "Uh, what are you doing?"

"Dancing."

"No."

"Roman, I thought you needed to piss."

Roman rolled his eyes until only the whites were left and they walked off, and Leo watched from the rear-view mirror as they disappeared out of sight behind a tree.

The engine's vibrations began affecting Leo's consciousness and he'd forgotten he hadn't slept since the day before. If he slept, the pain would go away. It would all go away and that thought soothed him. So he let sleep overwhelm him.

thirty-one.

"I hope he doesn't pass out," Roman said as they walked along the side of the road.

Hedges and bushes surrounded them, and the sky was lightening every minute, not yet sunrise, until they reached the sign for cows again. And the unpaved road.

"Me too," replied Elena. And the piece of information she so wanted to desperately blurt out was at the tip of her tongue. She could just spit it out.

"You look like you're about to cry." Roman looked confused and slightly worried. "Don't worry, I'll just be round the corner."

"It's not that," she laughed awkwardly. "I should've told you this before. Told both of you before but…"

"You love me?" he offered.

"No."

"Leo?"

"No."

"Robyn?"

"Shut up," she snapped. And took a deep breath. Too deep she began feeling dizzy. "Remember the scream?"

"Which one?"

"The one you heard."

"Give me more detail. Was it angry? Sad? Scared?"

An itch of annoyance crossed her features. "The one you and Leo heard from the basement."

"Oh, almost forgot."

A gap in her speech as she took to find the courage. "You guys didn't mishear it."

"Why would I mishear it? We aren't deaf."

It came tumbling out then. Like a burden unburdened, a problem halved.

"Robyn attacked me."

Roman blinked.

"I was asking questions about herself and she backed me into the corner and gave me a lecture on being nosy." She recovered a bit and recollected her thoughts. "She punched me. Really hard. So I screamed for help, what else could I do? But then she told me if I went to tell any of you, she'd kill you. All of us. In the moment, I thought she was just touchy on the subject, but in hindsight, I think she might be… she might not exactly be a victim here."

Roman's face contorted in disbelief. And then denial. Then anger. "Why didn't you tell us?"

"She said she'd kill us. I can't do that!" she exclaimed.

Roman dropped his gaze to the floor and shook his head absently, shock waves traversing over his face.

"Okay, I get it… but why did you stick up for her before? When we were voting?"

She stuck the tip of her foot in the ground and shuffled, making a hole. "It's a little stupid, but I thought she'd stick true to her word. So I pretended."

"God."

"I'm sorry."

"God."

"Yeah."

His face scrunched up and she allowed him to his thoughts. She thought he was going to say something but stopped himself. Then opened his mouth to speak. "Look, I gotta pee really bad, it must've been the ice cream. You wait there, okay?"

Elena took a few yards back and waited. He didn't take his eyes off her and she thought that maybe he'd blow up again. Old rage. But none. It was like the old Roman had gone. That rhymed.

"You're not gonna watch me pee, are you?"

"Ew," she cried and turned around in the direction of the car while Roman walked ten yards further down and disappeared behind a tree.

She didn't want to idle so she walked to the fence and ducked underneath it, dodging her arm from the wooden frame. A little walk to stretch her legs after being bent down replacing tyres for so long. For once, she was glad she paid attention while she watched Mark fix cars. It was always his own or a neighbour's. A stroke of pure luck she found two spare tyres and Robyn had only punctured two as well.

The grass rustled the way grass did when you walked on it after it had rained, her heels digging into the mud. Pink dominated the skies above her head and blended with swirls of blue, masking out the stars that had once been there. If she were at home right now, she'd still be asleep in her hoodie and sweats after a night of watching nothing special on her laptop. Her dad slipped into her thoughts again for the hundredth time that day. He had never left, he was always there, watching from the side lines. Why had she never realised he took drugs? Heroine, out of all things. She froze and pieced it together. He'd told her the injections he took were insulin and she'd never questioned it. She forced the unwanted tears back with a thick barricade and carried on walking. Already, she'd gone half a circle, so she completed the full one and went on again. The air was cooling the sweat that slathered her body and she was grateful for once for the cold. She never really liked the cold, always favoured the heat because it relaxed her. But nothing could beat the euphoric feeling of soon going home.

Another small circuit completed around the giant field and she stopped. Why was Roman taking so long? She realised she'd walked a further hundred metres without noticing in the other direction, but she could still see the black Mercedes. Something in her back pocket nudged her, telling her it was still there and forgot she'd pocketed Roman's phone. She checked the time. It was six fifty-two. Way too long to be peeing. So close to seven. And then a click from behind her, so close to her ears she thought her earring had come undone. A hand halfway to check but a voice interrupted.

"I'm gonna have to kill you."

Her breath hitched and tangled in her lungs somewhere, eyes widening in trepidation. She stayed like that for a few seconds before feeling light-headed, so she took in a few breaths of air. A major sense of déjà-vu occurred to her but she turned slowly, her right hand still dangling close to her shoulder.

Their eyes met.

Elena could feel everything drain from her head to her heels. A shaky breath, a lick of the lips. She tried speaking but it didn't come out. Tried again and then realised it was because she was whispering.

"Robyn," she gasped hoarsely.

Gun aimed straight at her head, eyes holding onto hers with ferocity. Standing so close, they could touch. For a few moments, there was nothing between them but the growing sky and the cold air. And the birds which chirped irritatingly. Why did birds do that?

"Robyn," she said again, this time firm. "What are you doing?"

Eyes steely and cold, she saw her own reflection in them.

"Put your hands down by your side. There, that's good."

"Robyn, what are you doing?" she repeated timidly.

Robyn looked down at the gun in her hand and frowned. "My name's not Robyn."

For a mad moment, she thought maybe that was her twin. Her evil twin. Her accent was a tad too thick for anyone in Runswick and she spoke quickly, like she was hurrying past every word. But her clothes. Still the same. Robyn's.

"Robyn's not home."

"She isn't?"

"My name's Renata," she said.

Elena was mystified and looked around. "Then where's Robyn?"

She rocked her head from side to side, looking to the floor and seemed ashamed. "I've taken over. Just for now."

"What do you mean you've taken over?" Elena took a careful step back, making sure she never took her eyes off Robyn. Or Renata.

"I wouldn't move if I were you," she said smoothly.

"Robyn. Renata, whatever you're calling yourself, we need to get back to the car. We're driving home." She stepped to one side so she could make a clean break for it if necessary. Robyn copied and they were soon circling each other, slow and jittery.

"Why are you in such a hurry?" Robyn asked.

"Well, they kidnapped you, didn't they? We need to get out of here."

Robyn looked confused. "Who's we?"

291

Elena thought she was joking and burst out laughing nervously, stopping with the circling and as did Robyn.

"You're kidding, right? Please tell me you're kidding. Leo and Roman? Who else?"

"You must be forgetting that I'm not Robyn. I'm Renata. I've been sent here to kill you because Robyn here tried saving your guts."

"Saving my guts?" she echoed.

"Fundamentally, you were the one to send me to my death." She jabbed the gun into Elena's chest like a poke. "I can't let that happen."

Elena was scared. She was beyond scared. It wasn't just fear, it was confusion. Was Robyn all right in the head? She'd never seen her behave this way. But after they'd left the house, she was acting strangely.

"I think it's wise if you just back down," she snarled. "Or I will kill your friends."

She didn't dare answer back. But then something popped into her head. A voice, her own voice telling her not to back down. Elena half-listened and it began to make sense. Who did Robyn think she was? This was all an act. Mark and Will probably put her up to this. But why? All she knew was it was not her time to die and not her friend's either. They'd done a full circle around each other and Elena saw in the far distance the Mercedes. Then snapped her eyes back to Robyn in case she followed her line of sight. However, it was too late. Everything she did was too late.

Robyn grinned. "You think you can run in those heels?"

"Yeah."

"We can test that out."

She waited. So did Elena. And when she timed it perfectly, she launched herself on top of her, both smashing into the grass, the gun spinning to the floor beside them. Robyn hit her head and complained, and Elena took that as a way in. She slammed her elbow against her face and Robyn cried out in pain, her hand going to her nose. Another hit to the nose and blood began running freely, seeping into her mouth and lacing through her fingers. In agony, Robyn began thrashing underneath her in panic. This was good. Elena snatched the gun from beside Robyn and pointed it close to her head while still straddling her. It wasn't steady in her hand as her thumb wasn't supporting it but made a show of looking scary. Robyn stopped struggling and they gazed at each other in a silence filled with gasps of breathing.

"You're not gonna do it," she remarked.

"Really?" she hissed.

A tremble of defeat in her eyes, so fleeting Elena thought Robyn was back. The real her. But instead, she raised her fist and plummeted it straight into Elena's head. She howled and another punch was inflicted. A tumble and Robyn was standing and Elena was on the floor, the gun back in her hands. Blood that carved itself like a mess over her face, a black eye waking beneath her eye and her jaw set grimly.

This was it.

She closed her eyes and listened to the songs the birds sang, the smell of grass so strong beside her and the feeling of rain between her fingers and bloody thumb. There was nothing in the world but those things and she concentrated on it hard, blocking out any other thoughts. Then she began wondering why it was taking so long and opened her eyes. "Are you stalling?" she asked.

Robyn had her gun lowered and was staring back at her, something sour on her face. She realised quickly she was trying not to cry.

Slowly, she sat up on her elbow. Everything hurt. "Why are you crying?"

"I fucked up," she mumbled, voice thick with tears. She'd never heard Robyn swear before.

"You didn't. All you gotta do now is walk with me. Don't you want to go home?"

"Yes."

"Jesus, don't cry. Nothing makes you cry," said Elena.

"Onions do."

Elena smiled. "Can you help me up?"

She laughed harshly in reply and the gun was back on her. "Ha. Tricked you. Scream and I'll make your death more painful."

So she screamed. She screamed Roman's name and then Leo's and alternated between the two as she scrabbled upwards and clung to Robyn's leg. Surprisingly, she fell and she was ready for it. A finger placed on the trigger at her head, but Elena beat a fit against her wrist and she released the gun, cursing. Elena was out of options, so she hauled Robyn up by the collar and wound her good arm tight around her neck, squeezing as hard as she could. She was right-handed so using her left wasn't as efficient, but she hoped for the best. Just to knock her out, not to kill her. Robyn's fingers clawed desperately at her arm and it was beginning to hurt but she remained there in a chokehold. A word escaped from her mouth, severed and soft but Elena ignored. She screamed their names again. Her arm was tiring and aching, so she pulled herself backwards, putting all her weight against her throat. Robyn wasn't letting up and started to thump a fist onto her arm. Agony with every hit and she bit back a cry. She reached her limit and let go, cradling her arm as Robyn gasped and coughed and looked at her with venom. So awake and so vindictive.

"Your death will be so painful," she grinned, and she recovered and reached for her gun, aiming at her foot.

A shot but Elena dodged just in time. Another at her arm but she rolled. She gripped her shoulders and shook. Hard.

"Robyn. All my life I've been belittled. Controlled. Manipulated. Into doing things for other people, and never for myself. You know how that feels?"

Robyn wasn't listening so Elena caught the gun in her hand and guided it away from herself when she pulled the trigger. It jerked and the shot rang in her ears. The gun was so warm.

"I'm not gonna listen to you. I knew you were evil from the start. But guess what? Roman wanted to leave you for dead while we cruised in a Mercedes, but I said no. Because you took my place, I was meant to be the dead one." She wrestled her back onto the ground when she attempted to sit up, and she seemed to be beginning to listen. "Robyn. I don't know if this is really you but you've gotta come back. Quit playing games. We need to get home."

Her betrayed face said it all when she heard two sets of footsteps marking their way towards them. Elena looked up. Leo and Roman. Leo slowed with every step closer and groaned. Roman stopped and looked at Robyn with astonishment. Then onto Elena.

"I told Leo everything."

"Good."

"Elena, get off her."

She stood and watched Robyn wipe her bloodied nose on her sleeve but didn't get up. A sign of defeat, maybe. Or thinking her way through a solution.

"What happened?" Leo questioned.

"She attacked me." But instead of coming out like a whine, her voice stuck in the air strong and sure. She squared her shoulders.

"Robyn, get up."

"It's Renata," she stood and wobbled alarmingly and straightened. Her brown hair was a mess and wisps of hair stuck to her face with blood. Eyes fell on the note in Leo's hand and she prised it off him. She skimmed it and balled it up, stuffing it into her pocket.

Roman gasped but Leo didn't say anything, just continued staring at her with guard.

"Renata. That's your name, right?" he said slowly.

"Yeah."

"If you wrote that, did you write any others? Maybe, warning Robyn of something?"

Elena didn't know why he spoke in such a way it sounded as if he were speaking to a child. Or a predator.

"I did," Robyn nodded and looked at him with understanding. "I was tryna help her. Help us."

"How did you know?"

"I'm smart, I'm resourceful. Robyn isn't as much as me, so I took over briefly. I can't make a definite appearance, or she'll know and go to a psychiatrist or something." She laughed and it dug painfully into the air.

The birds had quietened down like they were listening.

"You knew this was gonna happen to us?"

"I overheard Will talking on the phone when I was out with him last time. Lucky I heard it, and not Ray."

"Is Ray another one of your personalities?" Leo asked.

Elena raised an eyebrow.

"Yeah, he's ugly and old."

"And how old are you?"

"Seventeen."

"Like Robyn?"

"Yeah."

"I'd like to ask a favour."

"Sure."

296

"Can we have her back? For a few minutes? Just to speak," Leo gave her a leery grin.

Robyn considered. Her face melted into a nothingness. Roman and Elena watched on with anticipation. She rested a hand on her nose and winced and then prodded it and yelped.

"Robyn." Leo embraced her and Robyn looked startled. She looked between Elena and Roman. Leo let go.

"Why do you all look scared?" Her gaze shifted to Roman and half an amused smile appeared. "Your shirt."

"I love Harry Potter, get over it," he grunted.

"Leo, is your shoulder okay?"

"Yeah. Come back to the car, we're going home."

"Oh, that's fun." She broke into a smile then caught sight of the gun by her feet and then looked at Leo.

"Leo, you dropped your gun."

"Oh yeah." He bent to pick it up and held both guns in two hands. She wasn't looking.

They walked back to the car, all three swapping uneasy glances between them that Robyn managed to pick up on. Nobody said a word until they were at the car.

"Can you sit at the back, Robyn? I kinda called shotgun already."

"Sure," she blinked dazed. "I thought I punctured the tyres."

"I fixed them," Elena told her.

She probably would have looked surprised if it weren't for the haze that lingered on her face.

Doors slammed and seatbelts clicked into place. Elena sat on the right and Robyn sat on the left, middle seat empty. For the best.

"Are there any tissues? I'm still bleeding. I briefly remember being hit, but by what, I don't remember."

Roman found some Kleenex and handed one to her which she took gratefully. She smacked it on her nose and grimaced.

"You walked into a tree," Elena said.

Robyn groaned. "Why didn't anyone stop me?"

"You looked pretty determined."

"I'm so tired."

"Does your head still hurt?" Leo asked.

She shook her head and smiled wanly.

"Let's go then," muttered Roman, hands draped on the steering wheel.

Leo adjusted the rear-view mirror for him and the engine kicked into motion.

"Robyn, why don't you go to sleep?" Leo said, smile straining.

"Sure." She shuffled in her seat, bringing her legs up and tucking them beneath her. Her eyes slid shut and she seemed to drift off.

"You asleep?" Elena mumbled. She leaned forward as far as she could against the seatbelt and blew lightly onto her eyelids. They didn't flutter, signifying she'd fallen asleep.

"What happened out there?" Leo inquired wildly, turning his head to her.

Roman snapped his head to her too. "You left me, there could've been cows."

"I went to stretch my legs and she was behind me with that gun and called herself Renata. I think she's actually crazy."

"I think she has DID." Leo looked unsettled back at Robyn.

"DID?" they repeated perplexed.

"Dissociative Identity Disorder. I take psychology, we touched on it once or twice and I did a bit more research on it. She fits the symptoms."

"Insanity?" Elena wondered.

"She called herself Renata. That's a personality. Robyn's the main one but people with DID have memory gaps and have two or more personas in their heads which sometimes swap in."

"What, like, for real?"

"It's really uncommon."

"So Renata is evil? Robyn isn't? You think Renata was the one who attacked me back at the house?"

"Maybe," Leo muttered and looked at his fingers.

"But what triggered Renata to come out and replace Robyn?" Roman asked.

"I'm not sure."

"Do you think we can trust her?" Elena whispered.

The three stared at her for a few seconds and looked away.

"I'm not sure about that either," Leo answered honestly.

"What if Renata comes back?"

"Renata knows Will and Mark came back to kill me because I was the one who shot at them."

"And not Leo and I?"

"Dunno."

"Should we vote on it?" asked Roman.

"No," said Leo firmly. "We can't just kick her out to die."

"I guess not."

"Renata actually wrote all those notes to herself, but how did they get everywhere?"

"Maybe she pocketed them, and they fell out?"

"Or Renata put them there on purpose."

"God, I have never been so confused. Leo, you're sure about this DID thing?"

"Not really," he admitted. "But what else could it be?"

"I'll google it," Elena took out Roman's phone and put it in Google. Scrolled down a website or two and nodded. "It's a real thing."

"What causes it?"

"Childhood trauma."

Leo frowned. "Her mother left two years ago but she hasn't mentioned anything else."

"Maybe only Renata knows?"

"Robyn must know it too."

"Let's ask."

"And wake her up?"

"Give me my phone back."

"Oh, sure."

Roman reached a hand and shook her shoulder. Robyn's eyes flickered open and gazed unseeingly at the headrest in front of her.

Then she blinked. "What?" she said grudgingly.

"We gotta ask you something," Elena replied.

"Wait. I've gotta do something first," Robyn unbuckled her seat belt and tugged open the car door, slipping out into the cold. She shivered and blinked.

Elena really wanted to go home.

Robyn turned back to them with a gleeful grin. "Catch me if you can."

thirty-two.

Shit. Actual shit.

Everyone was out within a split second and all of Roman's hopes of going home washed away when he saw the same van from before. Robyn— or Renata ran towards it and it slowed down. He could see she had the gun she had before was gripped in her right and Leo held his own. Roman stood by the driver's side, shivering his ass off without an extra layer and watched the scene play.

Will got out but Mark didn't. He strode over to them with a rifle. Not a small handgun like Leo's, a rifle that he clasped in his arms. They were going to die. Will's face held only one emotion and that was resentment. Pure resentment that shone like a neutron star in space, collapsing in on itself.

"Mark's dead."

Heart reeling in his chest, anticipating what was to come.

"He bled to death. You all killed him."

"No, you shot him." Elena stood forward, blotches of drying blood all over her lilac sweater, tips of her hair flowing with the breeze. "You were aiming for one of us and you got him in the leg. That's on you."

"You don't know what this has cost me," he raged on.

Robyn stepped to him. "I'm not gonna let you kill me."

"Not now."

"Don't dismiss me. I know your schemes and I know what you're planning. Kill them, not me. Robyn needs me."

"You really believe that?" he snapped, gun aimed true to her head. This time, he would have zero chance of missing.

She faltered. "C'mon Will."

"No, I'm going to end this now. Now without my brother, I'm going to have to do this alone. This time, there will be no survivors." He changed his aim right at Roman and he froze.

"If you shoot, you're a psychopath," he said, his voice crackling at the last word.

"Come on, Will. All this for something your parents passed down. Isn't that such a burden on you?" Leo urged.

"Oh, it's not just that. You may know of a Clyde Jackson? One years old when it all happened?"

Roman didn't know where he was getting at.

"As a team, the four of you – you solved it. You brought me here so we can finish what my parents started. We let you leave so you can lead us to him. And you did just that."

He didn't know what happening, but Leo gasped in shock like he put two and two together. Roman didn't know what.

Will then turned his attention back to him. "We're not blood related but it's close enough."

Just before he could shoot, he yelled at the three to run, and began sprint-limping in a zig-zag motion towards a random direction, too scared to think straight. Bullets behind him fired in quick succession, pinging off the earth around him. He trundled into a gathering of trees he'd hope would stop him from being seen, weaving himself past each one. After two minutes, his heavy footsteps were cut short when he tripped over his own shoelaces, stumbling flat on his stomach against grass. A pain broke out like a rash in his ribs, drawing daggers across his chest and ripping a painful cry from him. Flipping himself on his back slowly and with agonising pain, he lay on his back, leg bent at a strange angle not bothering to right it. He could see the sky through the trees, searing the colour pink deep into his memory and he shut his eyes. His grip on the real world deteriorated and all he could do was listen to Leo's distant screaming and Will's psychopathic laughter following him in.

thirty-three.

There was only one thing she knew right then. Her whole life may have been fuzzy in some places, but this situation was real. It was acting on sheer instinct. And that was to run.

Robyn watched as Roman ran in an unpredictable way, dodging left and right like something blocked his path with every step. She knew it was keeping him alive though because bullets peppered around him but did not touch, just exploded with noise.

"Will, please stop." It was Leo and he began edging tensely to one side, trying to get to him.

"Aren't you all going to run?" he snarled to the rest of them. "Let's do something to make this more fun because you're losing anyway. I count to ten, eyes closed, while you run and hide. How does that sound?" He didn't wait for an answer and aimed the gun next on Leo who screamed as Will charged at him. He shot off into the fields around them and Robyn ran blindly after Roman. She only hoped that Elena had ran too, if they all scattered, there would be more time he dedicated into finding each one and more time for her to hide.

After several minutes of running wildly, she took a swift look back to see how much distance she'd put between them and she gasped, stumbling backwards.

A bullet to her stomach like a whip cracking out the lights. Hand to her belly, she staggered awkwardly until her back hit a tree and she collapsed. Pain sprouted like uncontrollable wildflowers as she looked at her hand and whimpered. So slippery and warm with blood she couldn't help but start to cry. Something in her mind was silent and watching, not intervening.

"I found you."

Robyn raised her head and looked desperately at Will. He was carrying the rifle, but he set it down beside him and knelt in front of her.

All she could do was make a strange gurgle at the back of her throat. She hoped she didn't start drooling blood because she knew she couldn't deal with that.

They stared at each other and Will seemed to smile.

"Y-you shot me."

"Good observation."

"Am I gon' die quick?"

"Ten minutes, give or take."

"…Fuck you."

"Do you know what happens if you're caught in this game?" he taunted.

She could only roll her eyes through the pain.

"They become like you." He stood and looked down at her, taking her gun she had pocketed and his own.

"Pl…" she gritted her teeth and forced her eyes shut, "please gimme the phone." The pain so raw it robbed her of her own voice.

"Losers don't get what they want."

"Please." She opened her eyes and took a deep intake of breath. So cold and numbing against her trachea.

Will looked at her in mock sympathy but to Robyn's delight, he slipped out her phone from his jacket pocket. "Why do you need this? Huh?"

"...dad."

"I'm afraid not."

"I'm dying."

"Can I ask you a few questions first? It'll only take a few minutes."

"A few minutes is all I have," she muttered, annoyed.

He chuckled. "You look like you're in pain. Do you want to text me your replies? Save your energy for later."

Robyn glared impatiently but complied. He handed her phone to her and she sighed in relief, it came out jittery. "I c-can't send messages."

"Don't you worry about that anymore. Just don't try anything stupid or I'll drag this out longer than it must." He typed something on his screen and a text message came through.

Do you know about Renata?
I know of her presence.
Was she the one who discovered my plans?
I think so.
And how did you, Robyn, end up knowing?
I read my search history and it came up.
Why didn't you do anything?
I thought I was wrong.
Never doubt your intuition.
Thanks.
You are so smart.
Thank you.
Too bad you're reduced to this.

You'll end up like this too.

He chuckled. "I hope not."

Why us? Why do you need to kill their son, haven't you done enough? She typed, eyes searching his.

You're all special.

In what way?

Just know that you were an important part of my life. Mark's too. Especially Elena.

Why did Mark need to cut Elena's thumb off?

He needed her phone to export a file from hers to his.

You're a psychopath. Did you ever love Leo? She held her breath which made her lungs feel like they were fit to burst.

You say so yourself. I'm a psychopath. I don't feel love like you do. But I think I did in my own little way for him.

Did you ever think of me in that way?

No.

She exhaled slowly and the tears seeped down her cheeks like the blood on her shirt. Stripes white and red now distorted with crimson.

He watched her with interest, following her eyes and every move. "Would you like me to keep your phone?"

She shook her head and tightened her weak grip on her phone, greasy between her bloodied fingers and cool against her skin. And then a sharp bite at her finger. The screen was smashed in the corner.

"Did someone break your nose?"

Robyn touched her nose and sniffed.

"I disabled your phone's ability to text and call out. Hope you don't mind."

"Sh-shut the fuck up—"

"I'm going to find your friends now, okay? You better hope they're good hiders."

"...no, leave them be."

"It was a pleasure knowing you, Robyn." And he left her to her pain, a parasite growing into every part of her. It made her body creak and cry with every movement as simple as breathing. She used her right hand to apply pressure on her injury and grimaced.

There was nothing around her but nature. All waking for another day whereas Robyn was wilting painfully. She missed her dad. She missed Leo and Elena and Roman. She missed Eliza. Yesterday, she never got the chance to properly say goodbye to her dad. He was mad at her for ditching him for a party. A party that killed her.

Her phone chirped suddenly. A notification to water her plant and feed the fish. Tears fell like evening rain and she did nothing to stop it. Her earring had ripped out of her lobe at some random moment and she didn't know where it was. Didn't know if she'd ever see it again.

Getting her dad's profile up, she scrolled through all their older chats. Her arm was beginning to ache, so she switched hands. It was difficult to type because the blood stopped the phone from recognising her touch, but it worked eventually.

I love you.

It didn't receive.

"I'm so stupid," she whispered to herself and tipped her chin to look directly at the sky. So close to sunrise and she couldn't make it to see the sun just one more time. She barely remembered what happened twenty-four hours ago, but she knew back then she was safe. All she could do now was look at the sky and think ugly thoughts while her

life

drained

away

before

her.

308

And for once, she could do

nothing to stop it.

thirty-four.

He'd solved it. When he first saw him in the light, he considered it. And when Will had told them, he knew it then that it was true. Clyde was very much alive, and he was on his way to warn him. His shoulder pulsed along with his heart and he knew soon he'd have to stop and get medical attention. But he didn't know when that would be, or if ever.

Running a twenty-eight-minute walk in ten minutes was painful. Just when he left, he'd seen Robyn run into the woods and Elena take off after him. They hadn't encountered each other since. He only prayed he didn't die on the way.

The familiar paving stones on the pathway building up to the squat of a house, quiet and secluded from the rest of the world. Leo hammered his knuckles on the door and waited, feet tapping awkwardly. The house was much nicer when it wasn't dark – the cracked grey walls didn't seem so cracked anymore, they were fainter somehow and the wild bushes either side weren't wild, they were speckled with growing strawberries so red in colour they looked like blood.

Something that sounded very much like chain rattled against the wood of the door and Leo took a polite step back.

The man looked back at him, only slightly shorter than him and the door was a few inches open.

"Clyde Jackson?" he said in breathless anticipation.

The man's eyes, blue like the girl in the picture, widened. "Are you here to kill me?" His eyes settled on the gun in his right.

"God, no. Can I come in?"

"You're with the group from earlier. Are you okay?" he asked and disconnected the chain from the door, so it swung halfway open.

"Yeah. Listen, you must get out of there. Someone is coming for you."

"Is this to do with my parents?"

"Yes... how did you—"

"Come in." His eyes fell on his shoulder for the hundredth time and grimaced. "We should call an ambulance too."

Leo was startled. "We don't have time, he's gonna come back and kill you."

"So you'd better come inside quickly."

He didn't know what else to do so stepped inside. Clyde locked the door, sliding the chain into place like it was going to keep Will out.

It was like stepping into an apartment, all laid out openly. There were no doors, just a rectangle of space where they should've been. Leo counted five rooms: the hallway they were in, the kitchen, the bathroom, the living room and his bedroom, all visible from where they stood. Floorboards that hushed the sound of footsteps and he could smell the faint trace of baking and leather.

He followed Clyde past the kitchen he'd seen him in, into the living room. There was a small armchair and another

311

opposite, both maroon in colour, a large circular rug that dominated the floor area, a shelving unit painted black, crowded with glass dogs and a TV placed on top of a rack. Overall, tidy.

"Your friend really liked those dogs," he said nodding to the figurines all neatly spaced along the shelves.

"She's funny like that."

Nobody sat. Leo took initiative and hovered beside one of the armchairs and gestured to it. "Can I sit?"

"Oh, sorry, of course. Sit."

Clyde sat and Leo followed and immediately launched into filling Clyde in about everything. The house, the four of them, a repeat of history. Clyde didn't say anything, just nodded in the appropriate places with an anxious expression sat on his face.

He was digesting the information and then nodded slowly once he'd listened at length. "I knew this was gonna happen."

"You did?" Leo blinked away the surprise on his face.

"Did you see the surveillance room? In the house."

"My friends did."

"My parents set them up because they knew they were gonna die, didn't feel safe. I dismantled the cameras a few years ago because I visit the place sometimes and they bothered me."

"Your parents knew they were gonna die? Why didn't they do anything to stop it?"

"Do you know why they killed them?" He leaned forward.

"Because they're psychopaths?"

"Well, not quite. They wanted the financial gain. Quite frankly, the house."

Leo blinked. Clyde sighed heavily to himself like he was exhausted and retreated back with his head resting against the chair.

"They killed them thinking they were going after their will, but instead, that got handed to me. Their son."

"I don't get how the police haven't arrested them."

"Not enough evidence, something like that," he muttered.

Leo scowled. "That's bull."

Clyde laughed. "It's what happens when you're white and powerful."

"Well they had access to your keys."

"Of course they did. They probably made a copy."

"If you visit the house, why don't you redecorate? It's stuck in the nineties."

"I don't visit often in case the people after me are there. I stayed there once with my friend and we left because we heard somebody outside."

Leo thought back to the clothes in the drawer. That must've been his friend's. And then a thought to what Robyn did to Elena. What Renata did.

"I'm guessing you guys are in danger then. Why didn't you just tell me before? How did you even recognise me?"

"You look like your mother, and well, we thought you might kill us."

His eyes widened in amazement. "Okay." His words were slow. Everything he said was slow and thought out.

Leo wriggled in the chair. It had started to become really uncomfortable sitting still and adrenaline still was very much prevalent in his blood. "We have to get out. They're coming for you to finish what they started."

"I'll be okay." He got up and Leo got up too robotically. "I'll take my car."

"I thought you didn't have one?" he said with a whisper of suspicion.

"I wasn't gonna lend my car to a couple of strangers. How old are you anyway?"

"Seventeen."

"And you can drive?"

"I passed, yeah."

Clyde nodded mildly impressed as he dug his keys out. "Took me three times to pass."

"Ha."

He looked at him thoughtfully and jangled his keys like he was shaking thoughts out of them. "Will and Mark are their sons?"

"You can say that."

"And they're here because they wanna do what their parents did, essentially kill me."

"Yeah. Mark's dead though so it's just Will."

"Oh dear."

"Will's got a shit load of guns so you're gonna have to be careful."

"I've been careful all my life." He stilled and the jangling halted. "I'm gonna drive us there to save time. I'll call the police and you find everyone."

Leo nodded, determination replacing the worry in his veins.

★

He swore he saw Roman run into these parts of the trees. They gathered with enough space in between so Leo didn't feel claustrophobic. It took them seven minutes speeding down the unpaved road without bends which wasn't too bad considering.

The sky was alight with grand shades of purple and pink now, not a star in sight, but the crescent moon still hung just below midway in the sky and offered him a beacon of hope.

He stumbled past a tree that jutted out at an odd angle, almost tripping and froze. A small coughing noise that came from an unseen direction. It scared him despite it being morning. Turning a full circle around him, straining his eyes through the trees until he could move on. Maybe he'd imagined it. And there several yards beside a tree was Robyn. Not stood stoically like she always did, but slumped against the tree, half sprawled and staring upwards.

His heart clenched and he called out her name. She didn't look which worried him even more, so he began running towards her. When he got close enough, he saw her hand was pressed to her stomach and red blemished her shirt. Her eyes searched the sky above, a layer of glassy tears over them like film and her parting in her hair had gone haywire.

"Jesus, Robyn." He knelt beside her and lightly touched her shoulder.

She flinched like she didn't see him there and she broke into a new wave of tears. "Leo." Her voice barely a whisper that pierced the air.

Leo couldn't stop looking at the red on her hands and it gave him memories of them in the bathroom hours ago.

"Listen, I only have a few minutes." She took his hand in her own, the one she used to put pressure on her wound and Leo tried not to shudder.

"They can't save me." She spluttered and covered her mouth with her sleeve.

"Robyn, don't talk, it's gonna hurt too much. Did Will do this?" Leo squeezed her hand and it slipped under his grip with the friction of blood. "I went to see Clyde."

She blinked in surprise. "He's alive?"

315

"He was the guy in the house. He's gonna call an ambulance and they'll get you better." Leo became aware he was crying. "You're gonna be okay."

"Leo. I'm not. I'm bleeding. So bad," she said feebly. "Leo, I've gotta tell you a few things, okay?"

Listening to her broken and laboured words made him break beneath her touch but he nodded his head like it was the only thing he could do.

"Will told me things. I know I have Ren-Renata in my head... I've always known.

"Listen, tell Elena her phone was used to export a file... okay? Tell her she's s-so strong and I'm so sorry." She broke down in tears.

"I will."

"An-and Will liked you. In a way."

The pain of the situation didn't make a difference and his eyes widened but he let her continue.

"Leo?"

"Yeah, it's me," he whispered.

"I think you're cool," she replied and blinked hard, letting the tears bleed from her hazel eyes. "You're interesting. You're brilliant and smart. You're different from the rest of 'em. I don't regret any time I've spent with you."

"Me too," he said. The information barely registered in his head but he left it for after so he could dwell on it.

"You're the only person I've felt that way with," she sobbed, and she wiped her free hand across her eyes, smearing the blood with her salty tears. "Don't worry that you don't feel the same. I'm dying anyway." She choked up a laugh.

Leo didn't know what to say. Maybe the pain was making her loopy and she didn't really mean it.

Robyn's eyes strayed from his eyes to the gun he still held and gripped onto Leo's hand with both of hers. Leo shook his head firmly and she moaned in pain.

"No, that's not gonna happen."

"Please… it hurts too much," she begged, and he realised his hands were trembling, breaking into a cold kind of sweat. "Just… point at the head. But don't miss."

"I can't," he said, notes of finality pinned to his voice. Seconds swept by where she just stared at him.

"Tell me a joke," she mumbled weakly. "I wanna die laughing."

Leo searched his brain for one desperately, but he just wanted to tell her he really liked her too. But for her sake, he pushed those thoughts back. "What did the angel say to the other angel?" His voice breaking up like static.

"I dunno," she muttered quickly like she didn't want to properly consider it.

"Halo," he said and grinned.

Robyn laughed after a second's pause, her laugh soft and twinkling. Then her eyes saddened again. "Please. Do it. It hurts so much… I can't go through this." Her voice decided and set even at the hardest of times.

"Are you sure?" he asked gently.

She nodded ardently and bit her lip back as tears came again.

He'd never seen her cry before. She let go of his hands and slowly he stood, joint cracking and shoulder throbbing. Checking the single bullet inside the chamber, hoping it miraculously wasn't there. It still was. With a gasping breath of air, he levelled the gun to her head, and she nodded encouragingly. His finger flitted to the trigger, but he didn't squeeze yet, just made it sit there.

Everything he'd gone through went through his head – the pain, the words, the fear. It didn't make a difference if he didn't make it out alive. If Robyn wasn't there with him.

"Leo," she whispered.

"I shoot now?" he asked.

"Yeah."

"You can always back out, there's time."

"No, do it now. Watch for the recoil... it'll surprise you."

He laughed through his tears and cleared them with his white shirt sleeve, making sure he had a clear view and didn't miss his aim. The gun centimetres from her temple and she gazed up at him with a fondness you gave to someone who made you proud.

"I'm proud of you," she said.

Say something. Talk to her, goddammit. This is your only chance, the last chance you're ever going to get. Don't leave words unsaid, they'll pick at your forever and you'll die with them in your grave. Buried beside you.

"You're really something, bus stop girl."

"Yeah." Was all she could say.

She began smiling and she let her grin consume her entire being before Leo pulled the trigger, sound blistering out his thoughts, eyes jammed shut.

In those few seconds of silence afterwards, he thought back to it all. The birds around him continued trilling rhythms they'd sang every morning, rustling of tree leaves every now and again and what the freezing cold winter brought upon the air. He thought of Robyn and her face and her everything. How could she be so brave? She had it together until the very end. All those times he'd wanted to die when he just wanted to live. To feel happiness, to feel relief, to feel something other than sadness. And now he hated himself for wanting to live when Robyn was dead. Those thoughts catapulted inside his mind and weighed him down until finally the tears stopped. Only then did he open his eyes.

He didn't realise he'd dropped the gun beside his feet but all he saw that would scorch into his memory forever was Robyn. It wasn't like in books where eyes stayed open and gazing to the sky, Robyn had hers shut but she was still smiling faintly. He could trace it with his finger, but he didn't, just watched her and the memories flicker by. A fatal shot to the head that still suppurated with blood. Leo covered his face, rasping cries that shocked even himself.

Leo blundered backwards a few steps looking anywhere but her. He didn't bother with the gun, there were no bullets left and he breathed in the cold like it was part of him. Mustering the strength, he turned and broke into a ran, a new objective replacing the old.

Robyn never got to say goodbye to Elena. Or Roman, or her friends. God, she never even got to say goodbye to her dad.

thirty-five.

Mark was dead. Mark was dead. She'd never see him again. Talk to him, hug him, listen to his laugh. Fuck Will, she never wanted to see him again.

She knew exactly where she was going, what she had to do in that moment – get to Clyde before Will did. With no phone on her, she looked to the sky, marking its colour in her mind. Closer to sunrise than she'd ever seen it before.

Knuckles rapping the wood of his door and a dejected kind of silence. She became impatient after a minute dwindled by and was startled by the sound of a distant engine noise. From the sounds of it, it may have been a sports car. It was barely audible, but it got louder and louder until she could see from further up the road a Mini. That was her chance. The car braked suddenly just before Elena could even obstruct its way, and the engine died. A woman in her thirties got out, yellow headscarf to match her car, grey sweater and jeans that hung loosely by her ankles. She looked at the blood all over Elena's sweater and gaped, stood by her open door.

"Hi. I was gonna stop you, but it looks like you already stopped," Elena smiled, bristling with confidence.

The woman nodded and looked her up and down with a look of uncertainty. "Is that the design or actual blood?" She jabbed a finger at her.

"Oh, it's my blood. I was gonna talk to you concerning that. Would it be okay if I were to use your phone? Reception doesn't reach here so we have to get to the junction further down."

"Are you okay?"

"Ha, no. There's four of us, a lunatic and another adult."

"I saw a Mercedes on my way here. And a van and a friend's car."

"Sorry, why were you driving this way? Nobody lives here." Her gut twisted in suspicion.

"I'm Clyde's friend," she said.

"What's your name?" she questioned. If she said the name Clyde had mentioned, it was her. It definitely would be, no doubt in her mind.

"Michelle."

It was her, and her gut relaxed weakly.

"Come inside, the car's warm." She ducked her head beneath the frame, sat, and put the ignition in, engine flaring back into life. It was a surprisingly loud engine for such a small vehicle. Elena hesitated and peered inside to the kitchen. Nobody there. Maybe he'd already left.

"I don't think Clyde's home, his car isn't there."

Elena jumped out from her thoughts. "He said he didn't have a car."

"He keeps in there in his garage."

She wandered to the side where Michelle was pointing and blinked three times. There was a garage and she'd completely missed it, morning and night.

"Okay. There's a guy who's got a gun and the four of us split, I don't know if they're okay."

"Well we better go then."

When they got to where the Mercedes was still parked, there was nobody in sight apart from another vehicle but it was empty and the van which parked facing the Mercedes. Elena had completely forgotten who went where but she remembered following Leo down the unpaved road. Maybe he had worked it out too and he'd already brought him to safety.

She sat in the passenger seat, seatbelt-less and shooting glances in all directions while Michelle decelerated and pulled the handbrake onto neutral.

"Sorry, you mentioned another car? Is it that one?"

Michelle slapped a layer of lip balm on her lips and gave her a smile. "Clyde's Ford, yeah." She eyed her sweater gingerly. "I better call the police. And an ambulance."

Elena nodded and tumbled out the car, shutting the car door and heading to the blue Ford, license plates almost twenty years old and dents and scratches carved into the body of the car. The window was half open on the passenger's side and she knew then with the blood against the seat about shoulder height was Leo's.

Elena raced into the fields, trying her best not to trip on her heels and she sprinted to the fringe of the trees. The tip of the sun's head peeked over the fields, startlingly orange and a deeper orange around it like an aura. Someone ran right into her, throwing her to the floor and deflating her lungs of cool air.

thirty-six.

"Leo?" she shrieked.

Leo swore and stood, hauling her up along with him. Roman stood beside him half keeling over and with a distressed look cloaking his face. If he didn't move, it didn't hurt so he just moved his eyes to clock on Elena.

"Sorry, Elena. God, I'm glad you're alive." He had been crying and he curled his arms around her shoulders. Then began sobbing.

"I'm glad you're alive too. Why are you crying? I found someone and she's phoning for help," she said and squeezed Leo.

He let go and sniffed deeply. Roman exchanged a withered glance at Leo then sighed. It came out jagged and laboured.

"What happened to you?" Elena said.

"I broke my ribs."

She winced and led them back to the tarmacked roads. A woman was on the phone, repeating phrases now and again. The service was spotty out there.

"Who's she?" Roman raised an eyebrow.

"Clyde's friend, Michelle."

Roman gasped. "Clyde?"

"He's the man I spoke to. The one you referred to as my best friend," Elena cried. "Leo, did you find him?"

"Yeah. I came back here and found Roman lying there half conscious. I only told him bits."

"Where's Clyde? Whose car is that?" Roman nodded to the blue car. A new addition.

"Clyde's. Look, where's Robyn?"

Leo stilled. Elena didn't need an answer, just read their faces like they were books and shook her head in an intense kind of disbelief. They confirmed it when they nodded, and Elena looked back to the trees that hid her body somewhere. Robyn engulfed in nature and the waking surroundings beside her, alone and withering away.

She sagged with resignation. "How'd she die? Where's Will?"

"I was with her when she died." Leo gestured to his stomach numbly. "Shot there. I dunno where Will is."

"Shit," muttered Roman and lowered his head. Even that hurt.

Michelle walked towards them, phone swinging by her side and Clyde by his car. "They're on their way."

PART IV
two months later.

thirty-seven.

Maybe it was the warmth. The rough tickling of the sheets between fingers or the voice he thought he'd never hear again. Perhaps the fact that there was the smell of coffee he always smelled every morning. Nevertheless, the relief came like it did the past two months.

He remembered the minute they got to hospital like he remembered his full name, something that seemed so unreal and almost impossible the hours before.

Leo's parents were breathing the same air as him; his mother by his side on a stool and his dad withdrawn from the situation by the door. That was normal. Normal was good. The clock opposite him on the wall read ten fifteen and the sky outside was an edgy and nervous blue, pinks and purples dissipating hours ago. A hospital so quiet at that time it spooked him.

His dad was the first to speak, clearing his throat and unfolding his arms. "I'll get you a coffee."

Leo the day before would've flung him a sarcastic comment right into his face, but he found that he couldn't speak. His throat was lined with hours of dryness and so he would have been grateful to drink anything.

Once his dad had exited the room, his mother edged closer and peered into his eyes, smiling a strained smile.

"You scared us."

"Oops," he said, not sure what else to respond with.

"Are you okay? How are you feeling now?" Her eyes fell on gauze taped to his shoulder.

"Holy shit, was I in surgery?"

"No, just a bit of tidying up."

Leo relaxed back into his pillow. Surgeries scared him.

"The bullet missed a major artery."

"Why doesn't that make me feel better?" he mumbled.

"How can I make you feel better then?" she asked softly.

Leo pulled a face. "I'm fine," he laughed nervously.

"Don't pretend."

"I'm not very good at pretending."

"Yes, you are. You're pretending right now."

"As I said, I'm not very good at pretending."

"What happened out there?"

"I was shot," he answered dryly.

Her blue eyes softened. "Why? What happened? We're not even in Riverton Hospital, this is Ficklebury. How did you travel so many miles away?"

"Things happen."

She sighed sadly and he suddenly remembered his friends and shot up.

"Where are the others?"

"You mean the two people with you?"

"Three," he corrected her and then his heart plummeted like a sinking ship. It was just two. Robyn was dead. He sat back. "When can I leave?"

"They said maybe this afternoon, they'll have to see," she responded. "But you can walk around, stretch your legs. I brought your earphones." She dangled his earphones in front of him which he took with a reassuring grin.

He got off the bed, realising he was in a hospital gown and took his phone from the table in the corner. Plugging it in and finding his playlist, he turned to his mother and smiled. She smiled back. But it was a smile on the verge of snapping it looked more like a grimace.

"I'm gonna find them. Where are they?"

"You'll have to ask reception."

"Okay."

"You were close to being concussed. Did you know that?"

"I did not."

His mother bit her lip and cast her gaze downwards in thought, so Leo waited patiently. "Your dad and I will be separating."

He blinked. "Oh?"

"Just for a bit, we'll see how it goes," she went on. "But your dad, he wants to try again with you. Be the dad you deserve."

That was bull and he knew it and he narrowed his eyes. He remembered his dad punching Carter, the only times they talked were the times they just argued and everything else. The bad outweighed the good, they always did in his life, so Leo shook his head. "Tell him he can try again later."

Now two month later, he regretted nothing. Apart from the fact it was a Monday and it was the first day back at school and he wasn't out of bed yet. He remembered the school's latest newsletter to parents about the death of one of their own, Robyn Wolff. A minute of silence would be held just before they left for lunch and an assembly to her year group in her memory. Two months and he'd never stopped thinking about it all. Her own funeral had been in mid-

December but only her dad attended to mourn in private. There came a point it burst his brains from his ears and when that happened, he usually spoke to James about it. And just at that thought, his phone chimed with a text from him which Leo used his foot to lazily drag across to him.

I stg if ur not ready.

A furtive glance at the clock. **relax, i just woke up.**

If ur not out in five mins, I'll leave without you.

Shimmying out of his t-shirt and sweats, and shovelling the textbooks in his bag was difficult, especially when it was almost completely dark inside and outside and he didn't want to blind himself with the lights that early in the morning. Still at seven thirty. One thing he liked about winter was that, but sometimes it got a bit depressing.

He froze with a staple halfway in his pencil case when he got a glimpse of something tall stood beside the door. He was still half-dressed and topless. "James, what are you doing in here?"

Shrugging the blond out of his eyes. "Your mum let me in. You weren't joking, were you?" He went over to his bed and lifted his shirt in the air to read the words on it appraisingly.

"I love pizza?" he read and turned to him.

Leo eye rolled and was very aware he was shirtless, so he grabbed his shirt from the door and buttoned it up. "What's your problem with pizza?" he mumbled.

"I think it looks like a dick."

Leo looked at James' reflection horrified. "Don't ruin pizza for me."

"Look at the shape of it."

"That's so unnecessary."

"I don't make the rules."

Leo got up to snatch his shirt off him and it was still warm from when he wore it. That won him a smirk from James.

"So, how are ya?"

"Meh." He continued to stuff things he needed in his grey backpack and realised he was missing his favourite pen so emptied out his whole bag.

James laughed and Leo could see in the mirror that he was staring back at him. It made Leo blood rush to his face. It was usually his face, but sometimes his ears.

"Me too."

"Stop looking at the t-shirt if you think it looks like a dick."

"Gross."

"Hey, your words, not mine." And remembered he put his pen with his books so stood to walk over. He found James stood right where he was meant to put his next step. Leo took an instinctive step back and his mind launched into a frenzy.

"Sorry," he apologised and brushed past him, breaking the moment of connection he had if any. Starving for it, but not needing it then, there were other things on his mind.

The bookshelf was about five-foot tall and consisted of four separate shelves at an equal distance between them. Leo had organised his books alphabetically, it hadn't taken long, but if someone replaced a book in the wrong place, he would piss the place down.

James was beside him in a second and retrieved a red book from the first shelf and flicked distractedly through it while Leo swiped his pen from the surface top.

"Don't bend the spine," Leo snapped, tapping his pen on the top of the spine and kept a cold gaze attached to him.

"Come on, Leo, we both know which spine you'd rather bend."

"You're right," he agreed calmly. "I'll break your back." He made to return to the mirror, but he halted because James was giving him that look again. It made him weak to his knees to be this close to him, someone who he used to love, and his gaze softened with his. A thought about Robyn entered his mind followed by Will, both smudged and just behind the loud thoughts of that present moment. His heart clenched painfully. "Why did we end, James?" His index did a little dance flicking between him and himself. "Why are you talking to me now? Was it because I almost died? Pity?"

James' face soon a warzone between sadness and guilt. More of the guilt really. Guilt of him being right. "Not just because of that," he started, and it seemed he needed to muster a tremendous amount of energy. "I missed you."

"But you left," he said. He knew how petty he sounded. "You shouldn't be sad."

James sagged beneath the weight of it all. "I lied. About everything."

"You did?" Leo raised an eyebrow.

"I didn't break up because we were drifting."

"Yeah, that was as a result," he said coldly.

"My dad found out."

His heart chilled of all emotion but horror. "Oh."

"Yeah, it wasn't you, it wasn't me, it was my dad."

"You left me regardless," he accused. "You could've told me. I wouldn't have cried every night."

"You cried every night?" He looked surprised.

"Sporadically," he murmured, annoyed.

"I'm sorry," he muttered hopelessly and dropped his gaze to Leo's feet.

"Yeah," Leo said through gritted teeth and that was the end of it. "We're gonna be late."

His mother held his coat while he stuffed his feet into his trainers and checked the time. Seven forty-seven. He could only hope James hadn't driven off already though he would've heard the screech of the tyres.

"Are you going to Robyn's memorial service at school?" she asked after handing him his coat.

He had his arm halfway through the sleeve and stopped. "Yeah."

"Okay."

Second arm through the sleeve and bag slung on one shoulder. "Bye."

"Bye, Leo."

The sky outside a dusty kind of blue with uneven slashes of orange every few places you looked, and the bright speck of white he only assumed was Venus. No stars today. Not since the sky dimmed with thick clouds hovering constantly.

His friendship with James now was quite uncertain as one could imagine. One minute they were as close as before and then next it was the opposite. He didn't know if he'd even class it as friendship. It was built only with the foundations and lacked any proper detailing, making it fragile to any hazards. So when his car was still parked on the kerb just outside his driveway, Leo thought they were ready to build the first storey.

He unlocked the doors gruffly without saying a word. Sure, Leo had his license, but when James heard about what happened two months prior, they'd started over. First, by offering him a lift which he accepted. Probably out of pity but this proved something.

Leo was glad to be out of the cold's presence and slipping into the warmth of the car. The same Corsa as always. The same one he hid his issues in. He slid the seatbelt across himself and clicked it into place, giving James an awkward smile which he looked away from. James with his sharp blue eyes and witty thoughts.

Their school was only fifteen minutes away by car and twenty-five on bad traffic days. Today was a quiet day so they rolled up into the parking lot of the sixth form with plenty of time to spare.

"Honestly, I don't know where you'd be without me," James said, killing the engine. The seat would go cold soon.

"I'd still be here, just not in your car."

He rolled his eyes and gave him a look. "I'll come to her memorial with you."

"It's okay, you miss third period and you have physics. Hard subject."

"I want to miss physics."

"You don't."

"Fine, I'll stay for half of it."

"That'll look weird." Leo clipped his seatbelt back and hurried out not wanting to be in the same place as him, smacking his head against the frame. It hurt. A text notification from his phone that he ignored for the moment.

Taking a step to the building with eyes pretending to search the floor. It was better like that because people wouldn't stop and try to talk to him.

"Hey."

"What?" And reluctantly met his gaze.

"I care, okay?" He gave him two awkward thumbs up like he usually did when he didn't know how to comfort someone. But somehow it made him feel better.

Leo got out his phone and looked down to the message. "I know."

Elena from her new phone asking to meet up. It brought the emotions building up again and he replaced his phone in his pocket and left.

thirty-eight.

Leo read the message and reacted with a thumbs up which assured her that everything was okay on his end with Robyn's school memorial. They hadn't seen each since they were discharged from hospital and she missed the two. She missed Mark the most. Mark's validation, the highs and the lows of everything, his jokes. Irrational as it sounded.

Elena looked at her thumb. Well, what was left of her thumb. It would not be until later that year she'd be able to get an implant. The hospital had tried their best in stitching but every few weeks, they'd rip at the seams and bloom with blood.

Her mum had let her stay off today because of her period pains, but that was just an excuse – she just didn't want to go back to school. She remained seated at her window in her own house with the TV on and relived the memory of the hospital.

She remembered her eyes had popped wide open.

"You mean he cut my thumb off just to export a file?" Elena gazed open mouthed at Leo, perched on the side of her hospital bed with one earphone in. Matching gowns and matching shadows behind eyes – the medication.

"I'm sorry he died. Even if he was gonna kill us. You liked him."

Elena nodded appreciatively. "Sucks."

"And Vienna."

"Thanks."

"And your dad."

"Roman's not awake yet," she said quickly before she started crying.

"I'm not surprised."

"Look at my thumb." She laughed as she put up her stitched-up hand. "They don't think they can reattach it back so they're gonna get me a new one from a donor."

"Involuntary donor. They're probably not alive."

"Maybe I'll be able to bring back the dead?"

"That's badass," he said.

She agreed and then fell in one of her contemplative trances.

"Poor Robyn. DID, huh. I didn't think I'd meet anyone with it."

"Yeah."

"I hope she's okay."

"Yeah, Robyn was really special."

She sensed he was holding something back but didn't push. "They're bringing the police in to talk to us."

His eyes enlarged. "Now?"

"Probably formally questioned at the police station."

"What do we do?"

"Tell them everything. Will abandoned his car and he's gone. They have the best chance at finding him. Or he might come back and kill all of us."

"Hmm." He pulled a face. "Doesn't really butter my toast."

"Then use jam." She shrugged and collapsed against the pillow righting her posture and gazed to the wall opposite. "Let's not play detective anymore. Look where it got Robyn." She didn't know where her clothes had wandered off to, but she was sure as heck she was going to throw them out. Burn them maybe. Not the shoes though, they were expensive. "Clyde needs to be protected," she said. "Will is probably after him "

"Elena!" The door was pushed open and held there as a small child with baby hairs framing her face hurtled in and threw herself over her bed. Elena froze and looked to who opened the door.

A woman with warm brown eyes and dark hair just like hers. One would age noticeably over the years, but some people really didn't.

"Mum?" she gawped.

Another squeal from outside and another small child this time a boy came bounding in. He stood by the bed and looked from Leo to Elena.

"Shall I leave?" Leo whispered.

She nodded and her gaze hardened on her mum. She shut the door after Leo and sat on the chair beside her dressed in a navy jumper that had a lyric scrawled across in red, grey sweats and flats. No words were traded until one of the children giggled awkwardly.

"I'm sorry about your dad," she said.

Elena forgot how deep her voice was, like an echo in a cave deep underground.

She nodded warily. "Are these yours?" Elena asked pointedly at the children on her bed. She guessed maybe they were both probably five or six.

"Yup, mine and Jane's," she replied and shot them both an affectionate smile which they eagerly returned with a giddy laugh.

Elena did a double take. "Jane?" she repeated.

Her mum's smile didn't dim, just brightened. "My wife," she said. The word wife was highlighted several times and stringing with confetti in Elena's imagination.

"I thought… you're religious," she said flatly.

"You can still be religious and love whoever you want. That's the point." She switched the leg she had crossed over.

Elena eyed her silver Crucifix necklace that laced itself beautifully around her neck and nodded slowly. "Okay."

Only then her smile wavered. "Are you okay with it?"

Elena laughed without humour. "It's just ironic because I know you would've said the exact opposite seven years ago." She cocked her head to the side. "I guess people surprise you."

Her smile flickered back to life. "I guess they do."

"Mama, can I get another cookie?" the boy whined and climbed off the bed to his mother's lap, joining hands.

Elena watched with an emotion she knew could only be jealousy. They had their mother, and their mother had them. Elena had nobody. She was suddenly angry at the children.

"You stole her," she snarled. "You think she's just gonna be there forever, don't you?"

The boy stared. Then he whimpered and the girl stopped bouncing on the bed, grin falling to the floor.

"That's not fair on them," her mum said.

"You weren't fair on me," she snapped and got out of bed from the opposite side. Shuffling into white clothed slippers, she made her way around the bed and had a hand to the handle.

"Elena. Please. We have to talk."

"Then talk here." She spun and crossed her arms, throwing the wickedest scowl she could find over her face. A flash of hurt in her eyes which stayed to cool and simmer.

"Not here," she said.

"What's wrong with here?" she leered shrilly. "We have good lighting and it's quiet. Not to mention it smells like—"

"Not with the kids," she clenched her teeth and appeared somewhat angry for the first time. A smudge of her old self in a new body she was trying to recreate. A person Elena never wanted to cross when that happened. Like torrential rain. So she sighed grudgingly and waited for her.

It was all that played in her memories over and over like a broken record. Except, it didn't sound pretty. She thought that kicking the year away under the carpet and starting a new one would make her feel better, but it didn't. It might as well have been the day after. Time, months, and years were all social constructs.

Roman had got back to her and agreed on the time she'd set. Five on the dot at Leo's mum's bakery shop. She wouldn't have to drive too far, just twenty minutes.

She jumped when she saw her door opening, and the pillow she had pressed to her chest fell to the floor.

Her mum smiled the dazzling artificial smile of hers with a tub of cookie dough ice cream. "Did I scare you?"

"No," she lied, leaning to the floor and placing the pillow in her arms. "Thanks. Roman ate mine."

"No worries," she scooped half of it into a bowl and took half for herself. "Hazel and Chance sent a message to you. Did you receive it?"

"No," she lied again, tucking her phone in her sweater out of sight and going for the ice cream.

341

It wasn't that she didn't want to reply, it was just weird. They were her half siblings and she felt no emotional connection to them. Maybe due to the fact they were both six and half her height and she'd never met them before. Jane was in Wales with them while her mum stayed in Strontham to fix things temporarily. Her dad's funeral was due to ever happen and part of her knew her mum was still being her old petty self.

"Elena." She shifted her weight awkwardly to the other side and bit her lip. "You know I can't stay away for more than three months from the kids."

"I never told you to," she said. Her hands broke into a tingling sweat despite the ice cream she was eating, and her phone began to loosen from her grip.

"I know. It's just… how do you like it here in Runswick?"

"I've lived here all my life," she replied. "I like it here. I have friends."

"You can still make friends there in Wales."

She looked at her horrified. "You're telling me to start my life somewhere else?" She could feel the darkness of the situation looming and she knew her mum was right, but she didn't want to believe it.

"Your dad is dead. You want to be like him? Sitting in your room all day doing nothing," she snapped.

Anger flashed like a loose bolt of lightning. "That's a little below the belt."

"Elena. You'll be doing this for the whole family. You'll like Jane. The kids miss you; they haven't seen you since."

"Kids miss anyone," she grumbled.

"You'll settle in just fine."

"I'll be moving out soon for university and I'll be eighteen in August." She scowled.

"You'll have to be out sooner than August," she mumbled and avoided her eyes.

Elena froze. "You're selling the house?"

The hesitation was her reply and she stood, pillow falling by her feet softly.

"Honestly, fuck you."

"Don't speak to me like that," she hissed, and she realised she was gripping the spoon she held, whites glowing beneath her knuckles. Elena wasn't listening, just wedged the bowl in the crook of her elbow and took off. Someplace to kill time until five. She knew of a place.

She disregarded the darting stares of students in the Main Hall and made her way to first period. The excuse she wrote down was that she missed the bus which wasn't exactly false. It was just that she missed the bus yesterday and not today. She wasn't even in uniform, just had her grey sweater and green jeans hanging loosely over her and the delicate silver bracelet that looped around her right wrist.

Onto the corridor that joined off to her maths classroom, she made eye contact with a teacher who was walking in her direction. She flashed a smile to him which he didn't return, and instead told her to stop with the hard-lined face of his.

"Are you a visitor?"

"Yes."

"All visitors are required to wear a red lanyard."

"I couldn't find reception, sorry," she smiled politely and plucked a piece of lint off her sweater and ran a hand through her hair. Her hand released the knots earlier than she expected and she had yet to get used to shorter hair.

"What's your purpose of being here? Another trainee?" He was growing increasingly displeased now and drew the back of his wrist across his moustache. Wiping off the coffee.

343

"Yeah, I'm teaching maths," she replied brightly.

"No, Elena. You're being *taught* maths."

Elena shifted.

"What's your excuse for not wearing uniform?" He glowered and took a slow sip of coffee.

"See, my boyfriend died, and I was—"

"I'm sorry to hear that. So sorry because I've heard you say that so many times now, I want to punch a wall."

Elena blinked. "I wouldn't if I were you."

"And that's jewellery, you're not allowed jewellery in school as it'll be confiscated."

"I think as a former school council rep., the rule needs to be reviewed," she stammered and couldn't look straight at him anymore. "Why does what we wear matter if you're telling us to express ourselves? A little bit contradictory, don't you think?

He took a menacing step towards her and she felt unease rising. "You think the rules don't apply to you?"

That's when the tears began cursing her vision so she could barely see his features. "Well, maybe just this once—"

"You're to go home and change. Until then, you're not allowed back in school." He finished his coffee, downing the rest as if it were a shot and scraped past her.

She brushed the tears away and breathed a sigh. So emotional. As sensitive as her skin.

thirty-nine.

"Wow. They're really pretty."

Roman inspected the icing of a cake at eye level and walking along and was in awe at the little cuttings of marzipan.

"Stop. You're running," Leo commanded.

He stopped, confused. "I'm not running."

"Running slowly is still running." He picked the tray lined with cake mixture off the table and placed it in the oven.

"Wow, I can smell them cooking already," said Roman.

Leo frowned. "I haven't turned the heat on."

"Oh." Roman sank back into his chair and watched the man from the very corner eye them, newspaper covering half his face. A frown settled on his face and he jabbed a thumb at Leo.

"He ought to leave that job for women. It's not very manly." He barked a laugh and nodded to Roman to laugh. He remained silent.

"Why don't you say that again," he said quietly.

"I said—"

"Do you leave the cooking to your wife?" he asked, interrupting him. His voice was very annoying.

"It's her job," he countered.

Roman stood and walked closer to the man. His frown deepened and he lowered the newspaper to the table.

"Then what's yours?"

Leo was back at the counter and stared at the scene.

"Why's that relevant?"

"What's your name, sir?"

"Drake."

He raised his eyebrows. "Like the rapper?"

"Like the sailor," he insisted angrily.

"Well, Drake. You're quite useless without your wife, then aren't you? You're so helpless, men like you. I wouldn't even call you a man, you're more like a…" He wrinkled his nose, "sack of meat."

"Excuse me?" He stood and was half a foot shorter than Roman which made his confidence soar.

"No, excuse you," he snarled. "You don't respect women."

"I respect the pretty ones," he answered disdainfully.

"That's not respecting women."

His large eyes narrowed. "Go to hell."

Roman started walking away.

"Hey, where are you going? I'm talking to you."

He turned over his shoulder. "To hell, are you dumb?" He stopped and turned to face him. "I think you should leave."

He got up curtly, adjusted his blazer like he had any business to and went to walk away.

"You didn't pay the bill."

The man glared, rifled around in his wallet and threw down a fiver, tipping a pound.

Leo watched him leave as Roman settled back in his chair.

"I hope he falls over today," Leo said.

"I hope his wife leaves him."

Leo turned back to the glass display and began wiping away the dust with a cloth. Chequered floor and beige walls boxed just the two of them inside his small bakery. The glass screen showing the pastry on display made Roman rethink eating dinner an hour early, cakes of all sizes and shapes, decorated with various colours of icing, sprinkles of different things surrounding it. Despite it being a bakery, it smelled more of coffee than anything else. Christmas decorations also draped itself across the room, tinsel and paper snowflakes and it made Roman smile.

Leo was stood in an oversized denim jacket with a collared shirt beneath, black jeans and dirty looking white trainers. It was nice seeing him not bloodied up.

"You cut a fringe," Roman said.

"Ages ago."

"And your shirt."

"What about it?"

"It's very nice."

"It's not the same one."

"Your shoes."

"I like them too."

"Your glasses."

"This is getting weird," he muttered and nudged his silver rimmed glasses up his nose. He didn't know he needed glasses.

"Where's Elena?" he questioned.

"I think she's running late. Said she was getting something." He leaned over the countertop with a thoughtful expression, arms folded and squinting into the darkening skies beyond the bakery. The pendant shades that hung overhead were doing a good job at lighting up the place despite them being filaments giving off orange glows.

Filaments reminded him of the house back in Ficklebury. It wasn't nice.

"You good?" Roman mused.

"I think I see her."

The closer the figure got, the more Roman knew it was Elena. She stopped just outside the door and raised an eyebrow at the sign.

"Are you still open at this time?" She pointed to the sign, her voice dimmed by the glass. Leo grinned and went over to flip the sign over to CLOSED saying nobody would disturb them to Roman. Elena kicked the door open and held paper bags stained with grease in her hands and a big smile on her face. She'd also cut her hair, so it just brushed beneath her shoulders. It was glossy and straightened.

"You cut your hair," Roman told her.

"I know. It was up to my ass, so I decided to cut it." She laughed nervously. "Can we eat, I'm starving."

"I just had dinner," Roman groaned.

"Well I'll just eat it like last time. Won't we Leo?"

"Sure."

Elena headed over to an empty table by the window and sat cross legged on the table. "I even got us cookies."

"I'll pass."

"You own a bakery," said Roman.

"Cookies are just hardened bread. They're literally made from the same stuff."

Elena shook her head in astonishment and went looking through the bags searching for something. Roman and Leo sat at neighbouring tables but Roman actually sat on a stool.

"New Year's Resolutions anyone?" asked Leo.

"Mine's to not die," replied Roman and grinned.

Elena frowned in thought and then smiled. "I've decided I don't need to be better. I love me already, there's nothing to change!" And stuffed a fry in her mouth. "Years are a social construct."

"That's great."

"Isn't it?"

"I haven't seen you both for ages," Roman said.

"That's why I said we meet." Elena broke off half a cookie and offered it to both and both refused. "Remember how the police questioned us?"

"I think they said insufficient evidence," said Leo.

"I think that's a bunch of shit."

"It is. Our injuries were enough evidence."

"And the license plates Elena and I memorised."

"They said it only helped them identify stolen vehicles."

"Well I know where Will is." She snapped her cookie into a quarter and offered. Roman took it but Leo shook his head grimly.

Roman blinked. "Will?"

Will hadn't shown up at school since the Friday before it happened and at first Roman was relieved he didn't have to avoid him, but now it unnerved him because he felt like it was a build-up to something even worse. To some big spectacle.

"Where? Have you contacted him?"

She looked sheepish. "I was hoping Leo would. You know, since he told Robyn he likes you."

Leo looked aghast and Elena offered her cookie which he declined once again.

"For God's sake." Roman broke into a laugh.

"And mine," added Elena.

Leo took it with an eye roll and ate it all in one go hungrily.

"You want me to talk to Will? Doesn't he want revenge for killing Mark? He'll probably kill us." His voice was uneven like an untarmacked road.

"I'm surprised he hasn't killed one of us," Roman said loftily. "I don't think he wants to."

"Oh, he does," Elena nodded firmly. "He's bought my house."

"What?" they cried.

"And he lives in the centre of town."

"You're serious?"

"When have I not been?"

"He kicked you out your home?"

"No, my mum's selling the house," she replied with a faint smile.

"Then where are you going?" Roman asked but he knew where.

Elena drooped. "Conwy. With her wife and everything. The kids too."

"Surely she can't expect you to drop everything like that," pondered Leo.

"She's expecting me to," Elena sighed, and her head fell against the wall. "Tomorrow."

"We have to find Will right now then." Roman brought himself up to his knees and dropped to the floor. "Where is he?"

"What, we're really doing this?"

"We can make the police go undercover with us and then throw him in prison." He could imagine it then, perfectly mapped out.

"Leo, do you still have his number? I deleted him."

"I blocked him," he said. "But I remember his number. What do I say?"

"Say you wanna meet."

A sharp tap on the door startled them, especially Roman who had his back facing it. Leo's mother was there, and she shrugged her shoulders upwards at the CLOSED sign. They went to open the door.

"The shop doesn't close until seven."

"We're doing homework," Leo lied.

"I don't see any of you doing that," she said doubtfully.

"The homework was to talk," he replied.

"Cross it off then." She breezed past them and into the kitchen.

They turned back to each other.

"Text him you wanna meet and…" Elena trailed off and looked at Roman for help.

"A hotel," he said. "You wanna run away together."

Leo looked repulsed and went red. Roman noticed he blushed easily.

Elena put a hand up to stop him from protesting. "We don't feel safe with Will still out there. You have to agree."

"Why haven't you called the police if you know where he is?" Leo quizzed. "Surely if—"

"Text him," she interrupted. "Trust me, it's so much easier than getting them to raid his house."

Leo stared at her, but slowly got out his phone and tapped in his number. He shot her another look from over his phone and waited for Elena to tell him to back out. She remained calm and staring back, nodding determinedly.

"You know, a few days ago I had a dream I was back at the hospital and Will was the one sitting next to me."

"Really?" Roman said. He thought back.

At first it was clear where he was – in the confinements of his room. If he opened his eye at that particular angle, he'd see his unfished assignments upturned on his desk and the shirt he always wore when he was home. Turn to the right a

351

bit and he'd be seeing the mirror and his perfect sleepy reflection and sometimes if he remembered to put it there, his bag. So when he opened his eyes and none of those things were there, he was forced to reconsider.

A hospital. A small room. So startlingly white and so was the clock, the exact same ceramic white, thoughtless in decoration. It was almost two o'clock and he shot up and groaned against the pain. His torso felt stiff and was wrapped in something that didn't restrict his breathing too much if he sucked in. Oh. They'd mended his ribs without him knowing.

He grinned. Neat.

He tested his ankle and frowned when he found he couldn't move it, so he flung a corner of the sheets over. Bandaged. Shit, he was basically a mummy.

Voices dawdled by the door and there was a shushing noise.

"Don't ssh me!"

"Guys?" he said, loud enough for them to hear.

Elena peaked inside and Leo just behind, both wearing warm smiles. He broke into a pleased smile.

"Roman," Leo said. "We were just gonna check on you."

"Ha. Well I just woke up." He did jazz hands which he cringed at. His tongue knocked sharply against his tooth. Still half missing. He didn't remember if he swallowed it or what, but he wasn't worried about that.

His dad pushed past the two and was yelling. "Where's my son?" He stood in the middle of the room and froze upon seeing Roman's face. Leo and Elena had gone.

"Roman," he said softly.

Roman burst into tears right there and turned his face away, embarrassed for himself. His dad went over to him and sat at the foot of his bed and encouraged him to let it all out until he finally stopped, eyes inflamed.

"Thank God my son is okay," he whispered.

Roman's face didn't match his as he remembered what he knew. What he could use against him. Wiping at his face, he glared. "Oh, *that* son. I just got confused because apparently you have two."

He expected him to stare at him with coldness, but he didn't. Just sat there in a strangled silence, face down. One could call is shame.

"Were you ever gonna tell me?"

He tapped the heel of his foot at a rhythm and stuffed his hands in his coat pockets before answering. "It doesn't matter anymore."

He felt the anger which came with his words. "Don't dodge the question."

His face showed betrayal and hurt and Roman didn't stop, he wanted to drag it out until it spilled the truth out.

"Does mom even know? How many more women have you slept with?"

"Hey, hey, hey, listen for a sec."

"Don't hey me. I'm leaving."

"You're healing so you can't," he said.

"You think I care about that?" he hissed but he didn't move. He couldn't – everything hurt. His dad opened his mouth to talk but he held a hand up to silence him.

"Can you give me a sec, I'm tryna think. You can get me a coffee."

"Sure." And left.

Roman searched his bed for a phone then snatched it from the table on his left, dialling his mother and ignoring the get well soon card beside it. It rang twice before she picked up and she sounded exhausted. There was also a strange whirring noise in the background.

"Is this Roman?"

"Yeah, it's me."

"Oh, thank God you're okay. Listen, I'm in London, I can't get to you yet, but I know your dad is there."

"London?" He frowned.

"I've been trying to find you."

An iron of guilt pressed to his chest. "Oh."

"I'm on the M1, I think I'll be there in three point five hours. Three if I go eighty."

"No, don't do that. Just drive the limit, I'm fine. But I gotta tell you something." He braced himself and dug his fingernail into his thumb. He hoped Elena was all right and decided to take a look at the card on the table.

"Okay," she said slowly.

"It's about dad."

"Is he okay?" Her voice rose a few octaves with every word. His dad didn't deserve her worry.

He opened the card and smiled warmly. "He's… uh." He really didn't want to hurt her. "He's not been exactly…" He used his knuckles to massage his temples.

"Is he okay?" she repeated.

He finished reading the message by Cahil and replaced it back where it was before, letting the warmth spread in his chest. "Yes." The words came spewing out. "Sofia and I weren't his only children. He cheated, mom. He had another child." His good foot began doing a weird dance which usually happened when he was anticipating the worst. She hadn't said anything and began questioning the cell service there. "Mom?"

"Honey, I know."

That had shocked him and it brought back the shock again in that bakery.

"Yeah. Weird dream," muttered Leo.

A text notification made itself heard and Leo paled. He titled his phone screen to them and Roman grinned.

forty.

Leo leaned over the side with his arms crossed, elbows on the ledge against the strong breeze. He wasn't afraid of falling but his stomach struggled to keep his dinner settled.

Below was the city centre, glowing amber with car lights trailing by each other like a river of fireflies, buildings like solid black blocks rising from the ground and halting at different levels around. He was at the very top of the hotel, pool just behind and a bar. But there was nobody there. Not a one. Just him. And soon Will.

He didn't feel in danger, but he didn't exactly feel safe either. This was no New York but it was pretty damn close.

Above was the velvet blue sky, cloudless and still burning orange in the very distance.

The tips of his shoes touched the concrete barrier and he nudged them back, worrying if he pushed hard enough, the side would break. He could hear someone up the stairs, ghost of footsteps passing every step. And there he stood. Will in his striped sweater, jeans and unlaced shoes. That could be an advantage and he kept his eyes to his, so he didn't realise. He did though and tied both twice. Will strolled over, eyes fixed on him with every step. He stopped a metre from him and smiled. Leo wondered if he could even feel happiness like he did.

"You called?" he said and thrust hands in pockets, surveying the city around them.

The sounds of traffic made Leo feel tense, so he took a step back from the barrier, closing the distance between them.

"You're here."

"I guess I am."

"I was thinking Iceland if you're still interested."

"I think I'd prefer Toronto."

"It's too busy there."

"Okay then Iceland."

"Iceland don't have a McDonald's," Leo stated. "If that changes your mind."

"We both know it hasn't." He laughed softly and Leo laughed along.

"Where have you been since?" he asked making sure it was casual sounding.

"Places." He shrugged absently. "Had to do things."

"And now you're here."

"I am," he smiled, and his eyes glinted in the lights of the city freckled on buildings and Leo put a hand in his pocket. Robyn's cigarettes nudged his fingers. They were still there after he moved them from his jeans in case his mother saw. Now he wanted to cry.

A painful jerk of a siren down below surprised Leo but not Will.

"I didn't pack," Leo admitted.

He smirked. "No? I didn't either. Just came for you."

Leo put his hand in his other pocket, reaching for his phone. Will saw.

"When were you going to tell me your friends were coming too?"

"I wasn't. They're not," he blurted a little too quickly.

"Okay."

"Let's go." He took both hands from his pocket and held out cigarettes to him.

Will raised an eyebrow. "Sorry, I don't smoke."

"Neither." He laughed like it was funny and craned his neck up to the tallest building he could see, his throat bare against the cold.

Will followed his line of sight and scoffed scornfully. "That's a law firm."

"It is?"

"I think there's something you're not telling me," he leered.

Leo frowned and looked back to him, smoothing over his mistakes. "Yeah. I forgot my passport."

Will took a step forward threateningly. "Are you sure?" he grit his teeth. "You know what liars get?"

"Hey, perhaps you'd like a joke? It could cheer you up."

He shook his head. "No, thanks."

"Aw, come on. Just one."

"I know that you got your friends somewhere here, they're watching us right now. Aren't they?"

"You know how I feel about people watching us." He took his hand in his and replaced the cigarettes in his pocket, gazing reassuringly at him.

Will faltered and met his gaze, conflict flickering across his face. Then he took both of Will's hands which were freezing.

"Iceland," Leo said, "is gonna be so beautiful."

forty-one.

Elena arched her eyebrows, staring downwards from the brightly lit office space. "I see the signal."

Roman peered downwards and squinted, then nodded. "Do it."

She hovered a finger over her keyboard in hesitation, worries of everything falling apart when they were at such a rocky stage. Her eyes felt bleak and tired and she had to yawn every now and again to keep her eyes from stiffening shut. It was almost eleven at night. Looking at Leo and Will then at Roman. But she had to try. And sent the message.

"Are you really leaving tomorrow?" he asked.

She nodded with sorrow. "I haven't packed."

"When do you leave?"

"Midday."

He looked at her regretfully. "Let's get going then," Roman said in a low rumble of a voice, letting him take her sleeve and tugging her from view.

forty-two.

They had time to spare which was always a good thing.

Roman watched Leo with two hands around a coffee and Will with a glum look on his face. It was weird seeing him after all that time. All that time he spent being scared.

He nodded to the man beside him and showed him. Elena was restless.

"Okay," he muttered. "Do you know if he has a weapon on him?"

Before Roman could even think about answering, Elena clamped a hand over her mouth and nudged them both to listen.

"That's it. The intercom. They're boarding now."

The man nodded to them earnestly. "Get in position."

forty-three.

Leo had never had coffee so late at night and right then he really needed the bathroom, but he couldn't leave him out of his sight yet.

Will sat beside him, his pensive eyes lingering on the planes outside and sometimes returning back inside to settle at Leo. He always avoided his stare and just pretended one of the planes sparked his interest.

It was surprising how calm Will was with the whole thing. Leo barely concealed the joy of the whole thing working out. A plane to the capital of Iceland one way. Will kept his blond curls flat against a grey cap, keeping away anyone who could recognise him. It was busy this time of year, a tall Christmas tree tucked away grandly in a corner.

In the past twenty minutes of waiting to board, he'd checked his phone once and only to check the time. He couldn't risk being suspicious when he had him so close to the edge. Not close enough he could push though.

"I really need to pee," he said and tapped his foot up and down in discomfort. It wasn't a lie.

Will's hollow eyes travelled from the night to him. "Then go."

"You wait here." He dropped to the floor and his feet ached from walking for so long, they actually throbbed.

"Where else do I go?"

Leo made his way to the bathroom and entered the gent's. There were two cubicles occupied in the row of twenty and he swooped a hand underneath the drier so they wouldn't hear his conversation and crept back to the entrance.

He dialled his number whilst keeping his eyes locked onto Will's back. Usually he hated calling people, text was easier and less awkward. But today wasn't usually. It rang six times and he picked up.

The dryer stopped storming out air and lapsed into silence. Annoying timing.

"Leo?"

"James. Hi."

"What's up?"

"The sky."

"Same here."

He drummed his fingers lightly against his thigh and kicked his untied lace from beneath his shoe.

"Uh, I rang you…" he began.

"I know," he said with amusement hanging from the other end. "It's almost eleven—"

"I'm at the airport," he cut him off. "And I dunno if I'll…" He picked at his fingernail. "I dunno if I'll make it back. I mean, it would be nice if I did but I can't guarantee anything."

"Huh? What was that? You're in an airduct?"

"What? No. *Airport.*"

"Ah."

"I said I don't know if I'll make it back." He looked back through the people walking, past the rows of seats people sat on, to Will.

"Why? Holiday already? It's the first day back."

"No."

"Then what?"

"I just wanna say that I'm glad we happened." His words came out rushed and ran into each other like paint. But he had no regrets, not any regrets bigger than leaving things unsaid with Robyn. He could've told her, but he didn't because he was too afraid and now was his last chance to ever tell anyone else. "Even if we ended up like this. I'm glad we're friends."

James was silent and Leo could hear the shuffling from the other end. Then the sound of wind knocking against the speaker.

He frowned. "Where are you?"

"I'm on a walk."

"Now?"

"Leo…" His voice held guilt and the smile Leo didn't realise he had vanished. "I'm glad we're friends too—"

"It's okay," he cut him off quickly. "I just wanted to get it out there. In case I die. I gotta go now. Uh, bye bye." He shoved his phone back in his pocket and ambled back over and darted a glance from the corner of his eye to the people who he knew were watching over him.

forty-four.

Her plan envisioned success. It radiated logic and durability. Fool proof and simple. Or so she thought.

She sat in a grey wig at the departure lounge which itched her neck horribly and a dress that made her vomit. Florals but make it eighties. Roman thought it necessary to be in disguise, which was true, but not dressed as the elderly. It had been difficult getting the police involved when they acted as if children weren't worth their time. First there was insufficient evidence, then it was one perpetrator dead, but they eventually agreed. That took another two hours and Leo's mum started to suspect something, but he'd quickly told her he was at a friend's house. Oh, the excuses people come up with.

A short dark-haired girl with a rainbow striped sweater and a squeaky suitcase tugging in her hand sat beside her and gave her a polite smile.

Elena smiled back and hoped it didn't show her true age. It was awkward because she didn't know if she wanted to talk to her, there were plenty of empty seats around them. She didn't know if her parents were anywhere nearby or if it was just her.

"What goes up, stays up for an amount of time and comes back down?" Elena asked, trying her best to make her voice strain with the years upon her. It was deeply unsettling.

The girl was rubbing her hands up and down her arms trying to get rid of the cold and her smile deepened.

"I'm not sure," she replied, and her voice was sweet, and Elena thought her voice was typically full of humour.

"Guess," she pressed.

The girl was her age she realised, maybe younger and her hand went to the silver necklace she wore without thinking.

Elena's face dropped. "I'm making you uncomfortable."

"No," she insisted. "I was thinking."

"Of what?"

"The answer to your joke." She dropped her hand to her lap.

"Oh."

"I don't know," she said finally.

"Planes."

The girl's face was wiped of expression and Elena barked an awkward laugh. "It's funny, right?"

"Yup," she said but her expression didn't change.

"Seriously, you're supposed to laugh."

"I didn't find it funny."

"Oh."

"You tried though," she offered.

She frowned. "It was funny."

"Maybe a bit," she conceded and shrugged her shoulders to her earrings. There were two studs in each lobe, and they were silver stars to match her necklace.

"They're pretty," she pointed and was dimly aware her voice wasn't disguised anymore.

The girl smiled appreciatively. "Thank you."

"Nice talking to you," Elena said as she got up after the echoing announcement made by the speakers.

A hand on the suitcase handle and a smile back on her face. "You too."

When she'd gone, Elena stared at her phone from her peripheral vision and kept her eyes on Roman by the bathroom. All she had to do was wait for his greenlight and everything would be okay. Hopefully.

Will and Leo got up, dumping their coffees in a bin and heading over to the gate leading out to their plane to Iceland. They laughed at something on Leo's phone and joined the growing queue waiting to board. She swapped her sight back to Roman and paled.

forty-five.

He couldn't get his phone to load any quicker. The percentage bar showing the progress of download was hardly halfway, so he edged behind the wall out of view, ignoring the groups of individuals walking by in both directions. So busy. Leo and Will were leaving right at that minute and it would be a matter of minutes before they boarded. Boarding wasn't part of the plan.

Hissing, he tried turning his phone off to reset everything, but nothing happened. It was an old phone, patterns of white decking the side from the time his dad's car had backed onto it. By accident, he'd been told whenever he cropped it up.

He peeked over from behind the wall to Elena who was trundling her suitcase to join the queue as well, looking doubtfully to the night outside.

This was all his fault.

The queue was moving every twenty seconds as the person at the gate checked boarding passes and passports. Leo and Will were eight groups of people from being their turn and Roman had to act.

Do something. Before they actually left for Iceland.

forty-six.

Maybe in the next ten seconds? Ten seconds ticked by and nothing.

Maybe in the next minute? A minute limped by and still nothing.

Leo found it difficult to remain still and kept crossing and uncrossing his arms. Will had noticed but hadn't said anything.

He gave him a sheepish smile. "I don't know what to do with my hands."

Will scoffed and his hand walked into his, replacing his cold with his warmth.

Two minutes passed and he got out his passport and boarding pass, as did Will and waited patiently for the family in front. The small child holding his dad's hand turned his head and stared at Leo.

"Why is he staring?" he whispered.

"He thinks you're attractive."

"You think so?"

The child then looked at Will. He pointed at him and they went on forward.

"No. Children are like that."

This was not how it was supposed to be.

The man from behind the glass screen gave both a sincere smile and checked their boarding passes, glancing once at their hands intwined. "Have a save flight."

"Thanks," muttered Leo.

Any time now.

He handed them to him with a flourish, and they walked under the exit and swallowed into the tunnel, side by side.

forty-seven.

Finally, she received the message and looked up from her phone, stripping the ridiculous wig from her head so her hair could finally breathe. Her eyes met the man's at the desk.

"Boarding pass and passport, please."

She leaned in. "I gotta tell you something."

forty-eight.

"Remember: leave it to us."

An echo of nods from all around and he grinned.

forty-nine.

His hand was still lodged into his and he didn't want to move it. Mainly because it felt comfortable, but also to make sure he didn't draw attention to him. Will remained in thought while they made their way down flights of stairs and onto the concrete where they were looking over earlier.

Orange floodlights and electrifying white light from inside draping themselves over aircrafts and their path, sky so clear it didn't appear grainy. People followed them and in front and they wrapped themselves closer together. Leo didn't. He embraced the periodic gusts of wind and occasionally tripped up on his suitcase. Will laughed every time.

For a second, his hand was still in his but then it was wrenched out and Leo began to sweat again. He sweat no matter what. A person several metres away aiming something straight at Will and he was about to interject but realised what this was.

People around gasped and rotated their heads to look while still walking. Nosy. Another figure popped up from the darkness and drew their weapon.

"Put your hands on your head." Voice firm and tone quiet.

Will did so and shot Leo a look of betrayal and didn't say a word.

"Does he have a weapon on him?"

Leo yelped and turned to behind him. Elena grinned and he forgot she wasn't as tall as she was when she wore heels. He embraced her, turning his back on his chapter with Will.

"We got past security so I don't think so."

"What about me?" A grumble from Roman.

Elena tugged him towards them and the three held each other. All they could do was embrace. Warm on one side and cold on the other where his back was exposed to the cold. He didn't mind.

A clink of handcuffs and two people stumbling by. Will turned back, hands behind his back as an officer kept a hold on him. He switched his gaze to each of them and he settled on Leo. They broke apart.

"I have to admit. You got me."

They stayed silent and watching.

"I knew something was up," he said and the officer keeping hold of him hauled him along, staggering a few steps. "You got me."

She snapped something at him, and Will quietened. One last stolen stare at Leo and he didn't look back.

Strings of people watched as they boarded, whispers scattering across themselves and eyes darting between the three and them. It should've bothered Leo, but it didn't because he was free of it all. Free of whatever control Will held over his head and Elena and Roman.

Robyn pushed his thoughts aside, revealing herself and he saw her smiling for the last time.

Elena raised her hand up and gave Will's retreating back the finger. Roman and Leo followed, like holding beacons over their heads in liberty. In a way, it was.

fifty.

"Sit."

The cat gazed back at her, green eyes appraising. It didn't budge.

"Roll over."

The cat blinked.

Elena grumbled and demonstrated to it. The cat looked appalled. Elena got dirt all over her top and glared at the cat. "You're no fun."

"This is so funny," said Roman in her driveway, watching.

"No, it's not. I'm not laughing."

She went back inside, Roman following behind and walked up the stairs and was out of breath by the time she got to the top. She sat by the window and grinned at the two. They were all in her bedroom, staring out at the main road traffic and laughing at license plates if they spelt out something funny. She enjoyed it thoroughly.

Elena remembered something she hadn't packed and went under her bed and retrieved a box taped over twice with tape. Her bedroom was bare, and it was all because of one thing. Tearing down her precious possessions and hiding them away in boxes, leaving the skeleton of her room behind. It wasn't nice and she missed her dad even more.

"What's in there?" Leo asked, both still at the window.

Elena hesitated. "Mark gave this to me when my dad died," she responded. "I never opened it until now because he told me not to open it until he was gone."

"I'd be so curious I'd open it right there," Leo said.

"Well I didn't really question it because I wasn't in the mindset to."

"That's weird," Roman scowled. "Gone?"

"I think he meant if we ever broke up."

"Ah."

"Do you have scissors? I swore I left them here but…"

"They're downstairs, I saw them," Roman said and nudged his way to the floor and out.

Both had helped her finish the last bits of folding things away into boxes and it was weird without Robyn. Weird because she would have probably been the one to tell her she was doing it wrong and she'd prove it to her. Or if Vienna or Mark were there, they'd sit and watch.

Her mum walked into the room with suede heels, gracefully planting her feet on the ground and surveying the room. She spotted Leo first and smiled. "Hi, Leo."

"Hi," he said. "How are you?"

"I'm great, how are you?

He started going red and laughed nervously in response.

"Do you want tea or coffee? Something to eat?"

Leo made a thinking noise which he drew out long. He looked up. "Can I have a pear?"

She frowned. "A pear?"

"Yeah, the green fruit. Sometimes brown. Depends what mood it's in."

She laughed brightly like she finally understood. "Of course."

She went downstairs and came back with a fruit bowl and offered it to him. "Wash it in the bathroom."

The glass bowl was assorted with individual fruits and Leo singled out a pear, but his face fell as his hand closed around it.

"Is this room temperature fruit?"

"I'm not sure I quite understand."

Elena turned back to the box, corners of her mouth lifting into a grin. She remembered she needed scissors and sighed. Roman was so slow.

"It's just that I prefer fruit refrigerated," Leo said. "It's just more... it's nicer to eat."

Her mum frowned. "I see."

Leo looked surprise. "You do?"

Her mum nodded. "Our fridge is not in the house, I'm afraid."

"That's okay." He shrugged. "I'll keep the fruit for later. Thanks."

"Okay." She turned to Elena in a way so her back completely faced Leo. "We're leaving in five minutes."

Elena rolled her eyes as she left and got up to Leo. "You're funny when you're awkward."

"You think so?" He blushed again, and it deepened when Elena laughed. "That's embarrassing."

"Yeah, you're, like, polite and your voice goes squeaky."

"Are you describing a child?"

"I heard this fact somewhere," she started. "People who go red easily are better to trust."

"What, because you know if I lied if my face goes red?" He raised a questioning eyebrow.

377

"I dunno," she admitted grumbling. "I just heard it somewhere."

"Right."

"I'm gonna miss you," she mumbled and heard a car lay it down on the horn outside. She winced.

"Me too," he agreed and wrapped her in a hug.

They rocked awkwardly like that in the time it took for Roman to come thundering up the stairs.

Breaking apart, Elena glowered at him stood by the door with scissors held securely in his hand.

"What's wrong with walking?"

"I just like to run." He held his nose in the air and handed the scissors to Elena when she walked over.

Elena sat, Roman squatted and Leo sat with his legs beneath him. She nudged the parcel between her feet and used one of the scissor's blades to strike across a break in the flaps. That took almost a minute because tape was circumferenced around the whole thing, refusing help from the others. Just before she opened it, she gave an unconvincing smile to the others.

"I wanna look at this privately."

"Sure," both said and went back over to the window.

She didn't know what would be inside. The box itself was medium sized and was light to hold, making her question whether anything was inside. One flap open and then the other and she froze.

fifty-one.

A silver Tesla sped past, breaking the speed limit and the speed camera behind a tree winked white light in its wake.

Roman smirked to himself and fantasised about the letter on the driver's doormat in a few weeks' time. Then with a shocked face, he replayed the license plate in his head and realised that was his dad's car. "Shit," he cursed.

"Guys," Elena croaked and sounded upset.

Leo and Roman went over and hunkered down beside Elena with her box wide open. Letters, notes and pages of writing spilled onto the floor around their feet and Elena pointed to the yellow note which stuck out. The only coloured bit of paper.

Roman picked it up. "*You have questions that Will will never answer, but I can.*" He managed to read through the difficulty and laughed at the double words. "You were dating Will too?"

Elena pulled a face but still looked bothered by something through it all. "No. Look." She sifted through some of the papers and passed them to both.

His eyes skimmed the first paragraph, it sounded boring and repetitive and then a word caught his eye. His own name. A profiling of where he lived, both Canada and England typed down, age, birthdate and other personal information. It wasn't an official file; it was just details copied and written down on a document and printed. He dropped it and picked up another one. It looked as if it had been crumpled many times over and pulled back out again to embody its previous state. He left it to the rest of the pile and sat back in confusion.

Leo looked up from his paper and Roman could tell from his peaky face that something was really wrong.

"Elena," her mother called from downstairs.

"Wait," she yelled aggressively and looked between the two.

"What is all this?" Leo stammered and held up a piece of paper shredded from its other half. Scrawled on it was a tiny inscription, a large paragraph if blown up to a legible size if the writing wasn't so hard to read.

"This is Mark's handwriting."

"You weren't kidding, his writing is terrible."

"He was dyslexic."

"Oh."

"Elena." Her mom walked in and hollered, jumping backwards to stop herself from walking into Roman. She threw Elena a strained smile. "We have to leave if we want to beat the peak of traffic."

Elena sagged and began piecing together the papers all over the floor, returning them in the box, standing and hugging it to her chest. Her mom breezed down the stairs and later a car's engine was fired up.

Elena looked at both, grasping at the last rays of time they had in each other's presence and her mouth thinned into a weak smile.

"I'll text every minute on the way."

"But we haven't found out what this has got to do with it all," Roman protested. "Will you send us pictures?"

"I will," she affirmed and let both give her quick hugs.

Roman squeezed her shoulders hard. He didn't need to worry about her arm anymore, or her hair getting entangled in his fingers. That was then.

Three forty-five in the afternoon, skies descending like the time upon them all as they wished her well, cars driving by on the dual carriageway. Venus hovered above the horizon, hesitant to reveal itself so early in the day.

Elena stood on the kerb, deep blue hoodie, and grey sweats for the cold. She held the box protectively in her arms and when her mom offered to take it, she shook her head. Their removal van had already driven off ten minutes earlier and left the small boxes to their own car.

"What is there to do in Wales?" Leo asked.

"Loads of castles," Elena's mom answered and grinned. "Did I tell you we also have a cat? It's ginger. You'll love her."

Elena scowled. "I'm allergic."

She didn't seem to have heard.

Roman beamed and held out a hand in front of her. She took it, shaking it and smiled through the corner of her eyes and gave Leo a one-armed hug, complaining when the corner of the box dug into his side.

"Don't worry. Once I'm eighteen, I'm out just like that. Uni will be an escape. A little bit like something to work for."

"Send us post cards," Leo reminded.

"Of course," she said and got into her black Audi.

Her mom waved at Leo and Roman who raised a hand half-heartedly to wave back.

The boxes stowed in the backseat and her own box resting on her lap, they backed out the driveway slowly. It took almost a minute because no cars stopped to let them out but eventually, they found a gap in the traffic. Roman didn't move, just looked on. When clear of the driveway, Elena yelled something through the glass which he thought was 'See you later, alligator', and drove off. Fast at first but decelerating until it was ready to take a turn, indicating right, and disappearing off the map.

It was just Leo and him left in the world of chaos which people called their home. Time continued with no sign of recognising their pain – didn't see it, didn't care. Time was a psychopath. And in the moment of it all, Roman knew he was going to feel so much more pain in his life. Pain of people leaving, hurting him, betraying him. It was so easy to hide but it was tiring but he was also going to feel hope again, happiness and relief. Those were parts of life, some had more bits that others, but in the end, everyone gets some.

"Roman." Leo jolted him from his thoughts and ripped his eyes away from the end of the road to his.

"Leo," he responded equally as calm, and his eyes were drawn to something white in Leo's hand. He blinked.

"I managed to take a piece of Mark's writing." He held it up, the writing so small and minute. "He knows why we were chosen. Everything."

Acknowledgements:

I'd like to thank the five months that I had to myself in lockdown because I wouldn't have had the time to finish this book in the amount of time I took otherwise. A special thanks to my English teacher who gave me pointers on how to publish. A big thank you to my parents who believed in me and encouraged me to pursue my passion even when I was sceptical, and to my sister who did nothing but judge – I know you love me. Now I mention my sister, thank you for editing (most of the manuscript) and being my favourite person. And lastly, thank you reader for reading my first ever completed novel. I hope it wasn't too bad.

About the Author

Charlie is a high school student who wrote her first novel Radio Silence when she was sixteen and currently lives in Manchester with her family. She has loved writing since she first opened a notebook at the age of six and wants to do criminal justice in the future.

Printed in Great Britain
by Amazon

46120923R00234